Samantha

SAMANTHA

R. L. PORTER

ARPress
45 Dan Road Suite 5
Canton MA 02021

Hotline: 1(888) 821-0229
Fax: 1(508) 545-7580

Ordering Information:

Quantity sales. Special discounts are available on quantity purchases by corporations, associations, and others. For details, contact the publisher at the address above.

Printed in the United States of America.

ISBN-13:   Paperback   979-8-89356-545-4
                  eBook   979-8-89356-547-8
                  Hardcover   979-8-89356-546-1

Library of Congress Control Number: 2024902803

toExcel

San Jose San Jose Lincoln Shanghai

To my sons, Burke and B.J., who encouraged me to pursue publishing arrangements for the stories I have written and thanks for the late hours you put in, Kathy.

Table of Contents

Chapter 1 1

Chapter 2 26

Chapter 3 39

Chapter 4 67

Chapter 5 88

Chapter 6 119

Chapter 7 136

Chapter 8 143

Chapter 9 176

Chapter 10 186

Chapter 11 207

Chapter 12 212

Chapter 13 219

Chapter 14 222

Chapter 15 227

Chapter 16 236

Chapter 17 241

Chapter 18 243

Chapter 19 250

Chapter 20 257

Chapter 21 262

Chapter 22 269

Chapter 23 273

Chapter 24 277

Chapter 25 281

Chapter 26 284

Chapter 27 290

Chapter 28 295

Chapter 29 302

Chapter 1

A balmy Friday in late August of 1953
Provo, Utah

It was part of her job and normally Delores would say something about the new girls taking their breaks together, but not today. Today was too important, too tenuous and too much was yet undecided. She had tried to talk to BB, wished he would have put more thought into the plan, but it was no use. BB just wouldn't listen to anyone else's ideas.

Delores Lebowitz was not attractive, had few friends and had always lacked confidence. She had but three dates during the two years she spent as a full-time student at Brigham Young University. She was often teased. "Just run on home like a good little girl," she remembered hearing dozens of times, with much more scathing remarks implied.

Once while in the student union building, Delores overheard herself being discussed. "There's that Lebowitz chick. I hear she prefers girls."

It irked Delores to have to put up with such condescension. Although she was a superior student and a committed career woman, she left the university after her sophomore year and took a job as the president's personal secretary at Zion Bank.

Mr. Shiply, the bank's president, considered Delores quite efficient. He liked her and made it a point to introduce her to the bank's most affluent unmarried male customers, especially those who he believed were candidates for matrimony. Several asked her to dinner, a few to movies and one older man took her to an air show in Reno, Nevada. Delores did not enjoy the men Mr. Shiply introduced her to. She felt inferior to them, could not relax or converse comfortably and only one asked for a second date, which he later broke, possibly sealing her lack of self-confidence forever.

Mr. Shiply remained persistent, continuing to try and find just the right match for his secretary. However, Delores began to spend several nights a week in bars and nightclubs. She found that she enjoyed the men she met in these nightspots. Most were very different from those she dated while in college and at the bank. Although many seemed irresponsible, most were fun loving, easy to enjoy and Delores eventually met two she favored, Dan and BB from Colorado. They were freight yard workers, inseparable hell raisers who partied harder than anyone Delores had ever known. BB made all the plans and Dan kept everyone laughing. He was a nonstop joker.

Before meeting BB and Dan, Delores had no idea there were so many exciting things to do. She couldn't believe she had been missing out on so much fun. She was actually enjoying being young and irresponsible, carefree. She began to want the mystery of the highway, the thrill of the unknown and the joy of experiment and challenge. Her serious moments were few, but not so few that she didn't grow to resent being shared by two inseparable friends. Although she was falling in love with Dan, Delores wasn't afforded the time alone with him that she longed for.

Jokester or not, Dan Newel had a beautiful heart and as the months flew by, Delores found herself wanting to spend her every moment with him. She loved everything they shared, laughing, crying, silently enjoying the road while BB drove, sleeping and making love. Dan often made fun of the insignificance of love making, but Delores knew he enjoyed it with her.

It wasn't the way Delores wanted things to work out, but it was BB who married her in Las Vegas the weekend before he and Dan enlisted in the army.

"Hey, Baby. You gotta marry me cause I called heads. Didn't I, Dan?"

"That's right, Delores," he laughed, struggling to open a bottle of beer with his teeth. "He won you fair and square. Where we takin the honeymoon?"

Delores chalked it up to fate, but had to admit that marrying BB wasn't such a bad deal for a few years. He and Dan got to come home on leave twice during training.

But, this thing today. It was just awful. It seemed like a joke last week, but they were going to do it, then go their separate ways. BB had orders for paratrooper school. Dan had an appointment to OCS, officer's candidate school, and Delores was to have a nice little house in the woods just west of Fort Benning that BB had found for her. Of course, he would take her to Seoul, South Korea when he finished paratrooper training. In a way, it was exciting. Almost like old times, but...Gees, what time is it?

Two twenty-two pm. Delores looked around the little kitchenette. The two new girls were just finishing their soda pops. The three old gals in records were taking chairs across from them and everyone but the tellers would soon be taking their breaks. Most brought sandwiches and ate them at the two o'clock break. This was going to be horrible, but it was time.

Delores spoke to the old gals from records, then slid her chair back and strolled calmly out of the kitchenette, through the consumer loans section and down the hall to the delivery door and eased it open. "Mr. Shiply should be by himself in his office," she whispered to BB, who had disguised himself with a bushy black wig and a nylon hose that was pulled over his face. "Where did you leave your car? Is it all ready?" asked Delores.

"Mine's in the alley behind the trash bin," whispered BB. "Dan's is a block away. They're both loaded and ready to blast off. Here," he mumbled, an undertone as he handed Delores a big repulsive looking pistol, then hurried through the doorway. "You might need this. Lead the way, then get out of the way. Just cover my backside." BB appeased too tense, which worried Delores.

Dan crept inside the bank and sidled down the hall, a big deer rifle held at his right side and a bundle of grocery sacks under his left arm. At BB's insistence, he'd slipped a nylon stocking over his head, too, but hated it because he'd done such a masterful job of picking his garb and painting his face. A rodeo clown with a big floppy hat, red pants and suspenders, white canvas shoes six sizes too big and a long blue coat he'd found in a trash heap at the dump. "Man, I hope we don't have to use these damn guns," he whispered, trembling, showing no sign of his usual air of merriment.

Never had Delores seen Dan Newel so serious, so visibly fearful. It was unnerving. She wanted to run out the back door screaming for help. But, poor Dan. She just couldn't. Delores took two deep breaths, then hurried up the hall to the president's office.

"Baby," whispered BB, grabbing Delores' arm as she passed him. "This should go down without a hitch, but you be ready with that pistol just in case."

Delores stopped. "BB please," she begged. "Let's don't do this."

"You do anything to fuck this up and I'll kill you. I mean it, Delores. I'll blow your ugly ass to smithereens," swore BB. Delores, shocked, turned and continued up the hall, whimpering all the way.

Mr. Shiply, a tall thin man with the normal alacrity of a turtle, shot to his feet as if he'd seen a ghost when the armed men barged into his office. "Good Lord," he whined, exhaling through a long suffering sigh.

BB leveled his rifle at the banker. "Mister, if you make a sound, you're a dead son-of-a-bitch," he snarled. "All you gotta do is take us to the safe," he added, gesturing toward Dan with a quick snap of his head. "We'll fill these sacks with cash and be outta here in a flash."

Dan held up two paper grocery sacks. "These here," he mumbled.

Delores stepped around BB, pointed a finger toward him and spoke to her employer. "This man demanded I take him to the president's office or he would shoot me," she whimpered, literally tearing toward blindness. "I just didn't know what I should do, Mr. Shiply."

The banker licked his lips and raised his hands. "Now you men just take it easy," he said, his voice that of a begging child. "We can stand a hold up, but we can't have anybody getting hurt. You'll get the money, but don't..."

"Shut-up and move," snapped BB, raising the big rifle in a vicious threatening gesture, his whole being creating an image of vile madness.

The heist went like clockwork. The sacks were stuffed full of every denomination of paper money printed in America. Mr. Shiply was left locked in the safe, the hall was empty, and no one was the wiser until an old security guard strolled down the hall to bring Mr. Shiply a piece of his wife's chocolate pie.

"What's happening here, Delores?" he asked, dropping the piece of pie, his eyes as big as the saucer that shattered on the shiny linoleum floor.

Dan dropped the sacks, fell to his knees and threw up his hands, causing Delores to panic. She lifted the pistol, pointed it at the old guard and pulled off a round. *Boom*, roared through the bank. The round hit the light fixture above the guard's head, startling him, causing him to faint and crumble to the floor. Then, everything went blurry for Delores. Dan scrambled to his feet and started crying, there were screams and yells, people running and all kinds of mayhem. Then suddenly, a bell started ringing.

"You ever say a word about me'n Dan and you're dead, Delores," she heard from behind her, then a thud.

"Oh God, BB," cried Dan, weakly picking up the sacks of cash. "I always knew you weren't gonna take her with you, but you didn't have to club her like that." Dan wiped his eyes. "Oh, Man," he moaned.

"Shut up," snapped BB. "I don't need a broad slowin me down. Just gimme one of those sacks, then run like a scalded dog before I decide to kill you, too. You weak ass bastard." It was eight minutes past three.

There was another drama unfolding that same afternoon in August of 1953, in Sherman, Texas. Although angry summer storm clouds were tumbling in from the northwest, there was a calmness about the foot traffic around the downtown square. It was mostly county farmers in blue jeans and hats and cowboy boots with high shines. Their wives and children were trailing along, looking at the displays in the storefront windows and carrying sacks stuffed with their purchases. Oddly, there were no men wearing irrigation boots. Big rubber knee-high boots that protected their pant legs when they watered the corn in the irrigation district. However, the crops had been laid by and it was time to watch and wait, relax some, visit with the old timers at the domino parlor, walk the streets and spend a little money.

The cornfields stood tall, thick with emerald green leaves, softly shuffling in the warm summer breeze, the tallest stalks drooping with heavy ears. Big bolls were popping in the cotton fields, massive undulating oceans of drab green speckled with dashes of brilliant white. Now that the corn had been watered for the last time, the melons growing between the rows, like pigs sleeping in the shade, would finally ripen.

Eisenhower was in the White House, the Korean conflict no longer dominated the news and the young men didn't feel threatened with the draft. Times were basically good and everyone in Grayson County seemed to be awaiting the coming bounty. Without exception, people seemed to feel compelled to take in deep breaths of the sweet summer air, exhale loudly and shake their heads, then say, "Hmmm, I just love this time of the year." They walked with a spring in their step, smiled quickly and exchanged courteous greetings when passing. Spirits soared.

Three people, an older man in a doubled breasted white suit and his female companion, followed by a teenage girl, stepped out of the courthouse into the broken shade of a huge cottonwood tree, its ocean green leaves whispering a happy song. The big tree was surrounded by cement benches known to have been placed there the day before the Butterfield Overland Mail Route first passed through downtown Sherman in 1858.

The man on the courthouse steps pulled a shiny gold watch from his pocket, something he was never without unless bathing or sleeping, it and its chain reflecting the sharp rays of sunlight that knifed through the whispering tree leaves, like mirrors. "Getting late," he said.

The older woman, dressed in an orange and white suit, shielded her eyes from the surrounding glare with a big brown envelope she held. "Are we in a hurry?" she asked.

The man looked up and waggled a thumb over his left shoulder. "Well, it might be wise to hurry along. Those are rain clouds to the northwest," he said.

The older woman took the envelope from her view for a second, then replaced it. "They're a distance yet."

The teenage girl made no comment, or observation. She was focused on the courthouse steps, seeming forsaken, wanting to go unnoticed. Her hands were gripping the strap of her small white purse, her pretty face vulnerably morose.

"What's wrong with them?" asked a round-faced lady across the street, who was bouncing a baby on her hip. There was something very wrong with those three people over at the courthouse. It could be felt in the air as well as seen on their faces.

"What people?" asked a young freckle-faced man, turning from a window display.

"That old couple comin down the courthouse steps with that young girl."

"Who knows? I know that girl, though. She's Frieda Wheeler's daughter."

"Frieda Wheeler? You tellin me that whore has a daughter that purdy?"

"Oh, Dottie, you're just jealous. Frieda's a genuine looker, too."

"Shut-up. You gonna get me a television or not?"

"I thought you said you'd lose some weight first."

"How bout you just gettin me one? Then, maybe I will."

The older woman across the street at the courthouse stepped from the stairs to the landing and pointed with the envelope she had been using to shield her eyes. "There's a little café over there where we could get some lunch."

There would have been time to walk across the square and get a sandwich, but Hiram Wheeler, a large man whose appearance suggested his confidence and success, made an issue of the weather, an effort to mask the excitement he felt. "We don't want to get caught in a downpour, Ladies. Let's wait until we get the girl home to eat." Hiram quickly rethought what he'd just said, wanting to kick himself for referring to the young lady, now in his keeping, as 'The Girl.' He wouldn't even refer to his own children like that. It was always Henry,

Joe Neil, or Lorraine, but never just my son, or my daughter. "I can't wait to hear what our Samantha has to say about her room," he added, winking, hoping these words more nearly communicated his heartfelt desire to ease the pain the young lady must feel with such a dramatic change in her life.

May, Hiram's wife of thirty-seven years, a tall trim woman whose appearance suggested her reserve and refinement, stepped from the sidewalk and reached for the door handle of a new white Chrysler parked at the curb. A large diamond ring, her twenty-fifth wedding anniversary gift from her husband, sparkled from the third finger of her right hand. "I don't know that it's going to rain," she argued.

"Look," said Hiram, to fifteen-year-old Samantha Wheeler, pointing high into the northwest sky, feeling the need to prove about the coming weather. "The bottoms of those thunderheads are heavy with rain," he added, then looked back to his niece and winked. "Samantha, waiting another hour or so to eat would be all right with you, wouldn't it?" he asked. "We'll be lucky if we don't see some hail before we get you home."

Samantha had short brunet hair, but it was full and shiny. Her neat white and tan summer suit suggested that she had taken care to dress for this special occasion. "Yes, Sir," she said, noncommittally. "Either way is fine."

"Then, hop in the back and we'll get on the road," instructed her uncle.

Hiram slid into the driver's seat, rolling down the window as he started the Chrysler's big V-8 engine. While adjusting the rearview mirror, feeling compelled to smile at Samantha's image, he backed into the street, then slowly made the loop around the Grayson County Courthouse square, exiting at the southwest corner. "I'll have you home in less than ninety minutes," he said, emphasizing the word 'home' this time, then pointed to a white road sign. Dallas-63 Miles, it read. "May's got your room looking better than any suite in the downtown Sheridan."

Neither Hiram Wheeler nor his two passengers were happy to be making this trip under the circumstances that had required it. May had given it the most thought and had spoken to herself about it. Now, rationalizing until proven otherwise, she was only going to discuss the best parts about having Hiram's young niece in her home for a few years. The kids could say and do what worked for them; it didn't matter to May. Neither of her two sons visited anymore and her youngest, Lorraine, and her husband had moved to Garland last summer. They had no say in May's and Hiram's affairs. Samantha could fill a few voids in the idle hours and give May someone to dote over a little, she had decided. It made no sense, considering the young lady's mother and father, but Samantha was so very pretty, actually quite lovely, and would be fun to show off when she was all dressed up for Sunday services.

Hiram perceived the situation with his niece differently than his wife May had chosen to. Adopting Samantha now, instead of eight years ago when the subject first came up, presented a new set of problems. He and May, now sixty-four and sixty-two, might find dealing with a teenager overwhelming. Hiram remembered the problems and adjustments he and May had encountered when their children were in high school. There were many times he just had to put his foot down when May and the children got into squabbles about dating and all the late hours. Hiram was a lot older now, had a definite heart condition and would have to consider that. He had to learn to handle things in a calmer manner and hoped May would do the same.

Being asked to adopt Samantha now, after Billy Ray refused to allow it eight years ago, was the worst thing his little brother had ever asked Hiram to do. One thing though, there would be a point made here. There damn sure would. Hiram would get Samantha on the right track. Hell, someone had to set an example for her and be around when she needed something. A person's teenage years seem to always be the most difficult. Now, he just needed to nudge her along until she got herself a good education, maybe even as long as it took to find a suitable profession that would be appealing to her. Finding herself a husband was going to be automatic for Samantha. The little thing was sure pretty enough and seemed to be a good girl.

Hiram and May had raised three children. Raised them responsibly and had gotten them set up right. Their worst fault, especially in the case of Lorraine, was allowing her to grow up with such endless greed. All the money in Texas wouldn't be enough to satisfy Lorraine. Hiram's two sons, Henry and Joe Neil, and his son-in-law, Ike, ran his building company now and were making money hand over fist, but wanted more. Even though there were no signs that an end to the demand for cheap housing would occur in their lifetimes, and the tract homes in the suburbs were selling as fast as Henry and Ike could throw them together, the kids were speculating in other areas of building. They had bid on several multiunit apartment projects, a high school in Richardson and a skyscraper in downtown Fort Worth. "A little luck and those kids would end up richer than their old man," Hiram said to himself in thought. "I hope they do, but I'm gonna make sure Samantha has a good chance, too. I'll make an agreement with her. Me'n May won't tell the kids, but we'll give her two hundred dollars a month for five years and buy her a car if she'll forget about Frieda and focus on her own life."

Unlike her aunt and uncle, Samantha had hardly had time to think about her situation. She wasn't expecting any significant changes in her life until last week. She was at the Fox-Fire Drive-in and had just gotten her paycheck when her mother and a strange man, who was in the passenger seat of a new black Buick sedan, pulled up at the side door. Samantha noticed the car when her mother honked the horn and waved. "I know who that is," said Wanda Reed, the little junior who wrapped takeouts and kept spare trays ready with straws, plastic flatware, napkins, catsup, salt and pepper. "You two look a lot alike, Samantha, but you ain't never gonna be that sexy."

"You're right," agreed Samantha, then put her check between her lips and hurried outside, tying her apron in back as she did. "Hi, Mom," she greeted, taking the check from her lips and putting it into her apron pocket. "Where are you off to?" she asked, noticing the clothes still on hangers that were crammed into the new car and the cardboard boxes that were shoved into any space that would hold them.

Frieda, Samantha's mother, removed her sunshades, shrugged as if asking why her daughter needed to know, then smiled as if filled with rapture. "I'll take care of that for you," she said, then reached through the open window and slipped Samantha's payroll check from her apron pocket. "Include your tips?"

"Uh-huh. Eighty-two for my hours and one fifty-six for tips."

"You sure? That would be over two hundred. This check's only for one hundred sixty-eight and change."

"Taxes, Mama. Mr. Biggio requires all the carhops to turn in their tips when they get them. Tips are subject to payroll taxes just like hourly wages."

"Uh-huh, sure they are. You bet," snapped Frieda, her big smile turning to a sneer of disgust. "I know Kyle and I'll kiss your ass if he doesn't keep what money you girls don't get back. Cocksucker buys Martha Rae's new cars and fancy clothes with it. Bet your butt he does."

"Oh, Mama. You can be so hateful. Anyway, where are you going?"

Frieda's big smile rushed back. She fluttered her eyelids. "Baby, if I didn't know you'd understand, Rob and I wouldn't be doing what we're doing," she said, in a dispirited tone, although her rapturous smile reflected another emotion. "We're leaving Sherman for awhile."

Samantha was lost for words, no questions came to her mind, no challenging statements. She said nothing, just stood staring silently, alternating her disbelieving eyes between her mother, the man in the passenger seat and the things that had been crammed into the car. "What's the matter out there, Samantha?" asked Wanda Reed, through the open takeout window. "Are you okay, Honey?"

Frieda, feeling no need for her daughter's friend to be nosing into family affairs, answered Wanda's questions. "Nothing's the matter out here, Young Lady, and Samantha's fine. Just close that window." Frieda needed to get on the road, so as soon as Wanda dropped the window, she spoke quickly and curtly. "Now, listen to me, Samantha," she began, slipping her sunshades back on and starting the car. "It's all arranged. You're in for a treat. Your father always said if something ever happened to me, he'd have his brother, Hiram, take care of you." Frieda paused and shrugged, then continued when her daughter appeared to be, as always, childish and stubbornly speechless. "Well, something just happened to me," she said, her expression one of stern commitment. "I left. Me and Rob have been in love for over eight years. He bought me this car, something your lazy old man would never even consider. Anyway, Rob and I aren't getting any younger, so we just decided to consider ourselves for once." The car started rolling back. "Have fun. I'll write you from Miami," said Frieda, waving over the steering wheel. "You might oughta take off early," she bellowed. "I left the trailer house in a bit of a mess. Oh, maybe you better tell your old man not to go botherin me'n Rob. You got it, Baby?"

Samantha, riding along in the back seat of the Chrysler, yet trying to think of what had happened to her, kept wondering what on earth she would do to ever find a job and a way to get to school in a big city like Dallas. Her mother and father's trailer home had been within walking distance of her job, her school and the shopping areas she used. She had worked since age thirteen at something, cleaning other trailer homes in the park and baby-sitting until she got the job at the Fox-Fire drive-in. That was a real good job, too. Her checks on the first and fifteenth were always over a hundred and fifty dollars. Even with paying her mother a hundred dollars each month for rent, food and incidentals, Samantha was yet able to buy school supplies and the clothes she needed. It was a real shame to lose that job.

Hiram, driving along silently thinking, kept cataloguing the things he was planning to do to properly provide everything a modern teenager needed. He wanted Samantha to feel that she was always on a level playing field with her peers. Hiram knew teens needed to develop a sense of not needing, although they were the most needful lot on the planet. The decisions they would face would come like machine gun fire, the rapidity making them need far better skills and more experience than they could possibly have gotten in about any environment known to man. That was what made the problem difficult, but love conquers all and that's how Hiram was going to deal with his newest dependent. Hell, he could love her to death, he was thinking, glancing into the rearview mirror, seeing her pain as she dug through the mess Billy Ray and Frieda had left her with. "Poor little thing now, but she's gonna be the strongest, prettiest and smartest one of them all if I have my say," thought Hiram, reaching for May's hand.

May, nervously wriggling in the front passenger's seat from time to time, was being strangely quiet herself. She was pretending to be concentrating on the crossword puzzle in the morning paper while considering quite the opposite of Hiram for her relationship with Samantha. May was troubled, also. She just couldn't arrange her thoughts of how to become a friend to a young woman almost fifty years her junior. Trying to assure her acceptance of the heartfelt gestures in the spirit they were meant was the biggest challenge, she felt. May, as was Hiram, was quite aware of the doubt that teens could feel for the loving ways of old folks that could never be part of their circle of friends.

Although Samantha, as confused as she was hurt and sad, set about her new life quietly and with as few interruptions to her aunt and uncle's home as she could manage, they went out of their way to make her happy and feel welcome. May showcased her at church on the first two Sundays she attended, then Hiram insisted Samantha be allowed to attend church when and if she cared to. He took her to the high school on registration day and introduced her to every faculty member she would be involved with, whether he knew them or not. "This is my favorite niece," he told each of them. "She'll be the best student in her class. You make a special effort to see she gets on fine here and let me know the minute you have any reason to think otherwise."

The big two-story home where Uncle Hiram and Aunt May had lived for eighteen years was built close to a line of low rolling hills on a long rectangular lot within heavily wooded acreage in far North Dallas. A gardener and a maid came in Mondays and Fridays and kept the estate beautifully manicured and squeaky clean. Hiram and May spent the early evening hours of most days sitting quietly in their wicker chairs out on a long front porch that ran the length of the house. Aunt May would talk about the lilac bushes that sat at either end of the porch, her knitting, or the doilies she crocheted and gave out every Christmas. Hiram gave his wife those hours, listening and commenting only to endorse her pride. "Yours are the most spectacular lilac bushes in all of Texas, May," he often said, or, "Everybody knows they'd have to give a five-dollar bill for one of your doilies, Honey."

Inside, the majority of the furniture was old, but flawless, second generation. The woods were kept glossy with varnish, the upholstery replaced if worn, but always protected with May's big draping hand crocheted doilies. The home had eleven rooms counting one that was kept locked. It used to be Uncle Hiram's drawing room when he was active in his residential building company, before his sons took over and hired an architect. The old couple shared an innate tidiness, but showed no concern those times Samantha's room didn't measure up to the order of the rest of the house. Her upstairs bedroom was once her first cousin's, Lorraine, who had made it clear that she would not be referred to as a stepsister, even though her parents had legally adopted Samantha. She did not care for such a questionable designation. "That makes it sound like either Mom or Dad would be your biological parent," explained Lorraine. "That kind of thinking wouldn't set well with me, Samantha. Do you understand? Well, of course you would," assumed Lorraine, not giving her cousin a chance to speak.

Lorraine was hardly understandable to Samantha. Outwardly, she could appear quite happy those times she wanted to, but never could she hide the unrest that lay just below the surface of her simulated air. She seldom smiled and never laughed. The woman, tall like her father, was thin and pale to the point of appearing anemic. She seemed to want to manifest herself as older than her years and was in fact quite old fashion for a woman of thirty-one. Lorraine, although her abundant hair was dark like her mother's and completely free of any visible graying, often wore it in a bun, or other styles that kept it close and tight. She wore dresses to her ankles and a sweater almost without exception, regardless of the weather.

The closet in Samantha's bedroom, a walk-in, had an end rack for long dresses, robes and pantsuits. That first day she peered inside, left for her to find on her own, a surprise May admitted to later, hung three colorful new dresses, a blue suit and a lavender bathrobe made of a soft terry cloth. May overly doted, but was loving and helpful. She seemed to enjoy shopping in the downtown department stores for school clothes and wanted Samantha to have a closet full to select from. She was fastidious and loved helping with any washing and ironing when Samantha needed that. A week before the fall semester began, May took her niece, as Lorraine advised she refer to Samantha, to the Preston State Bank in Highland Park and opened a checking account for her, making an initial deposit of two hundred dollars. "Young ladies need to be able to make their own decisions with money these days, Honey. Hiram nor I will meddle in yours," explained May, with a smile and a pat on the leg.

On the way home that same afternoon, May stopped at an office furniture store and bought Samantha an oak desk, then kept a crystal vase filled with fresh flowers on one corner, changing them every other day.

Although May seemed to glow whenever Samantha helped her with any simple chore, the home's kitchen was her private domain every morning. Her spreads were always artfully displayed. Regardless of the season or occasion, there would be fresh fruits and fruit-filled pastries, eggs prepared to order, toast or biscuits and three choices of breakfast meats. Hiram didn't eat lunch and May only snacked on crackers or potato chips. She liked to pick at snacks while visiting with Samantha as she ate, simple things like salads, a sandwich, or a bowl of soup. Dinner was the only meal that began with the blessing. It was also the time to review the day and Hiram liked to be first. He would begin while checking the time on his gold watch. "Another day," he would say, then sometimes tap his wife's big ring, a mock chiding to remind her that she too had a piece of fine jewelry. May would often offer a gesture indicating that she didn't need a reminder, a cute exchange to perpetuate the mock conflict, assumed Samantha. "Okay, Ladies," her uncle would almost always say, then tell what the day had held for him. "Tell us all about your day, Samantha," was his usual conclusion. Aunt May liked to be last, telling of her day after she had served and everything had been passed around the table. Before relating the events of her day, she inevitably began with words of contrition to point out her lack of triumphs and underachievement. "Now, I'm just not going to be as interesting as you two," she might say. "After all, what old woman would be?" She ended with the same question every night. "How did you feel today, Hiram?"

Samantha's uncle continued to drive her to school until Christmas when he bought her a new turquoise 1954 Ford Victoria. The car was registered to his building company and insured under the blanket policy that covered the fleet of cars and trucks his children and the site foreman drove. Samantha was so overwhelmed with the new car, smiling through welling tears, her lips trembling while she cried with joy inside, that she hardly heard her aunt and uncle's warnings to drive safely, let alone the part about getting an allowance of two hundred dollars a month for the next five years. Hiram seemed to understand

and waited several days before reiterating the important points of what had already been said. It was at the dinner table and May had just explained that Samantha would have to pay attention to the odometer on her new car and have the oil changed every three thousand miles. "You'll have the money, Samantha," chipped in Hiram, then reached into his coat pocket and took out an envelope. "I've written it out just in case I expire a little before you do," he said, a shy smile crossing his lips. "I guess you might say, at least it's the way we feel, that this is sort of your aunt's and my commitment to you. Your checking account will get an automatic credit for two hundred dollars by the 10th of the month. That's every month for the next sixty. We want you to be happy, Hon, be able to go to college and not have to always worry about the next meal. We want you to be completely free to accomplish all that you think you want to. To be independent in your thinking."

"I don't know what to say," whispered Samantha. "You and Aunt May have done so much for me. I was thinking about that just today while staring at my new car in utter disbelief, I guess," she sighed, seemingly completely overwhelmed. "Gees I feel helpless sometimes."

"Samantha, Honey," said May, her loving tone like a plea. "I can't imagine the day you could ever be helpless. You're a very capable young lady."

Hiram reached across the corner of the table and placed his left hand on May's right, his forefinger automatically finding the big diamond ring, rocking it back and forth. "We understand," he said to Samantha. "May and I are aware that you're going through an adjustment period. It's that time in your life. A person just naturally goes from being dependent to having to become independent. It's a confusing time. A time you'll have more questions about life than you may ever. We want to help you," assured Hiram. "Yes, we both do, but some of the most successful men and women in the world look to the heavens for their answers. God, they believe, as May and I do to a degree, holds all the answers they will ever need to find peace in their lives. Now, I believe you'll find that one's ability to achieve his or own complete independence is one of life's greatest blessings." Hiram paused, placed a hand on Samantha's shoulder, then continued. "Honey," he began, "I want you to get yourself a good education. If you will, you better enable yourself to find peace and reach your goals. You'll achieve a certain confidence and independence, and you'll like yourself for doing it." Again, Hiram paused, winked at his niece, and continued. "Now, tell me if you agree," he said. "I think a big part of being happy is liking yourself. Liking Yourself is easier if you will always be an honest self-critic. Even those times when you do things you shouldn't, if you're honest about it, admit you were wrong and correct any damage you can, then vow to change your ways and do so, I think you'll always have the pride it takes to like yourself. What do you think?"

Samantha, choking back tears while listening to her uncle, blotted her eyes with her dinner napkin and looked down into her plate. "I think I love you and Aunt May more than I ever believed I could love anyone in my lifetime, even myself," she said. "Thank you both for all you've done and if I ever disappoint either one of you, please tell me. I don't want to and I'm going to pray I don't."

Life with her Uncle Hiram and Aunt May was good for Samantha. Her days were always on the sunny side of the street. The old couple made her part of everything they did. She began joining them when they attended church and was baptized of her own volition. Hiram was always willing to help Samantha with her schoolwork and he and May paid an additional tuition for her to attend a summer session that earned her credits in art, literature and science.

On registration day her junior year, Samantha met Arlene Ott, a bubbly blue eyed blonde who had transferred from a high school in Oak Cliff. Arlene had a candy apple red 1951 Ford convertible. Her father, Frederick Allen Ott, was a dental surgeon. Arlene was immediately popular with the junior and senior boys, but expressed her disinterest diplomatically and almost equally as immediate. Although she was a poor student and had trouble with required courses, Arlene was very committed to the studies she liked and wanted to one day become the governor of Texas. She was elected junior class president in a landslide election, getting over eighty percent of the votes.

Samantha became fast friends with Arlene Ott and began to help her with math and science. They often spent nights studying together, each welcome to stay the night at the other's house. Hiram liked Arlene and she liked to discuss political issues and current events with him and May. Arlene's mother, Elizabeth, was the secretary to The State Board of Regents and spent four days a week in Austin. She was interesting to Samantha; however, Dr. Ott was quite boring and only talked, when he would, of things relating to his profession. He was very obvious, though, and Samantha knew the doctor liked her and approved of her friendship and possible influence with Arlene's overall grades.

"Well," he began, one Tuesday evening while Samantha was sharing Chinese food with him and his daughter. "Arlene wants to be a politician. How about you, Samantha?"

It was the first time the doctor had opened a conversation on any subject that didn't relate directly to his work. Samantha shrugged, then smiled and wiped her mouth, suddenly understanding that the doctor's question would lead to his work in time. "I haven't really thought about it," she said. "I guess my grades will..."

"Your grades are the best," interrupted Dr. Ott. "Arlene told me that, so what do you think you'd like to do? Become an actress? Seems you have what it takes. Good looks and smarts."

"Thank you, Sir, but I'm not so pretty as your daughter," responded Samantha. "By the way, I didn't know smarts were required for actresses, but you just inferred..." Samantha paused, allowing the older and more insightful adult to explain what he meant.

"Hmmm. Well," he began. "I guess there are some real goofs who act, but being intelligent goes a long way toward anything a person tries to do."

"And being smart enough to figure out what to do would help, too," said Samantha, smiling. "I'm still working on that."

"Good idea. Any special interest?"

The doctor, appearing innately shy to Samantha, always averted eye contact with her those few times he had anything to say. It seemed quite unusual. Unlike his wife, Elizabeth, who was short and plump, he appeared strong and healthy. Maybe even a bodybuilder. Other than his big hands and obvious strength though, Dr. Ott was medium everything. Maybe five feet ten inches tall and one hundred and seventy-five pounds, his face almost featureless, but in no way harsh or ugly. "There is something, Sir," began Samantha again, wanting to let the doctor know that she was, as well as interested in his work, interested in his personal accomplishments. "You make dental surgery, especially the things you've done, sound so interesting that I've actually asked two of my teachers about it. One said, and you can imagine what he teaches, that any surgery is an exact science. I can believe that, Sir. You seem like a brilliant scientist to me. Mr. Barns said..."

"Ha," interrupted Arlene. "When old big belly Barns told you that surgery is an exact science, you should have known it's anything but that."

"No," corrected Dr. Ott, evenly. "The man's right. There are latitudes any surgeon has to consider from time to time, but intricate surgery must be quite exacting. I'm far less than a brilliant scientist, Samantha, but I'm far more impressed with you," he added. "There's a journal in my study that I'd like you to take home and read in your spare time. I've marked two pages, not only because they refer to me and my work with a young woman, but...Well the lady had a traumatic automobile accident and I had to completely reconstruct her jaw. The journal thoroughly explains the procedure to do that. The lady's everyday pain was quite a serious matter, of course, but another problem was her very exaggerated overbite, both a result of the accident. Anyway, if you've read those few pages by Thursday, and have the time to come to my clinic Friday afternoon, I'd enjoy showing you some before and after pictures. It just might be what really sparks your interest in some phase of medicine. Possibly surgery, or something related. Prosthesis design, maybe."

Samantha and Arlene finished a math assignment, then played some records and showed the doctor their new dance step. The North Texas push, a swing step with lots of turns and spins. They went to bed at ten, but Samantha was up most of the night with the journal Dr. Ott had suggested she read. It was not only interesting, but also intriguing and the article played in her first interest for her own academic and professional endeavor. She felt she wanted to be able to have a positive effect on people's lives and their health, as Dr. Ott was doing.

At two o'clock Friday afternoon, Samantha walked into Dr. Ott's clinic with her science notebook in hand. A student eager to learn. She had worn a red and white high school sweater, a red pleated skirt, a light brown beret and brown and white saddle oxfords. A preppy look she and Aunt May liked. The doctor, almost immediately emerging from his office, wearing a white surgical frock and wire rimmed glasses, spoke to his receptionist in a serious tone. "Excuse me, Mrs. Baker. This is Samantha Wheeler, my last patient for this hectic week, thank God. She's experiencing some post-surgery trauma and I want you to take her to room C or D and prepare her for X-rays, then you can go. No paperwork will be necessary for Ms. Wheeler. I'll only be offering some advice," said the doctor, his tone professionally instructional, but once winking to Samantha.

Mrs. Baker, a woman in her fifties, close cropped hair and grim features, suddenly turned all smiles with childlike enthusiasm. She rose from her desk and extended her hand. "We'll fix you right up," she said, also winking, but offering a bright grin as she took Samantha's hand. "Just follow me. Were you in an automobile accident? There's so much of that these days."

Samantha, playing along with the doctor's charade, tried to speak as earnestly as did he. "No," she sighed. "It was a plane crash. The pilot missed the runway and hit a train. A hundred and ten passengers on board and over three hundred on the train and I was the only one hurt. Such bad luck."

"My, my," said Mrs. Baker, opening the door to room C, where a radio tuned to soft music played from a countertop. "Sounds to me like a whole lot of other people were quite lucky, though. There's so much goes on these days that I'm quite content to work all week, then stay locked away in my house until Monday morning. If I hurry, I can always get home before three on Fridays. The doctor lets me off early just so's I can beat the five o'clock rush. Anyway, just remove your little hat and, uh, well, put that notebook and your purse on the counter, then lie back in that big chair. The doctor will be right in. He'll make a visual check or two, then do the X-ray work himself. Okay?"

"Okay."

"Well, take off your hat and get rid of your things," instructed Mrs. Baker, pressing a foot pedal to fully recline the big dental chair.

Samantha removed her beret, slid her notebook and purse between the radio and a small stainless-steel sink, held by a Formica topped counter, then stretched out in the chair Mrs. Baker had readied for her. She was wondering whose charade was at work here, Dr. Ott's or his receptionist's. Did this happen often? Quite soon though, the doctor came in, turned and locked the door then took a stool beside the reclined dental chair where Samantha lay. "Now, Ms. Wheeler, where does it hurt?" he asked, placing a hand on her forehead.

"Oh, everywhere. You see, I swallowed a piece of the propeller."

"Oooh," sighed the doctor, yet serious. "We'll, you don't have a fever that I can detect. Where do you suppose that piece of propeller is now?"

"In my stomach, I guess."

"Well, it must be small," said the doctor, placing a hand on Samantha's stomach. "Such a little stomach," he observed, his hand pressing lightly.

"I guess it could be anywhere then."

"I see," said the doctor, moving his hand just below Samantha's left breast, pushing the base of her bra up slightly. "Oooh," he sighed again. "Then, it could be very large. Such a big, beautiful chest you have, Ms. Wheeler."

"Huh?"

The doctor finally smiled and stood, then turned to the little radio and increased the volume. It was too loud. "I just can't work without music," he said, then turned back to face Samantha. "Now, I'm glad you came, but why did you, Samantha? Are you really interested in what I do, or is it something else?"

Samantha sat upright. "Oh, well, I would like to think that someday I could be like you and..."

"Be like me?" asked the doctor, a slight surprise before speaking from a mask of strange and sudden change, his tone soft with attempted charm. "You like me, don't you." Doctor Ott placed his hands on Samantha's shoulders and laid her back down onto the black leather chair gently, allowing his upper body to follow hers as it lay back. Then, almost instantaneously, his face, distorted with a cynical smile, a mix of hunger and anticipation, materialized above Samantha's. Suddenly, he pressed his lips against hers, smothering her as he slid his left hand under her sweater and his right up her skirt, his body weight pressing Samantha to the chair. Before she realized what had happened, or could even fight to free herself, Dr. Ott had his whole left arm under her sweater, the forearm between her breasts, his hand over her mouth. With his right, he pulled her skirt above her waist and slid his hand inside her panties, the top of his head against her right cheek. She shoved at his muscular shoulders, beat on his hard back with closed fists, but the doctor wasn't fazed. He was concentrating, his eyes appearing to be watching his right hand as it cupped her pubic hair.

Samantha continued to beat on Dr. Ott's back, flailed her legs, kicked and squirmed and tried to gouge his eyes, pull his hair, but he was too strong and too determined. She was beaten, but continued the fight, moaning and mumbling, although knowing she would not be heard over the radio and through the closed door even if there was anyone else still in the clinic.

"Lay still, Samantha," wheezed the doctor, the raspy warning of a speeding predator closing in on the kill. "You'll like this," he assured, yet through a strained wheeze, but less forceful as he watched the work of his big right hand.

Samantha tried to shake her head, her eyes like saucers, blurring with tears and feeling like they'd pop out, her heart pounding against the doctor's big forearm, her fists pounding his back, his hard shoulders. "Oh yes. Oh, yes you will, Samantha," repeated Dr. Ott, his left hand yet on her mouth and his weight yet holding her down, his head now pressing harder against her right cheek, shielding his eyes with the bend of his arm. These were physical forces beyond what Samantha had experienced and the doctor seemed trained to prevent his own injury.

Suddenly and painfully, a finger of the doctor's right hand probed viciously at Samantha's vagina, again and again as he watched it force its way between the lips. In and out it slid and again and again until the long finger delivering the hot amber of pain had reached the depth. "Oooh, that's it," he wheezed, a whisper to himself. It was as if he knew he'd found a sensation that would trigger a thrill to camouflage this horrible event. "Better?" wheezed the doctor, a question for Samantha this time.

Again, Samantha tried to shake her head, which ultimately brought about the conclusion. "Don't tell me this is your first time," stated the doctor, evenly and without the grotesque wheezing.

When Samantha tried to nod her head to confirm that she was experiencing her first sexual violation, Dr. Ott raised up and looked into her eyes for a long second, possibly the first he had since pinning her to the reclined chair. His expression was one of question. "Really?" he asked, just as Samantha's right hand smacked his face.

Dr. Ott, as if he'd been standing in hot coals, quickly lifted his left hand from Samantha's mouth and slid his right from her panties, then jumped out of her reach, only to be shocked with the blast of her sudden scream. "Get away from me. You're a beast. A filthy beast," ripped through the clinic.

Samantha jumped out of the chair. "Just a minute," pleaded Dr. Ott. "You said that you..."

"Shut up. I'm telling my uncle and...and he'll kill you." The doctor shrugged, lost for anything to say or do. "Get out of here," repeated Samantha, whimpering this time, a plea instead of a scream, her body trembling, her face awash with tears. "Just...Just get away from me. Please." Dr. Ott turned and left the room.

Samantha, distraught, tense and tearful, arrived at her home at ten past five and immediately asked her aunt to be excused from the dinner table. May agreed after being convinced that Samantha was not sick. In her room at her desk, Samantha sat and thought for over an hour, then took paper and a pen from the drawer and wrote her uncle a note. *Dear Uncle Hiram, I'm sorry I missed dinner with you and Aunt May, but I would greatly appreciate it if you would come to my room about eight tonight. I need to talk to you about something that happened to me today. I'm okay, but I just feel that it would not be wise if I didn't seek your advice. Thank you. I love you.*

Samantha put the note in an envelope, went downstairs and left it on the dining room table, then went back upstairs and bathed, then waited for her uncle.

Just after seven, Hiram came upstairs and sat on the corner of Samantha's desk while she explained the events of her day. She left nothing out, including how the doctor watched his hand and basically used it to rape her. Word for word, she tried to recall the exact words he said. Her uncle interrupted her while she was describing the doctor's wheezing. "Tell me," said Hiram. "What has Dr. Ott ever said to you before today?"

"Not much really. He's kind of quiet. I was a little surprised when he talked to me Tuesday evening. He said, uh, something about Arlene being interested in politics and asked me if I wanted to be an actress, adding that I had the looks and smarts to be one. But, he usually just talks about the work he does. Like operations and all kinds of procedures on people's gums and their mouths and even extracting teeth. It's interesting, but he isn't."

"Are you all right, Hon? Both physically and mentally I mean."

"Yes. I'm okay, Uncle Hiram, thanks to you."

"That's the most important issue, but there are others. One, I hope you'll never regret coming to me, Samantha. That's because I want to help you anyway that an old man can. Remember, everyone needs help from time to time and when you find that you do, the final responsibility is on your shoulders to get it. Two, and I'm sorry about this, but I hope you'll find a way to understand. You're going to lose Arlene as a friend. That's too bad, because, although she'll never measure up to you, her aspirations seem sincere, and I find that a quality I can appreciate in people. Plus, I think the two of you just plain had fun together. May and I like Arlene, too."

Samantha nodded, smiling lovingly. "I know you do," she whispered.

Hiram looked solemnly into his niece's eyes. "Samantha, my dear. Do you understand why your experience with this doctor will ruin your friendship with his daughter?"

"Well, I'll never know what Dr. Ott told Arlene unless she tells me and she would surely have gotten a far different version than what really happened. I might find myself wedged between her and her father."

"Hmmm," said Hiram, nodding, arms crossed now, his chin resting on an open palm. "I agree, Samantha, and you can rest assured that I won't let an affluent creep like the good doctor Ott drag you through our court system. I won't let him and his pack of dirty lawyers try to turn you into something other than the victim you were, unless you want me to. I won't go after his money either, unless you want that. His money would seem dirty to me, but make up your own mind. What I plan to do, unless you object, is run the sleazy son-of-a-bitch out of town. I know the Chief of Police here in Dallas. We go back pretty far, to our army days in fact, and all I have to do is relate parts of your story and the good doctor won't be seeing another patient in Texas. You think on it and tell me what to do, Samantha. Now, wanna go downstairs and tell May nothing happened that you and I can't handle. Okay?"

"Okay, but I don't have to think about anything. You know what's best, Uncle Hiram, and I would have wanted to do just what you suggested anyway."

Samantha saw her friend Arlene at school each day for over three weeks, but their association was icy at best. On a Monday at the regularly scheduled assembly held in the auditorium, the school's principal, Arlene at his side, stood before the entire high school student body and announced that the junior class president was transferring to a private school in Austin. The announcement was first met with boos and catcalls, then cheers and claps and two speeches from junior class officers based on how the faculty and each individual student would surely miss such a born leader and fine person as Ms. Arlene Ott. Row by row, the students filed by and shook Arlene's hand, kissed her on the cheek, or hugged her, as did Samantha, who never saw nor heard from her friend nor Dr. Ott again, but never forgot either of them.

Chapter 2

The last semester of Samantha's senior year was her most enjoyable. The extra credits she had earned in the previous summer session allowed her the time to take a trip to Europe. One Saturday morning in April, she left Dallas on TWA and returned in the late afternoon two weeks later, having spent a week in Paris, three days in Madrid and four days in Rome. The long flight back across the Atlantic and home to Dallas was almost dreamlike, maybe a little nightmarish, too. It seemed to take a lifetime and Samantha's anxiety grew with every minute. She had never before been completely on her own, and although the only thing that happened to upset her during the trip was a roller coaster ride in Paris that made her sick to her stomach, she feared every man who had approached her. Even the most harmless conversations reminded her of how easily she had been enveloped into Dr. Ott's grips. And, there was always something missing. It seemed she had seen in every situation, so much less than she had in her life with her aunt and uncle. Paris was supposed to be a city of romance, but Samantha only saw its lacking or its seemingly artificial attempt at achieving its reputation. However, for her, the exhilaration of being in Paris, affected her in a way she felt others would be fortunate to experience. The city and its people merely raised her awareness of those she loved who also loved her in her very own home. There was no argument with Samantha, Europe had beauty in its storied history, but not being able to share it with her aunt and uncle diminished her appreciation.

As the big jet slowed and dipped its nose to descend into the traffic pattern at Love Field, Samantha raised her window curtain and looked out for the first time. Until then, she hadn't wanted to watch the ocean or eastern seaboard states crawl by. It would have only made her heart race and anxiety zoom to heights that might make her sick. With the realization of the vastness she saw below, she also saw the growing potential of her life, the security she felt in the care and control of her honorable uncle, his unrestrained love. Aunt May was one to love and appreciate, but Uncle Hiram was one to be loved by, to always have his trust and understanding. Samantha realized that last year when he was so supportive and helpful after the horrible experience with her friend's father.

The long final approach to Love Field, the endless taxiing to the gate, then getting her tote bag and getting off of the big jet was worse than the last hours before Christmas morning finally arrives for Samantha. She couldn't see over the line of people or distinguish a single sound until the woman in front of her turned and asked her to quit pushing. "Sorry," said Samantha, trying to look around the long line of people. "I just can't wait."

"Trust me, you will wait," snapped the woman, then turned away.

"Welcome home, Honey," greeted May, with a kiss on the cheek and a big hug the second Samantha stepped from the plane. "After my kids graduated high school, I never thought I'd miss having young people in my house again, but we've missed you so much. Your uncle has just been beside himself."

Hiram was standing behind his wife. "Now, Samantha, don't pay any attention to your aunt," he said, smiling. "We had a good time while you were gone and if you ever earn another trip, you just take it and don't worry about us."

Samantha fell into her uncle's arms, almost tackling him. "I had a great time, too, Uncle Hiram," she sighed, in a broken voice. "But my next trip will be with you, or I'm not going."

Soon after her trip abroad, Samantha began to feel a spirit of triumph. Whether she had really enjoyed Europe or not, she had done something entirely on her own, traveled across an ocean, took care of herself in foreign lands, was able to see some of the historical sights of Western Europe and was never really threatened. However, she suspected that part of her triumphant feeling came from the fact that she returned to the same world, the same loving arms and understanding hearts of Uncle Hiram and Aunt May. The following Sunday, and most nights thereafter, Samantha prayed for God to grant long, happy, and healthy lives to her aunt and uncle and to help her overcome the fear of strangers she'd felt since her experience with Dr. Ott.

Although it didn't begin that way, Samantha grew to love May and Hiram differently. She knew she would always feel a special bond with her uncle. It started with his immediate trust and respect for her and was sealed with his handling of the matter with Dr. Ott. Samantha would never doubt Hiram's unwavering covenant to love her, an indisputable reality that was all-new in her life. Her mother and father were always too busy with their own individual concerns to take notice of the needs of anyone else. They hardly noticed each other, which led to the demise of their marriage.

Hiram Wheeler was a graduate of Southern Methodist University in Dallas and wanted Samantha to consider enrolling for her freshman year so she could commute to the campus and continue to live at home. However, the tuition for full-time students was much more than Samantha could afford on her allowance and she wanted to pay her own way. She agreed to enroll at SMU, but put a condition with her acceptance of Hiram's suggestion. Samantha would enroll only if she could work days and take night courses, no more than three per semester. Hiram would have paid for her books and tuition, but was delighted with Samantha's responsible choice. "Well, thank you," he merely said, hugging his niece as if he'd scored a victory. He loved her beyond his own understanding.

Hiram went with Samantha to the campus on registration day and introduced her to the director of the registrar's office. "Hello, Mrs. Baker," he said. "This is Samantha Wheeler, the finest young lady I've ever known. I'm blessed to have her as a niece, blessed that she lives with my wife and me and could be even further blessed if you'd put her to work somewhere here on campus. She'll be taking nine hours her first semester."

Samantha's freshman year was an experiment for her. Every night after her classes, she tried to walk to her car and drive home without thinking of any possibility of harm coming to her. While walking along, she would sing or hum, review assignments sometimes, or try to remember different passages in The Bible she'd discussed with her uncle. As the days went by, she became more and more comfortable when alone, almost brave.

The first semester flew by for Samantha. Hiram coached her on study habits that had helped him and asked her questions from her notes every morning at breakfast. May adjusted her breakfast hour from seven am sharp to around midmorning in order to facilitate Samantha's later hours due to her night courses and labs. Samantha made two A's and a B on the nine credit hours she earned that semester. However, she made two B's and earned only six credit hours the second semester, having dropped a biology course when her schedule became almost unmanageable. The problem was somewhat due to her popularity with the junior and senior boys. "Either you tell'em no, or give up something, Hon," advised her aunt. "How about that art course on Tuesday and Thursday nights? It's just an elective, isn't it?"

"Yes, it is, Aunt May, but I love to paint. I should think about biology though. I'm behind and I want to do well in the courses required for my major."

During the first semester of her sophomore year, Samantha began dating Ken Valentine, a law student from Houston. Her feelings for him could never approach what she felt for her uncle, but somewhat like Hiram, Ken wanted to be helpful. So far, he had been considerate and seemed genuinely fond of Samantha. Ken was unthreatening and made her feel even safer when on campus. He was a free spirit, was always in a good mood, which never failed to uplift everyone around him. He began his romantic charade with notes left on Samantha's windshield, a chronology of make-believe meetings between a goddess from Venus and a lonely Martian exiled to the planet earth for his celestial war crimes. After a month of daily stories with hilarious plots, along with Samantha's becoming increasingly anxious to meet the man behind the notes, she left a message on her windshield for Ken. It was an invitation to dinner at her home. The night he found her note, she was watching from the shadows of the administration building. "How did you know who owned that car?" she asked, once she knew the notes she'd gotten weren't some trick of Dr. Ott's. Her uncle had warned her that sometimes criminals strike a second time.

"I have my ways," said the note writer. "My name's Ken Valentine. I know yours, Ms. Samantha Wheeler," he added, extending his hand. "Thanks for responding to my fumbling way to get to know you."

Ken showed up at the Wheeler home in shorts and a tee shirt. He was barefoot, his exposed skin was stained with green cake coloring and his hair dyed red. May enjoyed Ken immensely, but Hiram had an immediate dislike for him and never changed his mind. "I agree, he's a funny young man, Samantha," said Hiram, while discussing the young law student after he had left for the campus. "He kept you and May entertained for sure, but that just goes so far. There's something about that boy that bothers me though. I can't put a finger on it, but it's more than his silly antics. I hope you'll be especially prudent in your dealings with him, Hon."

"I will, Uncle Hiram," promised Samantha, then kissed him, a little quick peck on the lips, the first time ever.

Hiram, wise with his years, knew that his niece's unusual show of affection came from different emotions. One, the care she felt for him, but the other from the amorous feelings brought on by the dinner guest. "Goodnight, Samantha," he said, then crooked a finger, indicating that he wanted to whisper something to her. "I truly believe that if you ever realize the wonder of you, Young Lady, those kisses will be reserved for only those you love. Ask your aunt someday. She was hard to get, but when I did, I slipped a ring onto her finger and never looked back. I knew I had me a wonder, like you, Hon."

The Christmas break that semester was shared between Ken's parent's home in Houston and Samantha's in North Dallas. While around his family, Ken was charming, but very serious, almost wooden with his constant formality. Samantha got the feeling that his parents didn't approve of something about their son, care for her, or each other. Sybil, his mother, while giving Samantha a tour of the Valentine home, showing off the many western art prints they owned, made an issue about Samantha choosing such an expensive university as SMU when she had to work to merely meet the tuition for a part-time schedule. Among other disparaging remarks, she made it clear that Samantha's interest in science and medicine was misguided. Her reason no more than 'a woman's intuition' when it came to abstract things like determining what life pursuits one should endeavor to accomplish. Surprisingly though, Sybil approved of Samantha's interest in art and asked to see some of her work sometime. "The world's full of wanna-be artists, Samantha," Sybil had said, with a surly smile. "Ninety-nine percent never sell a piece of their work, because it isn't any good. I know and I've been told by several successful gallery owners that I have the eye. I've owned some of the finest work of recognized artists from all over the world. And, Dearest, I am completely qualified to advise you about your own work. I'll know if you have enough talent to ever do anything with your paintings. So many beginning artists go years before having to admit it."

Ted, Ken's father, was only home for one evening meal, avoiding more than a quick introduction to Samantha while he was serving cups of hot eggnog.

Almost immediately when classes resumed after the Christmas break, Ken went from a funny man to one who was in serious pursuit of a wife, namely Samantha Wheeler. His campaign included frequent romantic dinners, sparing no expense. A movie now and again and weekend outings that often required an airline flight. Once to Nashville to see the Grand Ole Opry, then twice to New Orleans, once during Mardi Gras and once to just hang out on Bourbon Street. In late April and twice again during the month of May, Ken took Samantha to different South Texas gulf resorts to lay in the sun and dine in swank restaurants.

Samantha was less than smitten with Ken Valentine, but grew to like and enjoy him. He was as persistent as anyone she had known and seemed equally as dependable. He never stood her up, nor was he ever late for a date and never failed to have set plans for an evening, or weekend's entertainment. He never studied either, which Samantha often asked about. Ken explained it away the afternoon he proposed. It was at the Cotton Bowl, during the final minutes of a football game. SMU was hosting Rice University and had just tied the score with a field goal. The stands, filled with red and blue clad SMU fans who were jumping and stomping, yelling and clapping, screaming and whistling, were shaking as if ready to cave in. "My Darling, Samantha," shouted Ken, trying to be heard above the reverberating sounds of the crowd.

"I love you. I want to marry you. I have to. You're the number one priority in my life and I'm going to fail at everything else I do if you continue to refuse me."

Samantha made light of Ken's proposal that day, assuming his reference to her refusing him meant his persistence that he be allowed sexual intimacy with her. She had not surrendered and would not bring the risks associated with taking such an irresponsible freedom into her aunt and uncle's home. She knew that outwardly they would be understanding, but inwardly they would be crushed and their hearts would break if something so severe as an unexpected pregnancy should happen. It would be the hardest on the one person who Samantha felt the deepest love for, her Uncle Hiram. She loved her Aunt May, but a mere approving hug from her uncle had become almost spiritual for her. He was, and maybe always would be, the only person in her life she could confide in fully. Samantha had told her Uncle Hiram everything he had ever asked her about her relationship with Ken.

As the semester continued, so did Ken's pressure for Samantha's hand in marriage, but she continued with her life's plan, enjoying how smoothly it was going, almost dreamlike with her uncle and aunt's interest and help. However, there were changes on the horizon for Samantha. They began like rumblings that precede an earthquake, then the great event, the eruption, followed by the aftershocks that appeared to have no end.

The first early warning, the rumbling that first rocked her peaceful world happened on a Sunday night. Samantha had just sat down at her plate. "Will Uncle Hiram be late?" she asked.

May said nothing until she had walked around behind Samantha, kissed the top of her head and dropped an unsealed letter onto her plate. "He won't be joining us tonight," she said.

"Is it his heart? Oh, I hope not."

"No, no," responded May, then corrected herself. "Well, in a way it is."

Samantha, began the short handwritten letter from Hiram. *Forgive me, but I no longer have the heart to see your pain. Although I soar with your every triumph, I'm too old and too much of an old fool to share what pains you. Your father phoned early Friday morning to inform me that your mother and a companion have been captured and are facing charges for grand theft in Birmingham, Alabama. Samantha, My Dear, I have fought all weekend with the decision I finally made to tell you about it. I pray nothing changes in your life now, you've done so well and you've made your aunt and me very proud. However, if you choose to visit your mother, May and I will pay your expenses and help arrange your transportation and a suitable place for you to stay. It is not mine or your Aunt May's place to make the decision for you. Always, your loving Uncle Hiram.*

Samantha dropped the letter and ran upstairs to Hiram's bedroom. He was standing at the window, looking out across the treetops that covered the low-slung hills behind the house. "I can't go to Alabama," said Samantha, falling into his arms. "My heart is right here in this house, plus I know you would be worried until I got back safely. Come on downstairs with us. I'm fine."

Samantha wasn't fine, but made sure that she gave every indication she was when around her aunt and uncle. Every time an image of her mother being behind bars crept into her mind, she would reject it as quickly as it had appeared. Like with Dr. Ott, she would dismiss the thought in favor of the words to a song, or something concerning her studies.

In time though, Ken began to see through Samantha's facade. His perception of her changed. He knew she was hiding, or fighting something. Her shield of independence, her needing nothing stance had cracked. Samantha was vulnerable and Ken liked her better for it. In his mind, her beauty, that look that made others feel lesser than they really were, had stepped aside and made room for him. In contrast to her phony iron will and stubborn stances on her own self-centered goal-oriented course of day-to-day living, she was becoming more and more pliable with each day. It only made sense. Samantha Wheeler's perfect world, naive as it was, had been penetrated by reality.

The first change in Ken's relationship with Samantha wasn't just a simple awareness. It was actually a reawakening. He had known for a long time that where others fell short in dealing with some silly anxiety, it was always just a shortage of brains and Ken knew he had extra in that department. The more he dwelled on that fact, the more Samantha seemed to be growing inferior to him. Her ideas and opinions soon became of no interest and Ken's seemed even more brilliant to him. She told him of her trip abroad. "Not bad, but I spent a month in Spain with my folks once." When she explained the two jobs she'd had, working as a carhop at the Fox-Fire drive-in and as a typist at The Registrar's Office on campus, Ken had a long explanation for her. It began with how jobs at a lower level than one should do to prepare for a career could actually be very harmful. "Too easy to get in a rut, develop bad work habits because you never have a stake in what you do," he explained, then pointed out how any work that was career related was so very important. "It's like building the foundation good and strong before you put up a house. That's what I try to do when I work with my dad."

Ken had a modicum of self-doubt, but it was beginning to feel less a part of him than at any other time in his life. Now, if he were to be asked to name the three most clever people in the world, he believed the only dilemma would be coming up with the other two names. Furthermore, if there proved to be others in the world who were actually as brainy as himself, Ken Valentine didn't need an association with them. That could cause discussions, debates, and attempts at polarization when their unwavering faith in his decisions was the only way. No, Samantha was perfect now. Tits and ass with no brains. He reasoned that her unawareness coupled with the selfish influence of her ancient aunt and uncle, were now the only reasons for her blind ambition and her hopeless cling to virginity. She needed to know her limits, in due time of course.

Another early warning, the most subtle, was the change that Samantha noticed in her relationship with Ken Valentine. He was always aloof when discussing anything but marriage and quickly became a nuisance on the subject. He dropped some of his courses and usually skipped class on those he didn't. He began to lie, although his excuses were usually understandable. "I just didn't want you to know. You have enough on your plate. Gees, I'm sorry, Samantha. I just didn't want your aunt and uncle to find out. You know how I respect them. I'm crazy about those two old folks. They don't like me so well, but I'm actually bigger than either of them in that reference."

Samantha raised a finger to silence Ken. " Don't fool yourself," she snapped. "Uncle Hiram is twice the man of anyone I have ever known or heard about. Aunt May is wonderful, too, but she doesn't try to have the influence on others that she could. You're wrong about my aunt and uncle, Ken. Completely wrong and I don't appreciate your opinion of them in the least."

Ken accepted Samantha's harsh stance and didn't see her until he stopped by her zoology lab that Thursday night, purporting to only want to walk her to her car. However, his need for someone to hear his diatribe of scathing words for his parents and older sister, Pat, proved to be the reason. A vicious conspiracy between them had suddenly formed. They had, as a family unit, decided to cut his allowance in half and stop paying his school expenses at the end of the current semester, giving him no choice but to drop out. Ken was a third semester law student, although after the current semester, he would have been at the university seven and a half years.

"What will you do?" asked Samantha. "Get a job and work like I do?"

Ken turned away and looked out across the campus as if he was saying goodbye to an old friend. "No. No, I shouldn't work," he sighed, pitifully as he hung his head. "It really can't be done in law school. The guys who work never finish with decent grades." There was a moment of confusing silence, then Ken turned to face Samantha again. "Hey girl. Cheer up," he said, smiling as if completely comfortable in the face of his sudden problem. "You know me better than that. I have it all worked out with my father. I told him how bad I want to marry you and guess what he said."

"That you're nuts?"

"No. No way," corrected Ken, his smile one of satisfaction. "Dad knows what I have in you. He told me that if we get married, and I do a tour in the army like he did, he'd take me into his firm and pay me just like I was already a member of Texas State Bar. All I have to do is finish law school at the University of Houston. Sound great? You can go to school full time down there, too. I'll have the means to support us both."

Samantha stalled, declining to further consider marriage until nearer semester's end. Then, one Friday in mid-December, the event proving to be the rupture that allowed her life's order to explode and steal away like molten lava running to the sea, came in a phone call. Samantha was working at her desk in the Registrar's office.

"Dad's dead," she heard. It was her cousin, Lorraine, calling from Parkland Hospital, a new facility with a fine trauma center where Samantha had dreamed of working one day. "Heart attack, of course," added Lorraine. "You might want to come down. His last words, at least according to Mom, was a jumbled-up phrase about her taking care of you. I'm sure that..."

Samantha heard nothing else. Suddenly, as if the receiver was too heavy to hold, she dropped it, then fell from her chair, dragging papers and the big black phone cradle down on top of her. When she awoke, she was outside on the sidewalk lying flat on her back staring at an angry cloud with a dark bottom like Uncle Hiram always mentioned as one heavy with rain and even hail. Blurry faces peered down on her, but the world around her was without sound, no one spoke or moved. It was as if she'd joined her beloved uncle in death.

Samantha blinked her eyes. "I, uh..."

A chorus of voices cried out like at a sporting event. "Yippee. We did it guys. We did it. Hey, everybody step back. Make room. Give her some air."

Hiram's heart attack was actually two. The first, a sudden jolt that knocked him to his knees, occurred while he was cleaning out his old drawing room so Samantha could use it if she chose to set up her own home studio. The second one, a massive one that took his life, happened while he lay flat on the floor, his head in May's lap, awaiting the ambulance she had called. His last words were not jumbled, but clear and complete. "May, you've been all I could ever want for almost forty years. I can't think of one complaint and I promise to thank you properly when you join me up there. You know I only told you one lie in my life."

"Please be quiet, Hiram. You should just try to lay still and breathe evenly. I know you're hurting but help is on the way."

"No. I've expired, finally expired and I need to tell you about the lie I told you repeatedly for twenty years. It's important, because I want you to tell a little fib for me. Please."

"Make it quick if you feel you have to. I'd kill for you, Hiram, so you know I'd fib if it was important," sighed May, her eyes full of tears.

"I did smoke," confessed Hiram, smiling, "Ten cigarettes a day at my desk down at the office. I quit on your forty-ninth birthday."

"I know, Hiram. It's a little late to lie about that. The kids used to tell me that you smelled of smoke. I just couldn't take that away from you. I didn't have many other complaints. Besides, I loved you then, just as I do right now."

"Ha," choked Hiram. "I think you're fibbing already, but speaking of love, I guess Samantha has reawakened us a little. From the day we sat there listening to that judge in Sherman while he read those adoption papers, little Samantha shaking like a leaf, I'm reminded of that long ago Sunday we wed. I see you every time I look at her. Til death do we part? Heck, neither one of us had any idea what we were saying. You know we didn't really plan anything so ornery as sticking together as long as we did, but we did and I'm going to my grave proud of it." Hiram paused, coughed and took a deep breath. "I've got too much to say, so I'll hurry," he struggled. "Do this for me, that's if you can, of course. I'd like you to try to keep Samantha from coming to the funeral. With all she's had to deal with already in her young life, something so unyielding as death just might be a little much. I still remember my father's service. I was bothered for a time, but I'm sure you remember that. Next, I want you to give my watch to Samantha. Take it right now. You know our greedy kids will make a fuss if they ever find out, so just fib a little. Tell them I wanted to be buried with it. Now think about this," continued Hiram, after May had his gold watch and chain in her apron pocket. "We have to admit that we consciously put Samantha at the center of our lives. We truly love her, so don't let my passing limit her life in any way. I'm happy you have her, May. She's a blessing, so you take care of her for us. I've left our affairs where you can easily. The kids will deposit your check in the bank every month just like they have for the past eight years. Now say goodbye. I'm going to sleep."

May whispered her goodbye, hearing the ambulance's siren as she did, then felt her husband's final spasmodic convulsion. Hiram Wheeler was dead before his body was placed onto a gurney.

Chapter 3

May whispered Hiram's final words to Samantha while they stood arm in arm at the wake held in the drawing room. Samantha listened as she stared blankly at the big body of her beloved uncle. He lay in peaceful silence, as if a mannequin sculptured to perfection, his eyes closed, his hair combed neatly as always, his cheeks and lips an apple pink, the pallor of his death hidden with makeup. A photo. Suddenly, her hand pulled from the grasp of May's and reached for Hiram's face. Samantha brushed his forehead with the backs of her fingers, sliding them down his right cheek to the cleft of his chin, then resting open palm in the center of his chest. "Uncle Hiram," she said, the unmistakable voice of a grown woman, pain filled but determined and strong. "I love you with all I have to love with, and I always will." Samantha bent over the casket and kissed Hiram's chin, then whispered, "God rest you until we meet again."

"Honey, your uncle is gone, and he would want us to go on. You…"

"Uncle Hiram will never be gone from me, Aunt May. I will go on, for him more than for myself, but my uncle will never be gone from me for one minute."

Samantha, acquiescing to Hiram's final wish for her, did not attend the graveside services, but turned from the casket and went to her room, where she stayed for four days. Her pain was exhausting and greater than all before it. Sleep was the only escape she could think of, although she was awakened many times by her own dreams. May brought a tray of food twice a day, Lorraine and Ken Valentine came to the room two times each. Ken's first visit was completely ignored. It was in the early evening hours the day of Hiram's funeral. There was a light tap on the bedroom door followed by it slowing opening then his whispering. Samantha lay still, keeping her eyes closed and hoping to return to the protective shelter of a deep sleep.

The dreams that tormented Samantha were of being lost, running from things unseen, calling for her uncle while falling and falling, or running and running, but never finding Hiram or reaching what awaited. Every dream included the face of Dr. Ott, his words, or just a sighting of him in passing. One dream included Ken. When she ran by what appeared to be the gates of Heaven, she saw that he was there on his knees, covered with blood, pleading to get in, but Samantha kept running. Running from whatever unseen evil chased her. That dream occurred the afternoon of Ken's second visit. He awoke her, a rose in an extended hand and an engagement ring in another, held behind him. "My Darling," he whispered, shaking Samantha, then bringing the shiny diamond ring around to show her the moment she opened her eyes. "I want you to wear this," he said, whispering through his silly perception of a sympathetic smile. "I enlisted today, and we can get married as soon as I get home from basic training. I report in ninety days, then, eight weeks after that, we'll get married at the chapel on campus. We'll have the world by the tail, My Dear."

"Go away," sighed Samantha, then buried her head in a pillow, considering Ken's words and actions tasteless sympathy.

"Okay, but I'm going to leave your ring on the dresser. I'll see you when you come back to work. I love you, Samantha. You're so beautiful."

Both of Lorraine's visits were longer and much different from Ken's. For one, Samantha wasn't meant to be awakened either time. The first one was just after Ken's second visit, when Samantha awoke to find her cousin snooping through her desk. "Can I help you find something, Lorraine?" she asked.

"What? Oh, no, sorry. It's just that I've never seen this desk. It's quite nice you know. Where did you buy it?" Lorraine emphasized the word buy.

Samantha explained that May had arranged for the desk and had paid for it, she assumed, then Lorraine's questions became more pointed. "And, your new car? Was that a little arrangement also? What do you live on? Is there another convenient arrangement there, too? Ken said you work part-time. Does your little job provide you with your needs? A nice car, your books and tuition and a closet full of pretty dresses? Hmmm, you must be a valuable commodity, Samantha Wheeler. Ken seems to think so, anyway."

Samantha, with even greater detail this time, explained everything that affected her existence, including the fact that she had been legally adopted, but Lorraine said nothing. She merely listened, then left the room. Later, Samantha was awakened by the light that spilled into her bedroom when Lorraine eased the door open and crept in. Her cousin turned and quietly pushed the door closed, allowing only a sliver of light into the otherwise pitch-dark room. Samantha quietly watched, pretending to be yet sleeping while Lorraine, a ghostlike image in the faint light, went to her dresser and slowly, one by one, searched through every drawer. Samantha knew who she was watching. Lorraine's long dress and frumpy appearance were unmistakable, yet Samantha felt a certain fear while watching her cousin. The fear was real, almost like that she felt when Dr. Ott was violating her. Suddenly, she felt very nervous, sweaty, unclean and as unworthy as Lorraine's words had been meant to make her feel. There was no Uncle Hiram to look to for comfort and there never would be again. Ken Valentine could never be that kind of influence in her life and no one she knew would ever love her as her uncle had.

Samantha waited until Lorraine held up the ring Ken had left and was examining its shiny diamond in the limited light. "Lorraine, what are you really looking for?" she asked. "I'll tell you if I know. Just tell me what it is."

"Oh," exclaimed Lorraine. "Good grief you scared me. Why didn't you let me know you were awake? I could have croaked just like Dad did."

"What are you looking for, Lorraine?" repeated Samantha, ire in her tone.

"Just this. Ken told me all about your plans. Congratulations. He's terrific and you'd better grab him. I'm getting a divorce, you know."

"Really?"

"Yes, really. Ike doesn't want a wife. He's a real...Oh, you don't care, except that I'll be taking my room back. In fact, you and I need to talk."

Lorraine had been talking most of the afternoon. She and May had sat out on the porch and discussed Samantha's situation thoroughly. The words Lorraine had for Samantha now were only reporting the results of what she had already affected. On June first, Samantha's car would be returned to the rightful owner, Wheeler Brothers Construction. Her allowance would be discontinued that day also and she would have fifteen days to find other living arrangements. "You're not our responsibility forever, Samantha," explained Lorraine. "You aren't actually family, and you know that. Mother has no sense when it comes to money. Heck, she admitted just today that she's never even reconciled her own checkbook. Dad always did that for her, but he can't now, you understand. I'll have to. Sorry, but I will see that you get an extra five hundred dollars the day you clear out."

Later that night May left with Lorraine, and Samantha didn't see her again until the following week. Samantha came home early Friday afternoon to eat and change clothes before her classes. She had agreed to see Ken for the first time since he came into her room to show her the diamond engagement ring. May was fixing sandwiches for Lorraine's nine and ten-year-old sons. "Oh, it's my Samantha," she screamed, through the open kitchen window.

Samantha hopped up onto the big porch and hurried into the kitchen, then into her aunt's awaiting embrace. "Oh, I've missed you, Aunt May. How have you been? Where have you been?"

May stood back to look her niece over. "Oh, Honey," she sighed, then buried her face in her hands. Samantha embraced her. "What's wrong, Aunt May?"

"The kids," she whispered. "Lorraine really, but Henry and Joe Neil are going along, too." May paused to look toward the staircase, then continued, yet whispering, but hurriedly so. "Listen, Honey," she said. "Don't do anything now, but there's an envelope hidden under my lilac bush at the west end of the porch. It's just something for you, but remember this. Lorraine has looked this house over for them and probably tore your room up in the process. You can never tell any of our kids, especially, Lorraine. Your Uncle Hiram wouldn't want that, Honey. We agreed that they would never need to know. Now,...Oh..."

Those were the last words May ever spoke to Samantha. Lorraine stepped into the kitchen from the dining room and grabbed her arm.

"Come on," she ordered. "We can go now. The boys will be happy to eat in the car."

Lorraine's boys, carrying their sandwiches, followed May and their mother outside, crawled into the back seat of Lorraine's silver Cadillac, then she zoomed away. Samantha changed, straightened her room, ate quickly, then hurried out to get the envelope May had told her about. She found it inside of a newspaper, sealed, with a penciled note on front. *Samantha*, it said. *Hiram won't need to know the time and I won't have anyone to show my ring off to, so we decided they should be yours. Other than each other, your uncle and I never loved another person as we do you. Goodbye, My Dear, and thank you for being such a wonderful part of our lives.*

Samantha, jolted and weakened by the gifts and note from May, did not go to her classes, but sat on the porch in first one wicker chair then the other and cried. There could never be an event, or any person in her life that could replace what she'd lost in her aunt and uncle, she knew. The love and trust they'd shown her had been immediate and their guidance would be everlasting. She would, she decided, keep the watch and ring forever, symbols of the purity of Hiram and May, two people who were icons of all good things that had happened to her. Samantha would never forget their love.

Samantha, although weary and too tired to even drive safely, met Ken at nine that night as she had agreed. He was waiting for her at Victor's, a restaurant on Lemon Avenue near the campus. "Hi, Baby," he said, pouring a second glass of champagne as she approached. "I feel like celebrating."

Samantha slid into the booth across from him. "I don't," she sighed.

"Well, just why not?" Ken passed a glass of champagne to Samantha.

"You should know, but maybe you don't understand me at all."

"Oh, I think I do. You're down in the dumps because you're about to be on your own." Ken paused to offer a toast.

"You insensitive idiot," said Samantha, a tired sigh again, then picked up her glass and clicked it against his, hard enough to break them both, although neither did. "You and Lorraine would make a perfect pair," she added, then placed her glass down without taking a taste.

"You think so, huh? Well, I know you're kidding, but maybe your stepsister, or cousin, or whatever you say she is, and I are somewhat alike," agreed Ken, then drained his glass and refilled it. "Yep," he continued. "I think Lorraine's a lot smarter than most ladies I know. Pat, my older sister, is just a little like you, Samantha. Stubbornly impractical you might say. Our parents have money and live like pompous brats. They could share the wealth. They just don't. Kind of like you, Pat never says a word." Ken took a long drink from his champagne, then plowed on with his commentary. "Well, you and Pat won't speak your minds, but I damn sure will. Just yesterday, I spoke out for you and me, Samantha. I get a partner's level salary starting the day I get out of the army. I don't know what you think, but I just want you to be able to go to school full time. That's all. Without you, I don't need anything, but I want you and I want what's best for you."

"What makes you think..."

"Samantha," interrupted Ken, one hand up as he poured himself more champagne with the other. "Lorraine bent my ear for an hour that day I came to see you. She told you that you're out on the street June first and you didn't say a word. She told me she thinks you stole Hiram's watch and May's ring, but I spoke up. I told her she was fuckin crazy. Yep, I let her have it and I know she appreciated my spunk."

"If you say another word like that, Ken, I'm leaving."

"Sorry. How about the watch and ring?"

"It's none of your business, but I just got them today and I'm not the least bit ashamed of having them. Aunt May gave them to me and told me that she and Uncle Hiram had decided they wanted me to have them. I don't..."

"Where are they?" interrupted Ken.

"In my car under the spare tire. Why?"

"Why?" echoed Ken. "You have to find a safe place to keep'em, Samantha, that's why? You must know Lorraine is a determined woman. She'll go to any length to get'em. I've got a lock box at the bank. Hell, you can keep'em in there as long as you want."

"Really? Well, how would...?"

"Let me finish what we started earlier, Samantha," said Ken, interrupting before taking a sip of the champagne. While appearing deep in thought, he twisted the glass in his hand, watching the bubbles rise for a moment, then took a longer drink and continued. "Face it. You could have negotiated some with Lorraine. You could have agreed to move if she'd give you a little more time on your allowance and another year or so with your car. However, nothing's going to change now, Babe, except that I'm offering something better than you have. I'll say it right here in front of God and everybody. I love you and I want to marry you. I'll take care of you for as long as I live. Period. End of report. Now, please, have some champagne with me and, by the way, wear that ring I gave you and let's put your aunt and uncle's stuff in my lock box."

The night lasted through three bottles of expensive champagne and until everyone had left Victor's except a sleek, dark-skinned man who came to the table, his eyes like black lights. He wore shiny black shoes with sharp toes, a three-piece black suit and a matching fedora. "Do you need some help getting home, Ken?" he asked. "I'd be happy to call a cab."

After an unsuccessful check of Samantha's glass for a remaining drop, Ken, his eyes gyros, looked up into the man's face. "How many are there of you, tonight, Raul?" he slurred, laughing at his own humor, his world of blurry images.

"Can you drive, Madame?" asked the man of Samantha.

Two kitchen workers helped Ken into the back seat of Samantha's car while she settled the check, one hundred and eighty-one dollars including a five-dollar tip, which brought an oriental style bow at the waist from the man in the black suit and fedora. "Gracias," he said. "Ken be excelente pasado manana," he assured, then turned and disappeared into the kitchen.

Samantha sat at the table wondering what she should do for several minutes. She finally walked out of the restaurant just as the two kitchen employees stepped inside, laughing until they saw her. "Night, Ma'am," one said, in an Alabama drawl. "Careful. Da dude puked in da back floboad. Sorry bout dat."

After driving to an all-night service station on Mockingbird and hosing out the mess in the back floorboard of her car, Samantha set out for her home in North Dallas. During the drive, experiencing the sensation for the first time, she felt like she would be intruding to stay even one more night in her aunt and uncle's home.

Ken, having been splashed with water several times while Samantha washed out the floorboard, suddenly awoke and climbed into the front seat, rolling down the window as soon as he was situated. "Wow, what a night. What a night," he said. "Are we going to stay at your place?"

"It looks that way, doesn't it," said Samantha, disgusted, but too distraught to express herself. "You'll be on the porch, and I'll be inside."

Ken was wide-awake by the time Samantha pulled up at the big house in North Dallas. The moment he stepped up onto the big porch, as alert as he normally was, he asked where the engagement ring was that he had given Samantha. "I'm surprised that Lorraine didn't take it, but it's right where you left it," she said, gesturing for Ken to take her aunt's wicker chair. "I'll get you a blanket and pillow."

"Can you go get it? Your ring, I mean. I promise I'll wait out here."

The final event that changed Samantha's life forever began to take form just after sunup on Saturday morning. For the next several hours, she dozed in Hiram's rocking chair while Ken sold and sold, pled and pled, promised and promised until Samantha finally asked the wrong question. "Where would I live while you're in boot camp?"

"Well," said Ken, the sheepish grin of a confessional crossing his face. "I lied about the army. I, uh…1 did go down and talk to a recruiter, but I used that to make a better deal with Dad. I get to stay in school until I get my law degree, another year maybe. That way I can get a commission when I enlist. We'll rent us an apartment for now, then you can keep it until I get us a place wherever I'm assigned. I'll be sending you an allotment you know. I think the guy said three hundred a month. You can work, too. You'll have my car. We know you're gonna lose yours June the first. Lorraine's the judge and jury on that."

Although reluctant, but feeling she had few choices, Samantha agreed to marry Ken while they ate a late breakfast. Her heart was heavy with the weight of all that had happened, her mind a dysfunctional mess in the face of the many changes to be endured. "Okay, I've said it," she said. "Shake on it." Samantha stood and extended her right hand. "Take my car and do whatever it takes to get yours from that restaurant we were at last night. I'm sure you don't remember, but you owe me at least half of our check. I had to pay a hundred and eighty-six dollars to bail us out. For now though, I'm going to bed."

Ken reached down and took his fiancee's left hand, gently slipped the engagement ring on her ring finger, kissed the back of her hand, then saluted, his face glowing with elation. "Lieutenant Valentine at your service, Ma'am. Get some shuteye. I have first watch and you can always count on me. I'm paying the total check. There'll be a hundred and eighty-six dollars in yo hot little hand befo sunset."

Ken left immediately, racing to the apartment he'd rented on Cedar Springs the day he talked with Lorraine. Before going inside, he took the watch and necklace from the trunk of Samantha's car, then hitchhiked to Victor's, got his car, then drove to his bank. There, he rented a lock box, stored the watch and ring, withdrew five hundred dollars, then rushed to the SMU campus and met with the pastor at the chapel. The meeting lasted less than ten minutes. The pastor was used to the many questions young people had about getting married. "If you're both twenty-one or older, just get a license and come back Thursday afternoon anytime after one," he said "I've started keeping my calendar clear one afternoon a week just for you students."

Ken hurried out of the chapel and drove to his apartment where he showered and took a nap. He was back to pick up Samantha just before nightfall, an extra apartment key and the one hundred and eighty-six dollars in his extended hand. "Well, here you are, Samantha," he said, handing her the key and the money. "Case closed. The famous watch and ring are in my lock box," he assured her, holding up the key. "I rented us an apartment today and you're going to love it. Two bedrooms, two bathrooms and a laundry right across the street." Ken paused to take a breath, then smiled and opened his palms as if addressing a room full of people. "We can get the license Monday and get married next Thursday afternoon at the campus chapel. I talked to the pastor just before I came back here. How's that for one afternoon's work?"

Samantha and Ken worked all day Sunday moving her belongings to the apartment on Cedar Springs, then were married the following Thursday. Her mind was jumbled and her heart was heavy all week, but Ken kept trying to champion the cause, doing all he could to ease her pain. He maintained constant enthusiasm and a special brightness, kept his appearance neat and conducted himself as if he and Samantha were yet dating, once taking her to his bank to prove he'd put her watch and ring in safe keeping.

Mood swings and doubts haunted Samantha though. She was well aware that her life had suddenly taken on an unexpected seriousness, regardless of Ken's attempts to ease her transition and raise her spirits. "I don't know. I really just don't know what I'm doing," she once said, her voice weak. It was the Tuesday before the wedding ceremony. She and Ken were eating a late lunch at the student union building. "I can't let myself relax, Ken. The minute I do, Uncle Hiram pops into my mind. Aunt May, too, but she's probably going to be okay in time. My uncle was such a loss. To many people really. He had a way of just being there. Always the one who understood and could make a problem seem so simple. You know what I mean, don't you?"

Ken, a likeness to an Ivy League preppy today, was dressed in black slacks, black loafers and a white turtleneck sweater. A strand of his blonde hair had fallen across his forehead. Lately, and again today, his blue eyes seemed to never quit beaming with his pride and elation. "Uh-huh," he said, responding to Samantha's question. "Yes, I do know what you mean. Hiram's gone though and, although you don't know it yet, I'm capable of taking his place and being more to you than he could," claimed Ken, winking, then wiping his mouth before standing in his chair. "Hear ye. Hear ye, all you good people," he requested, turning about, focusing on the high ceiling of the student union building, his arms raised as if summoning the attention of every angel in heaven.

Suddenly, and in complete contrast to the normal rumble of chatty students eating and discussing their various interests, an unusual quietness began to win over, almost as if the air had suddenly rushed from the big dining room. "Attention everyone within the sound of my voice," continued Ken, his focus now on his audience. "Please mark your calendars for two important reasons. First and foremost, Ken Valentine, that's me, and Samantha Wheeler will wed this Thursday in the campus chapel at two pm. Come give us your blessings, please, dear people. Secondly, my bride-to-be isn't pregnant. It's important that you make note of this date. We will not be parents until nine months from Thursday. Thank you for your attention," he concluded, as Samantha was yanking at his pant leg. Ken had lost the interest of his audience, the quietness now a clap or two in afterthought accompanying muffled laughter and constant murmur.

Samantha and Ken lived in the apartment in Dallas for just over a year subsequent to his graduation, then moved to the Houston metro. The delay in moving due in part to the birth of a six-pound little girl, Karla. The small apartment Ken leased was in Baytown on the East Side, the La Porte Freeway a straight shot to center city Houston where he worked with his father in his law practice. There was a shopping mall within walking distance of the apartment that had everything Samantha needed, but a grocery store. There was a branch bank, where Ken opened a household account and rented a lock box for the safekeeping of the watch and ring, a laundry with six washers and dryers and several small stores where Samantha could stroll with the baby when needing to while away her idle hours.

Ken's days began early and ended late, often after nine pm. He had no interest in his new baby unless in the presence of his parents when having dinner with them once a week. It was the only social life Ken had to offer his new family; his work demands the culprit. Samantha, although unable to gain the affections of, or even a reasonable rapport with her in-laws, looked forward to having dinner in their home, a change she could plan on. Her days, always alone with little Karla, had quickly grown boring and seemed to hold less and less interest for her as time went by. Samantha's only outlet was the time she found to spend on her hobby, oil painting. She seldom talked to adults and began fighting to keep from communicating in baby talk when she did.

It irritated Sybil and usually drew harsh words if it happened during dinner. "Sarnantha, cut the baby talk," she had said more than once.

In fact, time became the traitor as Samantha's life droned by with few changes, her anxiety mounting daily and her growing discontent an emerging problem. To deal with it, when Karla was two and a half, she enrolled at the University of Houston and took two correspondence courses. She dug into the work, driven by a painful hunger for the challenge. Soon though, her studies could not fill her time and the idle hours of before seemed even emptier, paralleling her life as she perceived it. Samantha couldn't keep from feeling lonely, starved for adult association. She loved and enjoyed her daughter, but had far too few adult relationships. People always noticed her at the market, but Samantha needed more than passing conversation. Pat, Ken's sister, had told her while on a run to the market, "Samantha, you make me feel like a bag lady. It's not your fault; it's just that you're so utterly beautiful. I'm surprised that you don't have a slew of friends. Men friends."

"Well, thank you, I think," said Samantha, wondering what Pat really meant. "Bag ladies must be pretty. You are, anyway."

Pat reached over and laid her hand on Samantha's arm, then spoke in an unusually serious tone. "Hardly. Anyway, the reason I mentioned how attractive you are is because if I were you, I'd dump Ken and find a more worthy man. Please forgive me for saying this, but it's true. Ken's the creep of our family. He's a worthless, fucked up, self-centered little shit and shouldn't be allowed to even touch you, or Karla."

Samantha, somewhat taken aback, sat silent until Pat stopped in front of the market, then stepped from the car and spoke while walking inside. "I'm not going to get mad, Pat, but tell me why you would say that about Ken."

Pat didn't answer, busying herself with getting shopping carts. Samantha assumed she didn't want to further expand on whatever point she was trying to make concerning her brother, if there was one. The time she spent shopping each week with Pat was like a small vacation to Samantha. It was her only real break. The neighbor, Mrs. Braxton, always volunteered to watch Karla and seemed to enjoy it. Finally, after rolling a cart toward Samantha and strolling away from the market's front door, Pat continued. "I know you must have thought you saw something in Ken, or you wouldn't have married him, Samantha. I know that, but I also know you were mistaken." Pat stopped in front of the bread shelves. "Wheat, right?"

"Please," said Samantha. "How could I have been so mistaken about Ken?"

Pat, always pressed for time, usually pushed her cart ahead, but tonight, she remained beside Samantha. "You know," she said, her tone soft, not to be overheard. "I thought I had Ken figured out when he was about fifteen or sixteen, but I really figured him out a few years later." Pat reached over and placed a hand on Samantha's shopping cart, stopped both carts, turned and put her hands on Samantha's shoulders, then embraced her, kissed her cheek and whispered, "I'm not going to say anything more, Samantha," she said. "I love you to death, and after all, I'm talking about your husband and little Karla's father. Ken is my brother and I'm supposed to love him, but he's made it very easy for me to hate him. I always will and if you ever decide to dump him, you'll have my blessing. Now, let's get our shopping done. I've got to get home and make dinner, then do some ironing."

Samantha thought about that conversation with her sister-in-law, such as it was, for several days. Pat seemed the most stable of the Valentine family and there had to have been something very serious happen between her and Ken to bring on this deep resentment, hate as Pat referred to it. Had he raped her? His own sister? Was it a feud over family money?

Although nothing happened to require any action, Samantha decided that the next time Ken tried to get romantic, she would confront him and hold her ground until she was satisfied that she knew what had happened between him and Pat. Ken seemed to sense it though. He began staying out later, working, visiting with clients and friends, even claiming to spend the night with Pat and her husband the next Monday. It was confusing. Was Pat conspiring with Ken to get rid of Samantha? That seemed unlikely.

The next Tuesday night, Ken came home in a new Chevrolet Impala. He hurried into the kitchen, waved to Samantha, opened the refrigerator and began shuffling through the cold-cuts drawer. "Well, what did you do today besides sleep, woman? Got plenty of that I'd bet."

Oh, he was disgusting, thought Samantha. "Just sleep. Just sleep and do three loads of washing. Well, I did iron four of your shirts and vacuum and clean the mess you left in the hall bathroom, which, by the way, included…"

"Blah blah, blah, yak, yak, yak," mumbled Ken, interrupting. "I'll bet you ten dollars that you would still be watching TV if you hadn't heard me drive up."

Samantha walked part way to the kitchen, then stopped, crossing her arms as she spoke. "Would you care to ask about your daughter's day?"

"Why? Isn't she here?" asked Ken, innocently.

"You idiot. Of course Karla's here," snapped Samantha, severely disgusted now.

"That's good," said Ken, sincerely. The little thing is a nuisance, but that doesn't mean she isn't supposed to be home in bed at this hour, thought Ken, then mumbled, "No ham? Oh, I see it, hidden back in the corner. Stupid place to put lunch meat," he said with bright exuberance. "Hey, Samantha, go look out front. I got me a new car today. Eight point six miles on the odometer when I took delivery."

"Idiot, idiot, idiot. Why do I live with an idiot?" asked Samantha of herself, giving in and walking to the front door. "Nice toy," she said, a tone insinuating her apathy. "Will it get me down to the market and back?"

Ken wasn't going to let anyone drive his new car. "Not tonight. Maybe I can run you down tomorrow. Where's the mayonnaise? Never mind, somebody stuck it in the door. No sweet pickles?"

Samantha closed the front door with a loud bang. "No sweet pickles, very little milk and I'm down to three eggs," she snapped, walking through the den to Karla's room. "Good night. I'll get to the market in the morning somehow."

"This stuff's old," mumbled Ken, struggling to get the mayonnaise jar open. "Hey, Samantha, I'm going to be spending tomorrow night with Pat and her family," he yelled, to the closed bedroom door.

While sitting on the floor by Karla's bed, Samantha decided that she must buy herself a car. She yet had the little amount of money she'd saved while working in the Registrar's office at SMU, plus the five hundred dollars Lorraine had given her for moving out of the big house in North Dallas and turning in her car without incident. Hiram's watch and May's ring were never discussed, leading Samantha to believe that her aunt had spoken out in her behalf.

The next morning, a Wednesday in late May, after arranging for Karla to stay with Mrs. Braxton, the neighbor next door, Samantha took a taxi to a cluster of used car lots that were bunched near the market where she and Pat shopped each week. Luckily, she was able to find something suitable quickly. It was a low mileage, 1954 Ford station wagon, $595.00 including a new spare tire. She had only spent $7.00 for the cab and would only have to pay $1.00 to Mrs. Braxton for watching Karla.

Samantha's day of decision and diversion, having again done something for herself, gaining such independence one's own car offers, with her own money, gave her the same triumphant feeling she had in those days after returning from Europe. She couldn't have loved the station wagon more if it was her own private airplane.

Thursday night, when Ken came home at seven, although Samantha had felt apprehension all afternoon, his attitude about her car fooled her totally. He thought it was a great idea and claimed to have been thinking about doing it himself. "Heck, you need to have something here to drive, Samantha," he agreed. "I was going to get something, but you know my hours. When have I ever even been able to take you shopping for groceries, much less a car? By the way, how do you get to the market and back?"

"Pat takes me every week now, but I've taxied a few times."

"Pat? Oh," sighed Ken. "Well, Hell fire. She claims to be as busy as I am. When can she ever take you to the store, Samantha?"

"Pat's very busy. She works sixty to seventy hours a week, so we both do our shopping at night. She gets here at seven and we're back by eight. By the way, Ken, how did you find the time to shop for your new car?"

"Don't be a smart ass, Samantha. It's none of your business, but Dad had a friend of his bring it to the office. I hope that meets with your approval."

"Would it matter?" asked Samantha. "Good night," she added, stepping into Karla's bedroom and closing the door.

The following Monday, Samantha left Karla with Mrs. Braxton again. She had made an appointment for a full-time position with three doctors at an orthopedic clinic in Pasadena. The interview went smoothly, and Samantha was hired as an assistant therapist and anesthetist, $122.50 per week. Her hours would be Monday through Friday from seven am until four pm. The schedule worked perfectly with Mrs. Braxton who agreed to keep Karla for thirty-five dollars a month.

Although little Karla had been a bright wonder, the past four years had been a draining experience for Samantha. To her, all she had lost and had to give up could never be replaced, but the independence of her own car and the new job brought hope back into her life. Ken, although he made it clear that Samantha would have to bear the expense of any baby-sitting her decision to work would require, felt that she was doing the right thing to broaden her interests, more nearly develop her potential and get to know the satisfaction of being self-supporting. He was no help, but neither was he a problem.

The balance of the summer flew by. Samantha's hours at the clinic each week brought life back into her world. Every morning, after parking her car in her designated spot and walking up to the front door, the clinic seemed an awaiting friend, her best friend. It seemed everyone, sparing the receptionist, who was vaguely nasty by nature, liked Samantha and wanted to help her. The doctors were friendly, but guardedly and professionally so. She met interesting patients, began to talk like an adult again and reveled in the learning experience. There were very few nights she didn't fall asleep while reading through any one of several professional bulletins or medical journals that came to the clinic.

One Thursday in early September while helping Dr. Benjamin prepare a surgical table for a patient, her back to the door, a man's voice startled her. "I was looking for Samantha Valentine, but I can see I've found her."

Surprised, or caught off guard, Samantha whirled around, dropping the roll of paper she was holding. "Sir?" she responded, realizing a split second later how foolish she must have appeared, dropping the paper and whirling around at the mere sound of her name.

The man laughed and reached for the roll of paper on the floor by Samantha's feet. "Good thing I don't wear a badge," he said, then apologized and extended his hand. "I'm David Mills. You and the good doctor here did a fine job on my boy and I just came by to express my appreciation." Dr. Benjamin stepped forward. He had surgically repaired a severely dislocated shoulder for a teenager named Donnie Mills. "Fine boy you have, Sir," said the doctor, taking Mr. Mills' hand. "Easy patient, too. Marvelous how the young heal, isn't it."

Samantha was studying Mr. David Mills. He wasn't much taller than her, quite trim and wore white canvas deck shoes, a perfectly fitted white double-breasted suit with a monogrammed handkerchief that matched his sky blue mock turtleneck. His smile was warm and constant, sending messages of interest. His hair was full, wavy, and black as India ink; his eyes a deep brown and locked with her own. "Could you excuse Samantha and me, Dr. Benjamin?" he asked, a certain warmth in his words and focus.

"Oh, yeah, if that's okay with Mrs. Valentine," said the big doctor, who waited a moment for a response, then left the room and closed the door. Mr. Mills, a puzzled look on his face, spoke as if tortured "I thought I heard the doctor say Mrs. Like married?"

Samantha was lost for words. Although he was at least ten years older, she was staring into the eyes of the perfect man. Appealing in his dress and demeanor, his fixed focus and voice reaching out with tendrils of comfort and trust. "Sir," she said, stalling, "would you repeat your name?"

"David Mills, but I guess I've made a terrible mistake. I'm sure you didn't tell my son that you were single. I mean, I did hear the doctor correctly, didn't I?"

"Did you really come by to ask me out?"

"Guilty as charged," sighed David, smiling, but sending a different message. "You see, I'm widowed, and my son is always looking for the perfect woman for me. Too bad he didn't think to ask if you were married. Sorry. You are married, aren't you?"

"Yes."

"Happily?"

"Miserably, but..."

David held up a hand, a gesture to silence Samantha. "I definitely want to hear more, Samantha. What time do you get off in the afternoons?" he asked.

"Four, but I have to pick up my daughter."

"Hmmm," responded David, squinting an eye as he rubbed his chin in mock thought. "Is there any arrangement we could make that would allow me a little time to talk with you?"

Samantha, as amused as intrigued with David Mills, began to laugh, then found herself ready to cry and turned away from him. Why? She couldn't understand herself. What effect did he have on her? Suddenly, startled again, she felt a hand on her shoulder. "I'm sorry," he whispered. I'll go. I just..."

"No, don't go," said Samantha, turning to face David. "I don't know what's wrong with me. Maybe it's just that I haven't been asked out, or even noticed by a man in...I have no idea how long it's been."

"Wrong. Very wrong, Samantha," said David Mills, reaching back to find the knob to the door. "Women with your looks get noticed all the time. It's just that I want to know you." David's hand found the knob, turned it and pushed the door open a few inches. "I'm curious. My son said that you're the most beautiful woman he's met, yet the nicest and most interesting. That, my dear, seems almost impossible. So, here I am and..."

Samantha, collected now, shrugged and turned back to the table she was working on. "Well, Mr. Mills," she said. "I'll be off at four, so let's have coffee. I'll call my baby-sitter and tell her I'll be an hour late."

At four that afternoon, David Mills was waiting in the parking lot beside his limousine, a stretch Lincoln as black as his hair. "Impressive," said Samantha, as he opened the back door on the driver's side.

"Arrogant actually," said David, smiling, his eyes welding to Samantha's again. "I rented it."

"Why did you do that, Mr. Mills?" asked Samantha, sliding into the back seat of the big Lincoln.

David slid in beside her and closed the door. "Well, I guess it was for the same reason I bought the white suit. To impress you."

"Why? What's wrong with the real you? What do you drive normally?"

"A pickup. I raise horses. Say, I brought some coffee. Want some?"

"Okay." Samantha searched for something to say for a moment, then asked, "Do you raise racehorses?"

"A few, but mostly show horses and riding stock." David took paper cups from a brown grocery sack and poured the coffee from a thermos. "Sugar, cream, or both?" he asked.

"Black is fine. Where are your horses?"

"Thirty minutes north. Would you like to see them?"

"Of course, but my daughter would enjoy it even more."

David instructed the driver to go to Samantha's apartment so they could pick up Karla, then to his ranch, a home surrounded by grassy acreage checker-boarded with perfectly square pens fenced with white pipe. There were one or two horses in almost every pen. "Mommy, can I pet one?" asked Karla.

David answered as the limo driver wheeled the big car into a long barn full of equipment, pickups, tractors and horse trailers. "Young Lady," he said. "If your mommy will allow it, you can ride my horse with me."

The evening lasted until just after eight when David dropped Samantha and Karla off at the clinic to get the station wagon. Karla, having had the most physical day of her life, had been asleep for an hour. David carried her to the station wagon. "Do you know what we have to do, Samantha?" he asked.

"What?"

"Get together again so we can talk about your marriage. What do you say?"

Samantha laughed. "Good night for now, but you're welcome to call on me again."

"Really?" David sounded like a little boy.

Samantha was sitting in her car, but stepped out, her actions all day beyond her understanding. "David," she said. "I have no explanation for my conduct today. I've never stepped out on my husband; but then again, I haven't enjoyed a simple afternoon or anything else since a few months before I got married. Thank you for today and..."

"Samantha, I'm going to kiss you unless you object," whispered David, stepping close, then putting more passion into the kiss than Samantha had expected. He wasn't a large man, but he loomed huge at the moment, hard and muscular. His lips were tender, his smell manly, a light musk aroma that lingered in her mind.

"I hope I don't regret this tomorrow," whispered Samantha, yet in David's embrace.

"Will you tell me if you do?"

Samantha nodded, then turned and got into her station wagon. "Good night," she heard, while backing away.

The next morning at seven, Dr. William C. Benjamin called Samantha into his small office. She knew it had to be about David Mills, but had no concern. There were two other employees she knew of who had dated former patients of the clinic. David, himself, wasn't actually a patient, nor was the outing actually a date. "Yes, Sir?" she responded, stepping into the doctor's office.

The doctor was affectionately referred to as 'Big Ben' due to his size, or 'Bullshit Ben', due to his constant mumbling of silly stories while in surgery. Of all of his antics, Samantha best remembered one afternoon while the doctor was closing the incision after a two-hour operation to reconstruct a patient's right knee. The patient, a middle-aged service station operator, had been involved in a motorcycle accident. "Hmmm," mumbled Dr. Benjamin. "I guess the lucky cuss won't have to have a wooden leg like mine. Have you ever seen it, Mrs. Valentine?"

Samantha played along. "No, but I've noticed that you have a limp."

"I do not."

"Well, you do, but maybe I shouldn't have mentioned it. I'm sorry. I suppose anyone would be a little self-conscious about such a noticeable disfigurement."

The doctor stopped what he was doing and laughed. "Disfigurement?"

"I apologize again," said Samantha, absently reaching down to clip an uneven thread from one of the doctor's stitches. "You should redo this one."

"Okay," said Dr. Benjamin, chuckling under his breath as he took the scissors from Samantha. "I wanna save some thread to stitch up your mean little mouth though. Disfigurement, huh?" sighed the doctor, yet laughing.

Samantha and Dr. Benjamin had become friendly immediately after she came to the clinic, although their friendship generally centered around jokingly finding fault with each other. The doctor was well over six feet, considerably overweight, had huge hands and feet and bushy eyebrows. Samantha found him easy to pick on, but liked him. Dr. Benjamin usually picked on her through a series of rumors he would whisper to her co-workers. "I saw Mrs. Valentine and the mayor dancing at the club last night. Boy, did she have that old man lathered up," he once told Clara, the caustic receptionist, which guaranteed that the fabrication would spread through the clinic.

Again, Samantha played along, making an effort to get the mayor's name and have something to say about him every few days. "We had a moonlight dinner on his yacht Saturday night," she once responded, when the receptionist asked her what she had done with the mayor lately.

Today, after Samantha stepped into Dr. Benjamin's office and closed the door, the doctor spoke without looking at her. "Please have a seat," he said, pointing toward a chair beside his desk with a pencil he immediately placed over his right ear. "It isn't policy, but I wanted to take a minute to let you know how my partners and I feel about you. You mind?"

"Certainly not," responded Samantha, taking the chair. "If it's bad news, I'll just cry a little," she added, smiling, but somehow uneasy, especially after the events of last evening. "Here's the Kleenex," he said, absently handing Samantha an unopened box while flipping through a file folder full of small notes. "You've never been late, Mrs. Valentine," continued Dr. Benjamin. "Commendable considering you have a small child, a husband and a boyfriend." The doctor looked up at Samantha and smiled after mentioning her having a boyfriend, then returned his eyes to the folder. "You're really quiet a woman," he mumbled, yet flipping through the notes in the file. "That's what my partners told me anyway. I haven't noticed," added Dr. Benjamin, unsmiling and mumbling. "They suggested that you should get a raise in your weekly salary. I'm totally against it, but you know me, I just try to get along, but then, I was outnumbered, too. Your next check will be one hundred forty-five dollars less taxes."

The big doctor held up a finger, "Now, here's my recommendation. Saturday afternoon at two, in the student assembly hall at Rice University, Dr. Nathan, a spokesman for the Western Surgical Association, is holding a seminar for anyone who's interested. There's been a lot of research lately on a subject that should be quite important to you." Dr. Benjamin closed the file folder, tossed it into his out-basket, looked up at Samantha, then folded his arms and leaned back in his chair. "In the short time you've been here, Mrs. Valentine, you've seen several patients who came in on gurneys flipping and flopping and cursing and spitting and being pretty darn abusive to all of us, haven't you?"

"Yes Sir, I have."

"Well, what you've seen around here is nothing compared to what goes on in emergency rooms of big hospitals," continued Dr. Benjamin. "We get most of our patients after some emergency room staff has stabilized them. Their shock and trauma have usually been arrested to some degree anyway. You know, people like you and me, smart and healthy and..." The doctor winked and awaited a comment from Samantha.

"Don't forget beautiful," she said, thinking of David Mills.

"Oh yes," said Dr. Benjamin. "We special people, most of us anyway, don't even consider the possibility of our needing trauma care and Dr. Nathan will be talking about exactly that. Recent research has rediscovered the importance of quick and positive care, deciding for the thousandth time that allowing a patient to suffer from severe shock for too long can result in his or her permanent physical, as well as psychological damage. You and I already knew that, of course, but hell, we'll just keep it our secret," added the doctor, his wink a playful beckoning to go along with his joke. "Anyway," he continued. "One good result of recent research is the new emphasis trauma care centers are placing on the importance of thoroughly trained anesthetists. Of course, I would prefer waiting until I see it in print before making any changes around here. However, my partners would like to offer you immediate assistance and the time to take two classes a week at the University of Houston, if you're interested. Your books and tuition will be paid for by the clinic; in addition, we'll reimburse some of your travel expenses. I suggested fifty cents a month, but my partners decided on fifty dollars. You know the deal. I was outnumbered again."

Dr. Benjamin leaned forward on his elbows. "I hope you're interested, Mrs. Valentine," he said, a serious tone this time. "You're certainly deserving."

"I'm very interested," whispered Samantha, fumbling to open the Kleenex box, her eyes beginning to show her emotions. "Thank you, Dr. Benjamin."

The doctor quickly stood and walked around his desk. "Don't you go to crying on me," he said, patting Samantha's back. "I'll be fine. Maybe I can find me a pet monkey to work Tuesday and Thursday afternoons. I hate to admit it, but you're the best employee we have here. I'll get along, but I'd sure hate to have to replace you on a permanent basis. Thank God the classes are only for one semester." Dr. Benjamin bent down and kissed the top of Samantha's head, then patted her shoulders. "Don't tell my wife I did that. She's not as big as me, but she's a lot meaner."

"No way. I'm going to tell her," whispered Samantha, trying to sound at least a little spirited.

"Oh yeah? Well, I'll blame you," said the doctor, patting Samantha's back again. "You know, we've got a patient who's probably bored to death. He's been waiting for us in room two since six-thirty. See you there," he added, then left the office and closed the door.

Samantha sat quietly thinking for a moment. Her employers had been almost too good, yet neither of the three doctors had done anything to indicate their appreciation of her until this meeting with Dr. Benjamin. She would attend the seminar, then enroll at the university as soon as possible, she decided, suddenly feeling that wonderful sense of triumph again. "Such good men," she said aloud, blowing her nose. Samantha tossed the tissue into a waste can and headed to surgery in room two, then suddenly stopped in her tracks, wondering if David Mills had anything to do with her raise, plus the time and assistance she would be getting from her employers. "Impossible," she said aloud, then continued to surgery.

At eleven-thirty that same morning, Ken came to the clinic to join Samantha for lunch. He was introducing himself to anyone dressed in white when Samantha stepped out of room two and into the hallway. Her heart jumped into her throat, seeing Ken for the first time since the morning before. Was David Mills a setup, her husband's doing? Pat's? "Hello," she said, weakly.

Ken flashed his affable smile and waved. "What a nice place," he said to the receptionist, then continued past Samantha, speaking to every employee, introducing himself, shaking hands with the doctors and generally acting the ambassador of good will. "Mind if I have some lunch with my wife?" he asked of Dr. Benjamin, who had followed Ken into the hall after an unavoidable five minute chat with him. Ken had barged into the doctor's office, taking a seat without more than introducing himself.

The doctor's voice showed his irritation with Ken's forwardness. "You mean to tell me there's something you actually ask about before doing it?"

Ken missed the innuendo. "Forty-five minutes and I'll have her right back here. Nice place you have. Very clean."

Samantha had slipped off her white smock and was walking behind the receptionist's desk to take it to a laundry bin at the end of the hall. Ken grabbed it from her, rolled it tightly, then threw it at the laundry bin, missing it badly. Throwing anything at the laundry bag was a pet peeve of the doctors. All employees, especially doctors and surgical assistants, were to take their smocks off, search through the pockets for anything belonging to the clinic, anything personal, or anything belonging to a patient, then place their smock in the laundry bin like a civilized adult. "Foul. I was fouled," exclaimed Ken.

Dr. Benjamin hurried after the smock, picked it up and searched through the pockets himself. Samantha, smiling, less nervous with her husband's unannounced visit, was awaiting the doctor's scathing reply, fully aware that it would be an indirect insult to her husband. Ken was holding his hands extended, appearing to expect another shot, his foul shot. "Samantha?" queried Dr. Benjamin, his bushy eyebrows raised, his big hand ripping a pocket of the smock off. "Where's those condoms of mine?"

Although at her wits end to control her laughter, Samantha managed to tell the doctor that she had left the unused ones in his office. "Good," he said, exhaling in mock relief "See you in my office after lunch."

The three doctors weren't impressed with Ken, but the female employees felt differently. Without leaving anyone out, he had complimented their appearance, emphasizing the confidence they must surely exude to patients with their professional manner, giving full credit to the nurses for the neatness and warm feeling of the clinic. In fact, the handsome young attorney was a hit with the ladies. "Really nice place you have here," he told each of them, smiling sincerely, easily winning their approval.

Samantha led Ken outside, then to a diner that was two blocks west of the clinic. While eating lunch, she daydreamed through Ken's busy antics and unorganized conversation. He conducted himself as if a nervous child, more obsequious than a first-day waitress. "Let me get that," he said, taking over when Samantha struggled to pull a paper napkin from its stuffed holder. "This saltshaker is dirty. I'll get another one. Do you want sugar in your tea? No, how about lemon? Here, I'll squeeze it for you. Ma'am," he said, raising a hand to summon a waitress, "I need a fresh slice of lemon over here."

Samantha knew there were messages here, but she was out at David Mills' horse ranch, resting her elbows on the top rail of a low corral, David's arm around her waist. Karla, astride a sleek black stallion, was riding toward them, out of the sunset, a ball of fire. Everything was bright, the fiery setting sun suffusing all darkness. In the distance, beyond and above the approaching stallion, were the smiling faces of her Uncle Hiram and Aunt May. Samantha smiled and closed her eyes in an attempt to store the images and convert them to memories. Somehow, over the smells coming from the diner's deep fryers and open grill, she could smell the long remembered scent of her uncle's cologne.

"What the heck's the matter with you?" asked Ken, shaking Samantha's arm.

"Huh? Uh, nothing that I know of."

"Nothing?" challenged Ken. He had been reading aloud from a brochure advertising a resort in Hawaii. "Okay then, Wise-ass. I'm gonna take you and Karla to Kona. Do you even know where it is?"

"Hawaii?" responded Samantha, reading the back of the brochure herself.

"That's right, on the west side of the big island. The Kona coast is the place to go if you wanna do some real marlin fishing." Ken held the brochure open for Samantha to see a picture. It was of a huge fish that hung from a crossbeam at the end of a pier. "Look," he said. "Nine feet four inches from the tail to the tip of its big, long beak. How would you like to reel that baby in?"

"I don't know. Looks like someone already did."

Ken spoke in a high-pitched singsong. "She just doesn't know. Well, I'll be darn. Okay, look at this then," he said, his tone normal as he opened the brochure to yet another page. "See this here? That's

Mauna Loa. It's a huge volcano. Thirteen thousand six hundred and eighty feet high. Boy, I'll bet you could see LA from the top of that."

Samantha, finished with lunch and ready to get back to work, shoved her plate aside and opened her purse. "Who pays?" she asked.

"Huh?" responded Ken, genuinely unaware that Samantha had finished and was ready to leave. "Oh, I want to," he said, evenly, but quickly continued more brusquely. "A genuine feminist, huh? You get a paycheck and suddenly you're all holy. Well, I'll tell you what. I don't wanna take anything away from you, Miss Independence. Just for you, we'll split the check." Samantha tossed four one-dollar bills onto the table and started for the diner's front door, but Ken caught her before she could open it. "Hey, slow down, Samantha," he said, opening the door, then following her out. "I came by so we could talk."

While walking back to the clinic, Samantha asked Ken if he was really planning a trip to Hawaii. "Of course. Doesn't everybody? I'm going to take you sometime. It'll be a family trip, when the baby is a little older, but that's not why I came by today. Mom and Dad want to see Karla tonight," he said. "You know, we haven't had her over there for dinner with them since you went to work. Time flies when you're busy, doesn't it."

"Really. Are your parents upset that I'm working?"

"Oh, no. Quite the opposite. In fact, Mom even had something nice to say about you this morning."

"Oh, yeah? Did it choke her?"

"Now, now, no smart-ass stuff. In fact, I'll let her tell you. It was nice, Samantha. Really, it was. Anyway, I'm off for the day, so I think I'll just go get Karla and spend the afternoon with her and Mom."

Samantha stopped, lowered her chin, raised her eyebrows and looked at Ken as if his suggestion was the shock of her life. "You and Sybil want to spend an afternoon with the little nuisance?" she questioned. "That's a laugh. Have you presented this proposal to your mother formerly?"

"Damn you, Samantha! You can be such a bitch. I just wanna let them get to know each other. That's all. Shit."

"I just wanted to make a point. That's all. Shucks."

"Okay," sighed Ken, pathetically, the point being quite clear. "Just tell me. Can you come straight over to Mom's after work? Say around four?" "I could, but..."

"No buts," said Ken, stopping a few feet from the clinic, all smiles now, a loving husband. "I'll grab your peach-colored pantsuit when I pick up Karla. I love it when you wear it braless, but I know you won't around Dad. He couldn't take it anyway. What shoes?"

"Oh, I don't care," sighed Samantha. "Anything white, but high heels."

"Good enough. I can handle that." Ken was backing down the sidewalk toward his new Impala, parked at the curb. "See ya later," he said waving. "This is a real nice place to work. I like it, uh, what's our baby-sitter's name?"

Chapter 4

Fridays at the clinic always seemed to fly by. The partners wanted nothing left undone, which kept everyone but Clara busier than on other days. It was nothing more than normal for anyone to be completely unaware of the time at days end. However, the hours after having lunch with Ken seemed like days for Samantha. She never got into her work and nothing went smoothly all afternoon. She kept having to fight off a feeling of anxiety, a dread, or a fear of something. Two of the partners, although she felt neither meant a word of it, made a special effort to say something nice about her husband, his pleasant demeanor and his professional appearance. Dr. Benjamin, his audience a surgery assistant, the curt receptionist and Samantha, expressed how pleased he and his partners were to have Samantha within their employ, but did not make mention of her husband's visit. Most of the girls had something to say about Ken's good looks, his blue eyes and blonde hair and joked of being so distracted when he was there that they weren't able to concentrate. "When I was in college, we called guys like your husband 'dreamy'," explained one of the single nurses. "I guess these days though, they're called 'hunks'. Like Paul Newman and Tony Curtis."

"Yeah," chipped in the receptionist. "Hunks. Like the mayor," she added, smiling, but obviously meaning to offend.

One on one, just before leaving for the day, Samantha expressed her gratitude to Dr. Benjamin's partners. "I was lost for words when Dr. Benjamin met with me this morning, but now that I'm more collected, I want to thank you two gentlemen, too. I'll make A's in both my classes just to show you how much I appreciate your kindness."

As Samantha stood at the door, she expressed her appreciation and understanding to the girls, although she had never perceived of Ken as 'dreamy'. He had come along in her life at a time when her dreams were filled with the aspirations she'd gotten from the many hours she had spent with her Uncle Hiram. Then came his unexpected death, which, Samantha knew, coincided with her lessening resistance to Ken's persistence to marry. Hiram always had high expectations for Samantha and she felt his force within her, but she felt a helpless void in his absence. Ken had claimed to be capable of taking Hiram's place in her world, which Samantha knew was not possible, but she did expect him to add more to her life than a child he wouldn't take an interest in.

Just as she opened the door, Dr. Benjamin stepped into the hall and crooked a finger, summoning Samantha to join him in his office. Once inside, the doctor, standing behind his desk with his arms crossed, began speaking before she could take a chair. "I won't delay you," he said. "I just wanted to take a minute to apologize for making that comment about the condoms. I know it was way out of line. I'm sorry."

"I thought it was funny," said Samantha.

"Well, maybe, but with my apology properly made, I want to add something a little more daring. I hope you don't take it wrong, but maybe that's the only way you could. Anyway, you're a lot of woman for that little boy you're married to, Mrs. Valentine. Would you like for me to tell you why it concerns me, or would you rather I mind my own business?"

The big doctor was looking right into Samantha eyes, intently, although his overall expression seemed benevolent. He was a good man, honest and caring, near enough to her own age to be understanding of her situation. "Please," she said. "I want to hear what you think. I appreciate your opinions."

Samantha slid into the chair she had occupied this morning, but the doctor remained standing. "We're friends, Samantha," he began. "Which means I can give you both barrels. I was in Korea with a slew of young men like your husband. Their actions clearly portrayed their inborn demeanor. They're the ones who always crumble under the first signs of pressure. I mean even times of alert, let alone an actual ground attack, artillery barrage or when we'd get a few incoming mortars and rockets." The doctor slid his chair out and sat at his desk. "Now," he continued. "Your husband is the classic. He never lets you finish a statement. He'll answer before he gets your point if he can. Like, you say do this and do that and do, then he says okay, before you complete all the honey do's. Then, he never finishes his own statements. I asked him about law school and his current job. His answer was SMU, then he asked who represented the clinic. I asked him where the two of you met and what he thought about you developing your career. Ken said SMU, then asked where I went to medical school. He was right here in my office and, as you see, my sheepskin was about five feet in front of his nose." The doctor paused, then stood again and looked out of his window. "Are you upset?" he asked.

"Yes, but not with you," responded Samantha. "It's Ken. He has a way of keeping me upset."

"That doesn't surprise me," commented the doctor. "I just wanted to make you aware of something, Samantha. My wife, my eleven-year-old daughter, Becky, and I live in a four-bedroom home ten minutes east of the clinic. If you ever need our help, just let me know and we'll be glad to have you and your daughter as our guests for as long as it takes you find whatever living arrangement that appeals to you. Your present situation can't last long, unless I'm terribly mistaken."

The doctor was silent for a moment, as was Samantha. She was lost for words and just a little confused. Finally, with his back yet to Samantha, the doctor continued, his tone softer, appearing even more understanding. "You're very naive, Samantha. There isn't another soul in the world with your looks and grace who wouldn't be so smug that no one could talk to them. Those words weren't meant to insult you, but to arm you. Just remember, once people get to know you, they learn to appreciate that you're smart and very capable, but you come off naive at first. Perhaps you intimidate Ken a little these days." The doctor paused and turned around. "Good night, Samantha." he said, softly. "It wasn't my intention to upset you. I just wanted to make you aware of...I was trying to make you aware of Ken's...Well, what I mean is that..."

"I think I understand, Sir," interrupted Samantha, standing, extending her hand. "Good night and thank you. Have a wonderful weekend. I plan to."

"Please do, Samantha," said the big doctor, taking her hand. "I have one more pearl of wisdom, then I'll really let you go. Did you take a look at the Mills kid's file after his father dropped by to talk to you yesterday?"

"No, Sir. In fact, he took me and my daughter out to his horse ranch."

"Well, I guess I was a little more curious. Our patient's bill was paid by a Mr. Jason Mills, the kid's grandfather. David is a suspended Louisiana Highway Patrolman who's over here looking for a job. He has a wife and another son in New Orleans, so says his father, Jason Mills, the real rancher. Just keep that in mind. It's none of my business."

Samantha, laughing at herself, stepped around the big doctor's desk and hugged him. "Okay," she said. "I'll definitely keep that in mind. Thanks again."

By the time Samantha arrived at Ken's parents' house, the anxiety she'd felt all day had tired her to near numbness. She sat in her car for several moments studying her day, analyzing her dread, her fear of something unknown, something unusual about to happen. Before today, Ken had never been to the clinic, never spent an afternoon with his daughter and his mother had never expressed any interest in Karla. Ken's interest in Samantha's work was understandable. He didn't want anyone to be dependent on him. That would not be a situation that served his self-interest. Samantha having her own car, her own income and a job she was happy with were things she wanted, but they were also exactly what Ken wanted for her. Maybe he needed that as badly as she did.

The meeting with Dr. Benjamin was quite informative, and although the revelations concerning David Mills were completely unexpected, his seeing through Ken didn't surprise Samantha. To her, Ken's inability to adjust to family life and its responsibility was telltale enough to illustrate his weaknesses.

Suddenly, while sitting there in her car thinking, almost like the effect of the second glass of wine, a calmness came over Samantha. She knew now and it was okay. Her independence was something she wanted. A blessing, as Uncle Hiram had said. The only difference in her striving to be independent today, that was unlike ever before, is that it was as much a necessity as a blessing. "Hmmm," sighed Samantha, then got out of the car to go inside. It was then, while looking about the big house that Samantha knew what had happened. One, which she'd never seen, there were several cars in the drive, Sybil's Cadillac, Ted's Lincoln and Pat's Buick four door. Cheryl Cooper and her husband's Plymouth Fury was parked on the street, but Ken's new Impala was nowhere around. This was a family meeting, there had been trouble and Ken was at the bottom of it. "Why am I here?" she asked aloud, then answered herself in thought. To pick up Karla of course, and maybe even get a whitewashed explanation of what happened with Ken. He just didn't want me to come home and find out that he'd packed and left. He wouldn't have the guts to tell me. Quite simple. Dr. Benjamin just saw it before I did.

However, just as Samantha stepped up onto the porch, an all-new possibility hit her. Karla. Had Ken ran off with Karla? No, there's no way he would ever attempt to manage the needs of a small child by himself, she wanted to believe, even though she was banging on the front door as if emerged in panic.

"It's okay, it's okay, Samantha," said Pat, holding Karla's hand as she swung the door open. "I understand, but we're fine. Aren't we Karla?"

Samantha knelt and extended her arms to her child. "Hi, Baby," she whispered, a tone expressing something between distress and elation. "Hi, Mommy. Guess what. I got a kitty. Daddy gave it to me."

Sounding brighter, as if suddenly energized, Samantha pulled Karla to her bosom and asked, "You do? Well, where is your little kitty?"

"Home. I mean, Mrs. Braxton has it. I fed it milk before I came though."

Pat took Samantha and Karla's hands, then led them to the den where she passed off the little girl to her grandfather, Ted Valentine. "We're all very sorry, Samantha," he said, lifting his granddaughter to a knee while sliding a brown satchel toward Samantha with his foot. "I bought this for Ken last Christmas, but he would never carry it. Maybe you can find a use for it, since you're the professional of the family. I guess bums prefer bedrolls and grocery carts. I noticed there's a shoulder holster and a little pistol in there. A nine-millimeter automatic. I don't know what Ken was doing with it, but I'm glad he didn't take it along, wherever the hell he went."

"Thanks, Ted. Don't worry about Karla and me. We'll be okay," said Samantha not completely sure of the problem.

"I'm sure you will, but Ken shouldn't have sold your jewelry to buy a new car," said Ted, averting eye contact with Samantha, his focus yet on the brown satchel.

"She probably didn't even know, Dad," responded Pat, as she continued to lead Samantha on through to the formal dining room. "Let's wait just a minute," she said, turning to look back into the den. The dining room was empty of people and conspicuously unprepared for use tonight, but Samantha couldn't care less. She wanted to be alone. There was nothing she had ever owned more precious to her than Hiram's gold watch and May's big diamond ring. She would never have sold them, nor would she ever have believed Ken could do something that hardhearted.

"Don't worry. I'll be along soon. Go with your father," said Pat, speaking to her nine-year-old daughter, Linda, who was beside her grandfather, her expression one of boredom and question.

The family all filed past the dining room, through the den and out the front door, including Sybil who was donning a jacket as she followed Cheryl Cooper out. "Let me get Karla and go," whimpered Samantha. "You have things to do and I'm sure your farther wants to go wherever everyone else is going."

"No, no," said Pat. "He and I will be staying. He wants to talk to you, and I want to be here. We're truly sorry about Ken. Maybe you should kill him. I'll even help if you decide to." Pat and Ted passed Karla back and forth as much as was necessary to explain Ken's situation completely without exposing the little girl to the things that would affect her. Samantha was told that Ken would be taking some time off before joining the Army and that Ted would be sending her a check for $150.00 a month to cover Karla's in home expenses. "I'll do that until Ken completes whatever training is required before he can have his family accompany him. In the meantime, I'll also pay Karla's day care expenses. If she hasn't already, Sybil will establish an education fund for Karla, which has been done for each of our grandchildren.

It will begin with a $4,500.00 deposit, then be increased annually by $500.00 until Karla is eighteen," added Ted.

Samantha did not respond, nor indicate that she had heard Ted's words. To assure he had her attention, he tapped her on the knee. "Is all of this okay, Samantha?" he asked, his tone like a plea for forgiveness. "You know that we regret our son's behavior, but we can't replace those pieces of jewelry he sold. I'm sure they were priceless to you. Ken hasn't been quick to mature, and we've always known that, but of course, we hoped. I fully expect him to be joining me in the firm again once he completes his tour in the army. I've wanted that boy in the service since he turned eighteen. It has to help."

Samantha finally responded, dully at first, but growing more forceful as she continued. "I hardly know what to say, Mr. Valentine, but...Well, let me start with thanking you and Sybil and I'll certainly express my gratitude to Pat before I leave. I have no objections to your help and wouldn't allow myself to even if something affected my pride. It wouldn't be fair to Karla. I hope you and Sybil will get to know her better. She's really a sweet little girl. As for my watch and ring, you're exactly right. Nothing will ever replace them, and I will never forgive Ken for selling them, nor will I ever again be a wife to him. Under any circumstances. Never," she snapped, repeating herself, then getting to her feet and adding less contemptuously, resignedly, "However, I guess I shouldn't be the first to take steps that could permanently separate my daughter and her father."

Ted got to his feet. "Well, I'm glad you're being practical, Samantha," he said, a tone of relief "I do want more time with little Karla, but, as you've surely observed, Sybil goes a lot of directions at once. She won't have the time for your daughter that I will." Ted waved for Pat to come to the den. "Will you help Samantha?" he asked. "I'm sure Karla needs to get home to her bed. I've gotta run if I plan to get to the club before Sybil and Cheryl have ordered."

If Samantha had doubts and fears of being on her own with the sole responsibility of a young child, she did not know it. She attended the seminar at Rice University at two Saturday afternoon, then spent most of Sunday boxing and storing any evidence of Ken in the garage. By Monday morning when she arrived at the clinic, Samantha was filled with all-new resolve. Hers was the first name on the roster when she registered for the two classes Dr. Benjamin had suggested she take.

September passed like the final hours of a fun vacation, each day dreamlike, stimulating and filled with the gratification of accomplishment. Her spirit climbed by the minute, but Samantha didn't see the change. It was Dr. Benjamin who first brought it to her attention. "The least you could do is let me in on your secret," he began, one Tuesday morning during surgery. "You're looking great and you're a lot happier lately. Let's have it. What happened?"

Samantha told the doctor what had happened with Ken and how she was enjoying her life in spite of it. She told him how the classes were going and how they had given her a better sense of self-worth in merely taking them. "I guess not living with the expectation of some jolting news when I get home each day helps, too," she added.

"I'm happy for you, Samantha," said Dr. Benjamin. "Don't burn yourself out though," he advised. "Make yourself take a night off every week."

Just before leaving for class that afternoon, Samantha met with the doctor in his office, agreeing to meet him and his daughter, Becky, at the First Baptist Church in downtown Pasadena the following Sunday night. "It'll just be a break," he said, drawing a map to the church on a crumpled candy wrapper.

Sunday afternoon, she took Karla and Mrs. Braxton out for an early dinner, then met Dr. Benjamin, Becky and her friend, Lois Winders. Samantha slid down the pew next to the doctor, Karla at her side and Mrs. Braxton following. Although it was only the second time she had been out to dinner and the first in a place of worship since the move to Houston, she did not break the routine until the week before Christmas.

Becky became attached to Karla, and slightly enamored with Samantha almost immediately, never failing to save room for them on the pew by her. "I think you're the most beautiful woman in the world," she once said to Samantha, then to Karla, "You will be, too, someday," kissing her cheek as she bounced the little girl on her lap.

Becky, tall for her age, had long blonde hair, light brown eyes, a pretty face and a quick smile. Samantha liked her and began inviting her over on Saturdays, taking her and Karla grocery shopping, to a movie now and then and roller-skating a few times. Once, as much for the adventure as anything, Samantha, Becky and Lois Winders spent a whole Saturday crisscrossing the metro on city buses.

The appreciation Samantha had for Becky was not due to the teen being so taken with her, but because of her maturity and friendship. Their talks were open and easy, each often finding answers for their own self-doubts and more often seeing the inaccuracy in the other's. One Saturday morning at the market, Becky said, whispering so Karla couldn't hear, "You were right."

"Oh?" questioned Samantha. "How was I right?"

"I started this week."

A few weeks earlier, Samantha had explained away Becky's concerns for being a late bloomer. Most of the other girls in her class had perky breasts showing through their sweaters, boys hanging around their lockers and walking them to classes, but most worrisome for Becky was the number who were carrying sanitary napkins in their purses. Mrs. Winders, Lois' mother, was a private nurse who often worked with Dr. Benjamin's patients who needed in-home care. Becky had tried to talk to her about several things that were causing her anxiety, but Mrs. Winders made light of the concerns. "Quit worrying about such a silly thing," she usually said. Mrs. Winders was sweet to Becky, often drove her to and from school, but didn't seem to want to advise her. Becky chose to look elsewhere for answers, hitting Samantha with everything at once.

"Okay, Becky," began Samantha, after giving the young woman's concern its due. "You've said you think I'm attractive a hundred times. Right?"

"I've said you're the most beautiful woman in the world, and you are," corrected the teenager.

"If you say, but here's my point," said Samantha, laughing off the child's absurd compliment. "When I was your age, a few boys made friends with me, but none really tried to date me. In fact, my first real date was after I'd gone to college. My uncle explained it this way. Teenage boys are easily intimidated. They're usually afraid they won't accomplish what their dad did, their mother, older brother, older sister, coach, or even some over-achiever their own age. It takes a while for most of them to work up the nerve to try to make friends with pretty girls. Brace yourself, though. When those same boys reach sixteen and seventeen, it will completely reverse. Some will think they've already exceeded anything anyone has done, or find a good excuse to downplay it as something that just wouldn't challenge their abilities nearly enough. You'll see. They'll keep you so busy that those A's you make will be as rare as a night at home alone. And, about your period, Becky, you should be prepared right now. If you're lucky, it won't start until you're closer to fourteen, but don't get caught unprepared. It could just as easily start this month."

At the market that Saturday, Becky didn't explain why Samantha had been right until she had put a box of Kotex in their shopping cart. "I should have been prepared," she said. "I didn't even have the right change to work the darn machine in the girl's restroom."

The Sunday evening routine of attending church with Becky and her father was broken but a few weeks later. It followed a Thursday afternoon when Dr. Benjamin rushed out of the clinic about one. Samantha hurried to the receptionist's desk. "What was that all about?" she asked.

"What was what all about?" asked Clara, popping her gum and flipping a page of a well-worn paperback, then adding, "Reading about kinky sex is almost as good as doing it, don't ya think?"

While finishing out her shift, Samantha became increasingly worried about the doctor not calling or returning to the clinic. One of the other partners was visiting his patients at County Hospital, but the other, Dr. Moore, shared Samantha's concern. "It just isn't like Ben to leave without telling someone where he could be reached. Let's find out what happened," he said, picking up a phone on his credenza and pointing to one on his desk. "Why don't you start with the Pasadena Police?"

Both Samantha and Dr. Moore made call after call to no avail, but finally learned what they hoped hadn't happened when the janitor at

Becky's school picked up a phone in the principal's office. "Huh? Oh I wouldn't know," he began, but added. "'School turned out at noon for Christmas vacation and everybody cleared out. I'm just trying to..."

"Did anything unusual happen?" asked Samantha.

"Can't say as it did less you wanna call a kid grab assin around and fallin down the front steps unusual."

"A kid?"

"Two girls I guess it was. Ambulance came a tearin, but that ain't unusual. You know parents these days. All the lawsuits over nuthin."

Becky dropped a book while she and Lois were hurrying out of the schoolhouse to meet Mrs. Winders, waiting at the curb. The book slid across the concrete landing like a sled on a snowy hillside. When Becky finally reached it and knelt to pick it up, she was knocked down the front steps by a crowd of anxious students dashing out to the buses, or to meet their rides. The back of her head smacked against a step, then again on the sidewalk where she sprawled out motionless and didn't make a sound. Mrs. Winders insisted an ambulance be called immediately, then rendered onsite aid until it arrived.

Dr. Moore called an intern he knew at Pasadena County Hospital and learned that Becky had been carried into emergency on a gurney around one-thirty pm. "Where is she now?" he asked.

"I don't know, but she was in the trauma unit for over an hour."

Samantha left the clinic at six and drove to her apartment like a mindless zombie. Dr. Moore had promised to call if he was able to contact Dr. Benjamin and learn anything further. The evening was awful, one of the worst Samantha could remember in a long time. She had grown very fond of Becky and maybe a little too fond of Dr. Benjamin. They, as if cloned, where both good people, fun loving and considerate of others, unpretentious and indiscriminate.

Dr. Moore called just after ten. Samantha was staring unseeingly at the television. "Hello."

"Samantha, the news isn't the worst, but it isn't good either. Becky suffered a bad blow to the back of her head and another one, which looks the worse by the way, just above her right eye. She..."

"But, she's going to be okay, isn't she?" interrupted Samantha.

"Of course. Now you get some rest and..."

"Dr. Moore. Please tell me. How is Becky?"

There was a long drawn out silence, then Dr. Moore hemmed and hawed through the explanation. Becky was in a coma. She had been knocked unconscious and several minutes had passed when she might not have even been breathing. "You know, Samantha, there are states of unconsciousness when a person's voluntary body functions don't, uh..."

The doctor faltered, neither he nor Samantha choosing to break the silence for several seconds. "Samantha," he began again. "Becky is on electronic life support. I know you want to run to the hospital, but Dr. Benjamin doesn't want that. In fact, he insisted that you, especially you, wait a few days before going to see Becky. His wife is...Well, she's a weird woman, which is none of my business, but I can just imagine. She's more than likely too busy laying blame to be of much comfort to Becky, or Ben. Do you know Evelyn?"

"No. I've never met her."

"Lucky you," sighed Dr. Moore. "Evelyn is an odd one. She joined a scientology group a few years ago and wow. All I can say is wow. The members who don't live at their commune meet six times a week just off the highway in a little town on the way to New Orleans. It's a town gone mad. I'm sure you've heard how outrageous holy-rollers are. For Evelyn's group, just triple that."

There was a numbness about the clinic on Friday. People moved from desk to desk, room to room and in and out with solemn faces. They stared fixedly at their work, or the floor, as they moved quietly through the clinic. Little fish swimming in a lake, hurrying to shelter, away from possible conversational encounters.

Without exception, everyone at the clinic loved Dr. Benjamin, his caring, his ever-present wit, his understanding and patience. And, they knew who was hurting the most. Samantha was favored by Dr. Benjamin, and he hadn't tried to hide it. When he took lunch out of the clinic, he asked her no one else, not even his partners. His questions about anything were directed to Samantha. "What do you think, Mrs. Valentine? Should we order additional surgical tape this time? How about a couple of extra instrument trays?" Samantha was the only one from the clinic who was invited to Becky's birthday party, a backyard dance with a five-piece band playing to twenty of her classmates, then a sleepover for eight of the girls. "Come on," had said the doctor. "You gotta help me chaperone. Evelyn's out of town. I'll be like a caveman around those kids. What could I do to communicate with them?"

The party had been fun for Samantha. She and Dr. Benjamin laughed, served snacks and soft drinks, danced twice and sneaked each other sips of champagne from a flask while the kids had a ball and totally ignored them.

The next few days at the clinic seemed morgue-like to Samantha, barely registering in her consciousness. Immediately upon arriving Friday morning, she went straight to Dr. Moore's office. "Sir," she said, standing in his doorway. "I need to know."

The doctor made a note in a file, folded it closed, then looked up from his desk. "Ben was here last night. He worked on this case record for a while and I think he plans to be here tonight. Now, I didn't tell you that, but..."

"Thank you, Dr. Moore. I might forget my purse when I leave today."

Samantha let herself into the clinic at seven that night. "How is Becky?" she asked, standing in Dr. Benjamin's office doorway. He was at his desk studying a medical journal. "I will find out," added Samantha. "You know I will, so tell me, or I'm going to go see her."

The doctor looked so different, red rimmed eyes, showing the pain storming within him. His hair was disheveled, as was the stained white shirt that Samantha could see above the desktop. "I know that," he sighed, then tiredly closed the journal and raised his big bulky body from the chair, slowly, awkwardly, like a puppet. "1 would have told you, but I'm in the dark myself. She's in a deep coma, but there just doesn't seem to be a reason for it. There was a lot of swelling in her cranial cavity at first, but that's improved. A neurologist I know flew in from Dallas last night and examined Becky this morning. About all that accomplished was my reading assignment. Look," said the doctor, pointing to six thick journals at the corner of his desk.

Dr. Benjamin took Samantha to the hospital at eight, warning her as they drove through the streets of Pasadena. "Prepare yourself a little. I know you've seen some gory stuff at the clinic, but you might find Becky's s situation a bit shocking at first. She breathes on her own sometimes, but not always. Her room is filled with machines that look to belong in the cockpit of a space capsule. There are four complicated apparatuses sitting around like guards. All colors of wires come out and meet at the end of the bed, then they're wrapped into a bundle like a huge umbilical cord as big as my arm. I don't know why it bothers me, but from the end of the bed, the wires, electrodes to her chest and the dome of her head, IV's, catheters, pumps and everything known to man, sneak up under the sheet and monitor Becky's every moment. I guess it just seems such a complete violation of her dignity."

Samantha was not prepared. She took two steps into Becky's room and fainted, awakening while Dr. Benjamin bathed her face. "What is..."

"What is, is that you bombed out on me just like Evelyn did?"

Samantha was lying on a rollaway bed in the hall just outside of Becky's room. "I did, didn't I."

"No, Hon. Comparing you to Evelyn was a little harsh. Tell me when you're ready and we'll try it again," said Dr. Benjamin, then bent down and kissed Samantha's lips lightly and quickly, speaking to a nurse who was observing when he stood upright. "I just couldn't help myself. We're in love."

The nurse smiled, then spoke over her shoulder as she walked down the hall, her words fading away. "Quite an improvement over your..."

Samantha and Dr. Benjamin spent the next hour with Becky, talking to her as if she was comprehending everything they said. It was touching, seeing the big doctor letting his heart go out to the comatose child with little or no awareness of anything else around him. "You'll be up and around soon, Sweetheart. Your mother was only kidding when she said you should jump up and tell us you're okay. I know you're okay, but what happened requires a little rest. I know that you know Samantha's here, but I'm not going to let you two go to a movie, or anything else until I've decided that bump on your head is all right. I'm sorry, Kid, but you'll just have to convince me."

It was Sunday afternoon while sharing a sandwich with Dr. Benjamin when Samantha found out what he meant when he told Becky that her mother was only kidding. "Dr. Benjamin, where is your wife?"

The doctor got to his feet and waved for Samantha to follow him out into the hall, where he explained the whereabouts of his wife. Evelyn had an outburst just minutes after the neurologist left to return to Dallas. She wasn't going to live with anyone, herself included, who was in a vegetative state. Even God would not expect that of anyone, she explained, then went on to rationalize that she understood what had happened wasn't anyone's fault. It was supposed to appear as an accident to those on earth, but it was God calling a lamb home. Becky was no longer of this world. She had gone to another. A better world. One of peace and love and an angelic life everlasting. Evelyn left the hospital room, went home and packed, then moved across town to live with another member of her scientology group.

The following Tuesday, Dr. Benjamin resumed his previous work schedule at the clinic, but he and Samantha met every night with Becky. The doctor would sit at a table and read, searching through the journals the neurologist had given him for hidden answers while Samantha worked with Becky. Night after night, the routine was the same, Samantha massaging every inch of the girl's body, bending her arms and legs, then bathing her and fixing her hair, adding a little gloss to her lips and color to her cheeks when the duty nurse wasn't looking.

One night, while Samantha was tickling Becky's feet and talking to her, Dr. Benjamin pulled a letter from his coat pocket. "Listen to this horseshit, Samantha. It came today."

Samantha let out a little sigh, one of relief. She had been conducting an experiment she had learned about in her classes at the University of Houston and was elated with the results. On a hunch, she reached under Becky's sheet and disconnected her breathing tube. Then, for a few frightening seconds, watched and waited. The girl was now breathing on her own, weakly, but without mechanical assistance.

The doctor misinterpreting the faint sigh, looked up from the letter, observing Samantha working with his daughter. Why was she so committed, so intent on helping? What was in it for her? A beautiful young woman, a good young woman with enormous responsibility of her own. "Shall we call it a night, Samantha? You probably don't care about my dingbat wife's informative letter."

"Huh? No, go ahead. I'm not through just yet."

Samantha was wearing jersey cloth warm-ups, leaning over Becky's bed, reconnecting the breathing tube, her back to the doctor. "My, my," he sighed, feeling a sudden hot pang of desire prick at his most manly instinct. The good doctor had never strayed, but he had never before known a woman like Samantha Valentine, purity with such beauty and appeal. "Thank you," he whispered, then began reading the letter. *Dear Ben. I wish you would try to understand me and get to know me again. People change over the years. You have and so have I. Surely you know I want our marriage, but for now, I must do what I'm doing. I'm happy. I'm learning more about the meaning of life than I ever dreamed possible.* The doctor paused, shook his head and looked up at Samantha, willing his eyes and imagination to appreciate her and not undress her. "Sound stupid?"

"No. A little 'all about me' maybe."

"I'd say. Evelyn seems to think the world is all about her lately," sighed the doctor, then continued reading from the letter. *And Ben, there's something I wish you'd do for yourself No doubt, you're an accomplished man, but you've become more of a believer in yourself than in God. l feel, because surgical techniques have so improved, you think you can perform some awful invasive brain surgery and bring back a person who The Lord has called. Even one who is catatonically unconscious like Becky. Please Ben. Lay down your scalpel and pick up the Bible. Even the earliest healers of our time knew there was a point beyond where man in his physical state could go. A subliminal place where spirits go to await redemption of their souls, to join God in his Kingdom and be cleansed of the tarnish of life on earth. Becky can't be brought back, Ben. Our God extended his hand and she crossed over. Any further existence on earth will have no meaning to her. You must accept that. Love, Evelyn.* The doctor crumpled the letter and tossed it into a bedside trash can, frowning as he looked up at Samantha. "What a bunch of bunk. Are you hungry? I can't remember the last time I ate."

Dr. Benjamin went after pizza and a six-pack of beer, then met Samantha at her apartment. They put little Karla to bed, then talked into the night. "Thank you," repeated the doctor, while exchanging a tired hug with Samantha at her door, wrapping up the long day.

"You're welcome and thank you for the pizza. Becky's coming around you know. She's breathing so much better."

The doctor, cheek to cheek in the embrace, clutched Samantha a little tighter, nodded, rotated his shoulders felt the magnificence of her, indulging, but knowing that if he didn't leave now, he may soon be too weak to. "Good night," he whispered, turned and left, feeling an unfamiliar wetness in his eyes.

On a Friday, two weeks later, Becky's first overt sign of awareness came suddenly, the result of Samantha's experiment. It was after her bath and just before Samantha and Dr. Benjamin had decided to leave the hospital for the night. Becky hadn't responded to electrical stimulation, but Samantha was quite sure she had seen her move her toes once when she tickled the bottom of her foot. "Come over and watch this, Dr. Benjamin," she said.

The big doctor looked up from his journal. "Okay, but when are you going to drop the doctor bit? I call you Samantha, so why can't you call me Ben?"

"I will now if you want, but you'll be Dr. Benjamin on Monday morning."

"That's fair." Ben sat on the bed and looked over at the hiccupping lines snaking across the EKG screen, reporting that Becky's heart rate was as normal as anyone's who was asleep. "She is improving, isn't she?"

"Yes, Ben," reported Samantha, smiling. She was holding three ice cubes behind her, which she brought around and held tightly against Becky's right arch, while also watching the EKG screen. Suddenly, there were two quick blips that jumped above the rest, then several followed suit. Becky tried to pull her foot from Samantha's hand. "Did you see that?"

Ben, startled for a second, suddenly began laughing, then jumped to his feet and grabbed Samantha, embraced her as he spun her around and around the room. "She's back. Becky is really back. You did it, Samantha. You little love, you did it," he whispered, tears sparkling in his eyes. "You're a miracle."

The ice worked the miracles. Wherever Samantha put it, she got a reaction. On Sunday, Ben showed the nurse. He put a double handful on Becky's stomach, and she moaned, flinched and moaned again. "Can you believe it?" he asked, laughing as if he'd pulled a great trick.

Dr. Benjamin made an arrangement with Lois Winders' mother the following week and Becky was released to his and her care on a Monday, a week and two days from the night she first responded to ice being held against her foot. Mrs. Winders came Monday through Friday at nine am and stayed until the doctor got home. Becky appeared to show improvement immediately. She had almost fully recovered by the end of December and wanted to spend three days with Lois and her mother. "Gee whiz, Daddy. What's the difference? Mrs. Winders will be there. I've missed so much and Lois is the only one who could possibly catch me up. Please, Daddy."

Ben couldn't say no. "I guess I'll just have to celebrate the new year by myself," he sulked, then picked up the phone as he watched Becky and Lois run upstairs to pack a bag.

"Hello."

"I hope you have to spend New Year's Eve alone," said the doctor. "Sorry to disappoint you, Ben, but Mrs. Braxton is cooking dinner for Karla and me," said Samantha, hoping her plans might change.

"What if I brought the champagne?"

"Hmmm. I'm sure that will interest Mrs. Braxton, so I suppose we'll see you at six-thirty tomorrow evening." Samantha immediately called Mrs. Braxton. She was excited and felt the doctor's visit would be quite an honor. "Splendid," she said. "Meeting that man at church is one thing, but you should have asked him over a long time ago. You don't have to spend every evening alone, Samantha. I'd bet one of my social security checks that Ken ain't alone right now."

"Can I do anything to help with dinner, Mrs. Braxton?"

"Heck no. I'm going to celebrate and do a standing rib roast. Six big heavy beef ribs. It's my favorite. Oh? Samantha, I know you prefer your beef rare, but how about Dr. Benjamin? And, uh. Well, I'll make yeast bread. Yes, two loaves," she added, almost inaudible, thinking aloud. "Everyone likes fresh baked bread. A salad. Uh-huh. Samantha, is there anything that's really traditional for a New Year's Eve dinner? You know, like turkey on Thanksgiving."

Dr. Benjamin sat at the end of the table, carved and served the roast, then fed himself and Karla while holding her, his hulk filling Mrs. Braxton's small apartment. He was a little overdressed, a navy three-piece suit, white silk shirt and a maroon tie with thin navy stripes. He ate heartily, drank lightly, thanked profusely and then bid his goodnight. It was just after nine. "Now Dr. Benjamin, you shouldn't give up this early on New Year's Eve," scorned Mrs. Braxton. "I've got Karla for the night, so... Heck, I'll be happy to keep her all week, Samantha. You kids go find a place to dance and ring in the new year."

Dr. Benjamin sat in Samantha's den and waited while she did her hair, a French twist. She freshened her makeup and slipped into a long, v-neck black dress Aunt May had bought for her high school graduation. She wore the only decent coat she had. It was a thin ankle length, black leather duster that Pat had given her rather than have it taken in and hemmed for herself. The coat was a little too full, but the length was close enough. "I'm as ready as I can get," she said, fussing with her hair, trying to get a rhinestone clip to hold the French twist.

The doctor whistled. "I'll get that," he said, jumping to his feet and taking the clip. He hadn't seen Samantha in black before, never had her eyes been so mesmerizing, the high fall of her breasts so intriguing. "I hope you have a toothbrush in that little purse," he whispered, touching his lips to her ear. "Mrs. Braxton said we could stay out late."

Ben left Samantha in his car while he checked several different nightclubs, finally finding the setting he wanted. It was a tiny, dark, waterfront blues bar featuring a band with a lead singer whose voice was deep and raspy, perfect for the Nat King Cole ballads he crooned white sipping Jack Daniels and chain-smoking Camel cigarettes. "I'm not hiding, Samantha," explained the big doctor, ordering the first drinks since dinner. "It's just that I haven't been out with anyone besides Becky in a long time. We have fun, but...Well, I wanted everything right tonight. I love a good blues guitar. Anyone can sing a blues ballad if the rhythm is on."

Samantha drank and danced and laughed, totally unaware of the time until the raspy voiced crooner started the countdown to the midnight hour. "Give me a ten," he moaned, and the crowd screamed, "Ten, Nine, Eight, Seven..."

Those who were partnered exchanged big kisses at exactly midnight, then ten minutes later all the lights came on and the band members started breaking down their equipment, getting ready to leave. "Dang," said the doctor, reaching for his wallet. "I could have danced all night."

Samantha was equally disappointed to see the night end. "Shall we try someplace else?" she asked, hooking her arm with one of the doctor's.

"You're kidding." Ben held the long coat. "Are you really game for that, Samantha? I don't want you to stay out just because of me."

"I'm game, and don't feel you have to stay out just because of me either."

Samantha slid her arms into her coat. Ben straightened the shoulders, then turned her to face him, leaning close, indicating he wanted to kiss her. "I'll be daring once again, Samantha. Would you object to my place?"

Their eyes met, then Samantha softly touched her lips to his, answering his question with her own. "Is there a reason?"

The big man paused, pondering, seeming lost or overly challenged, his brow wrinkled in thought, his eyes squinted in query, eventually explaining himself. "Yes, and I should give you that reason, Samantha. It's double daring, though. I want to be alone with you because I'm in love with you and I'm afraid I will be until I'm dead and buried."

The doctor's words weren't jolting. They were like an embrace from one who had suddenly appeared after being lost for years. Samantha leaned into him, his arms automatically closing around her, holding her against his phone booth size body. "I don't know if I'm in love with you, Ben," she whispered, peering up into his face, "but I know I love you. There's a difference, but I'm very happy tonight. How about you? Does being in love with me make you happy?"

The doctor pondered again, then went on, "I have plenty to be happy about, Samantha. In fact, I just couldn't help but think about something that my mother said a few months before she died. She was sixty-eight and had been the happiest of her life for six or seven months. I asked her why and she admitted to straying on my dad, a cranky old devil who had forgotten Mom years before. Anyway, Mom winked at me and said something about good seeds always growing in fertile soil. She told me that she had never loved my dad, and had never been happy until she finally fell in love, finally found out what love was all about. I can be happy just being in the same room with you, Samantha, but I feel both blessed and happy knowing that I fell in love with such a fine person. Win, lose or draw, I'm in love with you."

Chapter 5

July 1964
Houston, Texas

A light sprinkle had just begun to fall across the metro. A very gentle sprinkle, the type most people ignore, or moments later wonder if they only imagined it. The day, midafternoon on a Friday, was as good as anyone could expect in South Texas during the summer. Big puffy marshmallow clouds were drifting in from The Gulf. A gentle breeze laced with the sweet smell of rain, a welcome relief from the torrid heat and humidity, had summoned the storm all day. Now that the wet blessing seemed inevitable, the light sprinkles a promise, a sudden sense of torpor spread through the busy downtown streets. Two men in suits walked out of the Gulf States National Bank building and looked to the sky.

One asked, "Think we'll finally get a good downpour, or just another little sprinkle? False hope."

"Who really knows what these clouds hold?" was his companion's response. "Feels good, though, and we really need a good soaking," he added, removing his coat, allowing the light sprinkle to pepper his sweaty white shirt.

In the shadows of the big bank building, double-parked at the curb, sat a shiny Jaguar XK-E, droplets from the light sprinkle beading on its shiny red finish. Sitting in the driver's seat, Sybil Valentine, a glamorous blonde in her late fifties, smiled to the two men who had just walked out of the bank. From the passenger seat, a little girl waved.

"Y'all better put your top up," said one man, through a smile, his East Texas drawl friendly. "It might finally come a rain."

"Let it rain, let it rain, let it rain," responded the classy blonde, smiling flirtatiously, a singsong tempo in her words.

Both men nodded. "Amen," said the one carrying his jacket, as he led his companion across the downtown street, both appearing only semiconscious of the traffic, but totally unconscious of the fact they were jaywalking. The blonde in the shiny Jag seemed to be the center of interest to the man following. "Wait up a minute," he said.

The man carrying his jacket, a happily married man who seldom strayed, even in his thoughts, stepped onto the curb and turned to look back at the glamorous blonde. "I guess you want me to watch the kid while you buy the blonde a drink, huh?"

"No way," said the other man. "I'm just looking."

Both men stood on the sidewalk across the street and observed the middle-aged beauty. "I'd settle for the roadster," said the man holding his jacket.

Inside the bank, Cheryl Cooper had allowed herself to get hopelessly frustrated, far too impatient, something she did often. Today though, she had done everything her mother insisted she do, but the silly teller had to get the transaction approved. This was outrageous. The lady in new accounts had said all Cheryl had to do was show proof of Mindy's social security number and get a receipt for the money. There wasn't supposed to be a hassle. Cheryl had things to do, and she had only come back today because her mother insisted she make this deposit before the weekend, forty-five hundred dollars to open a savings account for the family to help build on. The money was for Mindy, Cheryl's six-year-old daughter, who was waiting outside with her grandmother. This morning, when Cheryl and her mother sat down to do the paperwork, a lady in new accounts had done everything but take the money, insisting that, since there wasn't an adult on the account, Mindy, a minor, had to have a social security number. "Damn it, you little twit," whispered Cheryl, through tight lips as the teller, who had been standing in front of someone's desk in new accounts for fifteen minutes, had only just now gotten his okay. Cheryl had never seen this man, who had purposefully and rudely taken an unnecessary amount of time to examine the paperwork, finally initialing something with a nod and a mumble.

All of this could have been handled on Monday. The hassle Cheryl experienced at the social security office this morning had already ruined her day and now time was becoming a concern. She had promised to go to an early movie and have dinner with her father at the club afterward, a Friday ritual with them. As the little teller finally approached her station, Cheryl opened her purse, ready to stuff what she was given inside and rush out.

"Okay, Mrs. Cooper," said the teller, smiling as she handed her the deposit receipt and paperwork she had just gotten approval for. "Mr. Brockmire initialed the entry in Mindy's passbook, but I'll handle it from now on."

"Yeah? Well, good," responded Cheryl, nastily, turning away as she stuffed the deposit receipt and paperwork into the passbook, then shoved everything into her purse. "I guess I'm supposed to bow down and kiss your ass now," she sneered, over her shoulder. "Fat chance."

Cheryl hurried out to the car and yanked the passenger door open. "So, is everything finally taken care of?" asked Sybil, looking beyond her, smiling to the two admirers.

Mindy slid against her grandmother to make room in the two-seat roadster. "It's gonna rain, Mama," she said, happily.

"Yeah? Well, let's go," snapped Cheryl, flopping into the seat, then banging the door closed. "Get in my lap," she added, pulling Mindy against her.

"Oh, we can get an attitude when we have to do things we don't want to do," said Sybil, flipping a finger wave to her admirers as she raced the Jag's big six-cylinder engine, its deep throaty sound reverberating through the enclave created by the tall buildings surrounding it. "You should appreciate the fact that I gave you the money for your daughter's college fund."

"Don't rag on me, Mother. You've done enough of that today," slurred Cheryl, speaking around the cigarette she'd just stuck between her lips.

Perhaps, had several factors not conspired against her, the heart lifting weather, the onlooking admirers and the fracas with her daughter, who only lit the cigarette because she knew her mother didn't allow smoking in her new car, Sybil would have noticed the big ambulance running through the traffic light behind her and the crash could have been avoided. The ambulance's speed was no more than thirty-five miles an hour, its colored roof lights flashing, but its siren silent, a company policy when carrying non-critical patients through the downtown area during daylight hours.

However, the big ambulance was right on top of the little red roadster when Sybil pulled away from the curb. The driver didn't even have time to hit the brakes, no squealing tires and no skid marks. The only sudden sounds were Sybil's scream ripping through the light rain, the shattering of glass, the metallic sounds of crushing metal, then a chorus of gasps and clattering feet as onlookers ran into the street.

The impact, the bumper and grill of the ambulance plowing into the Jag's left rear quarter panel, tossed little Mindy from her mother's lap like a toy. She landed fifteen feet in front of the Jag, her head and right shoulder smacking against the pavement. The little roadster rolled over twice, its first rollover leaving Sybil and Cheryl lying face down on the street, right in the path of the big ambulance. Their bodies were crushed like eggs under foot. Three lives lost one beautiful Friday afternoon on the streets of downtown Houston. Tragic fatalities that created a new life for another.

Two years later

Office of the Commander

Fort Dix, New Jersey

It was 3:15 pm the Wednesday before Thanksgiving, and already the day had been worse than any other all year. Six staff members, including his executive officer, Major Lane, had begged off at noon, all wanting to get an early start on their four-day weekend. There had been a parade of officers, all sympathetic well-wishers who just had to stick their heads in and get noticed by the senior officer on the base, the man who would have the final review of their OER's, officer's efficiency reports.

"Hope you have a nice holiday, Colonel Bishop, you old goat," chided Lieutenant Colonel Elliott, the post chaplain. He had a single rose in his hand and tossed it onto Martin's desk. "You know you're welcome to have dinner with me tomorrow. I don't think anyone should be alone on Thanksgiving, or any other day that's specifically set aside to praise The Lord."

"No way, Padre," smiled his boss, placing the rose on the credenza behind him. "Thanks for the flower, but we won't have Thanksgiving dinner together this year. I'd just sit and watch football all day while you got drunk."

"You're such a bore," said the chaplain, strolling out of the office.

"Happy Thanksgiving, Colonel Bishop," greeted a baby-faced captain who was standing just outside the colonel's doorway.

My gosh, thought Martin, the assistant finance officer, of all people, saluting like a goofy recruit. What next? A squad of latrine orderlies? Martin snapped a halfhearted salute in response. "Thanks, Captain Muncie," he said. "The same to you and yours."

"I'll tell Martha you said that. Her orders are for me to be ready to cut the turkey at exactly two o'clock tomorrow afternoon. We both wish you could join us."

I'll bet you do, thought Martin. "Thank you, Captain. And, Martha, too, of course. I'd love to stop by, but you understand, I'm sure."

Then there was Major Lane, trying to go unnoticed, smiling like a naughty kid when he was seen sneaking out at noon. "See you on Monday, Sir."

Maybe it was best the major chose to leave without being noticed, chose not to engage in any conversation, thought Colonel Martin Bishop, but he suspected otherwise of his XO. Somehow, for reasons he was yet to understand, the major seemed to be going through a number of odd charades lately. Although Colonel Martin Bishop, Post Commander, Major Lane's immediate supervisor, hadn't paid real close attention, he felt that his XO had been avoiding daily briefings with him, even casual one-on-one conversation and unnecessarily skipping a few command functions. Martin had noticed that his XO left the office early several times a week, but had decided to tolerate that, hoping he was merely taking good care of things at home. That was something Colonel Bishop wished he, himself, had done a better job of while his wife was living.

Martin considered Donna, his late wife, for a long moment. She was good in some ways and bad in others. A princess when she wanted to be, but more often a pain in the ass. Donna was an invalid, born with an enlarged heart. Her physical activities had to be limited, her condition constantly monitored and controlled with medication. She and Martin had been married two years before he learned the seriousness of her condition. He was bitter, remained that way throughout the marriage and secretly felt cheated.

"Sir," announced Priscilla, easing Colonel Bishop's door open. Martin thought his lanky secretary looked like a goose every time she stretched her neck to look around his office door. "You've got another one. Mrs. Lane, the major's wife. I'm sure you remember her." Priscilla was civilian, DOA, Department of the Army. She was single, twenty-eight, pretty enough, long red hair, boasted that she was five feet eleven, one hundred and forty-one pounds, admitted to, and was hopelessly in love with herself.

Colonel Bishop, who was stunned just now, wasn't that impressed with his secretary. To him, all she had to offer were the big tits most men think they want, but her big butt made her long legs, which weren't that shapely, look clumsy and far too skinny. He also knew that the seductive appearance she maintained, and worked every angle of, tight sweaters with low necklines, skirts hemmed above the knees and those monstrous spike heels, would be and maybe had been, the ruination of some poor married soldier. "What? Carol Ann Lane?" sighed the colonel, closing the book he'd picked out to read this weekend. Quickly, responding to an old habit Martin snatched a Kleenex from a box on his credenza and wiped the glossy top of his desk, mumbling to himself as he did. "This is a first. A subordinate's spouse dropping by to wish me a happy holiday. Hmmm." Martin tossed the soiled tissue into a cuspidor he used as a trash can, then spoke to his secretary. "Priscilla, didn't Major Lane sign out already?"

"Yes, Sir. He said he was goin to Atlantic City."

The contempt in Priscilla's tone irked Martin. "Well, let me make a couple of calls, then you can send Mrs. Lane in. Get her a cup of coffee. Is there any left? Fresh, I mean. Don't give her any of that leftover grease."

Priscilla batted her big eyes. "It's gone. Do you want me to make some?"

"Oh, no. Please. Let me," snapped the colonel, to his secretary, then to himself, "Dumb-ass. No gray matter to spare in that head," then again to the big secretary. "You go out there and ask Mrs. Lane if she wants coffee, then make some if she does. Very simple," he added, picking up his desk phone. "Very simple," he repeated, disgust in his mumble.

Within the minute, Carol Ann, a pretty brunette in her late thirties, cowered into Colonel Bishop's office in the shadow of his big secretary. She was trailing along slowly, looking about the neat office while avoiding eye contact with the colonel, whose desk was to the right of the door, facing across the room. That seemed odd to Carol Ann. For no reason she knew of, she was expecting the colonel to sit facing his office door, staring right down the throat of anyone the second they stepped into his space.

The small office was smartly furnished and manly appointed, a plank floor, one thick royal blue throw rug in the exact center of the room, dark paneled walls and one picture hanging over a small wet bar next to an open closet in the corner. There was a row of six leather chairs seemingly standing at attention in front of a big oak desk, a long credenza in back with a box of Kleenex and a single rose laying on it. The American flag was on the wall above the credenza and a brass cuspidor full of dirty sand, cigarette butts and crumpled paper was on the floor to the left of the flag. There was a little brass cannon on the colonel's desk that appeared to be used as a paperweight and a row of combat relics surrounding a desk lamp, a tiny model airplane on a thread hanging from its shade. A hardback novel, *All The King's Men*, was at the colonel's left elbow.

"Have a seat if you want," said Priscilla, gesturing for Carol Ann to select anyone of the stuffed armchairs. "Sir, the major's wife didn't want no coffee, or nothin. Would you like somthin?"

"No," snapped Martin. "Thanks, I guess. You can go back to doing whatever you do," he added, unsmiling, then stood and extended a hand. "Hello, Carol Ann. It's a pleasure to see you today."

"Thank you," she said, shaking hands with her husband's boss. "1 didn't know you flew," she added, noticing silver wings on the breast of his tunic.

"I fly for proficiency only these days, Mrs. Lane, but, yes, I did complete the army's flight training program," explained Colonel Bishop, smiling appreciatively, admiring Carol Ann for finding a simple way to appear less self-absorbed than some of the officer's wives. "My last assignment was commanding an assault helicopter battalion in South Vietnam. Please take a chair. That's certainly a beautiful skirt and sweater, although I'll admit that I'm a little partial to white," he added, feeling compelled to reciprocate with an observance of his own. "How have you been since the parade Sunday? I hope your old man told you how nice you looked in that blue suit. I noticed a few young men in the grandstands who must have thought you were a stunning sight to behold. They sure didn't watch the parade."

"Thank you, but I don't think I've been stunning since, uh, well, I never felt that I was. Oh, that blue suit? It's so old that...Well, anyway I've been all right, Colonel Bishop," said Carol Ann, looking down at her feet, suddenly concerned with the shoes she'd picked out for today and wondering if they matched her maroon purse. "And, how have you been?" she asked, automatically, as she slid into an armchair. "Good," she sighed, seeing that the flats she had on were in fact maroon and white.

"Good? Was that a statement, or a question?"

"Excuse me, Sir," said Carol Ann, momentarily then looking away as she checked her earrings, feeling a pang of doubt when she failed to recognize them by feel.

"Nothing," said the colonel, smiling again, but suddenly embarrassed with Carol Ann's neurosis. "Please call me Martin, and I've been doing well enough," he added, then crossed his arms, leaned back in his chair and asked, "Aren't you and your husband going someplace for the holiday weekend? Atlantic City? Seems I was told that."

Carol Ann shook her head, bowing as if in prayer. She had worried about this meeting all day. Although Colonel Bishop couldn't be much past forty, and was surely younger than her husband, Carol Ann always felt like a high-schooler in his presence. He wasn't as tall or as handsome as Howard, but had a look that women respond to and remember. A comforting look, older than his years, strong and steady. Fatherly. The colonel had unusually large hands, very dark features and beautifully thick blue-black hair with a hint of gray at the temples. To Carol Ann, his overall bearing was one that seemed to invite trust. He was in his greens today. Below the silver wings on the breast of his tunic lay a giant badge of medals. His build, small waist and big shoulders, fit the buttoned down, spit and polish image all officers wanted to achieve. A statement in itself. For that reason, Carol Ann had never been completely satisfied with her own appearance when in the company of Colonel Bishop. The white skirt and sweater she had selected for today was no less than the sixth outfit she'd tried on, looking for a soft image, without it being one of pity. "I'm sorry I wasn't able to give you a little warning before dropping by. I should have called, but I wanted to find a time when Howard had left early."

"I see," said the colonel, having no clue what Major Lane's leaving the office early could have to do with this visit.

Although things had changed with this duty assignment, Martin Bishop and Howard Lane were once good friends, old campaigners with the natural bond that comes from sharing the trials and trenches of combat. They met in Italy in 1944, second lieutenants, Platoon leaders in the same infantry battalion. During the Korean War, again in the same battalion, they were company commanders. Theirs was not an odd friendship, the men being secretly quite alike. Martin could not admit it to himself, but Howard Lane had certain abilities that he envied. One, unlike Howard, Martin had never had the confidence to lie in action or word. He had moved along in his career in constant fear of failure. He dealt with it by trying to be perceived as the meanest bull in the pasture, the one not to be challenged. He tried to appear to be what he was paid to be, a professional soldier. Although he hated the irony of living a life of pretense, he had done it well.

It was really Howard Lane who caused Martin to realize how unhappy he was with military life. Howard perceived his career as an escape, a road to early retirement where a man could live in the shadow of others and seldom be seen. As a career infantry officer, his occupation was supposed to be a commander of fighting men and everything that requires and entails, but Howard would readily admit that he hadn't remained in the service of his country to take the responsibility for, command, or lead anyone. Martin understood completely, felt the same way, but would not admit it to even himself.

Lately though, since Colonel Bishop had arranged for Major Howard Lane to be his XO, his tolerance was being tested because the major wasn't keeping up with the demands of his job. Martin hadn't specifically caught him yet and hoped not to, but suspected that Howard had been lying about the reasons he needed to leave the office early, as often as three afternoons a week sometimes. Another thing that irritated Martin was that Major Lane kept boasting that he had only hung on as an army officer for the advantages of an early and liberal retirement, as had Martin himself, but he did not want to be reminded of it.

Howard Lane wasn't aware that his attitude had driven a wedge between him and his old friend, Martin Bishop, until one Friday night last year when they discussed it at a surprise birthday party for Doctor Logan, the post's most popular orthopedic surgeon. A man who Colonel Bishop suspected was far too liberal when it came to prescribing pain pills. A matter he planned to look into before signing off on the surgeon's OER.

Howard had just slid back his chair to join his wife. "Stay right where you are, Major Lane," ordered the colonel, his right forefinger banging the table like a jackhammer, explaining exactly where the major was to stay. The two old pals were at the officer's club alone, while everyone else pitched in to sing happy birthday to the doctor. "I feel it would be dereliction of my duty if I didn't have a talk with you, Howard. Lately..." Martin stopped mid-sentence and pointed a finger into the major's face. Lately, Howard had a provocative way of smiling, reminiscent of the taunting twist in Elvis Presley's lips during some of those crazy interviews about his gyrations on stage. And, Howard just seemed too damn happy, something Martin was not. One thing that had always bothered Martin was that everyone looked up to Howard. He was tall, blonde, and handsome and looked like Martin perceived a wealthy California sun worshiper might. He always appeared to have spent a lot of time in the sun, yet there were no wrinkles anywhere on his face, a movie star look.

Perhaps, as much as Martin Bishop disliked his big secretary and believed her to be stupid, she might have said it best when she described Major Lane's appearance. "Geemannee crickets. Who's that?" she gasped, the first morning Howard sauntered into the commander's office. "He looks like Rock Hudson with blonde hair. Will he be working for you, Colonel Bishop?"

Handsome, subtly flamboyant, provocative or whatever, Howard grated on the colonel. "Don't waste that chicken-shit grin on me, Major Lane," he said. "I've been around you so long that I know exactly what you're thinking."

"Certainly, Sir," said Howard, biting his lip, fighting the urge to laugh. His moods had swung like a pendulum for months, from depths of despair and rage to days when he felt like a teenage kid and couldn't control his mirth, like today.

"That's better," said the colonel, his eyes like lasers. "I know right now, you're thinking that I'm just going to ask a few questions and make a few of my routine demands. You're right, I am, but that's not the half of it. Why are you leaving work early so often and what are those little white pills you take every hour or so? Is there something wrong with you?"

Major Lane shrugged, allowing only the slightest straight smile to part his lips in hopes of defusing his boss' manner. "It's my back, Sir. You remember how I suffered in Korea. The pills are called Soma 350, or something. I don't know, but they sure relieve the pain. There's no problem with them."

"I see. No problem huh? What's with this leaving early then?"

"This is embarrassing, but you'll find out anyway," sighed the major. "My wife has been having the problems. It's…"

"Your wife?" interrupted Martin, frowning as he propped his chin on a closed fist. "Hmmm, so the wife's the problem," he challenged, half statement, half question. "Well, go ahead, Major Lane. Try to sell me on that one."

"Honestly, Colonel Bishop. She says it was the same with her late mother. Runs in their family, I guess." Howard paused to catch the attention of a waiter. "Young Man," he said, holding up a hand. "Two more over here."

"Young Man," said Martin, waving a hand. "No more over here," he requested. He wanted another drink, but denied himself and his XO out of sheer spite. "What runs in Carol Ann's family, Howard?"

The major, about to bust a gut to keep from laughing, did his best to put on a grim face. "Sir, it's referred to as the change of life. Some women won't do anything, but sit around and bitch when they go through it. I have to do…"

"That's enough," interrupted the colonel, raising a hand as he did for the waiter. He knew the major was contriving, which bordered on lying. "Your wife's awfully young for such a condition, Howard. However, if that's the case, I can sympathize with her. I've heard that some women have a terrible time emotionally and never really understand why. I guess menopause doesn't usually have many obvious symptoms. However, I've also heard that the condition goes away in time. You just have to be patient. See if you can get her to go see a doctor. Carol Ann's worth it if any woman in the world is. She's always very pleasant and I'm sure that you don't have to be told how her even nature and social skills compliment you. She's never overdressed and never underdressed, but I've never seen her wearing anything that wasn't tasteful. Very tasteful, very tasteful," repeated the colonel, breaking eye contact with Howard as he looked around the club, spotting Carol Ann clapping as the doctor tore the wrapping paper from a small gift-box. "Your wife's the most attractive woman here, Howard," mumbled Martin, meaning it and again, feeling envious of his XO. "Take whatever time you need, but if you don't see any improvement, or say she has times when she's just too emotional or depressed, get her to a good female doctor right away. There'll be some pills that will help her, too."

Howard caught the inference and almost burst out laughing. "I've already considered it," he said, quickly turning away, nodding as if to confirm that his wife did look good. "Seems to be enjoying, uh, herself," he said, the falter in his voice caused by the near uncontrollable hilarity he felt. "In fact," he added, "I'm taking her to New York City tonight just to see if a change of pace helps out. 1 booked two nights at a downtown hotel and it's gonna be a weekend of room service and grown-up games. I'll talk to her about seeing a doctor, too. Fact is, I'd better go toast the good doctor, then whirl my wife around the dance floor once and get started. It's a long drive and I have to run by the house to get our bags."

"Okay," agreed the colonel, through with Howard, but enjoying making him squirm. "First though, I need to mention a couple of other things. Your drinking for sure. I have a drink or two every night. It's a harmless habit, but I never come to the office reeking of booze like you have lately. I can't imagine how you can handle liquor along with those pills you take, but you're drinking too much, Howard. Another problem I have with you is your frame of mind for the last two years. You think that all you have to do is hang in the army for what, three more years now?" Martin paused, feeling completely hypocritical as he awaited the major's comment, then continued when he saw that Howard wasn't going to have one. "Three more miserable years of doing nothing more than you just absolutely have to, plus avoid a command in Vietnam at any cost. All you want to do is assure yourself of making another rank so you can get the hell out with twenty-five years of service and a fat benefit package. Well, Major Lane, let me be completely frank with you. I can't..."

"You always are completely frank, Sir," interrupted Howard, unable to control his laughter for a split second, allowing an unexpected guttural sound to slip out, but quickly coughing in an attempt to camouflage it.

Colonel Bishop did not tolerate being interrupted by a subordinate, but would not have reacted quite so harshly at another time. However, his XO had a way of bringing out the worst in him. "Shut-up, Major

Lane," he snapped. "Shut-up right now and don't you butt in again until I'm finished with you. For a man with a bad back and a wife who's in questionable health, you've been acting very strange lately. I regret that you're in my command, but you are, and that's unfortunate for you. There are plenty of senior field grade officers who would just rubber-stamp your previous OER's, but you know I won't. You'd be wise to consider retirement right now, Howard." Martin had to think fast to keep this diatribe going. "It might be the best thing for Carol Ann, too. I would hope so, but I know you're not happy with the service and surely you know that you will never wear a silver leaf."

The colonel paused. Howard turned away, unembarrassed, but having difficulty keeping a straight face. It was the risk that thrilled him. "Okay," he began, then turned back around and looked Martin right in the face, squinting his eyes in mock seriousness. "With all due respect, Sir," he said, trembling to hold off the giggles. "I plan to do the twenty-five years if I don't get orders for Vietnam. I guess I'll have to accept that I might be retiring in my current rank, but I know I'm not bad for the service, and I'm not that bad of an officer."

"I don't know the extent of your personal problems, Howard, but I'd guess there are more than we've discussed. I'm not sure I even want to know anymore about you than I do. I don't claim to be very helpful with personal matters, but I will say that your choosing to stay in the army three more years would be a poor decision. I don't advise it," said the colonel. "That's all I have for now and let's hope that I don't have to say another word about your drinking. You should slow down on those pills, too." Martin paused, then continued with a challenging smile that would let Major Lane know he hadn't been convinced of anything. "My heart goes out to your wife, but it's because I'm unsure of all she's really having to deal with. Now, go on and dance with her. Dance with Carol Ann, Howard," instructed the colonel. It killed him to think that every woman in the club would take any tongue-lashing their husband wanted to give out just for a dance with Howard Lane. "You did hear what I said, didn't you Howard? I said dance with Carol Ann, not Captain Valentine's wife."

"Yes, Sir," said Howard. "Goodnight," he added, happy as hell to get away from the self-righteous bastard. Strolling toward a fire exit door, head down to hide a big grin, he snapped the thumb and finger of his right hand. "Let's go, Carol Ann."

Howard Lane, tall and trim, and although he was beginning to look a little frail these days, was elegant in his every movement, thought Martin. He was even envious of the major's walk, which looked choreographed. The younger company grade officers, those single predators who hung at the bar every night, considered him the best dancer in the club. There was a day, painfully remembered the colonel, envious as he watched the major's wife dutifully followed him out the back way, when the less outgoing young men would depend on Howard Lane to relax and break the ice with any woman who came into the officer's club alone, get her to laugh and joke, dance some and maybe even too drunk to say no. Howard laughed easily and it never failed to rub off on everyone around him. It irked Martin to admit it, but he wished to hell that he could see how it felt just once.

Today was no exception. Although his old friend had tried to upset him, Howard only saw the humor in his boss' inability to convince him of his concerns. Poor little wife with a head problem. You really care don't you, Martin. I'm drinking too much. Shit, thought Howard. He knew the colonel would tie one on every night if he had the guts. The pills? Completely harmless. The best attitude adjusters in the world. Hell, the old cranky colonel oughta try'em, mused the major, imagining Martin Bishop allowing himself to shake with a good belly laugh. Maybe not though. It would only take a big grin to crack his face. Take all the time I need? Well, okay, Sir, Colonel Bishop, old buddy. I was going to anyway, but it sure is nice for a man to have his boss' blessing.

Howard had always considered his marriage and career as protracted jokes, ongoing acts. His earliest ambition was to be a comedic actor. While in college, although on a ROTC scholarship, he majored in drama and worked hard at it. He wrote and directed four plays during his freshman and sophomore years and several scripts for different acting teams, plus worked up a slew of comedy routines for himself. His ROTC Commander and drama teacher let him perform any one of them at student assemblies during the last semester of his junior year. The student body as a whole expected Howard to be in the movies someday.

Howard Lane could act out his whole life if he had to. He had won high marks in several of the more difficult undergraduate courses. He simply acted alert, but was not interested. He would have never given up acting had things not changed just before his graduation, when the four years of ROTC began to pay off. Howard was commissioned to the rank of Second Lieutenant and started drawing O-1 pay. Then, as quickly as inevitably, the security of Uncle Sam's army was too appealing, and Howard entered active military indefinite status. Although it was the biggest mistake he ever made, his bachelor's degree and minor, journalism, aided in his assignments and he had been able to avoid several command positions. Once though, as a high time-in-grade captain, in danger of being passed over for lack of command time, he was assigned a company during the later stages of the Korean War. Howard hated the duty, but due to his claims of chronic back pain and time spent in the infirmary, he was replaced after only 131 days. Nevertheless, his record would always show that he made it through the only command assignment he ever had with a near perfect ninety-three on his OER.

"What's wrong, Howard?" asked Carol Ann, as he shoved her into the car.

"Not a thing," he said, smiling. "Tomorrow is Saturday and we're off. I just told Martin that we had plans to spend two uninterrupted nights in one of the finest hotels in downtown New York City. I think he was jealous."

"Why did you tell him that?"

"I don't know. I guess I just feel so damn good tonight," said Howard, sliding his right hand under his wife's dress, up to mid-thigh. With his mood so high tonight, it was impossible to worry about retiring before making another rank. Having to accept early retirement, which he assumed would red flag any other man as having had a very undistinguished career, was just another joke to add to the list for Howard.

"I wish you wouldn't do that," sighed Carol Ann, leaning away from her husband. "I'm tired and by the way, I'd just as soon stay home this weekend."

"You got it," said Howard. "There's a few things I can do Sunday anyway."

Howard's apparent ease in lying to his immediate superior prompted Carol Ann to begin checking into what else he treated so casually as his word. He hadn't paid any attention to her for the past several years and his mood swings had become more profound. She started asking questions, tried to find out what he did with his spare time, where he went on the afternoons he left the office early and how often that was. She was soon quite shocked to hear how brazen her husband had been about a certain captain's wife. It seemed Howard had completely disregarded Carol Ann's feelings. Had he even considered the damage to his career that such an indiscretion with a subordinate's wife would lead to, if he were caught?

Carol Ann had not come to Colonel Bishop today to ask for his advice, but to bolster her recent convictions, get a divorce and start her life anew. However, regardless of her disdain for Howard, she did not want to adversely affect his career, or keep him from getting help. "Well, thank you for noticing today and last Sunday, Sir," she said. "I have several white outfits, but that suit you saw is the only navy blue anything I own. I'm sure Howard has been a little too preoccupied lately to notice anything I do or wear though. It would take a week for him to even suspect something awry if I shaved my head."

"Please call me, Martin," said the colonel, uncrossing his arms, then resting his elbows on his desk, the fingers of his big hands forming a steeple, a shiny silver diving watch loosely hanging from his left wrist. "Now, Carol Ann, I'm sure you don't expect me to believe that you don't get your share of attention anywhere you go. You're a beautiful woman, but I'm sure the fact that I think so has nothing to do with the purpose of your visit, so feel free to begin at any time you wish." Martin resented Howard Lane and was itching to get some dirt on him, but couldn't communicate that to his wife yet. Cat and mouse. "Let me say this though, if your visit has to do with Howard's mysterious attitude of late, trust me, I'm quite aware of the problem."

"You are?"

"Yes, I am. And Howard blames me, right?" asked the colonel.

"That would be quite unusual, especially if we're talking about the same problem, Sir," said Carol Ann, nervously squirming in her chair, her eyes fixed between the colonel's shiny watch and the single rose on his credenza. "Do you know Captain Valentine?"

"Yes, I do. Ken works in the JAG office. Uh..." Martin paused, wondering what he should say here, hoping Carol Ann wasn't mixed up with Captain Valentine. He was another officer Martin resented. Ken hung out in the officer's club about every night, and much like Major Lane, he could have fun and make sure those around him did. There was one thing very strange about the young captain though. His living arrangement. Ken Valentine was married, but resided in the bachelor officer's quarters while his wife, a wholesome appearing and exceptionally beautiful young woman, lived off-base with their school-age daughter.

Ken Valentine's wife, as the colonel remembered hearing him explain repeatedly, was an emotional misfit. She, which Martin had trouble seeing the possibility of, was prone to hero worship and crushes on people in positions of authority. That seemed in such contrast with most people who had as much going for themselves as Samantha Valentine appeared to. The young captain had also said, which was a little easier for Colonel Bishop to accept, that his wife was especially vulnerable to high profile preachers and church leaders. For some reason, Martin could understand anyone's being friendly with preachers, considering them harmless and the last to take advantage of them, but Ken Valentine seemed to believe quite the opposite of a certain civilian minister and Samantha. Supposedly, the minister and Ken's wife had been involved in an illicit affair, possibly even at the present. Ked had caught them red-handed shortly after Samantha joined him from their home in Houston. They were right in his own bed.

Quite soon, according to the young captain, his wife left the house and got herself an apartment. Ken, hoping to reunite the family unit for the daughter's sake, had stayed away, but had phoned with wholesale, no strings attached pleas for his wife and daughter to come back to the base and live with him. At this point, Martin had been told, Samantha was considering it, but only on the condition her husband could get reassigned from Fort Dix to a base near their home in Houston, Texas, where she could enroll at the university. Due to his being less than convinced when hearing Captain Valentine's account of his marital situation, Martin had only led the young man to believe he had researched the possibility of a reassignment. "Captain Valentine isn't at all thrilled to be in the army," continued the colonel, wondering why the conversation had drifted to this particular young man. "He's impatient to get started practicing law as a civilian. I can't blame him for that, or the fact that it would allow him more time with his wife and daughter. Mrs. Valentine is a very sweet little lady, but somehow she manages to teach a Bible class at the post chapel every week, work with outpatients as a Red Cross volunteer, raise her little girl, plus work several hours a week for Doctor Logan right here at the base hospital.

The colonel paused in thought, repositioned himself in his chair, then continued. "Ken tells me that he met his wife while in law school at Southern Methodist University in Dallas, Texas. Samantha worked in the registrar's office and went to school at night. Studied medicine. I think he said that she's a licensed anesthetist. I suppose that's how she assists Doctor Logan. She's quite a young woman, blessed with good looks, energy to burn and a lot of talent." Martin nodded in the direction of the painting above the wet bar. "Her name is Samantha, isn't it?" he asked, knowing that it was.

"It certainly is. I couldn't forget that."

"Yes, I remember it is Samantha," said the colonel, then continued as if thinking aloud. "Beautiful brunette hair. Eyes as blue as I've ever seen. Ken gave me that oil painting she did, including a lengthy explanation." Carol Ann glanced over at the picture, uninterested. "You see," explained Martin. "It's just a simple desert scene. A big black buzzard soaring among some puffy white clouds high over a parched landscape. According to Captain Valentine though, it presents most of the colors common to the New Mexico deserts. The sky, rich and blue, the clouds, soft and white, accented by the shiny black feathers of the buzzard." Martin leaned toward the picture and pointed as he further explained it. "There's the green of the cacti, some red and yellow in the flowers. There's a hint of mauve along the horizon and several pastels.

See the big cliffs in the background? They're sort of a burnt orange, or terra cotta I guess it's called, and then there's…Well, you can see how many colors there are."

Martin returned his attention to his guest and cleared his throat, wondering if he was boring her. "You see, Mrs. Lane," he began again, hoping an explanation of Captain Valentine's reason for giving him the painting would somehow be pertinent to Carol Ann's asking if he knew him. "One night at the club, Ken was telling some of us about a cabin near Santa Fe that he and his wife own. I chipped in that my late wife and I had been to New Mexico at a time or two when I was in flight school at Fort Wolters, Texas. Clovis a couple of times, Roswell and Ruidoso once that I remember. Anyway, we weren't talking about the same part of New Mexico. It's a pretty big state. Ken and Samantha's cabin is in a high mountain park way up close to the Colorado border. Lost Mountain Park, to be exact. I hope Samantha didn't object to Ken giving me the painting. I've seen her a few times, but haven't actually talked to her."

Carol Ann, always wanting to be fair, to consider the wisdom of the older and wiser, the more accomplished and more objective, reflected on her perception of Samantha Valentine before she spoke. The young woman, possibly thirty, was in fact pretty. Although she had successfully avoided Samantha and never tried to get to know her, or even look at her closely, Carol Ann perceived her as being loose and lecherous. Her eyes were remarkable indeed. "It's a nice picture," she said, of Samantha's work. "Where did you grow up, Colonel Bishop?" A question merely to change the subject to anything, but Samantha Valentine, a young woman who Carol Ann could never have an ounce of respect for.

Martin pointed to himself, eyebrows raised in question. "Me? Oh, I'm from Camden." Such a quick change of direction, he thought. Few women had ever shown an interest in him. Did Carol Ann actually want to know where he'd grown up, or was she just moving the conversation a safe distance away from Ken Valentine? "Camden is across the river from Philly. On the New Jersey side. My parents are gone now, but I have two sisters. The oldest, Toni, and her husband have a market five blocks from the old house where I was raised. They have a troubled son who I used to try to spend a little time with. Good looking kid. Well, he's a man now, twenty-six, name's Adam Richardson. He'll be home from Vietnam in a few months. I couldn't wait for the army to get hold of him. Six or eight more months and the kid can get out, but I hope he re-ups for at least four more years. He used to get into a...Well, anyway, he needed some direction. Why did you ask where I'm from?"

Carol Ann, smiling sheepishly, looked away again. "Oh, you don't seem like someone from the West. I just wondered where you were from. That's all."

"I see, I think. Where did you grow up?"

"Texas. Same as Ken and Samantha, I guess. Dallas instead of Houston though. It's a big state, but it certainly has a few little coincidences."

Martin's curiosity was pricked. He wanted to extend this meeting as long as he could, hoping to get to know the major's wife even better. She was so appealing; her figure so ordinary that it invited without challenge and her face was so literally feminine that any man would take notice. It wasn't the face of a screen star, but one with soft features that were believable and interesting. She was a complete package; one that Martin would like to study under different circumstances and Carol Ann might just be trying to say the possibility existed without actually saying it. "I'm afraid that's a little beyond me, Mrs. Lane. Big state, little coincidences?"

"Well, there probably are some, maybe like two little towns with the same name or...Well, I was really referring to Samantha. Such a coincidence. My husband's lover's first name being the same as my late mother's."

"Aah." Martin nodded, then casually smoothed and straightened his perfectly straight tie. "Texas," he said, smiling as he changed the subject, confident that Carol Ann would come back to it. "The Great State, Big Country and all that, just like Gregory Peck said. I guess a Texan would know who's from the West," he said, righting himself perfectly straight in his swivel chair. "Ahem," he began again, clearing his throat. "So, Mrs. Lane, have we covered the purpose of your visit?"

"Oh, I'm sorry," she said, wondering if she should say nothing of her plans to the busy colonel and seek support elsewhere. Carol Ann did need to hear someone say that she would be justified in filing for divorce. For now, though, as she had done that day Priscilla told her of Howard's blatant indiscretions, maybe she should just cower out, go back home and get into an interesting novel. Perhaps it would be better. How could a man she barely knew be of any help? "I guess we have. I hope you have a nice holiday, Colonel Bishop. I'll be having dinner…"

"Please, Carol Ann," interrupted Martin, raising a hand. "Why did you come to me? I can't have a nice weekend if I have to spend the next four days wondering what I did to make you too uncomfortable to trust me." That sounded very good to Martin, a challenge, a challenge, but a gamble, as challenges are.

Carol Ann shook her head and looked at her feet. "It's nothing. I…"

"Now, now, it's something," interrupted the colonel again, just as his caller stood to leave his office. "Of course, if you've changed your mind about talking to me, or you just feel that I'm not trustworthy, I'm certainly going to try to understand."

Carol Ann, her back turned to the colonel, took a step toward the door, then turned and flopped tiredly back into the armchair. "Well," she sighed, exhaling as if she had been doing calisthenics, her nerves like jelly. "I guess Captain Valentine's wife has several talents, but she's far from sweet and further from being a lady." Carol Ann paused and straightened her white skirt.

"I see. You don't like Samantha. Would you tell me why?" asked Martin, hoping to hear the old line about the way she just doesn't understand her poor husband. That could open a door and set a course for Martin himself to need understanding, too.

Carol Ann spoke while yet focusing on her skirt, a little girl in trouble. "I mean sweet, talented, or whatever, Mrs. Valentine has my husband carrying on like a teenager, although he sure seems willing enough," said Colonel Bishop's XO's wife, just above a whisper. "I'm not sure I even care anymore, but I've heard they've been seen being more than friendly in the back seat of Howard's staff car a few times.

Your secretary told me she caught them right out there on that sofa in your office foyer in the middle of the day once."

Carol Ann was speaking so softly that Martin was having trouble hearing her. "Priscilla said that?" he asked, leaning forward in hopes he could hear every single word this pretty lady had to say about her husband's indiscretions.

Carol Ann finally looked up at Martin. "Yes," she responded, her tone more forceful. "I've heard they were seen once at a motel in Trenton and more than once at the Colonial Inn in Cherry Hill. I assume they have lots of love nests, but, like I said, I don't care anymore."

Martin, feeling the need to add something here, leaned back in his chair and cleared his throat, started to speak, but Carol Ann plowed on, her words coming faster and more pointedly. if Samantha Valentine wants my husband, she can have him. He's very abusive and quite mean when he drinks too much, which has been going on for over fifteen years. Now he takes pills along with his booze. Those pills, which he over does, make him happy one minute and crazy the next."

Carol Ann suddenly paused and shrugged with her palms up. Martin assumed the gesture was her way of asking for his advice. He was confused, especially with the complete reversal in the story he was expecting. He had to stall, give himself enough time to put the scenario into a perspective he might understand and be able to use. He needed to keep Carol Ann talking, if only answering his questions. "Mrs. Lane, I don't doubt that Howard's drinking and the pills you mentioned are serious problems for you, but you've only been told about a possible affair with Samantha Valentine." Martin paused, looked down at his desk, but held up both hands, indicating that he wasn't through. In truth, he was reflecting on all Captain Valentine had told him about his wife, finding it more believable now that Carol Ann had attested to an affair involving her husband and the young captain's wife. How could that help Martin though? He needed to know more of how Carol Ann felt about this affair of her husband's. Did she want a little revenge, get even this weekend? "You've heard rumors, but you're not sure they're true. Is that right, Mrs. Lane?"

Carol Ann focused on Samantha's painting. "What's not to be sure of? Their next move? I might worry about it if I cared. I don't though."

"We are talking about, uh, about..."

"We're talking about adultery," interrupted Carol Ann. "From what I've heard, before this weekend their affair was just a series of prearranged meetings that had to be fast and furious, but now this two-day thing. I don't know, but maybe I should..."

"Those son-of-a-bitchin fools," interrupted Martin, jumping to his feet, then stepping around his desk to sit on the arm of the chair closest to Carol Ann, hoping he'd timed this right. Nothing was clear yet.

Colonel Bishop felt he was an adequate leader of men, but knew he had problems with civilian women. Regardless of his rank and position, they just didn't respond well to him. Another problem, Martin had never felt safe in trying to cultivate an intimate relationship during stateside duty. That's why he preferred combat assignments. There were no rules in war zones, all's fair in love and career war. Moreover, career officers lived in fishbowls during their stateside assignments. Martin had always tried to set an example, knowing all the while that he was the only one missing out. As hypocritical as it was, he had even counseled several young officers over the years about infidelity not being a victimless crime. Its emotional intrusion on the innocent party was about the same as rape, he had said. "I'm very sorry," said Martin, once seated by Carol Ann. "You've been terribly wronged. You have to care. I know you do. I guess I'm out of style, but I haven't adjusted to some of the things that go on between men and women who are married, but not to each other. What do you think we should do?" Martin lightly touched Carol Ann's shoulder with a fingertip, applying a little pressure, but broke the contact when she did not immediately move closer. "Maybe we should take the weekend to talk about it, but one thing you should know is that I can always send Captain Valentine and his wife to Germany and Howard to Vietnam."

"Well, I guess it's something to think about," said Carol Ann, forcing a smile as she leaned into Martin. "Believe me though, I don't care anymore."

The colonel stood, put his big hands on Carol Ann's shoulders and applied enough pressure to imply he wanted her to get to her feet. "Scotch okay?" he asked, taking her hand as he led the way to the small wet bar. "Damn scoundrels," he mumbled, under his breath while stealing a glance at Carol Ann.

"Scotch is fine," she said, meekly.

"Please don't be upset. I..."

Priscilla bolted into the colonel's office. "Uh, excuse me please, Carol Ann. Colonel Bishop, Sir," she said, a cowering shrug to indicate that she had a dreadful situation to deal with. "I just have to go now."

The colonel responded as if he had expected her. "Good," almost immediately. Carol Ann was amused at both of them, the outrageous look of the big secretary assigned to a distinguished colonel and his appearing to be just waiting for her to explode into his space at any moment.

"Good?" questioned the young woman a confused air about her. "You did say good. Right, Colonel Bishop?"

He turned to face her momentarily, then returned his attention to the wet bar. "I probably said 'Goodness' when I saw you, but just go turn off the phones, then lock up and go have yourself an old fashion blast," he ordered, as if commanding a stockade release. "I hope you meet a rich young man who takes you to a faraway island where the two of you live happily ever after."

"Well, thank you, Sir," said Priscilla. "That sounds so wonderful."

"Doesn't it sound just peachy," mumbled the colonel, then turned to Carol Ann when he heard his office door click closed, followed by his big secretary's spike heels clopping back to the reception area. "Do you drink your scotch straight up, with water, or do you prefer it with soda, Mrs. Lane?"

"Water and ice, please," she said, a light laugh to follow.

"I know, I know," responded the colonel, turning to mix the drinks. "It's just that Priscilla is one painful person for me to have to be around. She knows I don't like to be disturbed when I have a special guest." Martin handed Carol Ann her drink, picked up the bottle of scotch and one of soda, then led her out to the empty reception area, stopping before the sofa she'd mentioned. It looked perfect, but was it? "Forget this," he mumbled, an order. "There's got to be something untainted around here."

Martin was as upset with himself as he was with Major Lane. Himself because he was always the one who was left out, Howard because the man had so easily manipulated him and was still having all the fun. However, the night was young and here he was with Howard's wife, who he hoped had no set plans for the four-day weekend. "Follow me, Carol Ann," he said, a softer tone than he had used in years.

Martin led the way through an open door that was down the hall from his office. "Let's sit here in the kitchenette," he said, sliding a chair out from a table with his foot. "Those scoundrels," he mumbled again, shaking his head in mock disgust. "Lies and lies and more lies."

Ann took the chair. "Thank you, Sir," she said. "I'm sorry I've bothered you today but now that I already have and it's too late for me to do anything about it, I can only beg that you just forget it. And, please don't stay late because of me. Really, I'm sorry I mentioned Howard and Mrs. Valentine."

"I'm not," responded the colonel, nervous, draining his drink with three quick swallows. "Let's put our heads together and decide what we want to do. I promise I'll try to be objective. Have you made plans for dinner?"

"I ate a big salad just before I came to see you. Sorry, but thank you just the same, if that was an invitation."

The possibility might have narrowed, but it wasn't hopeless, thought Martin. "Where is Howard right now?"

"He and Mrs. Valentine are probably in the bar at the Colonial Inn in Cherry Hill. I heard Howard make the reservation Tuesday night. He thought I was in the shower, but I was listening on the extension in my bedroom."

"Your bedroom? I see. You and Howard don't sleep together?" Was Carol Ann so neglected that she might be easy?

"In light of what you know, does that surprise you?" she asked, looking through her purse.

"I guess it doesn't, but I find it hard to believe."

"Why?"

Martin didn't have the nerve to offer up the right answer for Carol Ann, explain that she was so utterly appealing that he would never miss a night with her, so he jumped up and stomped out. "You just stay put," he said, over his shoulder. "I have some in my office."

Carol Ann was yet searching through her purse when the colonel hurried back into the kitchenette. "Here you are, Mrs. Lane," he said, handing her a box of Kleenex and the rose from his credenza. "I was just thinking. Having to constantly shuffle the necessary truths and lies to maintain an illicit affair must be a nightmare. Can you imagine how hard that would be? Where are you going, Honey? Oh, I have to run to the cleaners, then get the oil in my car changed, then stop by the bank, then, then, then, etceteras, etceteras. If this affair they're involved in has been going on as long as I suspect it has, their minds are probably flying twenty-four hours a day." Martin suddenly realized that he was doing all the talking. Maybe he had talked beyond what was necessary. Maybe Carol Ann was already angry enough, angry enough to mold, enough to want a little revenge. "If this question is too personal, just tell me," he said, nervous, but as confident as he had been with Mrs. Lane. "Have you ever been involved with someone? Say an affair outside of your marriage that just sorta...?"

"No, and why do you think I should care what Howard has to go through to hide his affair?" asked Carol Ann, moving the box of Kleenex aside.

Martin cocked his head and gave her a look of question. "May I ask, if you weren't searching through your purse for a Kleenex, what did you need?"

"Oh, I'm sorry. It's a habit," explained Carol Ann. "I lost my car keys one night when I was trying to spy on Howard and Samantha and had a time of it getting home. I don't want to go through that ever again."

"I'm sure," said Martin. He was mixing fresh drinks.

"Where were they?"

"My keys, or Howard and Samantha?"

Martin was asking about Howard and Samantha. "Ah, yes," he responded, deciding that courtesy was all that was required here. Carol Ann nodded. "I found Howard in the lounge at the Holiday Inn in Bordentown. He was hanging on the bar talking to a waitress. I never did see Samantha, even though I hung around that place for almost four hours, three of which I spent searching for my keys."

"Sony," said Martin, handing Carol Ann the fresh drink, then taking the chair beside her. "Things were bad enough without a problem with your keys."

"You know, Sir," she said, leaning into him, feeling the magnetism of his nearness, "I don't know why I even bothered, but I do know I'll never snoop around to spy on Howard again. I really don't care what he and Samantha do."

"Okay, okay, you don't care, you don't care, so to speak, but what are you actually going to do?" asked the colonel, wondering how Howard Lane would cultivate a possibility like this. Would he just pop the question? Would you like to get a room somewhere and, and...? Martin had no idea how to proceed.

"Okay, okay," echoed Carol Ann. "I want a divorce," she said, smiling.

"That's a big step, Carol Ann," said Martin, slipping an arm over her shoulder. "That's a very big step," he repeated. I guess though... Well, have you considered just having it out with Howard? I don't mean physically, but like a sit down...What?"

Carol Ann, shifting her weight under the colonel's arm, was slowly waggling a finger in front of her, her hand close to her chin. "I wouldn't be interested," she said, explaining her meaning.

Martin hesitated, his train of thought lost in the contrast of his desire to strip this woman and knowing he didn't have the nerve to try. "Oh. Well, uh, I uh," he began, floundering to speak his mind. "I suppose if you're convinced that reconciliation isn't a possibility, maybe a divorce is best. Where will you live? Dallas? I know you don't have children to take into consideration, but I uh, well, that's a plus. Have you thought about what you might do out there?"

"Not even once," responded Carol Ann, her smile one of unconcern. "1 guess I should though, since there's no one else to. In fact, the only family I have left are two aunts and one uncle and a bunch of cousins I haven't even as much as met. Seems like I remember that my aunts live in Washington. Maybe all of them do. Anyway, I don't even have any friends that aren't in the army." Carol Ann paused for thought. "Well," she continued, "maybe the Johnsons who've lived across the street from my Mom's place for twenty years are kinda like friends. At least they would say hello to me and Howard, but as I think about it, we don't have many friends, or very much of anything else." Carol Ann paused and looked down at her big diamond ring. "I do have this," she said, smiling apologetically.

The colonel, embarrassed, quickly looked away. "I've noticed that," he said, lying. "It's quite nice. Did Howard give it to you?"

"No. It was Mom's. She had several pieces of nice jewelry. Like that angel brooch with all the diamonds I wore to your party Christmas. Do you remember it? About everyone who was there thought it was beautiful."

"Uh-huh, yes," lied Martin again. "I noticed. It is very beautiful."

"Hmmm. Howard never cared for it, but Colonel Elliott liked it. Howard sold it to him for his..."

"Colonel Elliott? Our chaplain? For how much?"

"I'm not sure," responded Carol Ann. "Maybe a few thousand, but..."

"Who did Colonel Elliott want the brooch for?" interrupted Martin, dying to know how the hell the chaplain was screwing someone when he wasn't. "You were about to tell me when I butted in. Sorry."

"His younger sister. She got married in July."

"I see," said Martin, irked. Colonel Elliott had but a brother. Who was he screwing? "Howard lied to you, but go on. That brooch was a memorable piece of art. I can't imagine..."

"It was okay with me to sell it, Colonel Bishop. I mean if you were thinking that maybe it wasn't," explained Carol Ann, unconvincingly, but feeling the need to be convincing. "I probably didn't appreciate it as much as I should have, but the new owner might. Anyway, what's done is done, but thank you for noticing it when I had it. I guess you don't miss much."

Martin crossed his legs, absently letting his arm slide from Carol Ann's shoulders to her waist. "There was a day when I didn't miss anything."

"Like today?" Carol Ann winked. "Enough on the brooch. Howard and I have a little furniture, a little in our checking account and my car. It's a 1962 Pontiac Tempest convertible." Carol Ann paused and slid forward in her chair, then sipped from the fresh drink. Martin, feeling a quick pang of alarm, removed his arm, assuming she'd slid forward to avoid it. "Well, Howard and I do have two CD's, thanks to Mom," continued Carol Ann. "She died a little over two years ago. I'm an only child, so naturally she left us her house, her car, and her money. The house is in Dallas, 3040 Holiday Trail in Oak Cliff actually. It's only three blocks from one of the most beautiful parks in all of Dallas. Kiest Park. Mom and I used to walk around it once a day, weather permitting that is."

"The house is vacant?" asked Martin, relaxing, making conversation.

"Uh-huh. There's no mortgage and I've been keeping it up with the money that was in Mom's checking account. Her car, a 1958 Buick, hasn't been moved out of the garage since she died. I started it in September, but I haven't been back since." Carol Ann paused for thought, her eyes drifting to the ceiling momentarily, then returning to the colonel. "Come to think of it, that's what Howard did with the money from that brooch," she said. "He gave it to me to make the trip to Dallas. Anyway, the Buick is blue and white. It's a four door and I think the tires are pretty good. The interior is like new, and the paint has not looked better than it does right now. I remember that Mom had a muffler installed about a year before she, she...Well, what's so funny?" asked Carol Ann, noticing that Martin had a big grin on his face.

"I don't know. I guess it's just that, right in the middle of a marriage crisis, you wanna describe an old car to me." Martin loosened his tie, then unbuttoned his tight tunic, wanting to get the conversation headed in another direction, but again, unsure about how to do it.

"Anyway," he continued. "If you don't mind my asking, approximately what is everything worth that you and Howard own. The primary values would be the house, the furniture, the certificates of deposit, the cars and whatever jewelry Howard hasn't sold, if it was part of the things willed to you and him jointly."

Carol Ann was feeling the warm glow of the scotch and getting more comfortable with the colonel. "The total value?" she asked, smiling as she leaned into Martin's shoulder and drained the last sip from her glass. "I certainly don't mind you asking me anything, Sir," she said, rattling the ice cubes, indicating that she'd like another drink. "However, I wouldn't have a clue what anything's worth, but the CD's. They're a hundred thousand apiece. This ring is three carats, but it's really old."

Martin took the glass from Carol Ann, added ice to both hers and his, then mixed fresh drinks. "When did you last work, Carol Ann, and what did you do?"

"I worked at a flower shop when Howard was in Korea, but I'm not worried about taking care of myself. I'll get a job doing something, but I'll have a little nest egg with the CD's and Mom's house."

"Yes, you will," said Martin. "And, you'll surely find another man to spend time with. Do you go out now?"

"I probably should, but so far I haven't thought about it."

Colonel Bishop and his XO's wife talked on for a few minutes, then called the Colonial Inn in Cherry Hill, confirmed that Howard Lane was a guest and would be for two nights, then proceeded to discuss Howard and Samantha Valentine's sordid affair while getting drunk on the scotch. They fell asleep sometime after midnight while discussing the lonely years Martin had experienced since being widowed, but the distant *whoop, whoop, whoop* of an ambulance awoke him at three fifty-six. He and Carol Ann were on the floor, the bottles were empty, and they weren't fully dressed. The colonel's shoes, tunic, shirt and tie were on the table. Carol Ann's shoes, purse and white sweater were in a chair. "Uh oh," sighed Martin, removing his arm from between her full breasts, the soft nipples proudly looking at him through a thin white lace bra. He could feel the familiar old choke hold of fear fighting the pain of desire as he let his eyes roam over the sleeping beauty.

Chapter 6

After his Thanksgiving weekend tryst he claimed was with Samantha Valentine, Major Howard Lane remained in the army eleven more months. Colonel Bishop kept him busy most of that time, an attempt to keep him away from Captain Valentine's wife and Carol Ann. He sent him on training maneuvers, traveling to two and three-day briefings at other posts and twice to ten-day training seminars for battalion commanders.

As time passed, Howard became openly disrespectful toward Colonel Bishop, almost arrogant with his claims of frequent rendezvous with Samantha Valentine. During another time, Martin would have severely reprimanded his XO, even transferred him out of the country, but he and Carol Ann agreed to let things fall where they may. Once, while at the officer's club, Martin, careful not to reveal the reason, confronted Colonel Elliot about the brooch Major Lane might have offered to sell him. Howard actually had and the chaplain offered him two thousand dollars, but the major declined, wanting five thousand dollars. Martin made an issue of Howard's lack of feelings for his wife's fine jewelry, but Carol Ann didn't care. She explained that since she had gotten her mother's ring, Howard could do whatever he wanted to with the brooch. "I don't care if he gives it to Samantha Valentine," she said, completely unaffected. She had resigned herself to the facts, as she understood them, deciding that if Howard wanted a life with another woman, all the better for everyone involved.

Howard, although fantasizing and sensationalizing for his pride's sake, did want Samantha worse than anyone he had ever met. He knew full well that things wouldn't be getting better with her marital situation. Through Priscilla, Colonel Bishop's secretary, and two of her friends, Howard had laid the groundwork through rumor and innuendo that would surely lead to Samantha's divorce.

Samantha Valentine's agenda had first begun to form in her mind a year ago. The decision to change her life was made the very morning she was going through the personal things belonging to Ken's mother and Cheryl Cooper, his younger sister. A tragic automobile accident had taken their lives, along with that of little six-year-old Mindy, Cheryl's daughter.

The sun was already hot and bright that morning. Except for her daughter, eight-year-old Karla, who was still sleeping, Samantha was alone in her in-law's big house in Houston, Texas. Ken had bummed around the country for over a year, spent the last of his money and sold his new Impala to survive, then came home broke and joined the army. Now, he had completed his training and flown to Fort Dix to report for duty, a three-year stateside assignment. After days and days of Ted's appeals to give his son another chance, Samantha agreed, quit her job at the clinic and dropped her classes at the university. "I'll do it for Karla and you, Mr. Valentine," she said. "As soon as Ken has base housing, I'll drive Karla to New Jersey, and I'll do my part to try and work things out."

Samantha was in the den sitting on the floor, lost in her thoughts, when the soft *bong, bongs* of an old grandfather clock in the foyer began announcing the ten o'clock hour. Before the clock had silenced, the doorbell rang. "I'll be right there," she called, softly, trying not to wake her daughter.

"It's just me and Linda," said Pat, sadly through the closed door.

"Hello, Ladies. Come in," greeted Samantha, swinging the front door open, surprised to see her sister-in-law and niece. She had only seen them in the big house a few times before, the night Ken vanished and occasionally on holidays. "How are you, Linda?" she asked, as the teenager tried to slip by her without being noticed.

"Hi." responded Linda, a near indistinguishable grunt. Except for twenty years age difference, Linda and her mother looked very much alike, tiny blue-eyed blondes, barely over five feet tall, as slim as fashion models.

Pat, now Ken's only sister, smiled and followed her daughter into the foyer. "Hi, Samantha," she said. "Where's Dad?"

"He went to Padre Island. That woman who left the graveside services with him came by and honked. He said 'see ya', then hurried out."

"I'm not surprised. And, Karla?"

"Upstairs asleep. I couldn't get her to bed until after one this morning."

Pat looked around the house, seeming to be verifying that no one but Samantha was downstairs, then turned to her daughter. "Linda, would you give me and your aunt a minute alone?"

"Shall I wait in the car?" asked the young lady, automatically handing her mother a sack she had been holding.

"Please. Thank you." When Linda stepped outside, Pat took the sack into the den and set it beside a big leather sofa. "First, could I get you to do something with these things, Samantha?" she asked. "I don't care to even look at them and Dad won't take the time. He called me yesterday and said he was going to have Good Will come in and clean out Mom's and Cheryl's closets. I wish you'd go through both of them first though, Mom's dresser and files especially. Take anything you can wear, but let me know if you find her life insurance policy. Cheryl's, too. Mom was always worried about having to take care of a grandchild, so she bought large insurance policies on all of us. A hundred thousand a piece."

"That was thoughtful. Who's the beneficiary?"

"The remaining spouse except in Cheryl's case. Mom and Dad were named on that one. I guess Dad will get payment on both Cheryl's and Mom's policies. A lot of money. Double indemnity. Four hundred thousand dollars."

Samantha sat silently thinking for a minute, then asked the first question that jumped into her mind. "Pat, what about Ken? Are you saying your mother bought an insurance policy for him?"

"Well, yes, and you too. I was at the bank Friday, but she only had a bunch of coins in her lock box. Hopefully, all the policies are here."

"Well, I'll certainly look," said Samantha. "Now, you're sure it's okay about the clothes. What will your father...?"

Pat interrupted. "It's perfectly all right and Dad won't care," she sighed, a touch of bitterness in her tone. "He wouldn't even go by the coroner's office to pick up their personal things, so I did Friday afternoon." Pat pointed to the big sack she'd placed by the sofa. "Do what you think should be done with them."

"Okay, I'll do something," agreed Samantha. "Could I get you a cup of coffee or some orange juice?"

Pat declined, a single shake of her head, then turned away and stared through the French doors that opened to the patio. "I've had mine," she said, her tone weak. "It's going to sound like I'm just a fountain of new information, but I need to tell you something else Dad or Mom, or me, or even Ken should have told you years ago. It has been killing me and I'm, I...Darn it." Pat's voice faltered, she whimpered, wiped her eyes with the back of her hand, then continued. "This is so hard," she said, pausing to wipe her eyes again.

"Just a minute," said Samantha, taking her sister-in-law's arm and leading her to the sofa. Other than Samantha's husband's weak efforts and the support payments his father had sent her the months Ken was traveling, Pat was the only member of the Valentine family who had treated her as if she were even a part of it. "Please have a seat," she pleaded. "Let's both have some coffee. I'll get it and you need a Kleenex. I'll bring a box of those, too. Just wait here."

Pat sat solemnly drinking her coffee for a moment, then, with several starts and stops, told Samantha what had her so troubled. She began with a question. "I'm sure Ken hasn't, but has anyone else ever told you why he joined the army? Why Dad didn't take him into his firm?"

Samantha answered Pat's question with a simple, "No," but her tone communicated a need to finally be informed.

Pat went into the explanation. When her daughter was between the ages of five and six, her brother, Ken, Samantha's husband, began showing the little girl too much attention. At first, it appeared to be a natural fondness for his only niece. In time though, the fondness began to appear as fondling masked with playfulness. Ken seemed to always hold Linda in ways that were questionable to Pat and her husband. He liked to tickle her, but the tickling often consisted of rubbing in the wrong places. Not wanting to cause a family rift, Pat and her husband decided to do everything they could to keep Linda away from her uncle until she was old enough to understand their concerns. Quite soon, the suspicions were all but forgotten and all was well with Linda, until her health education teacher brought her home one Monday at noon.

"The teacher was explaining simple hygiene requirements to the girls in her class, but Linda decided to explain what she'd learned when her uncle used to bathe her," further explained Pat, looking into her coffee cup as she spoke. "It was terrible, and I don't even want to talk about what happened later, but I suspect a lot more went on that I don't know anything about. Anyway, a year or so later, Linda talked to me about it. It had to do with her washing Ken while they showered. That was when he first worked with Dad, before you went to work at the clinic. Long before your...Well your thing with that doctor." Pat paused for thought.

Samantha stood, then strolled around the den in thought herself. It was a thing with Dr. Benjamin all right, she admitted. A wonderful thing that grew from the seeds of need, blooming just weeks before the doctor's wife came home. Samantha yet felt the shame of having committed adultery, but the love she had shared abated that.

The week following that first New Year's Eve she spent with Dr. Benjamin, Samantha knew she was experiencing her first love. Unlike with her uncle and aunt, this love drove her to touch, to make love and want to. However, it was her love for the doctor that drove her to end the affair. "Ben," she whispered, while lying in his arms one night in a Galveston hotel. "I have to give you up for your daughter. I know she needs two parents for now, so I'm not going to see you away from the office as long as I'm employed there. I can't. I love you and it's too hard."

The big doctor understood but suffered visibly. Samantha could hardly look at him without wanting to comfort him, touch his hand, kiss him, and hug him. She did not though. It was painful and she knew she had only agreed to join Ken in New Jersey because she might not have been able to bear that pain much longer.

"Samantha," said Pat, breaking her thoughts. "I was trying to explain why Ken had so..."

"Yes. Go ahead," said Samantha returning to the sofa, dropping the sad thoughts of losing her first love. "I'm sorry, I think we're both a little scattered today. We can talk about this another time if you'd like."

"No. You've been in the dark too long as it is."

"Okay. Yes, you're right, I guess I have. So, how did Linda deal with that experience as she grew older? Is she okay now?"

Pat shook her head. "There are problems yet, but we're working on them," she said. "Of course, Ken was no problem. He didn't even bother to deny it when I confronted him." Pat paused again, watching her sister-in-law for a reaction, then continued when she detected none. "I couldn't have handled things worse, Samantha," she said. 'You and Ken had been married almost three years when I confronted him. You hadn't started to work yet. Karla was about two and I was worried about her. I talked to Mom and Dad a few nights later, whitewashing the most salacious parts for sure, but basically telling them what had happened. We had a pedophile in the family. Mom hardly listened to anything I said. I think she wanted to kill me and Linda both. Dad was plenty mad, but, like me, he didn't know what to do either. Finally, six or seven months later, maybe the following August, Mom and Dad took Linda to their cabin in New Mexico. They were there about a month, and by the time they got home, they'd heard the uncensored version. For months after that, Mom had very little use for me and even less for Linda. I'm pretty sure she didn't talk to Ken about it. Dad did though. He told me the next morning. Ken didn't deny anything, nor did he offer explanations."

Pat slid forward on the sofa, appearing to be ready to leave, but Samantha placed a hand on her arm. "So, nothing was done about it?"

"Not nearly enough," sighed Pat. "Dad told Ken that he wanted him to leave the firm, so…Well, that's when he sold your jewelry, bought the car and left town. You know the rest. Ken bummed around for a year or so, then came back and immediately joined the army."

"Joined?" queried Samantha. "Ken told me he was drafted."

"He enlisted," responded Pat, disgustedly. "Anyway, I've said my piece and I feel better for doing it. Cheryl was going to tell you, but…"

"Cheryl and I got along fine," said Samantha, refusing to let the white-hot rage she felt enter the conversation with her sister-in-law. "Thanks for telling me, although I'm sure it wasn't easy."

Pat quickly finished her coffee and left. Samantha carried the sack upstairs, checked on her sleeping daughter, then went to her late mother-in-law's bedroom. Sybil's, Cheryl's, Pat's and her husband's life policies were in her closet in a steel file cabinet, but Ken's and Samantha's weren't, leading her to believe they didn't exist. After slipping the three policies Pat asked about into a big brown envelope and addressing it to her, she put it into her own suitcase, then went to Cheryl's bedroom, untouched since her death.

Cheryl Cooper and her young daughter had been living with her parents for two years prior to her death, her husband being an early Vietnam casualty. Although a year older than Samantha and single until she was twenty-four, Cheryl had never held a job and would never have needed to had she lived. She was her father's favorite.

"Gees, I wonder what this is?" asked Samantha, taking a strongbox from a dresser drawer. "Oh, a fireproof strongbox. Full of what?" She was alone with her thoughts in Cheryl's bedroom, talking to herself, an attempt at keeping her mind from wrenching back to the ugly reality of her life. She and her daughter had been, and soon would be again, living with a man who had repeatedly molested a little girl, very near Karla's age when it was happening. Samantha could see the scene if she allowed the thought to stay in her mind. What she couldn't see is a reasonable alternative to joining her husband in New Jersey. She had to consider her responsibilities, the temporary loss of her independence and her limited ability to change either immediately. What should she do? Try to go back to the clinic, work days and go to school nights until she finished her education? Neglect Karla again? Sue for a divorce immediately? Samantha knew both might happen in time, but neither could now.

"I don't doubt one thing Pat said," she whispered, wiping her eyes as she opened the little strongbox, staring silently inside for a minute, blanking her mind before leafing through a few of the papers that were on top. An automobile insurance policy, expired. A marriage license, an envelope full of wedding pictures. A picture of little Karla and baby Mindy licking at each other's ice cream cones. "Cute," she whispered. Samantha found an old thin ring with a tiny diamond and held it up to the light. "A treasure once for someone," she said, gently placing the little ring back into the strongbox and closing the lid. On a hunch though, assuming there had to be something of value in a stuffed fireproof strongbox, she took it and the paper sack to Ken's old bedroom and dumped the contents onto the floor.

After looking through everything and finding nothing worth going to the trouble of storing in a fireproof box, sparing Cheryl's marriage license and birth certificate, Samantha dumped the contents of the sack Pat had brought onto the floor. She went through the women's purses first. Sybil's seemed as she assumed it might, a little over a hundred dollars in cash, a driver's license, credit cards and the usual makeup items, all neatly arranged. However, Cheryl's was stuffed. A half box of unused Kleenex, folded and shoved to one side. Three cigarettes in a crinkled pack and a gold lighter were among a hairbrush, hair spray, sunshades and four one-dollar bills at the bottom of the purse. Cheryl's driver's license and four department store credit cards were in a side pouch with a checkbook closed over a bank statement, its balance reflecting that Cheryl had eighteen dollars and six cents in checking.

Next, Samantha opened a little blue savings passbook that was folded over several pieces of paper. "I see," she said, noting that the savings passbook, which held Mindy Cooper's social security card and birth certificate, had an impressive balance, forty-five hundred dollars. The balance, which agreed with the only entry, also agreed with a deposit receipt that was in the passbook. The receipt was dated the day of the accident.

Suddenly, Samantha's thoughts filled with questions. *Who could know about this? Pat knew about the insurance policies, but did she know about the deposit made for Mindy?* Recalling the night Ken left town, Samantha could almost hear Ted's words when he told her all that he and Sybil planned to do for Karla during their son's absence. For one, Sybil was supposed to open a savings account, as it appeared had been done for Mindy, but just like the insurance policies, it was not done. *Sybil didn't care for me or Karla.*

Samantha repacked the strongbox, adding little Mindy's savings passbook, birth certificate and social security card to a packet that held Cheryl Cooper's, the little girl's mother. After straightening up in both bedrooms, she took the strongbox out to her station wagon and wedged it between the spare tire and the firewall. When she returned to the house, she went to the bedroom that Karla slept in and started packing her things for the trip to New Jersey. The next morning, she mailed the life insurance policies to Pat, then went to the bank that held Mindy's savings account and, using only the little girl's social security card and birth certificate, withdrew the forty-five hundred dollars.

Samantha left for New Jersey eight days later, her route including a stop in Dallas, where she opened a savings account for her daughter at the Republic National Bank. Deposit, forty-five hundred dollars.

Although Samantha loved Cheryl and Mindy, she had never felt less than completely justified in taking the money that was in Mindy's savings. In fact, what she had learned from Pat that day, and the ease of walking into a major bank and taking another person's money, made her current agenda seem completely plausible. Now that Howard Lane was getting a divorce, she could start working toward its end.

Although Samantha hadn't expressed it, nor fully admitted it to herself, the things Pat had claimed of Ken back then, weren't complete revelations. She had heard things, and seen things that should have sufficiently warned her of her husband's character flaws, but Samantha was naive on such matters and her senses had merely whispered among themselves, unable to get her attention.

Perhaps, Samantha conceded, she had been too self-centered, concerning herself with how she had been wronged, and letting herself fall so deeply in love with Ben. She would have given Ken up in a heartbeat, but would never have given up her career had he, or even his parents, been honest with her. Until the day Samantha learned that Ken's father had sold his practice, she had been led to believe that when Ken got out of the army, he would join his father as a high paid attorney. She had hoped for that. Her plan was to divorce Ken then, a time when he could afford child support. Samantha could work and pursue her medical training again. Someone should have told her that it would never happen long before Pat did.

Ken had even lied about being drafted. He enlisted, according to Pat's account. Now that Ted had stripped his estate of most of its value and moved to Canada with his new bride, he would never have an ounce of concern for little Karla. Samantha loved her daughter, but if that wasn't the case, the little girl would have no one to care for her. Ken's father did try to keep his children from feeling completely left out when he sold his practice and remarried. Pat had gotten the big home in Houston. Ken had gotten sixty thousand dollars of the life insurance proceeds and the family's small summer home, a cabin in the mountains northwest of Santa Fe, New Mexico.

Samantha had been to Lost Mountain Park in the New Mexico mountains when Karla was a baby, but Ken wouldn't let them spend the night at the cabin. He insisted they stay at an old motel up on the highway, across from the little dirt road that led to the park. She and Karla spent three nights, joining the family twice for lunch out on a pier by the mountain lake behind the cabin. One other day, Ted took everyone on a fishing trip where they caught big trout below the bridge over Rainbow Canyon and pan-fried the catch. Lost Mountain Park, nestled in the shadows of the big peaks to the west, was a beautiful setting, remembered Samantha.

The first day she and Ken visited the cabin, his mother had driven Samantha and Karla to Santa Fe. It was a long tiring day. Sybil was either showing off, or actually wanted to buy every Remington print in every gallery in Santa Fe. When prints instead of original oils didn't seem to adequately impress Samantha, Sybil bought a big Remington bronze of a cowboy on a horse for $7,500.00. "Well now, Young Lady," she said, making a point to address baby Karla as she admired her purchase. "When your mother can do something like this, I'll consider her an artist. Isn't it just breathtaking? So real, such a perfect representation of the actual anatomy of the horse," spending several minutes, and adding comments as she traced the lines of the bronze horse's muscle formation, concluding with, "I think Remington's bronzes prove to we, critics, that he was truly a horseman. What do you think?"

"It's wonderful work," commented Samantha. Karla had dosed off.

Samantha knew she could easily find the way through the forest to the mountain Park where the cabin stood among others by the little lake. There was a small sign across the road from the motel that said the 'Lost Mountain Park' and pointed to the narrow dirt road that led to the cabin and beyond. Samantha knew she could get the little cabin for Karla and herself, along with her old Ford station wagon and the sixty thousand dollars plus accrued interest, if she chose to accept that as a one-time settlement agreement when she filed for divorce. She could get a lot more than that if the right lawyer got the case and Ken had a lot more to lose. The lawyer would butcher Ken and the jury would send him to jail, but what would that do for Karla? Label her for life? Samantha hadn't made up her mind what was best for her and Karla, but regardless of what she decided, the most pressing issues in her life revolved around Major Howard Lane, who had vowed to free himself of his marriage as soon as he retired.

During those last few months while Howard Lane awaited his discharge, Carol Ann began meeting with Colonel Bishop whenever and wherever the opportunity might present itself. They had dinner together once a week, went to movies, to two different plays and the Army Navy football game one Saturday at Veterans Stadium in Philadelphia. Martin took her to a Christmas party in Camden with his sister and her husband, a New Year's Eve affair in Atlantic City and skiing twice in upstate New York. They spent two different three-day weekends boating and fishing off the Florida Keys. Other than flying in small airplanes, which Carol Ann had refused to do, there wasn't much she didn't enjoy doing with Martin.

Equally as fast as time seemed to fly by, Carol Ann fell hopelessly in love with the distinguished colonel and began to experience passions she had previously believed were only written about in romance novels. She felt she had found her first and only intimate love in Martin Bishop. He had explained how his life and ideals had changed dramatically and how much he must have needed that change. Martin would not profess to loving Carol Ann, explaining that if there was such a thing as love, it was surely much the same as madness. An emotion that he did not understand, or possibly need to experience. He wanted to be with Carol Ann because he was happiest when he was.

Of course, Carol Ann did not want to hear Martin's opinion of love and chose to believe that he did love her. He, as he explained, just did not understand. Surely, he would one day, but Carol Ann did wonder if he would really ever be able to make the harsh decisions necessary to permanently unite them as more than lovers. He seemed to be willing to settle for something less, an affair forever kept secret. One that was driven by sex as a reward for showing her a good time.

Carol Ann did understand some things about Martin. Deeply ingrained within his psyche were needs to work, to be a part of the fraternal order of the army, to maintain an impeccable image, and not one of a senior officer who slipped around with the wife of another.

Martin understood himself. He wasn't above lying, but was afraid to, could not live with the consequences of being caught and, for that reason, his word had been his bond since childhood. He wanted to do the right thing by Carol Ann, but didn't know how to go about it just yet. Long ago, Martin had learned that once his mind was set to a course, he did not waver. When and if he grew to love Carol Ann, as she described love, their life together would be the goal he pursued until it was accomplished.

After several weeks of discussion, Carol Ann agreed that Martin needed more time to make his commitment to their relationship than she did. One Friday night during a quiet dinner, she suggested that he would be better off not making any immediate changes that would affect his career. "I think that would be best, Carol Ann, but maybe I already have," responded the colonel. The inevitable vicious talk around the base, partly due to his position, had already begun to boil among the ranks. "You'd think I was the first person to step over the line and breach all those ironclad rules that govern the conduct of military officers."

That weekend, a soul searching one for sure, Martin took Carol Ann to Niagara Falls. They never left the room, merely talking until they reached a decision. Martin chose to end their affair, if only temporary. Carol Ann claimed to understand, agreeing to resume a life without him, divorce Howard and move to Dallas, but it was tragic for her.

It was midafternoon Sunday. Martin had crossed the bridge and was on Interstate 90 East when Carol Ann collapsed. She leaned forward as if sick, then fell against the passenger door of his car. Martin panicked, stopped along the interstate, rushed around her, and lifted her to her feet. Seemingly, within that same instant, a New York State Highway Patrolman stopped to render assistance. The Patrolman took over the situation as if he'd dealt with many of the same nature. He immediately called forward to a hospital in Syracuse, then led Martin right to the emergency entrance, roof lights whirling, siren intermittently used to clear the way through traffic.

Carol Ann was admitted to Mercy Hospital, sedated and was deep in sleep within an hour of her collapse. Martin was waiting in the hall outside her room when the emergency room physician first addressed him. "Sir, I'm Dr. Mundale. I don't think you have a real emergency on your hands. My only recommendation is that your wife stay in bed for...She is your wife isn't she?"

"Yes. Yes, she is. Did you talk to her? What did she say? What does she need? Surely you're not saying that all she needs is bed rest."

The doctor gave Martin a long challenging look. "I talked to her," he finally admitted. "Are you worried about what she might have said?"

Martin felt the doctor was justified in that remark and let it pass. "I'm only concerned with what my wife needs, Dr. Mundale."

"That's good. I didn't mean to sound like a detective, but you... Never mind. Carol Ann needs rest and understanding," said the doctor, his words less pointed. "You might throw in a little love, too, Colonel Bishop. I'm not a psychologist, but I'd bet a tall martini that your wife is merely exhausted. Not physically, but mentally. You should know what she's been going through, so do something about it. We'll keep her lightly sedated for a day or so, then give her something to help her sleep for the next week. She'll be in your care, so if she needs more, I suggest you address the problem immediately."

"Her..." Martin caught himself. "A girlfriend of Carol Ann's told me that she might be going through the change of life. That she..."

"I think the friend must have been referring to herself. Your wife is a long way from that unlikely situation, Colonel Bishop. Just do as I said. Good night."

As soon as Dr. Mundale went about his business, Martin requested that a rollaway bed be brought to Carol Ann's room. He wanted to stay by her side until Dr. Mundale released her, hopefully when he made his rounds the next morning.

For hours on end that night, Martin struggled with the decision he knew he must make, rid himself of everything that might interfere with his ability to make a life with Carol Ann Lane. There were many things he wanted to and could have done over the years, but did not. Martin had fooled others, but never himself. He knew his life's successes could be attributed, in part, to caution and fear of unknown consequences, paying some awful price if he did some of the things he wanted to. "Life's a bitch and fate's a bastard, but I'm going to live my life with Carol Ann," he said aloud, finally leaving her side to take his own bed.

"Good morning, Colonel," greeted Dr. Mundale, finding Martin in the bathroom shaving. "How's our patient?"

"She rested well, but I don't know."

"I'll ask her," chided the doctor, shaking Carol Ann awake. "Good morning, Mrs. Bishop. I hear you slept like a baby."

"Huh? Oh, Dr. Mundale. Good morning. Where's Martin?"

Martin wiped the shaving lather from his face and hurried to Carol Ann's bedside. "Sweetheart," he announced, a tone as if taking a sworn oath. "I'm going to put in for my retirement the minute we get back to the post. I've had a good career and I'm young enough to start another one. I will..."

"Just a minute, Colonel Bishop," interrupted the doctor, placing his stethoscope at the rise of Carol Ann's left breast. "I think maybe I understood what brought on your wife's problem, but why don't you two talk it out on your way home. I'm satisfied she's ready to travel."

Carol Ann, both amused and amazed, sat quietly as Martin drove back to Fort Dix. He had never had so much to say. Nonstop. "Just rest and hear me out, Carol Ann," he began. "Correct me if I'm wrong, but I think you're anxious to file for a divorce, so do it. Get it over with." Martin put an arm over Carol Ann's shoulders and pulled her against him. "Here's another suggestion," he began again. "I think you want to sell your mother's home. So, if that's the case, get it started and I'll get started finding us a place. I don't care where it is either, but I will admit that Washington State is my favorite kind of country. Have you ever been to Seattle?"

Carol Ann, enjoying Martin's enlivened spirit, wanting him to talk on, kept her response short and simple. "No, but I'd like to go."

Martin plowed on. "Seattle is an old town, but the air always feels fresh and clean. There's a constant ocean breeze. It rains a lot all over the Northwest, but the summer nights are cool, and the winters aren't too bad. It's a magnificent part of the world, Sweetheart. Big, beautiful mountains and vast forest lands, the ocean, endless blue skies?"

Carol Ann wanted to shout, but spoke calmly. "It sounds wonderful, but I'd live in a rain forest if you were there."

"Oh, I didn't mean it rains that much, you silly, and don't you worry about me being there. I'll always be there, wherever there is. Every morning you can just kick me outta bed and tell me to get you an umbrella and your coffee and I'll hop right to it." Martin paused and looked at Carol Ann for a long moment, smoothed back her hair, then continued. "I feel great, Sweetheart. That little spell of yours was quite a spooky time, but I endured it. You're so utterly beautiful these days, but I won't complain if you wanna go around looking like a sponge. With so much rain in Seattle, I mean."

Carol Ann took Martin's hand in hers. "I'm thrilled that you want to go on with our relationship, Martin," she said, her tone soft, but challenging. "You seem happy about it, but I want you to be certain about retiring before you do anything. I want you for me, but I want you whole and happy for you."

"Try me. Get yourself a good seat and watch," chided Martin. "Since I've made up my mind, I can't wait to get started."

The day after he returned to duty, Colonel Bishop, just as he said he would, quietly put in his request for retirement. Martin was committed to a life with Carol Ann Lane, but due to old habits, he didn't want the senior officers around the base to know anything about their plans. He especially didn't want anyone trying to talk him out of calling it quits on his career. That decision was the proverbial love-hate type for Martin Bishop. He loved Carol Ann, but hated what he had to do to really have her. When he gave up his quarters, he found himself making up a story about finally deciding to buy a house. The story seemed a harmless lie, but it wasn't. There were no secrets in the bachelor officer's quarters, too much drinking, too fraternal. Quite soon, Martin felt the only way to prevent exposing his lie about buying a house was to live with his sister in Camden and commute back and forth to Fort Dix.

Martin's sister gave him a small bedroom and the use of the guest bathroom. Due to the limited space, he and Carol Ann met once or twice a week in Philadelphia or Baltimore finalizing their plans to live together in Washington. Martin was able to arrange his retirement ceremony without the normal pomp and circumstance accorded other field grade officers. It was a closed-door affair held late on a Friday afternoon in his office. The official separation day would be March 15, 1968, twenty-five years and eight days from his date of enlistment.

He and Carol Ann had agreed that he would proceed to Washington and find a rental near Seattle, then decide on something to buy when she joined him. She planned to move to Dallas when Howard officially separated from the army, file for divorce, sell her mother's home, then start her life anew in Seattle with Martin Bishop.

Tonight, Carol Ann was sitting beside him in the restaurant at the old Lord Baltimore Hotel where Martin had gotten a room. It had been overcast, gloomy all day, dark as twilight. A cold wind sent snow flurries whirling about like ticker-tape confetti, lightly covering every surface, then immediately melting and turning the world into a big drip like Carol Ann felt she was right now. She was being very quite, almost silent while folding her paper napkin for the fifth time. Martin, concerned, slid his arm around her waist, then whispered into her ear. "We've talked about this, Carol Ann. I've already said that I'll go to Dallas and stay until your divorce is final, but you want me to go find us a place in Washington. I can't do both you know."

Carol Ann didn't understand herself. Her mind had been a busy montage of plans for weeks. There was so much to do. "I know," she sighed tiredly. "I was just thinking, feeling sorry for myself, I guess. I've gotten spoiled, being able to talk to you and see you as often as I can now, but I know I won't be able to when you get to Washington."

Martin kissed Carol Ann's cheek. "Silly," he said, playfully. "You know I'll have a phone wherever I stay, and we can always write."

Carol Ann held his face with her hands, kissed his forehead, each cheek, a peck for his lips, then looked into his eyes and made a tsking sound "Shame on me," she said, finally smiling. "I'm just being a big baby. I could get so excited, but I'm afraid to let myself. I know that's little girl stuff, but we've both seen how life can go. You lost your wife when the two of you were so young. Then my marriage, if it ever was a marriage, just evaporated overnight. I don't want to have to go too long without seeing you, Martin. Remember? You said it yourself. Life is a bitch and fate is a bastard."

Martin leaned away from Carol Ann for a second, then chuckled and slid even closer. "So, you were lying there in that hospital bed listening to me while I thought you were about to die, huh?"

"Uh-huh, and it was one of the best nights of my life. I even got up and took a shower when you started snoring," confessed Carol Ann. "If it takes me a long time to get things done in Dallas, will you come to see me at least once?"

"Only once, huh? How about ten times if you don't get out of there quick enough to suit me. Without you, Sweetheart, Seattle might as well be Russia. It's a long way to Washington, but when we get set up there, we'll be miles and miles from wherever Howard and Samantha live."

Chapter 7

Samantha Valentine had no plans to live with Howard Lane. She never had. In fact, she'd tried to call his wife twice and had written her once, each an attempt to explain that there wasn't anything going on between her and Howard. On both calls though, Carol Ann had hung up the second Samantha announced who she was. The letter was returned unopened, a vicious note scribbled on the back. *Don't you ever call me again. Don't write. Don't speak if I ever have the misfortune of having to occupy the same foul space you do. You've taken what you want and you're welcome to it. Now leave me alone.* Samantha didn't know Carol Ann personally, but believed she was as vicious as her note.

Although her little apartment was cramped and allowed no space for her hobby, painting with oils, Samantha had grown to prefer living alone. A single mother, alone with her school-age daughter. A year and two months after she had gotten to Fort Dix, concern for Karla being near Ken and growing doubt of him drove her out of her home. She searched until she found an apartment she could afford on her earnings, finally finding a tiny one bedroom. It had a huge hall closet that could be converted into a bedroom for Karla. A hospital bed, one of the throwaways from the base, had fit perfectly.

Karla even liked the little apartment and found the perfect corner for her cat, the one her daddy had given her the day he left her the first time. She had raised it from a tiny kitten to a big eleven-pound friend, one that didn't want to let Karla out of sight. However, "He who giveth can taketh away," she learned from her father. Ken dumped the big cat somewhere on the streets of downtown Trenton the day Karla and her mother moved out of base housing.

Samantha chose the little apartment due to its close proximity to the base, and it was only ten blocks from Karla's school. Moreover, it was close enough to her work to walk if the old station wagon ever really quit. Samantha's limited means required she take advantage of her PX privileges, those of the commissary and base hospital, at least until she made up her mind what to do on a more permanent basis. However, her mind was made up for her. It followed a physical confrontation with her husband, which developed spontaneously one Monday night when Ken showed up at the apartment with a new canary yellow Ford convertible, three brochures advertising different Hawaiian beach resorts in hand.

Samantha knew Ken's standard procedure. He wanted something and would promise a family trip to Hawaii to get it, then never deliver, but she wasn't about to give him the chance tonight. "If you're going to suggest a trip to Hawaii with Karla and me, save your breath, Ken. I can't take the time and wouldn't if I could. Just tell me what you want."

As it turned out, Ken needed time to pay the one hundred dollars he had agreed would be his monthly support payment for his daughter. He'd spent about every dollar he had on the new car, but loved it anyway. It was the first car he had ever paid for himself, and felt completely justified in doing so. "You took the wagon, so I had to buy something."

Samantha, thinking back, should have agreed, but allowed the pang of resentment she felt to get out of hand. The station wagon was thirteen years old and had over a hundred thousand miles on the odometer. It blew black smoke out the tailpipe constantly, the windshield wipers and heater had been intermittent at best for over a year. "A brand-new car," sighed Samantha, under her breath. "I'm driving your daughter around in a piece of junk, but you never consider the needs of others. No, not you. Not Ken Valentine. He has to have a new convertible." Samantha threw her hands up in disgust "Why don't you just go to Hawaii by yourself. Karla and I will just have to make out somehow."

"Make out? Who moved out? Who bought that old derelict laying out there in the parking lot? You created your own problems. Don't blame me."

Samantha held her tongue, thinking what should be said as she walked down the hall and closed the door to the closet that served as her daughter's bedroom. Karla had been in bed for an hour. "Okay, you're right," conceded Samantha, calmly returning to the den, standing in front of Ken, who was seated on her sofa. "I was the one who chose to breakup our marriage, but I had several good reasons. You know I did."

Ken chuckled, crossed his legs and leaned back, yawning as if bothered to have to await the final curtain of a boring play. "Name one reason," he said.

Samantha didn't choose to go into her reasons for leaving Ken, deciding to present him with her complete plan and what she would request in a divorce settlement instead. Although his expression immediately changed to surprise, he was absolutely silent throughout the entire dissertation. Samantha felt that, by his lack of reaction, her husband had acquiesced and would handle a settlement much as cowardly as he had handled things when his father confronted him about the indiscretions with his sister's little daughter, Linda. She was completely fooled. Ken reacted quite the opposite. His look of surprise was immediately replaced with his first comment, a denial of any surprise at all, his lips quivering with ire, his expression a twisted scowl.

Ken's late mother had warned him repeatedly, he claimed, stating she knew Samantha had only married him for his money and would one day want a divorce, then attempt to extort him in any way she could. Although her 'woman's intuition' was Sybil's only basis for the rash prediction, Ken turned violent when it appeared to be proving out, a monster wielding a red-hot branding iron with his words. "You're just a money-grubbing whore," he screamed. "I would have never given you the time of day if you weren't the best fuck in Dallas. I'll give you that Samantha. Hell! There must be hundreds of men who'd give you that. Right? Is it hundreds, or is it thousands? You're trash and you're stupid. I know all about your kinky fling with the big pig you worked for at that clinic. Hell, that's the reason I left Houston."

Samantha fought back with her own scathing words. "Kinky? I'm stupid, huh? Well, I sure can't say that about you, Ken. You're a clever pedophile. I have to give you that. How many times have you gotten away with molesting a child? A thousand? Or is it a..."

"Shut your mouth or I'll kill you," screamed Ken, interrupting, pointing at her, his thumb and forefinger forming a pistol, his face a hateful mask.

Samantha was startled. She had been caught completely off guard, having expected her husband to cower through a silent denial, much as he did with his father. Just as she was starting toward the door, feeling that she should end the meeting by suggesting he leave, Ken sprang off the sofa and knocked her down. All she heard was a loud pop before tumbling over an armchair, landing sprawled out face down on the floor, the vicious slap blindsiding her. "Get up if you want some more," he snarled, gasping to breathe.

When Samantha rolled over and sat upright, Karla was standing over her, whimpering, eyes like saucers. "Go to bed, Kid," snarled Ken, raising a hand as if to slap her.

"You go away, Daddy," she screamed. "Don't hurt my mommy anymore." Ken whirled and went to the door, opened it, then turned back to face his wife and daughter, their eyes telegraphing fear and shock. "Look," he said. "I'll agree to your demands, Samantha. You take the wagon, my money, and the cabin. I'll be fine. I've got two hundred grand coming right after your accident." Ken paused, a sudden satisfied smile crossing his face. "Whoops. The stupid little whore didn't think about that did she," he said.

"Ken," sighed Samantha, hugging her daughter, holding her face hidden in the small of her neck. "I'm going to tell Colonel Bishop about this."

"Oh, please do. We're just like this," said Ken, holding up two crossed fingers. "Old Martin knows about you and your latest sucker. Poor Howard Lane," he added, then walked out the door, shouting to any and every one within the sound of his voice. "Can you believe it, folks? That whore up there stole fifty dollars. Trust me, she ain't worth it."

Early the next morning, Samantha called Ken's immediate superior, Major Brooks, the senior officer in the JAG office. The man only listened, proving to be the epitome of a 'no comment' attorney until Samantha asked if he was in fact listening. "Yes. Certainly, Mrs. Valentine. I was listening. After all, it's your story, but I do have one question," he said.

"Go ahead."

"Will you go along with this? If nothing happens between you and Ken that poses a threat to you, can you keep the events between you and him to yourself until I get back to you? Give me a week."

"What do I do if he does show up? He threatened me you know."

"In the heat of battle, of course. We all say things we don't mean when we get upset, Mrs. Valentine," explained the JAG officer. "It's called speaking before you think. Just this morning, I told my son that I was going to break his leg if he left his bike laying in the driveway again. It wasn't a threat. I don't plan to break my son's leg even if he leaves that darn bike in the drive until I run over it, but I said I would. However, you can call in a firing squad if your husband shows up and you feel he's a threat. It sounds like you'd be entitled to."

The JAG officer, Major Brooks, presented with an unusual problem concerning a military officer, his own staff officer no less, called the post commander for his advice. "Well, that's quite a problem isn't it, Major Brooks. However, I know Ken Valentine, and, in a way, I'm surprised, but in another I'm not," said Colonel Bishop, seeming to be thinking as he spoke, less spontaneous than the senior JAG officer had experienced before. "Let me think this out. Call me back in thirty minutes," added Martin Bishop, ending the call.

Major Brooks sat at his desk awaiting Colonel Bishop's return call for the better part of an hour, his mind blanked with confusion. The young captain had a loose tongue when it came to his wife. She was a gorgeous young woman, but a complete fraud, and supposedly, quite a problem, if Ken Valentine's account was in fact accurate. Samantha was an emotional hand grenade who kept a finger on the pin. She had been involved with some preacher and now with some senior officer on the base. She was uncaring, insensitive, and considered hers and Captain Valentine's young daughter no more than a burden. Major Brooks could understand how any young man could lose control having to deal with a woman like that.

When his young staff officer didn't show up for work at his usual nine o'clock hour, Major Brooks picked up his phone and called Colonel Bishop again, catching him in a completely different mood.

"Listen, Brooks," snapped the colonel. "You call Ken Valentine in and, if you so much as believe half of what his wife told you, give that man one choice. Take it or leave it. He either agrees to his wife's demands and volunteers for overseas duty, or faces a full-blown court-martial proceeding," ordered the commander, his tone leaving no question in Major Brooks' mind. The commander's word was not subject to debate on the matter concerning Captain Valentine and his estranged wife. "Thanks for enlightening me on this, Major Brooks. You might tell Captain Valentine that a civilian attorney will be provided for Samantha at no cost to her," he added, an afterthought just before he hung up.

Major Brooks had three meetings with Ken Valentine, one that lasted from two that very afternoon until midnight. He arranged for an attorney just as Colonel Bishop suggested, then contacted Samantha via letter. It was early Friday morning of that same week. A staff corporal, serving as a courier, delivered the sealed envelope to Samantha's door. It contained two letters. One, with Ken's notarized endorsement, was his agreement to her terms of divorce. The other, a letter of instruction from Major Brooks, the officer Samantha had talked to on the phone. The instructions named the civilian attorney who, at no charge to Samantha, would handle all transfers and file the uncontested plea to officially affect the divorce proceeding. A postscript in longhand explained that Ken had only requested that he be entitled to a certain bronze statue of a man on a horse that belonged to his mother. The bronze was in the New Mexico Mountain cabin and Ken would like to pick it up when he returned from Vietnam. He had volunteered for duty and had been advised to be ready to ship out in ninety days.

As agreed, Samantha got custody of their daughter, ten-year-old Karla, their savings, her station wagon and the summer cabin. Even though the transfers were quickly accomplished via quick claim and the civilian attorney had completed the final filings, she remained in her apartment near the base and waited for the official date when she would be free of Ken Valentine forever, the 30th of October, 1967. Never again would Samantha have or even see, Uncle Hiram's watch or Aunt May's ring, but never would her ex-husband see his daughter or have any of the things she was awarded in the long overdue divorce.

During Samantha's wait for her divorce to be final, and until the lease on her apartment lapsed, she continued to help Doctor Logan, wanting to stay proficient just in case things didn't go well. Several times, on nights she and Karla came home after dark, Samantha noticed an MP watching her apartment until she was inside and had locked up. She assumed Ken's supervisor, the helpful JAG officer, had made that arrangement.

Chapter 8

On January 31st, 1968, Howard Lane officially retired. The next morning, packed and ready for the long drive to Dallas, he stopped by to see Samantha and give her the two-thousand dollars he'd gotten for the angel brooch, which was to cover her moving expenses. She was shocked. It was the first financial help anyone had given her since she separated from Ken.

Howard was drunk, far too drunk to be driving, but had somehow made it without crashing his wife's little convertible. "You be careful," he slurred, attempting to indulge in a departing kiss, then his eyes suddenly filled with hauteur when Samantha pushed him away. "Hey, didn't I just give you some money? What the fuck's wrong with you?" he asked, then immediately forgot he'd asked her anything and turned to walk out. "Carol Ann and I are leaving for Dallas as soon as I get back," he slurred, staggering as he swung the apartment door open. "Don't you waste a minute, Samantha. I'll have everything waiting when you get there, money and...Hey, where's my pills?"

"If you weren't so drunk, you could see them," she said, pointing toward two bottles of the Soma pills that were sitting on her kitchen table.

Keeping the pain pills available for Howard was for two purposes, each leading to the conclusion of Samantha's plan for him. One, they made him less of a threat. Two, he was totally unpredictable when denied.

The pills had actually led to Howard and Samantha's acquaintance. One day while at work, the major came in to see Dr. Logan. "Good morning, Howard, old boy," greeted the doctor, then introduced him to Samantha. "Meet Mrs. Valentine. Feast your eyes but keep your hands in check. I have to. Is she a spittin image of Natalie Wood, or what?"

"Well, she certainly is," responded the charming major.

"Samantha, this is Major Lane," continued the doctor. "He has a back problem, severe pain that originates in the lumbar area. It's caused by sciatic nerve irritation. You can dispense whatever amount of Soma 350 he wants. As you know, I keep plenty here in the office."

Howard began as an interested pursuer, understanding and seeming to just want to offer a little social life to a separated mother who was strapped to make ends meet. He constantly asked her out to no avail, so began showing up at her Bible classes. Finally, Samantha met him for lunch. That led to another, then another, then dinner, and then more dinners. As time went on, Howard grew difficult to deal with, his conduct and persistence bordering on that of a stalker. He often showed up at Samantha's apartment at odd hours, drunk and loud. No wasn't an answer he would hear. "Howard, if you ever come here uninvited again, I'm going to go straight to Colonel Bishop," she once warned. "Now you listen to me, Howard Lane. One more of these late-night disturbances and I'm going to tell your wife," she threatened another time.

"My wife?" he slurred, laughing ominously. "You won't call Carol Ann, but I don't give a shit if you do. I have things all worked out with that woman. You wanna know the details?"

Samantha wasn't interested in hearing more stories about Howard's relationship with his wife that particular night. However, a few nights later, when he showed up at her apartment after two am, insisting that she hear him out, help him, become his ally, she listened and became even more alienated from him than she already was. "Now, see here," he began. "I got two hundred big ones that my daddy willed me five years ago," he lied. "Carol Ann has a house her mother willed her about the same time. I figger the money's mine and the house is hers, but she don't figger it that way. She wants half the money and keep the house. It ain't gonna happen though. I'm takin what's mine. She's only gonna get what's hers, plus a little surprise."

Howard went on to explain his intentions, of which Samantha explained the pitfalls and possibilities of a new plan that would be more fair to Carol Ann. Whether he was convinced or not, he seemed to be, as nothing was said about his marital situation for several days. Samantha's decision to make the change followed another night after the Bible class when Howard showed up at two-ten in the morning scratching at the door like a cat. Samantha quickly donned a robe, rushed to the door, then whispered through it. "Howard, please go away. Karla has to go to school tomorrow and I have to be at work by seven. I don't want to see you for awhile anyway."

"Open up for just a second. I've got a surprise."

"Sh," pleaded Samantha. "You'll get me thrown out of my apartment."

"Open up, then." Samantha opened the door, but only inches. Howard bolted inside, shouldering her out of his way. He wasn't completely drunk, but had more booze with him, two bottles of wine, one in each hand, held like clubs. "What on earth is it with you?" demanded Samantha. "I can call the MP's, you know."

"You can get us each a glass and a corkscrew, or get your head bashed in," responded the major, unsmiling as he raised a bottle of the wine. "We're gonna get drunk and I'm gonna spend the night."

Samantha, not knowing what to expect, vividly remembering Ken's attack and his implied threat regarding the life insurance policy she had become to assume existed, reacted on instinct born of her experience with exactly that. She didn't know what could be going through the dark mind of a desperate man being denied anything. She turned as if to search for a corkscrew in a cabinet drawer, but took out a small butcher knife and wheeled around to face Howard, holding the knife in both hands. "You get out of my home right now and don't ever come here in the middle of the night again. You're..."

Before Samantha could finish, Howard brought one of the wine bottles down hard and knocked the knife from her hands. It went flying down the hall and banged against the bathroom door jam. There was a moment of silent disbelief, then Howard dropped the bottles of wine and grabbed Samantha's throat. "Get naked," he ordered, yanking her against him, his big hands ready to crush her windpipe. "You can't keep me waitin forever."

Samantha tried to scream, but Howard smothered her quivering lips with his, hard and wet. She bit his lower lip, but he would not be denied. He clamped a hand over her mouth and dragged her to the floor, ripping buttons from his shirt. Samantha, helpless, willed herself into unconsciousness, witnessing nothing more of the violent attack, more of which was observed by a ten-year-old child, than by herself. "Mommy? Mommy, wake up," she heard, a teary plea as Karla covered her naked body with the blanket from her bed. "That mean man left."

Samantha, knowing full well that local civilian authorities would always sympathize with base personnel, chose to tell no one of the assault. Howard Lane, even if found guilty, would never face more than an unofficial reprimand, maybe some minimum fine. That would not satisfy Samantha Valentine. She could not allow it to end there.

In the ensuing days, Samantha made every effort to go on with her life as if nothing had happened that horrible night. She decided to avoid discussing Howard's attack with her daughter until Karla herself brought it up, which occurred one night while she was helping with the dinner dishes. "Mommy, why was that man holding his thing when he laid down on the floor by you?"

Samantha, anticipating a difficult question, had chosen her words carefully. She knew fabricating about what her young daughter must have seen would be like trying to stick to the Santa Claus myth after the child learned she'd been duped all along. "Sweetheart," she began, picking Karla up and sitting her on the kitchen cabinet, eye-to-eye with the little girl. "Your mother made a terrible mistake," she explained, part mendacity, but partly true. Ever having anything to do with Howard Lane was a mistake, but the violent event that resulted was not of her volition. "Someday soon, when you're a little older, I'll tell you what I did wrong. Meanwhile, if you'll forgive me, I promise it will never happen again."

Karla seemed to accept her mother's rationale, but was constantly concerned with the changes that would affect her. For several days, she asked about her father, her grandfather, her aunts, Pat and Cheryl, and the things she remembered about Houston. "Why do we live in New Jersey?" asked the girl, one morning before going to school. "If Daddy isn't going to live with us, can't we just go back to Texas?"

Although Karla soon stopped asking questions, Samantha knew her attempts had not eased her daughter's concerns. Instead, she felt that Karla had chosen silence over getting more confused. The little girl began to avoid conversation whenever possible and didn't have another question until the morning Samantha gave her employer a week's notice. Karla was with her. "Are we really moving, Mommy?" she asked.

"Yes we are and you're going to love our new home."

"Will that old mean man hurt us if he finds us?" asked Karla.

"No, but don't worry. He doesn't want to find us."

The pace of that week Samantha began her move to New Mexico was as hectic as any she'd experienced, always with no help and never with adequate time to rest, or merely relax while eating a meal with her daughter. Once she'd gotten started, packing what she needed for the trip was the least frustrating. She could control it and Karla usually sat with a TV tray and ate while watching anything that was on the set. Otherwise, she kept herself occupied with a book or her crayons. Dealing with Karla's teachers, the bank and other service people, or about anything that hinged on the inefficiency of others was nerve racking and far more time consuming than she had expected.

The day after she gave notice at her job, Samantha closed her checking account and bought traveler's checks with the balance, three thousand thirty dollars, which included the money Howard had given her for the move. While at the bank, although having to wait for an officer to approve the transaction, she bought a cashier's check with the balance of her savings account, the sixty-seven thousand three hundred dollars she was awarded in the divorce. During the next few days, as time allowed, she said her good-byes around the base, making a personal call on Colonel Bishop.

"Mrs. Valentine," he greeted, meeting her in the hall before she reached Priscilla's reception area. He wasn't going to give his big secretary a chance to spread rumors about his, Howard Lane's and Samantha Valentine's leaving Fort Dix so near the same time. "It's completely unnecessary to thank me. I just hope I did the right thing. Where will you live, Mrs. Valentine? The mountain cabin in New Mexico? Lost Mountain Park I guess it's called."

Samantha, shocked the base commander knew of the mountain cabin, its location, even the name of the park, faltered with her answer. "I, uh, no. I'm planning to sell the cabin and live in Dallas," she lied.

"Well, good luck, Mrs. Valentine," said the colonel, dismissing her, anxious to get across the river to Philly where he and Carol Ann were meeting in the lounge of a downtown hotel. "Goodbye, Samantha. You'll find some beautiful scenes to capture on canvas when you get to the New Mexico mountains."

Martin watched from his window as Samantha drove away, noticing the cloud of black smoke boiling up from her old Ford wagon. He felt a brief wave of satisfaction, having possibly helped a nice young woman who must have needed a break. Martin had seen Ken sporting around the base in his new convertible a number of times. "Just go buy yourself one," he said to the window, smiling, picturing Samantha motoring down a shady boulevard in a red convertible, her beautiful face and blue eyes stopping traffic.

Over the next few days, while arranging to have her mail forwarded and household items shipped to New Mexico, Samantha couldn't keep from wondering just how many of Howard's friends knew of her cabin and if Howard himself knew. She finally dismissed the thought when another spark of doubt caught her while packing. Samantha couldn't find the brown satchel that Ken's father had given him when he worked at the firm in Houston. She had been using it to store important records, W-2's, the current insurance policy on the Ford wagon and other documents that had to be available those certain times they were needed.

At first, the most troubling issue with the missing satchel was the deposit receipt and passbook Samantha had gotten when opening the savings account for Karla at the Republic National Bank in Dallas. *Anyone could lose a receipt and a savings passbook and financial institutions are surely required to keep backup records*, she assured herself, then remembered the little pistol. "Oh, no!" She sighed, her heart leaping. "Ken's acting crazy enough to use that thing." Samantha checked the time. One-ten pm. "I've got to report it."

Colonel Bishop was busy when Samantha tried to reach him by phone but returned the call at four that afternoon. He was irritated.

"Mrs. Valentine, I'm quite pressed for time. I've done what I can, you've thanked me and that was enough. What else is it?"

Samantha told the colonel about the satchel and the important papers, then stressed her concern about Ken having the pistol. "Did Major Brooks tell you about Ken threatening me?" she asked.

"Mrs. Valentine," sighed the colonel. "I'm sorry you're frightened, but most men own some sort of gun. I have a dozen. Please, just forget it. If Ken didn't have the one you mentioned, he could get another one. Anywhere."

The colonel's words were true enough. Ken had never shown interest in the pistol, or any gun. It just wasn't going to be something to add to everything Samantha had to think about, she decided.

After studying a road map to determine the time needed, she called the airlines to confirm their flight times and schedules. She then wrote Howard to notify him of the exact date and time an American Airline flight originating in Philadelphia would arrive in Dallas. She allowed herself a month and a day from the time she planned to leave New Jersey, to accomplish what she needed to do at her mountain cabin, then fly to Dallas from Albuquerque, New Mexico, arriving on March 18th at five-thirty pm. That would put her there an hour and ten minutes before the American flight from Philadelphia arrived at Love Field. Samantha and Karla would be waiting at the American gate and Howard should never suspect they had come in from New Mexico.

Early in the morning of February twentieth, a cold and windy day, Samantha left New Jersey on the long drive out to New Mexico to meet the movers. Her little daughter, yet choosing to remain silent, immediately crawled into the back seat and slept until the first stop for fuel and refreshments in Richmond, Virginia. Karla, although a little cantankerous, finally had something to say. "Mommy, where are we gonna spend the night?" she fussed. "I don't like driving in this awful old rain."

After too many years of misery, the feeling of finally being free of Ken was so exhilarating for Samantha that she could have driven coast to coast nonstop, regardless of the harsh conditions. "Now, now, don't be that way," she said, handing her weary little daughter a soft drink and a package of chips. "We can have our snacks in the car and go a little further."

Karla finished her snack, then crawled into the back seat and dozed off again. To add to the cold and windy day, a steady rain had been falling since Samantha reached Baltimore and was continuing across Virginia. She was in Eastern Tennessee, on Interstate 40 south of the Appalachians before the sky began to clear. Karla, as if aware of the change in weather, awoke and crawled into the front seat. "Can we stop, Mommy? I'm hungry and I gotta go again."

"Good timing. We need gas and I need to find a restroom myself."

Samantha exited the interstate at Knoxville, refueled, rested a few minutes, then drove on to Memphis. Her head felt like it would split, her eyes were burning, her mind a tangled web of plans and contingencies. The threat against her life that Ken had made, however subtle, loomed like the fear of something sinister hiding in the dark. She had been pushing herself too hard, and although an exhilarating anticipation for the all-new life awaiting her was holding steadfast, she was physically and mentally exhausted. A few days of nothing but rethinking and rebounding were long overdue.

There was a brightly-lit motel on the outskirts of Memphis, its flashing neon sign advertising double occupancy rooms for $19.99 per night and a restaurant with 24-hour service. Samantha registered for two nights, hoping to do nothing but rest and spend some uninterrupted time alone with her young daughter. Since the day the little girl realized that her father had left her, Karla had been dull and despondent. She had told her teacher, along with a curious neighbor who wanted to know why she carried a big clock to school, that since she lost her cat and her daddy went away, her clock was her only friend. After the teacher persisted to get the details of her daddy going away that day; the little girl all but refused to leave the apartment, seldom speaking to anyone unless it was absolutely unavoidable. Samantha hadn't been ignoring her daughter, but considered the stance a necessary battle that Karla would overcome. "Honey," she said, folding back the covers for her daughter, "I know you brought your clock along, but Mommy needs to sleep tomorrow. If you'll let me, and be very quiet, the next day will be yours. I can take you shopping, then to a nice restaurant, a movie, or whatever you want to do. What do you say to that?"

"Okay. My clock's in the car. Goodnight."

Samantha hung a 'Do not disturb' card on the door of the room, then went to bed and slept until eleven the next morning. She awoke when her daughter came back to the room from the motel's restaurant. "Mommy, I brought you some milk and this," she said, holding up a saucer with four slices of toast.

Samantha was touched. "Put them down and come here," she said.

The little girl did as she was told. "What?"

Samantha sat upright and hugged Karla. "Thank you, Honey. Mommy appreciates it when you do things for her," she said. "It's being thoughtful."

"Okay. You're welcome."

After a day spent entirely with Karla, including shopping, an afternoon movie and a late dinner back at the motel, Samantha drove from Memphis to Amarillo, Texas and got a room for one night. Early the next morning, she continued on the long drive, across the barren lifeless landscape of the Texas high plains and into New Mexico. Karla was asleep within an hour of Amarillo, but Samantha was intrigued with the sights, sounds and feel, she told herself. An attempt to fill her mind with thoughts other than those that inevitably haunted her, those she was defenseless against.

The whistle of the wind seemed as if were a living thing, unseen, but heard and felt, like one's heart. Although Samantha saw no one, no wildlife, no cattle, no horses and only big rig after big rig mindlessly roaring east and west, she knew the splendor of the West was there. There were no beautiful rivers or majestic mountains, but there was a special beauty in the uncompromising vastness, its unyielding stance after centuries of man's attack with chain saws and bulldozers. The sky, witnessing it all, its clarity an enormous eye, was unrestricted by smog, or even clouds. There were no distractions of a city's constant confusing hustle. The horizons revealed no limits, but merely slipped from sight beyond the curvature of the earth.

Mile after mile, hour after hour brought little change in the landscape, Eastern New Mexico being an extension of the vast Texas plains. The highway was becoming hypnotic, tiring now, its stripes tracking due west as straight as the flight of a bullet, their path unwavering, as flat as a table. It was then the inevitable memories came creeping back, a gang of hecklers, flashing by slowly like flipping through photographs, each image lasting until replaced by the next. There was her mother, uncaring as she waved goodbye when Samantha worked at the Fox-Fire Drive-in. The little closed off room in Dr. Ott's clinic where he violated her. His wheezy words, his right hand like a long hot sword. Then, Lorraine's heartless scorn as she all but took everything dear and familiar to Samantha away. Ken's cowering life of lies and deception suddenly turning to rage just before he struck the side of her head, then Howard Lane's horribly malicious rape attack that Karla must have witnessed parts of.

Tears were welling now, but Samantha wiped her eyes and drove on. As always, when the dark memories came, it seemed that her mind was trying to vomit all the bad that had happened, but she knew it was as impractical as unreal to think that could ever happen. Would the day ever come when Samantha would be free of the words in Ken's death threat? Could she ever forget the vivid images of Howard's sudden attack? "The man is a despicable beast," she sighed aloud, knowing the closure of his chapter had not yet occurred, but must, and could soon.

Maybe she was destined for a life of lonely pain, thought Samantha; the ills of her past only cured if she could do it herself. Since the day her aunt and uncle were taken from her life, the only true adult love Samantha had shared were those few stolen moments with Dr. Benjamin. Would she ever find another who would love her and want to help her? Who else could she confide in as she had her uncle and Dr. Benjamin? Karla someday? But, would Samantha live until her daughter was old enough to help her? After what Karla might have seen, would she ever respect her mother?

Samantha knew Ken had never loved her as his wife, but she had never really loved him either, their union evolving due to her needing a place to run and him needing a naive companion. "Now," thought Samantha, "All I need is the independence Uncle Hiram said I should achieve, but I want a life of something besides running with the pack, chasing the prize. The all-American dream."

Without even a subtle warning, as if another photograph popping into Samantha's mind, a little town began to rise from below the horizon spreading out as the distance closed. It was the village of Moriarty, no more than a crossroads, or truck stop. Samantha had exited the highway onto the off-ramp, unaware of doing so. The landscape had changed, and the ever-present wind was now swirling through the little town, carrying thin bits of sand and little puffs of dust. Distant mountains with high clouds hanging above could be seen to the north and west and there were people. A man on a horse, children running after a boy on a bicycle, storefronts with cars and pickups parked in front, others pulling in, or backing out. An old man, his face shaded with a wide brimmed hat, waved from the bed of one of the parked pickups. The dark skin of his face suddenly twisting with a grin as he pointed toward an intersection, the only one in sight that had a traffic signal.

Samantha nodded to the old man, then looked ahead. Beyond the traffic signal, a stalled big rig was blocking the entry ramp to the highway, creating a torrent of excitement. There was a group of curious locals watching from across the street, seeming equally interested in the long line of passenger cars waiting for the truck to move out of their way. A few of the drivers were intermittently honking their horns, but most appeared patient, as if enjoying an unfettered moment of their own. Samantha stopped at the end of the line, rolled down her window and breathed in the cool clean air. It would be hard, she decided, to be upset with a traffic delay in a place so at peace, so seemingly pure.

People. How interesting they can be, she was thinking, stopped now, watching as a tow truck made its way past the stalled cars. The truck stopped by the big rig, where two men in khaki pants and stained tee shirts were crouching near the eighteen wheeler's left front tire. Suddenly, again as if a photograph had materialized within the halls of Samantha's mind, a huge blonde man on a black motorcycle appeared at her open driver's side window. "Hi," she said. "I guess we may never get through."

The big blonde motorcyclist spoke without facing her, his focus on the stalled big rig. "Never say never. Where ya headed, Ma'am?" he asked, smiling as he turned to face Samantha, the mirrored lenses of his sun shades making twin clowns of her face. The man's unusual size, his mass, his big arms and shoulders carried such bulk that Samantha felt intimidated, suddenly lost for words. "On west, it appears to me," he said. "You okay?"

Samantha nodded, her eyes seeming to weld to the big man's right shoulder. "Oh, uh yes. Santa Fe, but how far is it to Albuquerque?"

The man was so close that Samantha could read the little red instruction tag for cleaning the bedroll tied behind him. Imagining now, playing a game to relax herself, Samantha tried to smell the freshness of the blue jeans he wore, clean and new, the legs stuffed into big black boots. His sleeveless cotton shirt, although beginning to show wear, did not look neglected. The man wore a black leather vest, *Vengeance* in faded red block letters across the back. "I'm going through Santa Fe myself," he said. "Albuquerque is about halfway, an hour for you," he added, smiling, his demeanor that of unconcern for the delay.

"What should I do? I mean, I shouldn't wait here. I have a little girl."

"I read you loud and clear. Just follow me, but don't try to keep up once we're back on the highway."

The man revved the motorcycle's big engine, *Barroom, Barroom,* then turned it around and started idling back toward the signal light, glancing over his shoulder just as Samantha fell in behind. His blonde hair was stirring in the wind, the sunshades flashing like beckoning beacons. Freedom personified. He waved when passing the old man in the bed of the pickup, then continued toward the highway on the same service road Samantha had entered the little town on. After pointing to the *Do Not Enter* sign on the side of the road, he leaned into the curve that came off the highway and rode right across it, over the sandy medium between the east and west bound lanes and stopped. There were no cars coming from either direction and no one from the little truck stop town could see what went on out here. Samantha eased to a stop beside the motorcycle, surprised the man did not frighten her.

"Be careful where you stop next time," he said, easing the motorcycle forward as he spoke. "Beautiful women all alone at a truck stop? Not a good mix in my books. See you later." *Barroom. Barroom,* and he was gone, his image shrinking as he sped toward the horizon, now turning blood-red as the sun sank into the low clouds.

Samantha watched for a moment, wondering if she was feeling a certain envy for the motorcyclist's apparent ease in dealing with his world, his obvious freedom. Maybe it's just irresponsibility, she rationalized in thought, idling onto the highway. He's probably some society dropout living on the muster-out pay he received when he got out of the army.

Again, along the highway to Albuquerque, Samantha took in everything, fighting to keep her dark memories away and her fear of what faced her from returning, and the many variables she must control. Although less immediate, but definitely the most challenging, the most threatening, would be putting a closure to her association with Howard Lane. No margin for error there.

Karla had missed the excitement at Moriarty, sleeping soundly in the back seat. Samantha awoke her at a gas stop in Albuquerque, not wanting the little girl to miss the drive into the mountain country of Northern New Mexico. Except for the time spent shopping, the movie and dinner in Memphis, Karla had slept away the whole trip. The few hours she had been awake, she appeared dull, or bored, no doubt apprehensive. "Honey," said Samantha, shaking Karla's leg until she awoke. "Let's find a restaurant where we can get something to eat. I'll bet if you'll splash some cold water in your face, you'll stay awake until we get to our home. Besides, Mommy doesn't want you to miss anything. It won't be very much longer and it's beautiful the rest of the way."

The little girl seemed to completely change after having a hamburger and a glass of milk in Albuquerque. She had new spirit, was more alert and seemed to brighten with the cooler mountain air. While driving through Santa Fe, Karla was talkative and asked questions about the plaza, the old cathedrals, the adobe homes and the people. "Where's our house, Mommy?" she asked. "How much longer?" she wanted to know several times. "Will it just be you and me?"

"If we hurry, we'll be there in an hour, Sweetheart. And yes, it will just be the two of us. Are you excited?"

"Yeah. Look at all these people, Mommy. They wear hats. Wonder where they're all walkin to. Is that old woman an Indian?"

Samantha hurried through the dusty streets of downtown Santa Fe, found the turnoff to Highway 84 North and drove the half-hour to Santa Cruz, then on to the little settlement of Abiquiu. Just out of town, across from the old motel she remembered, stood the little sign, almost impossible to see in the final minutes of twilight. *Lost Mountain Park*, it read, an arrow pointing to the dirt road that lead west through woods. "You and I stayed there once, Karla," said Samantha, pointing to the old motel.

The little girl shook her head, disagreeing. "Uh-uh. I never was here."

The landscape had changed steadily since Santa Fe. The scrub brush, pinyon pine, dwarf cedars and juniper trees had slowly given way to tall fir and spruce trees, ponderosa pine and thick alpine cover. The rough dirt road zigzagged through a narrow section of the Santa Fe National Forest, no more than five miles in width. Darkness covered the forest like a black cloak. The sun had hidden behind towering peaks in the distant darkness, lordly as they loomed like black frames against the horizon. "This is scary," said Karla, enjoying it.

Samantha wasn't enjoying being in the forest at night, alone except for her small child. To her, the woods belonged to itself. A near impenetrable barrier enforced with endless wall-like stands of tall trees and thick tangles of vine-like undergrowth that hid deep clefts and dangerous ravines where a person might fall and never be found. A broken leg or even a turned ankle could render a human easy prey for wild animals. Ken's father had warned Samantha about these woods, replete with bear, wolves and big mountain cats, hungry hunters, powerful and fast with razor-sharp claws and big teeth, capable of tearing through a person's throat in an instant.

Although shivering against thoughts of danger lurking in the blackness of the forest and the chill of the night, Samantha tried to keep a smile on her face, a perky appearance to hide her apprehension from her daughter. "It's sure pretty up here, Karla, but neither of us should ever go into the forest alone. You have to promise me you will never do that," she said, suddenly wondering what would happen if the old station wagon finally quit. In the broken moonlight, walking out of the forest would be like teasing fate. "Okay?"

The little girl didn't answer immediately, but sat silently looking out her window, unseeing beyond the big trees that lined the road. "Mommy?" she finally uttered. "Would something eat us if we got lost?"

Samantha reached over and patted her daughter's leg, a gesture of assurance. "Mommy knows the way. We're not going to get lost."

"Better not," responded Karla, softly. "There's bears in the woods."

The old station wagon leaned and struggled as the little road twisted and turned, breaking out of the blackness within the tall trees and into little moonlit clearings on the flanks of ridges, only to be quickly enveloped within darkness between the big trees again. Samantha, through an unblinking stare, kept scanning the dark and narrow mountain road for deer, or any yet un-thought of wild animal that could cause her to crash the car. She held the speed down, slowing for every curve, every ravine and stopping once on a one-lane plank bridge to observe and listen to a small waterfall. An orange ribbon in the dim moonlight, cascading over boulders and splashing into a pool a few feet from the little bridge, baneful music in the night. "Look at that, Mommy," said Karla, pointing to the pool below the waterfall, a puddle of swirling moonlight where big droplets were steadily bouncing up, then returning to the churning surface. "It looks like boiling blood."

"Oh, Honey," challenged Samantha. "Now, that's silly. You've never seen such a thing as boiling blood. Besides, that's not nice to think about."

"I saw it on TV. These mean people were boiling a witch and the water turned yuck and red and..."

"Sh, sh, now, Karla," said Samantha, not knowing what the little girl had seen or what should be said. "That was just a silly story. It never happened."

The little girl spoke softly, a whispered thought. "Uh-huh, it did. The old witch cooked up, too."

Samantha drove on. From the bridge, the little road climbed up to a clear mountain pass and around a hairpin curve, then went back down switchback after switchback, finally breaking out of the thick woods at a lower plateau. To the right, accessed by an even narrower dirt road, was a collection of loose buildings. One was a huge hut, maybe an airplane hangar. Ken's father had mentioned flying to the park and camping in Rainbow Canyon once during deer season, but Samantha assumed he had flown to Santa Fe, rented a car and drove on to the park.

"Look, Mommy," said Karla, pointing to another sign, one Samantha didn't remember. "What's that sign say?"

"It says Lost Mountain Park. Private Road. Keep Out."

'Why?" asked Karla, wanting to know everything. "Don't we live here?"

"We sure do. That sign is just for the people who don't."

Just yards beyond the sign, Samantha could see the twinkling lights of the little village, slumbering at the edge of a clear mountain lake, a mass of sparkling crystals and blurry orange streaks, its surface picking up the magnificence of the starry sky and the lights of the surrounding dwellings. The lake was formed by the Abiquiu Dam and was fed by the Gallina and Arroyo rivers that wound out of the high mountains in the San Juan Range.

The little road, now the main road, continued on around the north end of the lake, but another turned off and led to the cabins, then beyond, disappearing into the dark woods. The cabins were bunched near the water's edge at the southwest corner of the lake. Samantha's cabin stood among several others, all facing away from the water, toward a wide grassy area that appeared to be mowed frequently. Then, the woods, stretching south to the desert floor.

Across the lake was a row of homes. It looked like five, no six, the reflection of their lights more uneven blurry orange streaks floating in the rippling water. Surrounded by huge mountains and dense forest, the little park, a remote world seeming sinister in its silence right now, created the feeling of a trap for Samantha, a box, cold to the touch, a minimum security prison.

Once outside the car, the stars above, appearing close enough to reach out and touch, seemed like millions of eyes that could see a person's every move. The North Star, an intimidating magnification, looked like a billion-power telescope that could stare right into one's soul. In the midnight darkness, the big peaks to the west seemed to be staring down like Monarchs from hell. Lost Mountain Park didn't appear to be a place Samantha could ever like.

It was different for her daughter. Samantha knew Karla had completely relented and given up her code of silence when she swung the little cabin's front door open. "Oh, Mommy, is this all ours?" she screamed.

"Don't be so loud, Honey," whispered Samantha, reacting to her feelings of something foreboding about Lost Mountain Park. "And yes, this is our home. I don't think we want anyone to stay with us. What do you think about that?"

"Promise me, Mommy. I don't like that man who took Daddy's place," said little Karla, then dropped her tote bag and ran through the cabin, the lights from the car lighting the way. "It's dark up here in the mountains," she whispered, taking her mother's attitude as a silent warning, but following with a long bombardment of shouts even louder than before. "Which one's my room?" she asked, then continued before Samantha could answer. "Hey, we have a washing machine like when we lived in that army house," exclaimed Karla, running to the utility room, pointing to the appliances. "That's what dries clothes. I member the one we had. You just gotta turn this here. This here knob," she repeated, then flipped on a light switch. "We got lectric," she said, turning around and around, her eyes showing the wonderment she felt. "Mommy, I love our new home. Look at all the cowboy pictures. I didn't know we had a fireplace like Papa Ted's. Is that my toy cowboy up there on that shelf?"

Samantha spoke with a finger to her lips. "Pipe down just a little, Sweetheart. That's your father's cowboy. It's a very expensive piece of art."

From the outside, the cabin, a rough mix of native timber and frame, looked exactly like six of those immediately surrounding it, each built by the same builder using a common set of plans. Inside though, Sybil had put her imagination to work when decorating. Besides the Remington prints and bronze, the furniture was all designer, brass and glass tables, rich leather chairs throughout, a small, but tasteful sectional in the den. The cabin was filled with the finest furnishings Sybil could find in Santa Fe and Albuquerque, Mexican tile floors in every room, a colorful patchwork of Native American throw rugs adding warmth to the ambiance. As Samantha looked around, it seemed like Sybil's haunting presence was still there and no one else had been.

Samantha remembered that one of the cabins had been converted to a small grocery and bait store, coffee free all day in its two-table eatery. Some of the cabins, including Samantha's, had big sheds in back the year-round dwellers used to garage their cars. The cabins had simple cement slabs that served as porches and step-ups for the front door. The last time she was out, four of the cabins were sharing a boardwalk with handrails that led to a small pier where the residents could fish, or moor their small boats.

Samantha, tired from the trip, brought only absolute essentials in from the car, then quickly prepared beds for her and Karla and went to sleep. When she awoke at noon Wednesday, her daughter was no place to be seen. Worried, she slipped on the things she'd worn the day before and hurried outside. "Hello," she said, to an official looking man who was leaning up against the station wagon, a clipboard held against his leg. He looked rigid and strong, wide shoulders and a thick neck. His skin and hair were dark, accenting the whites of his eyes, making the pupils look like dots of coal. The man wore a dark blue parka, neatly creased khaki trousers and military-type jungle boots.

"Are you lookin for that little girl?" he asked, unsmiling, pointing toward the lake. "She's fine. Just been down there at the pier being quiet as a mouse and watchin old Dolly fish for her dinner. All she needs is a heavy coat. It got down to thirty-four degrees last night."

"I felt it," agreed Samantha, closing the door behind her. "That little girl who's being so quiet might just need a paddling, too. She knows better than to go outside without telling me," she said, shielding her eyes as she looked out at the placid water, shining as if on fire, then turned back to the man with the clipboard. He looked far too official for such a remote part of the world. "Do I scare you to death?" she asked, smoothing back her hair and trying to smile away her uneasiness with the man's presence. "Sorry, but I think it was almost midnight when we got in." The man chuckled as he rocked his head from side to side, seeming to be toying with opposing possibilities. "Okay, don't tell me, but will you share that thought?" asked Samantha. "I deserve a little humor to start my day, too."

The man's smile quickly went away as he shook his head. "Strictly business," he said, standing rigidly. "You're not going to like me anyway" he added, lifting his clipboard and running a finger halfway to the bottom of the yellow legal pad it held. "Ninety-six dollars plus three hundred eighteen and fifty cents is what?"

"Over four hundred, why?" asked Samantha, sitting down on the cement slab, smiling to herself, amused at the man's sudden return to seriousness.

"Somebody has to pay, or I have to cut off your power and water," he said.

"Is the bill overdue?"

"A year."

"Well," sighed Samantha, then asked, "Is cash okay?"

"Works for everybody I know," responded the man, yet unsmiling. Little Karla ran around the corner of the house. "Mommy," she said, her tone and eyes condemning. That lady down there caught a little bitty fish, but she just threw it right back in the lake. I wanted it."

"She's supposed to if it's little bitty, Honey. It'll grow up, then you can catch it and I'll cook it for you. Will you run inside and get Mommy's purse?"

Karla looked at the man with the clipboard. "Is that so?" she asked.

The big man seemed startled to be addressed by a little girl. "Oh, a good fisherman always throws little ones back," he said, his rigid demeanor yielding slightly.

Karla, disgusted with this revelation, turned and hurried inside. "What's your name and what do you do?" asked Samantha of the man with the clipboard.

"I'm Chip Parker. The local jack of all trades. I do a lot of things," responded the rigid man, gesturing toward a heavily loaded flatbed Chevrolet truck that was parked in the middle of the road. "Those are drums of gasoline," he explained, noticing the question in Samantha's expression. "Everybody needs gas for their cars and trucks and it's a long way to town." The questioning look in Samantha's expression held. "Boats, too," added Chip Parker, his tone a plea to convince before further explaining what he did. "I handle trash pickup and do some custom hauling. I even fight the weeds and grass all summer and collect for utilities around here. We're co-op, case you don't know."

"Here," said Karla, leaning out the door to place the purse on the cement.

"Thank you," said Samantha, catching the door just before it banged closed. "Okay now," she said to Chip, feeling an unexplainable sense of doubt about Mr. Parker. "Tell me what I'm paying for, Sir."

Chip's all business demeanor resumed. "Well, it's ninety-six dollars for water. That's eight dollars a month. The rest, three eighteen fifty is for electricity. Totals to four hundred and fourteen dollars and fifty cents."

Samantha suddenly felt an urge to test Mr. Parker. "Can I pay five hundred dollars and the excess go toward next month?"

"That'll be fine," he said, nonchalantly. "Trash service is ten dollars a month when someone's here."

Samantha handed Chip five one hundred-dollar bills. "Thank you," she said. "Now, would you be so kind as to tell me if I can still get a cup of coffee down at the store? I have some, but I don't know where I packed it."

Chip looked less putout, less challenged, but equally as unfriendly. "I'd bet old man Valentine left plenty somewhere in that cabin," he said, walking away. "Just look around. Chances are you'll find it."

Chip was right about the coffee. Samantha found what she needed in one of the cabinets. After having her morning cup, she went to work unpacking, hanging or storing her pictures, cleaning and dusting, then ended the day with a shopping spree at the little store.

It was only four-fifteen when Samantha left the store with her two little bags of groceries, but the sun was already behind the big peaks to the west, their shadows reaching to the center of the lake. The whole park seemed void of life, except for an odd looking man, as round as he was tall, who was walking a big black dog out across the expanse of grass in front of the cabins. He bent at the waist, shielded his eyes against the remaining glare of the lake for several seconds, then waved. "Hey, welcome back," he said, holding the big dog by its missing ears "Want a puppy for your little girl? I got two males and a bitch sired by this beauty. They're free."

"I'll think about it," said Samantha, nodding as she hurried past the boardwalk thinking of her experience while in the little store. The proprietors, Jay and Ada Redwine, had to be in their seventies. The odd thing was they're offering a helping hand at anything, but Samantha couldn't help but feel that their hospitality was less than genuine. Both seemed nervous, as if something in their world wasn't quite right. Jay, wearing greasy lumberjack boots and an old faded red flannel shirt, full bearded and robust, appeared stressed. He was missing two front teeth, which Samantha decided might explain his guarded smile. His harsh brown eyes, staring like lenses, made Samantha think of a cat, ready to pounce onto a mouse it had cornered. Ada, thin and drawn, appearing to have new dentures, clicking them often when she wasn't talking, seemed more like a professional interrogator than just a local gossip fountain. She and Jay both had dull gray hair, complexions like prunes and seemed too old to be working.

Odd people, thought Samantha, reflecting on Jay and Ada's reaction from the minute she walked into their store. "Come in here, Little Lady. Need one of us, just say so. We always helped yer daddy and we ain't gonna mind pitching in if you need something," explained Jay, turning to his wife for endorsement.

"Yep," agreed Ada. "We been here abouts nigh on a century," she added, taking a deep draw from a filtered cigarette that she held between her thumb and forefinger, its smoldering tip in toward her cupped palm. "Helped everbody time and again," she sighed, painfully, then clicked her teeth and continued, holding the smoke in her lungs as she spoke, her voice high and weak. "Yore Daddy was gonna let us know if he would sell us his cabin, but he never did."

Jay chipped in. "You tell'em we're still interested when ya see'im."

Ada nodded in agreement. "He probly just forgot," she murmured, then paused in silence for a moment. Samantha was yet trying to decide if she should say anything about the ownership of the cabin when the old lady continued, breaking her thoughts. "If you ever want me to keep yore little girl, don't you be a bit bashful," she said, then exhaled a puff of white smoke, immediately taking another drag from her cigarette, speaking again with her lungs full. "Ain't seen'er since that summer she was still in diapers, but I bet we'll get along fine. When's yer folks gonna be comin up? Be another year?" she asked, coughing once.

Samantha, still undecided as to what to say, responded with a shrug and a smile. The old woman gave her a blank look, then exhaled the thick smoke through her nose, clicked her dentures and dropped the glowing cigarette butt into a coke bottle. "Well, maybe yer daddy don't wanna sell. Hell, I can understand that. I don't care if I ever get so far away from the park that I can't see the lake out there."

Samantha's mind was awash with crisscrossing thoughts of new possibilities, possibilities needing time to consider. "How do I get my mail?" she asked, deciding to change the subject.

"Mail?" Ada didn't appear to want to talk about the mail. "Nobody has no complaints about the mail. Jay picks it up in Santa Fe every other day. You'll get yours."

Ada turned around, tiptoed to reach a fresh pack of cigarettes from a high shelf behind her. "Thank you," said Samantha, taking advantage of the pause, hurrying away from the counter to complete her shopping. Before leaving the store, she met three of the locals. One was a teenage boy with long blonde hair. He wore a dirty black jersey, jeans and big knee-high rubber boots like she remembered the irrigation farmers wore back in Sherman.

"Hi, Ma'am. I'm Sonny," greeted the teenage longhair.

"Hello, Sonny." Samantha spotted the dairy case and started down an isle toward it.

"Need some help?" asked Sonny, then followed Samantha throughout the little store, asking questions, making conversation. There were two middle aged men near the end of the dairy case, one standing and one kneeling by a wooden crate half-full of mud. The man standing was Jack Cox, clean-shaven, small and frail, a brow beaten expression about his skinny face. Both men wore khaki pants and shirts and knee-high rubber boots like Sonny was wearing. The man kneeling was BB Douglas, who looked like an ex-marine with a buzz cut, a very rude one, thought Samantha.

"Ma'am," had greeted Jack, nodding his head when Samantha and Sonny walked past. "Saw ya come in last night."

"Hello," Samantha said, avoiding eye contact with either man.

"Anything ya need, you just let me'er Sarge here know," offered Jack, pointing toward the lake. "We live on past your daddy's place, two up from the end cabin. Saw yer brother. Funny tang. He was crawlin..."

"Hey," cut in the man referred to as Sarge, neither speaking to Samantha nor acknowledging her in any other manner. "Help me here, Jack," he ordered, holding up a slimy earthworm. "We didn't get all the big ones yesterday. Those pools in Rainbow Canyon's full 'em."

Jack smiled sheepishly. "Pardon me," he said, then knelt by the bait box.

Samantha hurried away, Sonny right beside her, the big rubber boots making him sound like a giant duck flapping its webfeet on pavement. "Mr. Douglas caught a two-foot long trout right off the bridge up at Rainbow Canyon when we came down from camp yesterday," whispered the teenage boy. "He used a feather fly. A red'n yeller'n Jay made."

"Run on, Sonny," ordered BB Douglas, his forceful voice a match for his drill sergeant appearance.

While paying for her groceries, Samantha asked if Ada would in fact keep her daughter in the event she had to go to Santa Fe on business the coming Monday. "Huh? Uh, well, I," stammered the old woman, totally lost for words.

Jay, although staring at Samantha, interrupted his faltering wife. "Now, now, Ada," he said. "I recollect you just sayin you would."

"Well, I did offer to watch Mindy and I..."

Jay finally turned to his wife. "Yes, you did and yes you will watch her," he said, smiling and winking to soothe any ruffled feelings.

"Your wife is right to be a little apprehensive," said Samantha. "It might be better if she and Karla got to know each other first." Samantha paused, then quickly corrected herself. "Get to know each other again, I mean."

"Suit yourself," said the old woman, obviously relieved.

Samantha paid for her things, picked up her grocery sacks and stepped outside. The boy with the long hair was doggedly angling toward the road that led past the cabins and into the woods beyond. "Sonny?" called Samantha, feeling sorry for him, thinking the man called Sarge had been unnecessarily gruff. "Would you like to come by my cabin and get some milk and a sandwich to take with you?"

"Naw," said Sonny, a tone of dejection. "Sarge says 1 gotta go to the camp, but I don't know why. I didn't do nuthin so wrong."

While putting away the groceries, Samantha considered Lost Mountain Park, wondering if she could actually endure it. Although she had decided to hold Karla out of school until September, where would she go then? Where do people work? What attracted the likes of Chip Parker, BB Douglas, Jack Cox and the Redwines?

Samantha, rationalizing, decided to dismiss her concerns, replacing them with the hope of always being able to sell the cabin and relocate. The Redwines seemed genuinely interested, although they seemed to believe they were talking to Ken's deceased sister. Should Samantha allow that to go further? Cheryl Cooper, although close enough to the same height, had much lighter hair and was thin as a rail. *Anyone could gain weight,* she said in thought. *Women dye their hair sometimes, too.*

"Mommy, guess what," exclaimed Karla, bolting into the cabin, bouncy and excited. "There's a boy lives around here who's gonna take me fishin up in the mountains this afternoon. I need some gloves. Do I have any?"

"Whoa, Karla. Who's this boy?"

"I don't know his name, but he's retarded and lives in a cave with his dog and a bunch of other guys. Member guys."

"Retarded? Do you know what retarded means, Karla?"

"Oh-huh. He can't read and add up."

"I see. Well, just how did you meet your fisherman friend?"

"We talked when I was watchin that Indian woman catch that little fish."

"What does your friend look like? Does he have long blonde hair?"

"Yeah." Karla nodded. "It's kinda long and he's got big boots." Samantha, unsure of anyone who lived in Lost Mountain Park, explained this to her daughter, denying her the fishing outing with Sonny. "I just saw him, Honey. He can't take you this afternoon though. He has to work. Now, there's something we have to do," she added. "I have business in Santa Fe and I need you to go with me. The next day though, I'll get us some fishing equipment and we'll catch one right off that pier down there. What do you think about that?"

"What about our house? That boy said we should watch it real good."

"Watch our house?" Samantha thought for a moment, wondering if she understood the little girl's concern. "Well," she began, then paused, choosing her words carefully. She needed to gain her daughter's cooperation without causing unnecessary concern. The house hadn't been watched for the last year, why now? Suddenly smiling, she reached down and picked up Karla, hugged her while turning around and around, then lowered her to her feet and kissed her cheek. "You just amaze me sometimes, Karla. You've gotten so smart and I'm so proud of you. I should have known you'd understand," she said, leading Karla to the fireplace. "We own this house, so it will be up to us to protect it." Samantha sat down on the hearth, facing Karla. "Honey," she began again. "Mommy will make us a plan and if we stick to it, always stick to our plan, people will leave our little house alone and we'll always have it."

Karla was confused, but feeling good about being part of something that sounded so serious. "Okay, Mommy. I don't ever want to leave here."

Samantha wasn't sure if she should share her own feelings about the park with her daughter. "Okay," she said, having decided to wait for a better opportunity, or see if either she or Karla had a change of heart. "Remember we have to go to Santa Fe Friday. After that, we'll have to make a trip out of town, but when we get back, we'll go right to work on our plan to protect our home. We have to. Your daddy went away for awhile so it's just us now."

"Why did Daddy go away? I wish he'd come see our house."

Samantha turned her attention to the fireplace, pushing an unburned chunk of wood off the grate. "Maybe your daddy just wanted to live somewhere else for awhile," she explained. "That's okay. We have a car and our home, and I think we'll be okay. Don't you?" Samantha, dividing her attention between the fireplace and her daughter, began loading the grate with logs for the evening fire. Karla silently stared at her feet for a moment, then reached for Samantha's hand and said, "Mommy, I know Daddy's dead."

Samantha, confused, didn't comment. She was wondering just how we'll a ten-year-old child could deal with the challenges of growing up without a father, especially if Samantha went to work. And, she knew she herself would be greatly challenged if she tried to step from her past and assume the identity of Cheryl Cooper. "No," she finally said. "Your father isn't dead. He's just on a long trip."

"No, he isn't," mumbled Karla. "Daddy went to a war place."

Samantha chose to change the subject. "We'll see about that. Anyway, did you tell the boy who offered to take you fishing what your name was?"

"Uh-huh, and I told him I was twelve. Why did Daddy...?"

"You shouldn't have told Sonny that you were twelve," interrupted Samantha.

"I did cause...Cause he told me he was fifteen."

"That's not a good reason, but maybe we're going to have to tell some fibs from time to time. After we get back from our trip to Texas though, we'll decide just what. Now, I don't want you to worry about your father. He must have wanted to go on a trip, so maybe he's glad he did. Maybe he'll have fun, but let's not think about it right now. Okay?"

Karla nodded, unable to understand and beginning to wonder if danger actually awaited her and her mother. "Okay, but I'm scared,

Mommy," her tone a plea. "Don't be mad at me, but I wanna sleep with you tonight. Can I?"

Samantha agreed, then went into the kitchen. The little girl followed closely, appearing unwilling to get too far away. Seeing this apprehension, Samantha got Karla involved in the evening chores, having her open and heat a can of soup, pour the milk, get out the spoons, bowls and crackers. Samantha busied herself in the utility room, loading the washer with soiled clothes, folding clean towels. After eating and clearing the table, she and Karla dressed for bed and lay down in the little girl's room.

Samantha read from an old outdated National Geographic until her daughter fell asleep, then checked the time, ten minutes until twelve. Karla's big round white-faced clock was sitting by her bed on the nightstand. It ticked off the seconds like a jackhammer. Samantha hated the clock but was all too aware that it was her daughter's friend. She put it on the floor, put her pillow on top of it and tried to sleep on her stomach, her cheek flat against the sheet. But, her mind was troubled. If Jay and Ada, and the little sad guy, Jack Cox, believed she was Ken's sister, would everyone in Lost Mountain Park? Were there possibilities there? Would the past be washed away, quicker if Samantha assumed a new identity? Could it be done. Samantha would have to rely on her ten-year-old daughter to successfully pull it off.

Samantha forced herself to shelf that idea. She needed sleep, but there was so much yet unresolved that her mind just wouldn't take a break, it wasn't the old memories resurfacing; it was an all-new fear of failure trying to blitz her every shred of confidence. You just can't think about it right now, thought Samantha, scolding herself, then immediately started counting backwards from a thousand.

Counting didn't help, nor did holding her breath while counting. Nor did the muffled ticking of the big clock. That was getting intolerable, like the shooting pain of a headache. And, the popping coals in the fireplace were beginning to sound like dueling pistols.

Samantha gave up at 5:20 am, moaned into the kitchen and splashed her face with cold water, the sting of a thousand needles. She started her coffee, then went to her bedroom dresser and slipped on jeans and a loose jersey. After pulling Karla's bedroom door closed, she turned the kitchen light on, then slipped outside. Darkness yet covered the park, quiet as a prayer, excluding the sound of rippling water slapping against the braces of the pier. Samantha's breath was like gray smoke, the chill of the damp air like a slap in the face. She breathed in deeply and looked around, feeling the ever-present uneasiness she'd experienced the moment she entered the park. Out on the lake a thin mist, gray in the predawn dimness, hovered above the water, its ghostlike tentacles reaching for the shore. To her right, just below the snow line of one of the tall peaks, were two flickering fires. They looked close enough to hit with a stone. Samantha rubbed her eyes, blinked and rubbed them again to better focus. "That's very weird," she whispered, the sheer size of the big peaks making her feel strangely helpless, but the fires suddenly a mystery more chilling than the damp air. "Bizarre. This is a bizarre place. Why would anyone even be up on those peaks? I don't know if I want to know what's going on, but Lost Mountain Park is strange and just might be dangerous."

Samantha went to her station wagon and searched through the back until she found the little fireproof strongbox she'd stuffed between the spare tire and the firewall that day down in Houston. Once back inside, sitting at the table, she went through the contents again, finding Cheryl Cooper's and her daughter's birth certificates and social security cards. After a moment of thought, she hid the birth certificates and social security cards in her bedroom dresser, then took the strongbox back out to her station wagon, placing it where it had rested all those years. "You have plenty of time to think about this," she mumbled, attempting to calm herself, resisting a quick look toward the big peaks.

Samantha was brave to the point of being careless when she was at least a little familiar with her environment and had a predetermined course to follow. Dealing with the unknown, though, kept her on edge and caused the anxiety that kept her awake last night. She hated it. It changed her, made her inefficient, ineffective at even the redundant. "I just can't," she mumbled, aloud, then in thought, I'm always afraid of something and I can't live with that, forever carrying that burden. Samantha had never found a way to combat the fears born from her past, but tonight with so much yet to do and not knowing what to do, she was exhausted and weakened.

As she stepped up onto the cement slab porch, spasmodically, Samantha's whole being flinched, a warning of an unknown presence, stoking the fear she had admitted to only a moment ago. Her heart suddenly began to thud within her chest cavity, her breath coming like having to be drawn through a heavy blanket. Slowly, with a movement that should only be perceptible to the most astute observer, she turned around, reached behind her and felt for the doorknob, then stood perfectly still, utterly immobilized by her fear, listening, staring unblinkingly, her eyes, with only the slightest movement, scanning her immediate surroundings. The predawn air was cold and thick and although there was no light to suffuse the darkness, it seemed to have all the properties of smoke rising from a flame, or vapor above a boiling kettle, the exhalations of a swamp. Samantha squinted, looking for evil eyes staring back at her through the stirring miasma. She couldn't see the evil, but there were sounds, the beat of her own heart and that of something else. Samantha could feel it, its closeness, could imagine the flare of nostrils and the whisper of the air being sucked into them as a living thing readied itself to attack.

She would be helpless against anyone with a knife or a gun, even more helpless if she allowed herself to consider how alone she was. Holding her breath against the rising adrenaline rush, Samantha rolled the knob and put her weight against the door. Then, she saw it, beyond the store, almost to the turn that would lead through the forest and back to town. An instant red glow. Did someone tap a brake pedal?

There was a long weary moment before Samantha's fear began to give way to utter exhaustion, her heartbeat slowly becoming inaudible, then suddenly there was nothing, no more sounds of something waiting and watching, approaching, stalking her. It even seemed the predawn darkness was melting away. "Well," she sighed, then whispered to herself. "How about it? Can you walk and talk? Do you think you're safe now?"

Samantha leaned against the front door for several minutes, her thoughts a hopeless maze. She was making her life a living hell and had to find a way to rid herself of the constant fear she felt and purge her mind of those torturing old memories. She hated the park, where she believed something bad could happen at anytime. What could she do about it? Nothing. What good would it do to worry about anything she could do nothing about? Samantha released the doorknob, crossed her arms and looked to the heavens, surreal and pulsating like some primitive life form. A massive living thing that Uncle Hiram had said held the answers to everything she did not understand. "God, please help me," whispered Samantha, closing her eyes. "I so need Your help. I know it says in The Book of Mark that he who believeth and is baptized shall be saved. Oh Lord my God, I am baptized, and I believe that You are the power of all that is. Please save me. Please help me to be strong and brave for my daughter and bless hers and Uncle Hiram's and Aunt May's souls and..."

"Are you all right over there, Ma'am?" came the voice of a dark figure stepping from the shadows beyond the cabin by the walkway to the pier. Samantha gasped, her knees buckling. "Oh," she moaned, too scared and weak to scream. "Please don't...Who's there? What do you want?"

"Want? Nothing at all, Ma'am. It's Sonny." The boy stepped closer, his big boots flapping against the damp grass.

"Sonny?" sighed Samantha. "Wh, what's that?"

The boy was carrying a huge metal tube. His face was blackened with something that looked greasy. "Oh, it's just a water pipe. I saw something around your cabin like a dog or somthin. You were out at your car, so I was gonna knock him in the head if he did anythang."

"Crawling around the cabin? Why?" asked Samantha, suddenly remembering that the little man in the store was trying to say he had seen someone crawling around.

Sonny shook his head. "Don't know. Don't know why I scered him neither. He had a little pistol, but he uped and ran off," explained Sonny, pointing toward the store. "He ran thataway."

"Well, thank you, Hon," sighed Samantha. She hated to even have to consider that there could be any truth to Sonny's story, but that's what Jack Cox was trying to tell her at the store when Mr. Douglas yelled at him. Ken had that little pistol, but like Colonel Bishop said, most men own a gun. "Why are you out so early, Sonny?" she asked, cocking her head in query.

"Goin to work. Guard duty today. Fact, I better hurry on. You okay?" "Well, I think I am," sighed Samantha. "Thank you again for being around this morning, Sonny."

"S'okay, Ma'am." As Sonny started for the road that led through the woods to the big peaks, Samantha suddenly shivered. Goose bumps crawled up her back and blanketed her arms. The chill of the damp morning air torturous now, but the awareness of her vulnerability was like a flashing sign. "Sonny," she called. "Come back. I've got something for you." Samantha turned and stepped inside.

Sonny walked back to the cement slab, leaned on the pipe like it was a cane until Samantha returned. "Take this and eat it on the way," she said, shouldering the cabin door open, then handing Sonny a plastic cup of black coffee and four chocolate chip cookies wrapped in a paper napkin.

"Gosh, Mrs. Valentine," exclaimed Sonny, dropping the pipe, taking the coffee and blowing on its steaming surface. "Thank you. Thank You, Ma'am," he added, holding a dirty hand out for the wrapped cookies. "I'm shore hungry."

Samantha felt a pang of pity for the ragtag young man. "Sit down here on the porch, Hon. Eat your cookies and I'll get us some more."

Samantha went back inside, brought out the sack of cookies, the coffeepot, a cup for herself and sat down by Sonny. "I'm hungry, too," she lied, pouring herself a cup of coffee. "Help yourself. I know there's at least one more sack of these cookies in my cabinet."

Several silent seconds passed before either spoke, then Samantha refilled Sonny's coffee and asked, "Why do you always wear those irrigation boots? Why does everybody?"

Sonny, trying to show his manners, waited until he had swallowed the cookie he was eating, then said, "It rains a lot more up thar than down here and everbody cep Mr. Parker wears rubber boots. He says they make his feet stink."

"Up there?" Sonny nodded and proceeded with the cookies. "What goes on up there?" asked Samantha.

"Not much anymore. The members is all gettin mad."

"Why is that?" Sonny dipped a cookie into his coffee, took a bite and spoke as he chewed. "I don't know xactly," he said, his concentration on the cookie. "Me'n Mr. Cox just guard the gate. We've seen some of the members run off though. One morning a Meskin tole me not to be surprised if everbody leaves."

"Leaves and goes where? To their homes?"

"I guess." Samantha thought for a second, then asked. "Sonny, do your parents live around here?"

"Dead." Sonny held up the cookie sack. "Can I take the rest of these?"

"Sure, Hon. Would you like to take a little glass of milk, too?" "Can I? They's nuthin like that up at the camp. Not much to eat no more neither. Members gripe about it all day."

Samantha brought out an unopened quart of milk, but sat back down and held it in her lap. "Where do you live, Sonny? Sleep and eat, I mean."

"Around. Mr. Parker's place sometimes, but mostly I sleep on Mr. Douglas' couch. I stayed in your shed with that big guy, Mr. Begay, twice before you moved here. He's nice. Even let me take his motorcycle fer a spin. I want one like that someday. Say I was to get me a job somewhere."

"I'm sure you could get a job if you wanted to, Sonny."

"Yeah." Sonny finished his coffee. "I'll get me a job someday."

The boy was making Samantha sad. She changed the subject. "So, Mr. Douglas and Jack Cox live together?"

"Uh-huh. Jack don't have no house of his own, but Mr. Douglas lets him stay at his cabin." Sonny paused for thought, rolling the top of the cookie sack closed. "Maybe Jack stays there cause it ain't Mr. Douglas' cabin neither."

"Oh? Whose cabin is it?" "Mr. and Mrs. Mennafee. They live in Arizona, but they don't like to come to the mountains no more. Ole Jay and Ada Redwine owns all the cabins cept four and wants to buy theirs, but Mr. Douglas won't let'em."

Samantha handed Sonny the milk. "Here, Hon." Hearing that BB Douglas was strong-arming someone wasn't a surprise. She suspected he did much worse. "Well, if I was in Mr. Redwine's position, I'd just report BB Douglas to the police. Anyway, I hope you'll let me fix you a big breakfast some morning," she said, sincerely, but hoping the show of appreciation would earn her one more answer. "Why do the Mennafees not want to come to the mountains anymore? They must have once."

"Mr. Parker and Jack says they got mad at Mr. Douglas, but he says they's just too old."

Chapter 9

"A week, I guess. Yeah, seven nights will do," decided Ken Valentine, unable to blow any more money in the Santa Fe hotels and bars. He was down to two hundred and fifty dollars, but then there was the bronze. Besides, Samantha had...Shit. Over sixty thousand dollars. The bitch!

"All right, Sir. That'll be one-forty. Cash would be appreciated."

"No shit, Sherlock. Half goes in your pocket, right?"

Paul Baldwin was the night clerk at the Pueblo Heights Motel in Santa Cruz, wedged between the high mountain ranges of Northern New Mexico. He was a longhair, new-wave hippie now, a beady-eyed shrimp who hobbled along on a cane, the result of a self-inflicted bullet wound in the left foot that got him off the front line and home from Korea. He couldn't be insulted. The chances of that had passed long ago. The jerks in the Veterans Hospital in Phoenix had worn out about every possibility before he got his discharge. This fuckin wise-ass pretty boy didn't have a prayer. "My pocket? Not necessarily," sneered Paul, his beady eyes peeking over half-rimmed reading glasses. "I might just stick it all up my ass. Less you wanna try."

Ken, unsmiling and not amused at Paul's insolence, reached into his pocket and painfully peeled seven twenty-dollar bills from the dwindling wad he'd carried since out-processing through finance at Fort Dix. "Here you are," he said, holding the money just out of Paul's reach.

If Ken knew more about the creepy little night clerk, he might even like him. They would identify and easily establish a reasonable rapport, but Ken's dislike for the little man was immediate. An opinion based on the runt's hideous appearance and the fact that he'd ignored Ken for five minutes while whispering on the phone. The motel's office was cold as a mountain stream. Paul had on a big coat and kept a foot resting on a buzzing space heater. Ken had just stood at the counter shivering and resenting the little guy. In fact, Paul could be useful to Ken, too. He could take him into the mountains and introduce him to BB Douglas and Chief for one, but most important, he could advise Ken to stay away from the big blonde biker named Chad. The guy was DOJ, part of a task force the Department of Justice in DC had established just to go after stateside subversives, government dissenters, traitors, skips, draft dodgers and any military personnel who had gone AWOL. Crimes against the US Government. But, Chad Begay was a dead duck. BB Douglas was in Special Forces and jump school with big Chad, knew he went into intelligence and had kept up with him through a National Guard Commander in Phoenix, too. Of course, BB told Chief, who immediately informed the entire army of Freedom Fighters to be expecting Chad Begay. "It is in the interest of our movement to capture this particular man," had said Chief, at a meeting six months ago. BB Douglas was always on his haunches at Chief's left side in front of Colonel Dan, who usually stood back and clowned for the troops. Paul liked Colonel Dan and the troops loved him. He was just a happy ass who never quit trying to get a laugh. Of late, he was the only one at the top who the members could stand. Most of the members felt they had been fleeced and weren't going to be any better off than if they would have just gone into some branch of the armed forces.

"Listen up, Gentlemen," continued Chief. "Mr. Begay's execution will be a violent one for sure. It may serve to make a statement for our cause, and it may not. It may only accelerate the inevitable clash of US Government agencies and the Freedom Fighters. We must work, Gentlemen. It's possible that we will be defending this fortress against every method of attack available to these agencies. Mr. Douglas and I want the guard towers and this headquarters area completed by mid-April."

While Chief was rattling on, the troops were watching Colonel Dan, who was standing back and going through a bunch of gyrations like he was shooting at something. "Headquarters cave will be our last line of defense," continued Chief. "I assure you though, never will we surrender to an illegal government. We will stand." Chief paused, tilted his head back and focused on the ceiling of the command room. After a minute or two, he put his hands above his head. "God Almighty," he prayed. "Look down upon Your flock. Your army of Freedom Fighters for the People will stand. From Your teachings through the prophet Luke, I repeat, *Then let them which are in Judea flea to the mountains.* We have, Lord, and it is here that Your army will stand in Your name. Give us the strength of Thy will and let it fill the very veins of these humble bodies who serve You. We will stand. We will serve. Amen."

Paul was actually beginning to believe that the members of the Freedom Fighters considered Chief full of shit. They didn't even bow their heads when he prayed anymore and usually whistled and clapped when he finally shut up, their disrespect meant as a challenge.

It was worse at the last meeting, which Paul would never forget. Before Chief was even finished, Gunner interrupted him. "Hey, Man," he shouted, stepping forward from a group of members who were leaning against the left wall of the big cave. "What the hell are you guys ever gonna do about food around here. Nobody has had a..."

"Shut-up, Gunner," yelled BB Douglas, jumping to his feet. Chief waved a hand again and the kid named Gunner laughed, but leaned back against the wall, mumbling to those near him. "Gentlemen," addressed BB Douglas, stepping forward. He had a little boy smile and spoke with quiet assurance in his tone, unusual for him. Paul knew that he and Chief didn't have the blind loyalty they wanted and wouldn't get it from the losers they'd let join the army. "We'll make our stand all right, but I'll order a retreat before I'll let overwhelming odds take us out," continued BB Douglas. "I know you men can survive in the caves, the ravines and clefts above and along the river in these surrounding mountain woods. Hell, they stretch up through the San Juan National Forest, through Rio Grande National Forest, up the Sangre De Cristo Range, through San Isabel National Forest and into Beaver Basin which leads to Taylor Park, my homefuckintown in the shadows of Mount Harvard Peak, fourteen thousand feet high."

Paul remembered that the troops perked a little, began to listen. BB had paused to take a deep breath and wipe the sweat from his forehead. A big blaze at the entrance was making the cave too warm, but BB Douglas had always seemed to love speaking in front of a group.

He could get really charged up, but normally left that part for Chief, who liked to do it, then end with a touch of reverence. Paul knew that was bullshit. He had noticed that Chief knew a line or two from Bible scriptures, but just a few, and he misinterpreted those, plus had worn them out. In truth, Paul was disenchanted with the militia. He felt that the little son-of-a-bitchin Indian and the bitter cocksuckin ex-army shit eatin sergeant were no less hypocritical than a sleaze bag lawyer arguing the defense of a serial killer. They were either pure criminal or pure stupid or both in his book.

"You men listen to me now," droned on BB Douglas. "If, which Chief and I doubt, but if the time comes for us to retreat, I'll lead the way. It'll be the biggest and best adventure of your lives. We'll hit and run, rape and pillage, then hit and run again. We'll strike every little town and every farmhouse and eat like kings all the way to Mount Harvard." BB paused. Some of the members were laughing. Colonel Dan had been snapping to attention and making his eyes big at every point BB made, mouthing, *Not yours truly. Not me. Screw you Pal.* BB felt his words were exciting the laughing members and went on in a louder pitch. "There's the biggest, deepest granite cave in the whole fuckin world on the north side of Mount Harvard. It's a thousand one hundred and thirty-six feet through a mine shaft to the cave, a huge opening half as big as Santa Fe. That shaft was started in 1918 and completed in 1924. It was dug by two hundred coal miners from West Virginia who were imported just for that purpose. The miners were lookin for gold and found some, but it ain't all they found. They discovered the biggest, deepest, purest underground lake that man has ever laid eyes on. I know, Men. I've been down there. I shit you not, there's still gold in the bowels of that big mountain, but do you know why the mine work was abandoned? Hell yeah, ever damn one of ya do. Rumor. The fuckin US govment started this here rumor that ever swingin dick in the world could get rich if they's to mine uranium in Utah. Do you know what happened as soon as the bomb was dropped on the Japs? Sure as hell ya do. The rumor was history and half the West Virginia miners were dead from radiation exposure. Those that wudn't looked like lepers with frog faces. Better'n half, I hear tell it, blowed their ugly heads off with dynamite caps soon as they saw themselves in a mirror."

Yeah, Ken Valentine could definitely benefit from an acquaintance with Paul Baldwin, but he might have to wait for that. "I'll just watch you stuff the money up your ass, Hot Shot," said the wise-ass.

The little night clerk snatched the twenties from Ken's hand with the quickness of a striking snake. "Your room's number seven, Motherfucker," he said, raising his cane as if to actually strike a blow.

Ken backed out of the motel office with his travel bag in his left hand and the middle finger of his right extended upward. "You little runt. I could crack your head like a walnut with the heel of my shoe. In fact, I'll let you know if I'm going to bother in the morning. Just in case you have someone who'd care to bury you, although I doubt anything but a starving junkyard dog would give a shit."

Ken's orders were to report to Travis Air Force Base in Oakland, California. He only had eleven more days of leave, less than two weeks to decide. But, he couldn't make a decision yet. When he first met Chip Parker and BB Douglas and attended an organizational meeting to test the interest in forming a camp where military objectors could stay and live without the constant threat of the US Government, Ken had gotten some interesting ideas. Although it seemed a rip-off at the time, the underlying theory was sound and a lot of money could be made. Ken had to find out if the group was ever formed and see if he wanted to join before he did anything so stupid as go to Vietnam. Maybe he could offer the Remington bronze as his tuition. Hell, if BB and Chip were worth their salt, they could strong-arm some art dealer in Santa Fe and get the tuition out of that. Plus, Ken had a law degree and experience as a military officer. That alone should qualify him for a role at the top of any loosely put together organization of ne'er-do-wells.

Paul Baldwin next encountered the pretty-boy the morning following his check-in at the motel. It was almost noon and both had just gotten up and out for the first time that day. Ken, standing at the open trunk lid of his canary yellow convertible, was tracing his finger from right to left on a road map. Paul, not using his walking cane, peg-legged from a vending machine by the motel's office door over to the new convertible and stood with both hands resting on the dusty hood. "Feeling any better this morning, Sir?" he asked, smiling, his tone friendly. "Sure a nice car."

Ken looked up from the map and smiled himself. "Thanks, and yes I am feeling better. How about yourself?"

"Not so good really. My ass is killin me and I still can't get them twenties out," explained Paul, very seriously, squirming a little as he spoke. "Hey, I'm sorry I was so darn mean last night. I was tired. What's your name? I'll buy breakfast if you'd like to come along."

"Paul Baldwin," said the little man, peg-legging around to the passenger's door. "Where you from, Mr. Valentine?"

Breakfast was from a limited menu at a Mexican bar, Cantina Clavado, as there wasn't an eating establishment in Santa Cruz yet serving breakfast at the time Ken and Paul left the motel, plus the cantina was owned by the owners of Pueblo Heights Motel. Paul nibbled on chips and salsa, drank draft beer and talked while Ken ate French fries, drank bottled beer and listened. He was amazed. The little night clerk, though cautious, knowing BB Douglas' consequences for a fuck-up, was trying to recruit him into the Freedom Fighters for the People. Ken, though lying, had merely told Paul that he had a cabin at Lost Mountain Park, then all he could do from there was listen to the little peg leg's pitch. "Absolutely amazing," said Ken, laughing through the word amazing, then proceeding to tell Paul what was so amazing.

The peg leg didn't think so. "Not really," he said. "I've recruited sixty-three people from right here in Santa Cruz. I just do an interview or two and make up my mind if they're a candidate. Hell, I need the money. I got dependents and I get ten percent of everything I bring in. Chief and BB are plenty weird, but they pay cause they need the ninety percent. What'd they hit you for, Ken?"

Ken shrugged and wiped catsup from his mouth. "Nothing was that clear to me, Paul. I'm an attorney and a few of the proposed members wanted me involved even if I didn't have to pay any tuition," he contrived.

"Riders, they're called. Like on a scholarship. Riders get a free ride as long as they make the grade. I can't say positive, but I don't think there's been a rider let in since that retired National Guard commander from Phoenix."

"Hmmm. Why was he let in?" asked Ken, calculating.

"Don't take this wrong, Ken, but I'd sure feel more comfortable if you'd show me some ID or something. You have to understand that..."

"Doesn't bother me in the least, Paul. Honest," assured Ken. "I've got my orders in the car if you wanna see them. I'm an army attorney. An 0-3 on indefinite status. I got swept off to Vietnam by a major and a no-good colonel because they believed my wife instead of me. I'm sure you can understand that. A woman screams and a man hangs. Fits like a glove."

"Yeah, I guess so, but..."

"Stay put," interrupted Ken, then wiped his hands with a napkin and went out to the convertible to get a set of his orders. "Read'em and weep. I did," he said, rejoining Paul.

Paul read Ken's orders, looking for duty assignment and dates mostly, but verifying that he was in fact a captain with a JAG MOS and was on indefinite status, RA, regular army instead of US, a draftee doing the last few months of his tour. Many young officers, Paul had witnessed, with at least a few years' time in grade, were easily lured into federal service by the aspects of early retirement, some as close as fifteen years from a paycheck for life. Ken Valentine though, had nineteen months to go, Vietnam most of that, which meant his chances of seeing military retirement above ground were slim at best.

"So," said Paul, sliding Ken's orders across the table. "If BB and Chief won't let you in the militia without paying a tuition of some amount, are you still interested in joining?"

"I can handle it, but tell me how the guard commander got in without paying. Did he have something besides money?"

"The guy's a stone-cold nut, but he had a lot to offer," said Paul.

"Tell me, Paul. I already know enough to bring heat down on BB and Chief, too, if I was going to do that. How did the guard commander get in without a tuition? A rider, as you say."

"Okay, but just hold it down," agreed Paul, chewing on the end of his reading glasses, his bad leg nervously tapping the floor, his eyes squinting and his tone soft as a bedtime lullaby. "It began after the unit he commanded in Phoenix set their summer arms training and bivouac schedule two years ago. He goes by Colonel Dan, but his real name is Daniel Newel, an old buddy of BB Douglas'. They made some juicy arrangements for the militia. Colonel Dan was supposed to have a bunch of M-14's and live rounds convoyed to a training area three days before the weekend warriors who had to qualify and get rated with an M-14 were scheduled to arrive. It's a gunnery range and bivouac site in the Prescott National Forest. Colonel Dan agreed, then BB decided that he wanted more. You see, Colonel Dan got himself mixed up in a little deal with BB and his wife in about fifty-three. It started like this, Colonel Dan and BB used to live in Utah. They were real good pals. Back before they joined the army, they met this girl named Delores who worked at a branch of The Zion Bank in Provo. It was a setup. BB even married her, then came up with a plan. A hit. Sorta like an inside job on that bank where this Delores worked. Well, they hit it. Hit her, too, and got off with four hundred of the bank's big ones. All cash. Delores wasn't killed, but she took the fall. She's still doing the last nickel of a twenty, probably afraid to get out."

"Wow. What a scene," sighed Ken. "That Dan and BB Douglas are bad boys. Whatever happened to the M-14's and that arrangement and what was the extra part Colonel Dan threw in for BB?"

"Everything connects, Comrade," whispered Paul. "See, BB had been pressuring Dan for years. Hell, he was scared shitless that Delores would eventually break and put the finger on them. BB is such a liar that I would have never believed him about that bank heist, but Chip Parker told me that he bought his folks a bunch of grazing land and two hundred head of cattle with the biggest part of his cut. The land's in Colorado west of Mount Harvard just like he brags it is. The extra deal was the colonel's way of buying a truce between him and BB, but things didn't go as planned and he had to ask for more. When the rifles and ammo got to the gunnery range, six troops were posted to act as dummy guards and baby-sitters until the whole unit arrived three days later. They weren't supposed to be armed with live rounds, but there were boxes and boxes of it in the convoy vehicles. So, when BB, Chief and eleven doped up loyalists showed up to make the heist, they were met with heavy resistance. The dummy guards were locked and loaded and, well, Chief and BB don'ts take no prisoners, so there was shooting and five dead Army soldiers were the result."

"Wow, Man! How many National Guard were there?" exclaimed Ken.

"Just six. Five dead and one who was wounded badly, but not so bad that he didn't overhear BB and Colonel Dan arguing. Mostly he heard Colonel Dan screaming and crying about the fact that there wasn't supposed to be a single round fired. The guard guy took some hits and fell into a pond or something. I don't know, but I do know that he just laid there and listened and watched this argument between Colonel Dan and BB."

"So, the wounded soldier knew the commander was involved."

"Exactly. He watched as BB, Chief and the loyalists left in five of the convoy vehicles and Colonel Dan in the jeep he'd come in. A long time later, long enough for the convoy vehicles to be to hell and gone, the colonel came roaring back to the campsite with a bunch of squad cars right on his tail. It was the middle of the night by then. The wounded soldier was sitting in some other vehicle that was there, dressing his wounds probably, but when the troopers came to help him, he spilled his guts. I'm guessing, but knowing what I do about Colonel Dan, he must have downed his way into getting out of there. Says he claimed he'd been knocked out. Laid on the road for six hours, but the soldier threw shit on that, so the colonel goes wild and says the wounded guy was a nut case and probably set up the hit. Claims the guard guy is half delirious all the time and is always seeing things. Like aliens and ghosts and spirits and spooks of every kind. The state troopers didn't know who to believe, so off to the hospital goes the wounded man and back to Phoenix goes Colonel Dan, however temporary that might have been. Regardless, it makes no never mind yet, because Colonel Dan showed up in Lost Mountain Park in a one ton truck loaded with what he thought he had to have. BB Douglas took the one ton and let the colonel join the militia. I'd bet a six pack that Colonel Dan hasn't been off Maiden Peaks since he showed up."

"Gees," gulped Ken. "What an outfit. Multiple murders, theft of government property, harboring fugitives of justice, armed robbery. What the hell else? How does BB, Chief and their lieutenants keep all the members together? Just keep promising to keep'em out of trouble or what?"

"Truth is, they're not right now. Members sneak off every night. Probably a hundred dead already. They head off the mountain with no food and no brains and starve, or freeze, or get killed and eaten by something. Militia's had money, but BB and Chief didn't spend much for food and stuff. They rat holed it for themselves. They tried to keep all the members content with dope. Weed and acid and promises, too. Like Ho Chi Minh keeps the Viet Cong loyal with opium and big hopes for all they ever want. The whole member body of the Freedom Fighters is just a bunch of fucked up kids who was in trouble fore they ever got drafted, or thought they might be." Paul paused, seeming to be in thought for several seconds before continuing. "For about a month now," he began. "I've been hearing rumors about a rebellion. Members are tired and hungry. They're not getting fed and they're tired of BB and Chief's promises. Any leader of men had better know he has to feed'em and keep'em busy, but that hasn't been happening in the militia lately."

"Where did they get the dope?" asked Ken, his interest waning. It appeared too late for a man to benefit from the Freedom Fighters.

"I think the acid was always a problem, but there's a group in Santa Fe that can get all the weed they want. Big bucks for everybody but BB and his loyalists, but like I said, they ain't buyin nuthin."

"Got the dope with strong arm stuff. What else?" Ken was searching.

"If all that's not enough, that extra deal the colonel arranged should pretty well fill your plate, Ken. You see, the Phoenix National Guard Armory installation was the commissary for all the Arizona Guard units, the staging area for their weaponry, equipment and initial payroll-processing center. That's been changed I understand, maybe just because of Colonel Dan. Two of the six trucks were loaded to the gills with extra M-14's, crates of rounds, artillery pieces, bazookas, mortars, M-60 machine guns and box after box of rations and everything else that's provided to soldiers in Armory units."

"What happened to the convoy vehicles?" cut in Ken. "They were parked in that big Quonset hut at the entrance of Lost Mountain Park when I saw them, but they're in the caves on Maiden Peak now."

Chapter 10

Carol Ann and Howard Lane left what furniture they owned on consignment with a secondhand dealer in Trenton, New Jersey, then shipped only the clothes and personal effects that couldn't be loaded into the Tempest to Dallas. They moved into the house Carol Ann's mother had left them, taking separate upstairs bedrooms. Now, since the little modification, Howard was in complete agreement with the terms of the uncontested no-fault divorce his wife had proposed, which was basically sell everything and split the proceeds regardless of how anything was acquired. However, the verbal agreement had been softened, modified just a little. Howard's input. If his plans were more immediate than Carol Ann's, she had agreed to let him take $75,000.00 of the $100,000.00 CD that was hers. She would await the sale of the house for the balance she was entitled to and get any overage. He was in full agreement and had already cashed both CDs and deposited the proceeds into their checking account. The old home, a three-bedroom, split-level brick, was in good repair and fully furnished. Some of the furnishings in the den and dining room were valuable antiques. A big round oak table, eight matching ladder back chairs and a hutch full of priceless china were known to be near a century old. In the den, being used as a coffee table, sat Carol Ann's grandmother's old English cedar chest. Pushed up to the home's biggest picture window, stood a cherry wood desk and a coat rack that were once in her grandfather's office when he was a federal judge. However, in the spirit of fairness, nothing was to be kept by either Carol Ann or Howard, except the old Buick if he wanted it. He'd been leaving it down at Kiest Park off and on for over a week with a *For Sale* sign in the back window. An even thousand dollars he wanted, because that's what Carol Ann said he'd have to pay if he kept it.

However, today Howard had suggested that he and Carol Ann go to a few automobile agencies over in Garland where she could trade her Tempest in on a new full size Chevrolet four-door, if she found one she wanted. He had been considering trading the Buick in on a new impala two door hardtop for himself and Samantha. "Look," he said, changing his mind just before noon, "I know it was my idea, but maybe we should just keep the cars until we get everything settled. Old Grady Johnson offered me six hundred for the Buick, but I know it's worth more than that. Besides, I don't feel right spending money when I don't even have a job. Maybe I should go put in an application at Dallas Baptist College this afternoon. It's close and if they have Army ROTC, I can teach. Hell, I know I could be a career counselor."

"Well, it doesn't matter to me," stated Carol Ann. "I'm satisfied with my car, but we have the money to buy new ones if we want. Isn't that partly why you cashed the CD's?" she asked.

"Yes, but..."

"Who cares?" interrupted Carol Ann, neither caring for an explanation nor wanting to get into a debate. "Anyway, have you decided where you and Samantha will live? You should think about that before you go job hunting." Howard shrugged as if he didn't know where he planned to live, an unnecessary lie, one of habit. Carol Ann no longer concerned herself with his interest in Samantha Valentine, or his rationale. "Well, Carol Ann, I guess I should try to find a place in Arlington or Grand Prairie," he lied.

Samantha and her daughter were due at Love Field at five-forty and Howard had already rented an unfurnished three-bedroom duplex in East Dallas for them. Between his and Carol Ann's and the apartment manager's, Howard accumulated enough furniture for them to get by on until Samantha's household goods arrived. The bedroom, he assumed would always be the spare, became a full-blown project for him to try and make into a home studio. He equipped the room with its own separate lock and a special lighting system, featuring six spotlights and ten forty-eight-inch florescent tubes controlled by rheostats. He bought three small tables on casters from a restaurant supply house for Samantha to use as workbenches, easily moveable from workstation to workstation. In each of the four corners of the room stood a big plywood tripod to hold canvasses that Howard had picked up from an art supplies distributor. He bought five big painter's drop cloths to cover unfinished work and found a rack at a junkyard, one originally designed to hold automobile windshields, to store finished work. He and Samantha hadn't discussed it, but Howard assumed her hopes were to find a gallery that would display her work.

"If you two are going to live on this side of the metro, you should consider using your part of the CDs to buy this house," suggested Carol Ann. "Do what you want, but let me know," she sighed. "I'm going by the real estate agent's office today and talk to him about buying it. If I were you, I'd take that *For Sale* sign out of the window and drive the Buick until I decided what I wanted to do."

Carol Ann left at one that afternoon. She felt that the real estate agent, Mr. Lincoln, who she and Howard had listed the house with, was the best candidate for a quick sale. Last week when he phoned about the appraisal, he had said that he was interested in making an offer to buy the home himself, complete with its furnishings. "My offer will only be around eighty percent of appraisal," he had said. "Just consider it an alternative. Sort of a standby if you and Howard are dealing with some time constraint. I own several rentals and I'm a cash buyer, Mrs. Lane. Plus, you won't pay a commission if I buy your home."

"Thank you, Mr. Lincoln," Carol Ann had said, then hung up the phone and quickly did the math in her head. "Eighty percent of one hundred and twenty-five thousand is what? A hundred thousand? Close enough."

Carol Ann had been so excited this week she had written Martin five times that she could remember. And now, being in the same house with a man she had developed an apathy for and over a thousand miles from the man she loved and missed desperately, had created just that very time constraint her real estate agent had baited her with. "When could we close, Mr. Lincoln?" she asked, walking into his office.

The agent, having grown used to the inevitable impatience homeowner's experienced when an offer was on the table, had written a contract on the Lane home. "Ten days," he said, handing a manila folder to Carol Ann. "You and Howard will net ninety-eight thousand, four hundred and sixty-six dollars after your share of prorated closing costs."

Carol Ann studied the sales agreement for a moment, then took an extra copy and left for downtown Dallas to see an attorney she'd called. The young man had told her to drop by his office anytime during business hours. If he wasn't there, he explained, his secretary would get her an instruction kit that would provide the information to put together a no contest self-help draft for the firm to finalize and file the divorce. She was a ball of nerves, completely exhausted and almost out of breath all the way downtown. By the time she found the right building, its parking area, the elevators and the correct suite, it was almost five in the afternoon and the young lawyer had gone home. Carol Ann was given the kit she had been promised, but was never asked her name nor introduced to either of the two young women she talked with. "You can just mail that in," she was told, just as she hurried back out to the elevators. Martin had promised to call at exactly six if he'd found a suitable rental.

In Santa Fe the previous Friday, Samantha and Karla had arrived at the driver's license division just minutes after nine in the morning. The little girl waited in the car while her mother went inside to get a New Mexico driver's license. She had Cheryl Cooper's social security card and birth certificate in her purse. "Good morning," she greeted, attempting to get the attendant's attention away from his morning newspaper.

"I agree," responded the attendant, his attention yet on the paper.

"Sir, what do I need to get a driver's license? I guess I lost mine during my recent move."

"No, Mexico license?" No eye contact.

"No, Sir. Texas, but I'd like to get a New Mexico license."

"Was your Texas license current?" Still no eye contact.

"I think so, but I can't really remember the expiration date.

The attendant, a tall thin young man with too much unkempt blonde hair, wore a dark blue parka, a denim shirt and wire rimmed glasses. He was sitting on a stool at a counter behind a half-wall. At another time in her life, when Samantha wasn't doing something she was unsure of, the man's manner, as he slowly folded his paper and slid it down the counter near an older man who was mopping what appeared to be the remains of a soft drink that had been spilled on the dusty linoleum floor, she would have considered him insolent. "Read that story about Deputy Knight on page three," he said to the older man. "That's one guy that didn't last long. Two federal dicks busted him for having marijuana in his patrol car. Forty-four keys."

"I saw the federal guys down at the plaza twice."

"What do you suppose old Knight was doing with that much marijuana?"

"Tune in, Gary. What's Knight do all the time?"

"How would I know and how do you know, Clyde?"

"Does anything go on in this berg that I don't know about? Your boy was sent home last Tuesday for smoking in class and Della's seeing the sheriff again and BB Douglas was down from the mountain yesterday, the bastard, and Hal bought Brady's horse trailer Monday a week ago and..."

"Okay, okay," said the man in charge, then turned to Samantha. "I'm so sorry," he said, getting to his feet as he removed his glasses, the reaction from being so close to beauty he could see from the waist up and vitality he could feel from the blush of his face to the tingle of his feet.

Samantha slept better last night than she had since arriving at Lost Mountain Park. Somehow, having had a prowler and escaping any harm had boosted her courage. Nothing had happened to evidence it, but she felt that Sonny, and maybe others, were watching out for her and Karla. Maybe, just maybe she was overcoming the fear that had haunted her for so long. Today though, she felt very uneasy with this first attempt as an impostor, but overall, she felt good and knew she looked good. Designer shades with black frames hid the brilliance of her blue eyes, but her cheeks were glowing with color and her slightly parted lips were shining with a clear gloss. Her rich auburn hair, set before she went to bed last night, fell to her shoulders, a big springy curl at each temple. Her outfit was one she had worn often when teaching the Bible class back at the base in New Jersey, a black open leather jacket over a long-sleeved olive blouse, black skirt hemmed at the knees, one that would flatter a figure even less appealing than her own. "No harm, Sir," she said, smiling, "I'm sure my problem won't be that difficult for you. It's just that I was a little shocked when I couldn't produce my driver's license the other day. I wasn't able to do something so simple as open a bank account. In truth, I guess I was more embarrassed than inconvenienced."

"We'll fix you up, Miss...?"

"Ms. Cooper. Ms. Cheryl Cooper. I'm one of the first Vietnam widows I think. Your name is..." Samantha paused to try and read the man's name tag.

"Gary Hardy, Ms. Cooper," interjected the attendant. "Do you have some form of ID with you? I can use about anything with your Texas address on it."

The attendant made a copy of Cheryl Cooper's birth certificate, then gave Samantha his card and advised her that, if all went well, she could return to the Department of Motor Vehicles in two hours and pick up her New Mexico driver's license. Samantha left the station wagon at DMV, took Karla and walked to the plaza where they ate fresh doughnuts and drank cups of hot chocolate that were being offered by a vender with a folding table and chairs set up on the sidewalk. The plaza was buzzing with muffled chatter. Indian artists and other street merchants were talking back and forth as they laid out stacks of blankets and baskets and rows of turquoise and silver jewelry. Their colorful paintings were standing against storefronts; pairs of moccasins and other wares were carelessly displayed on the sidewalks. There were similar displays being set up around a big statue in the center of the plaza.

"Hello, young lady," greeted a tall man, addressing Karla, as he slid out chairs for himself and his companion, obviously his son. "Mind if we join you and your sister?" added the man, winking.

"She's my Mommy," answered Karla. "My name is..."

"Please have seats, there's plenty of room," interrupted Samantha, hoping nothing more would be said.

The man took a chair, introduced his son, then himself. "This is Aaron," he said as the younger man joined him at the little table.

"Aaron Hall and I'm Lloyd, Aaron's old man. Are you a buyer?" he asked of Samantha.

The men, although there was a considerable age difference, did have similar features, but something else that seemed to compel Samantha to stare at them. Like Howard, they were both well over six feet tall, had blonde hair, but were built like marathon runners. The men looked enough alike, but there was more. Something in their underlying persona. Were they the federal men who arrested the local deputy? "Am I a buyer?" she finally responded. "Oh no. We're from Texas. I am an artist though, but I've never sold anything. I hope to someday."

"That's the spirit," responded Lloyd, his pale blue eyes scanning every inch of Samantha's face. "Let me give you a card," he said, then reached inside his jacket and produced his calling card, his eyes yet at work. "Now, don't you take this wrong, but I buy any kind of art," he lied. "Paintings and Indian jewelry mostly. I'll buy the finest Navajo work, or even this ragged junk you'll see right here today. I don't care if the price is right. My market isn't that tough, and it spreads from coast to coast. You call me when you're ready to show some of your work. I'd be a buyer if anyone would be. Right Aaron?"

The young man might have nodded, but Samantha caught very little change in his expression, one of disinterest. He spoke through a terse smile that was only a hint to acknowledge being addressed by his father, his deep blue eyes scanning the plaza. "In truth, neither me nor uh, my old man here have an eye for paintings, good or bad," responded the younger man, then turned to face Samantha. "However, Ma'am, jewelry and ancient artifacts are different matters entirely. Then again, it's rarely a concern. Mom gripes a little. You'd understand if you saw the house, but everything sells in time. You see, we use the market as judge and jury. We just show our wares and whatever sells, we go after more. It's that simple, but we seldom admit it."

"Well, thank you, Gentlemen," said Samantha, getting to her feet, averting eye contact with either man by focusing on Lloyd's calling card. "Don't be surprised if I call. I have a few pieces ready now. Maybe I'll have you test them sometime. It would be most encouraging to sell something. Come on, Honey." Samantha took her daughter's hand and turned away, watching from the corner of her eye as Lloyd got to his feet. "We have to hurry," she added, hustling the little girl along.

"Your name, Ma'am?" she heard Lloyd call.

"I certainly will," she said, pretending not to have heard the question.

"You horny bastard," mumbled the younger man. "Get you out of Washington and you try to hit on every good-looking leg we run across. Why do you? You just have to lie. And, those stupid calling cards. Gees, you're impersonating a legitimate civilian."

"Hell, I am legitimate and we ain't seen anything finer than that woman, Partner. Good looking don't describe her," said the older man. "By the way, that was nice fabricating. Maybe you ought to be an actor, Aaron, old boy."

"No thanks, and I won't see anything finer because I don't go around sniffing hemlines twenty-four hours a day. That just might interfere with my job, which reminds me, where the hell's Chad and Franco?"

"You know where they are."

"I do? Where's that?"

"Late," said Lloyd, finally taking his eyes off Samantha. "Chad and Franco are always late, but it never bothers me. Why do you always want to get back, Aaron? You're single and you can find broads anywhere just as well as in the bars around DC."

"Forget it. Chad and Franco are independent bastards, but I don't see how they get away with being late all the time. Four days counting today."

"I don't know about Franco, but Chad don't give a shit. He put in for retirement at the end of this year. Between his military duty and time with DOJ, he's got twenty-three years of government service. Word is, he bought a big motorcycle and plans to tour the world on it next year."

"Hell, Chad doesn't look forty," argued Aaron.

"I think he's thirty-nine. Joined the army when he was sixteen," said Lloyd, absently. "Whatever, he's sold his house and has everything he owns in storage. The man's just marking time. Can't say as I blame him."

"So, he is. What are we waiting for? Let's make the arrests and go home."

"Well, I could give you a dozen reasons," drawled Lloyd, trying to be less metropolitan. "What would be the charges?"

"At least five counts of murder in Arizona. And, where do you think Dan Newel is? You know damn well he's hiding in those mountains. How about theft and conversion of stolen property. Government property no less. Armed robbery in Utah. Possession of an illegal substance. Conspiracy to commit..."

"Whoa, Stud," interrupted the older man. "You're proving my point, don't you think? I can't tell you why, but that Delores Douglas is lying to cover for Dan Newel and BB Douglas. Her statement indicates that she fired the only shot because she was the only one armed. The old guard claimed he didn't see a thing. He's dead now. The bank president saw two big men carrying rifles, one with a blackened face and the other dressed like a clown. By all accounts, Dan Newel is a clown, but that don't prove nothing, so how could we get a judge to give us a warrant without some physical evidence. You know the trucks are long gone. I think you've just got a hard-on for Chief Ironsides and that BB Douglas."

"Yeah. I hate the bastards for causing me to have to come all the way to New Mexico," sighed Aaron, looking across the plaza for Chad or Franco, then toward the corner where the pretty brunette and her daughter had disappeared. "There's women everywhere all right and that was a classy looking one for sure," he said, conceding the last elements of the conversation to his older partner, as he always did. Lloyd was always right, and he was just as right about Delores Douglas. She lied. She was afraid to testify against BB Douglas and loved Dan Newel, always would and would always protect him.

Samantha Valentine led her daughter to the Merchant's Bank just off the plaza, which they had passed when walking from DMV. Inside, she left the little girl sitting in the lobby, then approached a customer who was standing in line awaiting a teller. "Excuse me," she said. "Do you know who I should see to open an account here?"

"Just walk over to Jim's desk and see him. Go right past that girl who's fooling with that vacuum cleaner," advised the customer.

"Sir," said Samantha, approaching an older gentleman who had watched her from the moment she walked into the bank. "I need to open a checking account. Well, savings too, then see if one in Dallas is still active, maybe get the balance at the same time. Can you help me with that?"

James Stockard, small in stature, was the bank's senior vice president, an accommodating man who worked with a fixed frown on his face and never said an idle word, asked applicable questions only. Samantha kept answering, kept smiling and kept asking Mr. Stocked for more service. He opened Merchant's Bank checking and savings accounts with Samantha's cashier's check from her bank in New Jersey, sixty thousand in savings and eight thousand in checking. Per her request, Mr. Stockard called a Mr. Benjamin Lewis Russell at the Republic National Bank in Dallas to verify that the savings account was yet active and confirmed the balance. Then, via wire transfer, deposited an additional five hundred dollars and converted the account to checking instead of savings. Mr. Russell, the officer at the Republic National Bank requested that Mr. Stockard verify Samantha's identification and have her sign two signature cards which he wanted sent directly to him as early as possible.

"Anything else, Mrs. Valentine?" asked Mr. Stockard, emotionless.

"No, Sir. That's it for now. Thank you very much," she said, with a wink and a smile. "I hope to be doing business all over New Mexico and Texas quite soon."

"I'm sure."

By the time Samantha picked up her new driver's license, spent the required minute of appreciation with Gary Hartly and made the long drive back to Lost Mountain Park, the sun was sinking behind the big snowcapped peaks, and the breeze coming across the lake carried its nightly chill. She and Karla were hungry and exhausted, both wanting to do nothing but eat quickly and get to bed. However, that was impossible. The furniture had arrived and the movers had stacked it on the grass in front of the cabin. Their big yellow truck was out on the road, colored running lights aglow and its engine idling.

Samantha parked on the road herself, assuming she would need easy access to the shed where the furniture could be stored for the night. When she approached the moving van, she found the two drivers asleep on big, padded quilts in the back. Although far too rough and less than eager to do so, they quickly carried everything into the shed before they left.

Samantha wasted no time getting herself and her daughter fed and into bed that Friday. She could hardly wait to rid the cabin of Sybil's furniture and be able to use her own. The next day began with a loud knock on the door at six in the morning. It was Sonny, the longhaired kid with the big rubber boots, BB Douglas, and little frail Jack Cox looming behind, his presence an apology.

"Ada told us you got some furniture yesterday," said Sonny, when Samantha opened the door, hardly a hint of light in the early dawn hour.

"Figger you'd need help," added BB Douglas, the man with the hard features who Samantha felt was so rude.

On their own, while Samantha made coffee and Karla's breakfast, the men carried everything from the shed back to the grassy area in front of the cabin. They were leaning against her car waiting when she emerged, coffeepot and cups in hand. Jack Cox was eager to break for coffee, but BB and Sonny opted to walk over to the little store and get sodas for themselves. When they returned, Jay Redwine, the old storekeeper and Chip Parker, the grumpy jack of all trades, were following along.

The men worked together with strange efficiency, BB and Chip helping Samantha direct the effort. By midmorning, the cabin was to her liking, something she had not expected to go so smoothly. Besides moving Sybil's furniture out and Samantha's in, the men assembled the beds and put the mattress in place. Sonny was the only one to accept anything for his help, a five-dollar bill he seemed to need BB and Chip's okay to take.

Jay walked away without even giving Samantha a chance to thank him. BB Douglas, Jack Cox and Chip Parker seemed happy enough to get some of Sybil's finer things, the glass and brass tables and two of the leather chairs. Samantha kept the big sectional, three chairs and the bedroom set that was in Karla's room. Chip and BB hauled what they were given toward the other side of the lake using two trucks, a huge Dodge with four back tires, and what seemed to be BB's and Chip's flatbed Chevrolet, Sonny riding along to hold the glass tables steady.

"Well, that's that," said Jack Cox, surprising Samantha. He was on his haunches near the front of her station wagon. She hadn't noticed that he'd remained behind. "Nice to get that part over with but I have to do something with that shed."

"Don't need to be getting in a rush," sighed Jack. "Whatcha doin Monday night?" he asked. "Maybe Ada could keep your daughter if you'd like to get out."

"No, no," said Samantha, not wanting to believe Jack Cox was asking her out. "I don't date and I don't plan to for a long time. If that's what you had in mind."

"Well," he sighed, "I shouldn't be asking you without clearing it with Sarge and Chip first anyhow. Sorry."

Samantha felt a stab of fear, but was curious.

"Clearing what?"

"Uh, invitin you to the meetin," explained Jack, his eyes darting out toward the lake. "Your brother's a comin again."

"Oh, yes. He said something about that," fabricated Samantha. "What's this particular meeting about?"

"The same."

"Well, let's just have some more coffee and you sort of explain it to me, Jack. My brother wants me to get involved, but he hasn't explained anything," contrived Samantha, her fear masked with a smile. "Shall we go inside?"

Jack sauntered in and took a seat at the table. Karla was dressed and ready to go out to the pier where she could watch the early fishermen. "Be very careful, Honey," instructed Samantha, zipping the girl's coat up to her chin. "Will you do that for Mommy?"

"Oh-huh." Karla was out the door in a flash, her little feet soon clattering along the boardwalk. Samantha poured fresh coffee, then sat across from Jack, appearing to be wrestling with a confusing quandary.

"Now," she said. "I think I remember my brother saying that he had attended several meetings. Where are they held and who organizes them?"

"Up on the peak at headquarters. I guess we all organize'em, but Chief runs the army. Says he's the overlord. Sarge is second in command."

"My brother did say that much, but he didn't explain anything about the army. Is Chief an Indian?"

"Navaho. A living legend. Chief says his lineage includes this great warrior that was nine feet and two inches tall. He was the exalted lord of the whole Rocky Mountain Range," explained Jack, his eyes beginning to dazzle as if feeling deep admiration. "Some of the men wanna call the army a militia, but Chief wants to becalled the Freedom Fighters for the People. That makes it fine with me," said Jack, nodding, taking a cigarette from his jacket pocket. "Ya mind?" he asked, holding the narrow shaft up for what seemed his own inspection, then continuing before Samantha could respond. "Now, Mr. Douglas and Mr. Parker don't like it so much, but Chief looks at the Freedom Fighters as family and I like to think of us in that light, too. Since I've been..." "

Excuse me, Jack," cut in Samantha. "Let me get you something to use as an ashtray."

Jack lit up while Samantha found a cracked coffee cup for him to dust his cigarette ashes into. "Thanks," he said, filling his lungs with smoke. "Since I been with Chief, the Freedom Fighters rather, I've learnt a lot, mostly from Chief himself. You see, people all over this country have to make a stand. Their rights are bein violated right under their noses and they think they have to accept it, like helpless lambs bein herded to slaughter. It happened to the Indians a long time ago, but now they's thousands of young men from ever background in this whole country bein persecuted and sent to Vietnam for no good reason a'tall. Like the Sarge and the overlord says, Chief that is, well people we're s'pose to be fightin for over in Nam don't want our boys over there and the commies dang sure don't. Kennedy might have cared, and Johnson even might, but nobody cept the poor boys and the sufferin families have any stake in their lives. Chief says that Johnson's just a career politician and he does what they all do. Goes along with the mob, labor and big bucks corporate establishments that make bullets and war planes and tanks and bombs and uniforms with ever American resource til their pockets is lined and can't hold no more. It's hopeless, worse than illegal search and seizures our govment lets the tax pigs do. There's worse shit the stinkin FBI and the killers in the CIA do."

Jack paused, shook his head and exhaled loudly, as if really disgusted with the U. S. Government, but Samantha assumed his show of emotion was more than likely picked up from Chief, as his opinions definitely were. "You really have a lot of respect for the man named Chief," she said.

"He puts it best. Says he'll be remembered as one of history's most noble revolutionaries. You see, when none of our elected leaders is willin to make a stand against this illegal war in Asia, Chief is. He says the war is just about spillin blood for votes and power," said jack' "Corporate profits, too, and for justifyin the existence of the parasites in the govment agencies, their paychecks and graft money. Chief told us that Kennedy and his brother was gonna get rid of the CIA. The Secret service, too, but those bastards got friends in the mob and they handled JFK. Had nuthin to do with Oswald. Chief says Oswald was just a handy pawn. A stupid one, but he was there and the politicians like Johnson needed a suspect fer a quick fix. Chief knows all about it and he'll tell you at the meetin Monday, if you wanna know." Jack paused, biting his lower lip and nodding, a testimony to his belief in Chief's words. "Anyway," he continued, "one of the big problems is what does our boys do?" Jack paused to take another drag from the cigarette and flick ashes into the cup. "What's in it for them and what choice do they have? You know, there was some real American heroes in World War II who were Indians. What'd they get? Not much more'n dead. All. Chief says the ones in the Freedom Fighters are Native Americans and they'll die on American soil or not at all. Whatcha think?"

"Well, I uh," responded Samantha, startled to be asked anything at this point. "I know there's a lot of rioting and demonstrating going on."

"Chief says it ain't doing a thang but gettin our boys throwed in jail, save them that has fled to other countries, Canada and Mexico mostly. He figgers our boys shouldn't have to leave their homeland to keep from goin to jail or gettin killed in the jungles of Vietnam. The Sarge tells me it's an awful stink hole over there and gooks you think is friendly will kill you just this quick," said Jack, snapping his thumb and finger to indicate the immediacy of a soldier's life being lost to an unsuspected enemy.

"That is so true," said Samantha, sighing to manifest herself as a sympathizer to the cause of the Freedom Fighters.

"You bet it's the damn truth," responded Jack, seeming to be getting emotional now. "Chief's nephew is MIA. Dead he figgers. Says he's been missin since early on in sixty-four. It ain't right for our boys to even be over there. Hell, we got battles right here in the USA. I really have to get busy, but I can check with ya Monday after I take my nap. I always take a nap on meetin days cause I get back so late. If you wanna take your car you can, but you can ride with me'n Chip if you're a mind to." Jack paused, looking for a response.

Samantha had drifted off. "Oh. Yes, I see."

"Good," said Jack. "I think you'll see that we offer our boys sanctuary right here in these mountains, but we gotta have some support to do it. Headquarters is, well, you'll see, but to give you an idea, is cut back into the solid rock that makes up Maiden Peak. It's a granite fortress that could take a direct hit from an atom bomb and never hurt nuthin. Took us two years with jackhammers and dynamite, plus a backhoe with a front bucket on it to get in a hunert and sixty feet. We're still workin and got that cave in over three hunert now. Takes money and takes men and these here Indian boys and kids that's AWOL ain't got nothin but time and big hopes that the Freedom Fighters can provide what all we plan. We will be able to hold off bout any attack the govment wants to come with. Shoot, the little cave the members of the army lives in goes straight down. Down more'n a hunert feet. We got a stock a ammo and gas to last til kingdom come. Used to be tons of rations, but I hear they're all gone right now. Be gittin more, I guess."

Jack paused, seeming to be awaiting Samantha's comment, but continued when she had none. "Like I said, I'd better be runnin along," he sighed, getting to his feet. "Need anything else, you just lemme know. I'll check with you over the weekend. Chief likes for everbody to paint their faces for the meetins, but if a guest has a little to throw in the kitty, he kinda overlooks that. Ain't so strict. You'll be all right. I'll ask Chief special for ya."

Samantha watched Jack walk out then sat and thought for the better part of an hour, the solitude only serving to convince her that she must leave Lost Mountain Park. Below the surface, there were more subversive goings-on than she had even imagined. Ken was hanging around with a bunch of radical militants, which might add to his unpredictability, dangerous enough as it was. Maybe all he wanted was to pick up the Remington bronze, but BB Douglas, Sarge, the man called Chief, and his militiamen were preparing for war against the US Government. The park could soon be a staging area for troops and equipment. No one would really be safe.

While absently preparing lunch of tuna fish salad, crackers and milk for herself and her daughter, Samantha considered the options she thought to be available to her. She was trained, experienced and could work wherever best to establish a stable life for her and Karla. That wherever just might be the West Coast. California could be too fast for a single mother, she felt, but Oregon or Washington might just be perfect. Yes, upon her return from Dallas, Samantha would find out if the Redwines were actually interested in the cabin; and if not, she'd list it with a real estate agent in Santa Fe. Moving further west would be more expense, but hopefully she would find an ideal neighborhood with typical suburban neighbors and a school suitable for Karla. Samantha had already had a career of dangerous crazies in her life and longed for something typical, even boring.

After putting her lunch spread onto a tray, Samantha took it out to the pier to eat in the midday sun with her daughter. The day was bright and balmy, clean mountain air, a shirt sleeve paradise in the warm sunshine. The lake, rippling ever so slightly in the soft breeze, seemed to be radiating the warmth of the sunlight fourfold from its shimmering surface. Its colors of greens and blues and even its existence seemed more imagined than real. The touch of an experienced artist to add passion to a sleepy mountain setting. Samantha ate sitting on the big planks of the pier, her feet dangling off the side. The little girl sat leaning against a gasoline drum, one Chip Parker must have placed on the pier for the boaters.

Samantha knew her daughter was pouting over something. "Why so quiet, Honey?" she asked, deciding to break the silence. "Are you sleepy?"

"Uh-uh. I just been wonderin why we didn't get somethin to fish when we were in that town. You said we would, Mommy."

"Yes. I remember I did say that. So, do you think we can find something over at that little store? I bet we can."

Karla shrugged. "Maybe, but there's some poles in the sha-yad."

"The what? Oh, you mean the shed."

"That place you can put the car in. You know what I meant."

The little girl was worn out and about to become cranky. "Okay, then I'll look through the shed, and if I find us some poles, I'll go down to the store and get some bait. Then, when you're up from your nap, see if we can catch our dinner. What do you think about that?"

"I gotta take a nap?"

"Yes, you should."

"Well, how long?"

"Until you wake up. You can't just lay down, you have to go to sleep."

"Can we really eat a fish?"

"Yes. We have to wash it and clean it, but then we just fry it like bacon."

"Will it be good?"

"I think so, now quit stalling and run inside. I'm going to look for some fishing equipment for us. I'll come up with at least one pole, that is if you're good and take a nice long nap. Otherwise, you have to go to bed real early tonight."

"Oh," sighed Karla, getting to her feet. "Naps is for babies," she added, then turned and trotted up to the cabin, again her little footsteps clopping on the boardwalk until she reached the grass, then nothing but the serenity of silence in the sunny midday warmth.

Samantha sat looking about her, the peaceful appearance of the cabins slumbering in the park, a facade. Across the lake, catching her eye, was an older couple struggling with a small aluminum boat. She could hear their playful exchange, their laughter riding on the breeze like the waffling ripples that lapped at the braces of the pier. The old couple seemed a happy lot, unaware of any pending threat to their peaceful world. Who and how many, she wondered, were connected with BB Douglas and his foolish attempt to marshal a resistance force to thwart the US Government and all of its resources? What was Ken up to?

Then, from behind her, came footsteps, heavy on the boardwalk to the pier, like those of a large man in boots. Samantha's head swung around as if sprung from a trap door, startling the man approaching, then startling herself when she realized who he was. "Gosh," she said, maybe a frightening gasp, for the big man approaching jerked to a stop with obvious surprise.

"Relax lady," he said, his mirrored shades hiding his eyes. "I promise I ain't carrying heat today."

"How very amazing," said Samantha, quietly. "Well, maybe not."

"You don't think so, huh?" responded the big blonde man, continuing his approach until he stood next to the gasoline drum. "I was hoping there might be some problem you need my help with again today."

"Depends. You might just get your wish, Mister," said Samantha, gesturing for the man to take a seat beside her if he chose to, his big frame like a building towering above her. "We didn't exchange names out on the highway to Albuquerque the other day. I'm Samantha."

"Chad," said the man, introducing himself as he sat down. "How have you and your little girl been since I last saw you stranded at the truck stop?"

"Fine, I guess, and you?"

"Okay, Ms. Samantha no last name."

"Well, that's good, Mr. Chad with no last name either."

"Care to exchange?"

"Care to take off those sunshades?"

"Sorry. A habit worse than my lying."

"My last name is Valentine," said Samantha, appreciating Chad's cooperation in removing the mirrored shades.

"Mine's Begay. Sounds Navaho, but I don't look it do I."

Samantha chuckled, the first time she'd laughed in so long she couldn't remember. "Mr. Begay," she said, yet smiling from the brief chuckle. "I'm afraid I don't know what a Navajo is supposed to look like. Judging by you, I'd have to assume they're all athletic. However, you're quite a refreshing sight to me today."

"You don't know what an Indian looks like? Hmmm, I guess you don't watch movies. Darn," exclaimed Chad. "I was planning to ask you and your little girl to go see a John Wayne picture with me."

"And, when did that thought occur to you?"

"Just before I walked out here."

"I see. I mean I see what you meant by your habit of lying."

"Bad deal, huh?" said Chad, playfully shoving Samantha toward the water.

"Don't, you big bully," she snapped. "I'll freeze to death."

"Never thought of that, but I guess I just saved your life. Now, tell me what you're doing up here in Lost Mountain Park," said Chad. "Pretty remote, this park way up here," he added, cutting an eye toward Samantha as if accusing her of something.

"I live here. You must have walked right by my cabin. What about you?"

"Why did I know that was coming?" asked Chad of himself, his big shoulders shrugging as he looked out onto the lake. "Now, let me see," he continued, appearing deep in thought. "What white lie might the lady believe?"

"Don't bother," said Samantha, deliberately. "I think I know. You're a friend of BB Douglas and Chip and Jack and..." She paused, wishing she hadn't said as much as she had.

"So, would it be a problem if I was friendly with BB and the boys?"

"I can't say. I don't know what to think about Mr. Douglas and his associates," said Samantha, resignedly, but hoping Chad had an opinion he would share with her.

"We might just have to talk about BB and the boys a little later, but I'd best be on my way for now," said Chad, getting to his feet, then wiping his hands on the seat of his jeans before putting his mirrored shades back on. "It was nice to see you again, Samantha. Mind if I come by this weekend?"

"It wouldn't matter if I did mind. I'm leaving for Dallas Thursday. Mr. Redwine has agreed to drive Karla and me to the airport in Albuquerque."

"Interesting," said Chad. "When will you be back?"

"A week or so, but I'm not exactly sure."

"I guess we can't set a date to get together then? That's if you don't know when you'll be back and, of course, you haven't said you're interested either."

Samantha, somewhat amused with Mr. Begay, looked the big man over, his expression one of challenge, although she didn't have the advantage of seeing his eyes now shielded by the mirrored sunshades. "Okay, Chad," she said wondering why she had. "Monday night. Not this coming, but the next. Come by any time after five and I'll fix dinner, then the rest of the evening plans will be yours. Is that a date?"

"A Monday night, huh? Uh, I don't..."

"I didn't think so," interrupted Samantha. "Can't miss the meeting, huh?"

"Don't be so quick to make assumptions, Ms. Valentine," said Chad, his hands up as if being arrested. "I'll be here at five-thirty. Is that a date?"

Samantha wanted to agree to the date, but wondered what Mr. Begay had in mind. She trusted him, but why? Maybe he really didn't know what she wanted to know anyway. For no reason she could put a finger on though, the big man seemed to have some role in the goings on at Lost Mountain Park. "Let's just wait until I..." she began, but Chad interrupted her.

"I'd like about any kind of vegetable salad or pasta," he said. "I'm a vegetarian, but you and your daughter have whatever you'd like. Tell you something I like with everyone else's steak though. That's a good red wine. I'll bring a bottle unless you plan on serving the fish catch of the day."

"Okay, okay," chuckled Samantha. "You bring the red wine and I'll have beef of some fashion. See you then."

Chad winked and walked away, turning toward the little store once off the boardwalk, then continuing a few yards beyond to his motorcycle, left leaning on its kickstand beside the dirt road. Samantha, although not apprehensive in the least, wondered if she should be, considering she had just agreed to a date with such a big, strange man, mysterious for sure, but so was her interest in him.

Samantha went back inside, checked on Karla, then concentrated on her furniture, arranging it as she felt it best fit into the little cabin. Her day, as she continued to review it, was as confusing as it was eventful. She had never thought about the possibility, but surely couldn't have expected to ever see Chad Begay after the chance meeting at the truck stop. And, little frail Jack Cox. It wasn't that hard to think of him as a blind follower of some more forceful man, but it was hard for Samantha to believe he could get so caught up in something as outrageous as a group of militants, no less fanatical than a religious cult, plus show such bizarre passion for its outrageous purpose.

When Karla awoke, sunset fast approaching, Samantha was able to get the little girl involved in packing for Dallas, fishing from the pier as far from her mind as yesterday's breakfast. They went to bed before nine, but Samantha had trouble falling asleep, unable to keep from worrying about her date with the strange man who rode the big motorcycle. When had she done something so impetuous?

Chapter 11

Howard met Samantha and her daughter at their gate and drove them straight to a restaurant on Greenville Avenue, just three blocks from the duplex he had leased. While packing for the trip, Samantha had coached Karla on what to expect in Dallas. "Honey, we're best friends now, so we have to trust each other," she began. "We're going to see that man you don't like. He lives far away and that means we'll have to fly. We might drive back, because I remember how you like to go on long trips in a car. Anyway, the man's name is Howard. Now, don't you be afraid. He's not going to hurt Mommy again. No one will. I'll make that a promise if you'll make me one?"

"Okay, what is it?"

"I want you to remember the man's name is Howard, but all you have to promise Mommy is that you'll never tell him where we live. Easy enough?"

"I guess, but what do I say if he asks?"

"My dealings with Howard are strictly business, Karla. We'll be in Dallas for a few days, but he shouldn't ask where we live. He thinks we'll be coming from our little apartment back in New Jersey to live there in Dallas with him. Just go along with that. That's what I'm going to do. We're not going to stay with Howard, but if he asks, we'll just have to tell one of those little fibs we talked about. You can never tell him about our cabin home. He might want to take it away from us. You wouldn't want that, would you? Lose your pretty room? The beautiful lake, the fireplace you just love? Hmmm?"

"No, never. Never, never, Mommy."

Howard was excited to see Samantha and near breathless in anticipation of her reaction when he showed her the studio setup he'd worked so hard to get just right. He had left a bottle of champagne chilling in an ice bucket on each of the worktables. Each tripod was left covered with a dropcloth; he had dimmed the lights, then looped strands of red ribbon over everything. "Honey," he said, clutching her hand as she perused the menu. "I've missed you so much. Let's hurry. We need some time alone and I have a surprise for you."

Samantha, although weak from worrying about having to do it, being able to do it, was here strictly on business and had to set the tone of her visit straight for Howard. "I want to know what you've decided to do about your wife before I go anywhere or do anything else but have my dinner," she said, flatly, pulling her hand from Howard's. 'Besides, Karla's tired. Why don't you drop us off at that place you leased, then you and I can visit tomorrow."

Howard frowned and shrugged his shoulders in defeat. "Gee, Honey, we have a lot to talk about. Can't we put Karla to bed and..."

"What am I going to drive?" interrupted Samantha, yet concentrating on the menu, searching for an out. "I hope that's your surprise. Is it?"

"No," sighed Howard. "I couldn't get you a car in my name. It would be half Carol Ann's. We can get one..."

"Just a minute," interrupted Samantha, raising a hand as she turned to her daughter. "Karla, give Howard and me a minute alone. You can wait over there by those pinball machines. Okay, Honey? Mommy won't be long." Samantha extended a hand to Howard. "Give her some change," she ordered, trying hard to be forceful.

Howard fished into his pants pocket and pulled out a few folded bills, then handed Karla two dollars. The little girl looked to her mother for permission to take the money. Samantha nodded, then turned to Howard. "Bring me up-to-date. You've filed for divorce, I suppose."

"Well, uh," he faltered, then leaned forward and whispered. "You know what Carol Ann and I agreed on. The only change is in her attitude. She's agreed to take her house without question, and I get my money. She contacted an attorney the other day and plans to file the papers just as soon as we sit down long enough to fill'em out. I can move in with you and Karla anytime. That's why I got a three-bedroom. One for us, one for Karla and one that's..."

"Howard," interrupted Samantha, shaking her head. "I don't think you've been using your head," she said, needing to plan a course for getting Howard to stay in his home until he had exclusive control over his money. "You won't get but half of the proceeds from your CD's if Carol Ann's attorney gets involved. He'll be representing her, not you. That's what attorneys do. They make every decision and make sure their client gets the most of everything. You just might be in for a big surprise. And, guess what. I'm not going to live down here in Dallas with no money. I've said that all along, so why am I here, Howard?' Samantha's heart rate was about to soar through the ceiling, but her confidence was falling through the floor.

Howard had a big smile on his face. "I haven't just been sitting around, Samantha," he said, proudly. "I've cashed the CD's and the proceeds, two hundred and eighteen grand, including the accrued interest, are in mine and Carol Ann's checking account. We're going to trade the cars for..."

Samantha raised her hand. "Just a minute," she said. "Can you write a check for the two hundred and eighteen thousand dollars?"

Howard shrugged. "Yeah. Sure I can," he responded, an air of accomplishment about him. "So could Carol Ann, but she knows better."

"Well?" sighed Samantha, interrupting, appearing to be thinking as she dug into her purse, hoping to hide her shaking hands. "Here," she said, absently handing Howard a bottle of the Soma pills he'd taken for so long, a ballpoint pen and a little yellow card. "I got all the pain pills Dr. Logan had in his office. That's a signature card for our bank account." Samantha tapped the little yellow card with a finger. just had my savings transferred to a bank here in Dallas. The funds will be available this coming Monday." Samantha was amazed with herself, contriving like an accomplished con man, even faster than she planned to have to, but finding it necessary since Howard's money might really be available. "If you can write a check for the proceeds from cashing your CD's, then do it and I'll deposit it immediately. You can settle with your wife later and you won't be in a praying position. I don't think you want her to get any funny ideas, do you? You know the story, a scorned woman and all that can entail."

Howard's expression changed to apprehension. "Write the check now?"

"Well, no," responded Samantha smiling to soften Howard's obvious concern. She was somewhat, but not totally convinced that he had in fact liquidated his CD's. "Not here, you silly man. We'll wait until we get to the apartment you leased for us. Let's eat and run before Karla falls asleep. We've had a very long day. Where is your wife now?"

"Home," said Howard. "She's probably on the phone with old Martin Bishop right now. They talk all the time. Good for them, I say."

Carol Ann was actually leaning against the kitchen counter waiting for Martin's call, her purse hanging over her shoulder as if ready to run someplace to meet him. He had been on her mind all day and she was worn out from her own anxiousness by the time the phone finally rang. "Hello, hello," greeted Carol Ann, grabbing the receiver on the first ring, stammering. "Who, uh, who is this?"

"Hello, Sweetheart, uh, hello Sweetheart, I love you, I, uh, love you," greeted Martin. "Do I have the right, uh, number?"

Carol Ann tossed her purse onto the kitchen table, closed her eyes and sunk to the floor, even weaker from the sound of Martin's voice. "Sweetheart, it's, uh," she sighed, pausing, a whimper in the falter of her voice. "It has been so long," she continued. "I love you, too, but I want to show you. You said you'd come to see me. When will...?"

"Carol Ann," interrupted Martin. "I have to be here tomorrow morning to sign the papers for your new home. It's a white two-story on a golf course lot that's within walking distance of the Olympic National Park. We're just three miles from Port Angeles. You can see the Strait of San Juan De Fuca from the kitchen window. There's seventeen hundred square feet of livable space, one small bedroom downstairs and two big ones upstairs. Ours, the master of course, has an all-tile sunken tub, just in case you're interested."

"It sounds just perfect, Honey. Did you buy it?"

"Lease purchase," said Martin, the excitement he felt coming through the receiver. He had set his mind and Carol Ann was going to be the center of everything he did for the rest of his life. "The place is perfect, Honey, and I know you'll go nuts when you get here and see it," continued Martin, talking faster, imagining Carol Ann in the sunken tub. "First things first though. I didn't tell you that I brought my nephew. Remember Adam Richardson? I told you about him."

Carol Ann was dying to see Martin, but the excitement in his voice was cheering her up. "Yes, I remember you spoke of Adam. He was in the Army."

"Well, he got his discharge, but I hope to talk him into reenlisting."

"How does he like my house?" asked Carol Ann, her voice picking up the excitement in Martin's.

"He wants to be your house boy, but no deal. Anyway, if you'll be at Love Field at six pm tomorrow, you can meet him. Adam will be going on to New Jersey, but I can stay awhile. How's that fit with your schedule.?"

After Carol Ann and Martin finished their phone conversation, she sat at the kitchen table and worked on the divorce kit until midnight, then went to bed.

Chapter 12

Samantha and Karla finished their dinner, then Howard took them to the apartment he'd leased. He felt better than he had in weeks, the euphoria produced by the Soma pills giving him the giggles. "The gold mine," he said bowing as he opened the door to his project. "Picasso never had it so good," he added, laughing as he demonstrated the effect of the special rheostat-controlled lighting. "Your own ribbon-cutting ceremony complete with champagne."

Karla fell fast asleep on the den sofa while Howard was showing off the in-home studio, but Samantha looked on with mock interest, expressed appreciation for Howard's handiwork and the spaciousness of the duplex. "Well, thank you, Howard. My workroom is perfect, and champagne was very thoughtful. I guess a little celebration is in order, isn't it. I'll make arrangements for a phone tomorrow and have my furniture brought in. The movers only gave me ten days, then we have to pay storage."

Howard and Samantha visited at the little kitchen table for a few minutes, then she opened two bottles of the champagne while he carried in hers and Karla's bags. From one bottle, she poured herself a full glass of the champagne, dropped ten Soma tablets into the other, then tossed the pill bottle with the remaining pills into the trash.

Samantha felt criminal for using pain pills to disarm Howard, to calm him and allow herself to feel more comfortable, but she also felt it would be best if he slept most of tomorrow. "Howard," she called, while he was putting her bags away. "How old is this stuff? It's sour."

"I don't know," he said. "I picked it up yesterday. Try another bottle."

Back at the kitchen table, Samantha drank from the glass she'd poured from the first bottle while the remainder drained out in the sink. "This is better. What do you think?" she asked, handing Howard a glass from the spiked bottle.

He drained the glass, then handed it back to Samantha "Tastes fine," he said, coughing. "Fill me up and sit down. I've got a toast for us."

Samantha sat down at the table beside Howard. "Okay," he continued, his champagne glass extended for the proposed toast. "Here's to good fortune and a happy life for you and me."

Samantha clicked her glass against Howard's. "Here's to you. Thank you and I hope you're as happy as I am," she said, then leaned close and quickly kissed his cheek, feeling a sickness as she did so. "How do you feel?" It was so hard to look into Howard's face, the image of his attack yet vivid in her mind.

Howard drank and laughed and fought to stay awake. Everything was funny. Samantha kept his glass full, kept laughing right along with him, easily getting the check and signature cards signed. The signature card was for show, a small degree of authenticity. It would go into the first live fireplace she ran across, but the check would go into her account at the Republic National Bank.

Just after one that morning, Samantha helped Howard into the Buick and drove him home, doing her best to keep him awake and alert enough to show her the way to Holiday Trail in Oak Cliff, then point out his home.

"Can you get back here tomorrow?" he once slurred. "All you have to do is find Kiest Park, then remember that Holiday Trail is on the south side."

"Of course."

"I'll pack up some stuff in the morning so I can stay at the duplex, too."

"No, no," said Samantha. "Not yet. We should give Karla time to get used to the idea first. A week or so anyway."

"A week? Hmmm, okay," said Howard, giggling. "We gotta do it on the floor first thing though. I tested that bed today. It's a squeaky son of a gun."

Samantha, getting sick from being so close to a man who had raped her, hurried across town, took a freeway over the Trinity River to Oak Cliff. Howard pointed out a big heavily wooded park. "Nothin to it, he said. "Just find this park, then turn up there," he added, batting his eyes to stay awake as he pointed to a residential area south of the park.

Samantha slowed the Buick and turned onto a wide street that led to the homes south of the park. The third street was Holiday Trail. "Here it is," said Howard. "Simple enough, huh? You just have to find the park." Before Samantha could respond, a sudden sneezing fit began to rack Howard's body. "Oops," he slurred. "Hay fever I guess."

"Where do I go from here?" asked Samantha.

Howard glanced to the right, several houses down. "Bingo," he giggled, pointing to the two-story brick home. "We made it. Hey, lookey there. Dark as a dungeon. Carol Ann's sound asleep in her domain. A beauty, huh?"

"It looks nice." Samantha turned off the headlights just as she pulled into the drive. She helped Howard out of the car and up to the front door, constantly reminding him to keep quiet. Once he'd fished his keys from his pants pocket, she unlocked the door and tried to assist him inside, but his knees buckled and he fell through the open doorway, sprawling out by an opening to the kitchen.

"Sh, sh," whispered Howard, giggling. "Come on upstairs with me."

"No. You go right to bed," whispered Samantha, helping Howard to his feet. "I'll be by before noon tomorrow," she lied, feeling a sudden fear reach for her. Why was she in here? Was coming to Dallas even going to be worth it? Yes, it was, she decided. If Howard had really gotten the money from his CD's, he had just settled his account. He was a despicable human being and needed to have to live knowing that he did pay, too, but was he going to live?

Samantha stood in dim light that was bleeding through a small window curtain in the front door and waited until Howard was upstairs. Had he overdone it on the pills this time? Mixing them with the champagne might have been the wrong thing to do. As hard as it was to care, she didn't want to be responsible for Howard's death. Soon, all seemed too quiet for a few seconds, then she heard Howard's muffled laughter. Good, she said in thought, but then she heard a weak groan, followed by a loud coughing fit and more groaning, then sneezing. Samantha reached for the door, wanting to leave, but wondering if she should. Was he going to choke to death or something?

Samantha crossed her arms and leaned against the door. Was Carol Ann even here? She looked about the house for any evidence, through the kitchen. A door. Did it lead to the garage? Was Carol Ann's car in there? Suddenly, Samantha saw a woman's purse laying on the kitchen table, papers beside it. She's here. Silly, she thought, feeling a sense of relief, the fear and doubt that coiled around her releasing. Deciding to leave, again she reached for the doorknob, but..."Hello. Is that you Howard?" came from upstairs, maybe at the landing.

Reacting automatically, Samantha sunk to her knees and hunkered by the door, hating that she had, but frightened again, too much so to move. She was no less than an unknown intruder to Carol Ann, who had every right to shoot and ask questions later. "Oh." Samantha let a whimper slip out.

"Howard?" repeated Carol Ann, a soft question this time. Samantha could hear her coming down the stairs. "Howard? Howard, I hope that's you," said Carol Ann, flipping on the kitchen light, her voice laced with question.

Samantha froze, immobilized with fear, but Carol Ann turned as if sensing her presence, her eyes suddenly saucer size, her face alert with surprise. "What on earth? Samantha Valentine?" she screamed, gasping. "Why you bold little bitch. This is..."

"Mrs. Lane, I'm very sorry." Samantha's voice was a weak plea. I was just making sure..."

"You get out of my house this instant. This is not Howard's house, it's mine. I keep a gun in the..." There was a stir at the top of the stairs. Carol Ann paused, turned around as if suddenly afraid. "Howard, you better..."

"Party time," giggled her husband, coughing, rubbing his eyes as he strolled down the stairs, yet fully dressed. "Let's break out the booze and put on some shit kickin music."

"You bastard. You and this..." Samantha didn't hear another word. She was on her feet, out the door and into the Buick like a leaping cat, the back tires squealing in protest as she zoomed away.

At the park, driving like a reckless fool Samantha turned on the headlights and sped through the surface streets to the freeway that led to the East Side, arriving at the condominium at twenty minutes past two in the morning. She was beyond tired, nearer dead or sick from fear and its exhausting toll. Just crawling out of the car and making it inside to check on Karla was a genuine struggle. "It's over," sighed Samantha, kneeling by her sleeping daughter. "We can go home. Home, Honey."

Karla rolled over and smiled. "Night, Mommy."

Howard, leaning against the refrigerator, and Carol Ann, sitting at the table, were entrenched in a battle of wills, bitter but both having hopes to soon be living with people they wanted. Carol Ann didn't care about Samantha and her husband's affair, but wanted Howard to leave the house immediately, never again to bring another woman into her home. "Just what were you two planning, Howard? A quickie down here on the sofa? You pig. You can have the CD's, I don't care. Just take your things and go away this minute."

"Cool it, Carol Ann. I'll get out of here next week," said Howard, turning to search through the kitchen cabinets. "Isn't there some bourbon around here someplace? Maybe it's good'n aged by now," he giggled, sneezing and coughing, wiping his red eyes with his sleeve, then batting them to adjust to the light. "Hey, by the way, how about the divorce papers? I'm about as sick of you as you are of me, so let's get it done."

"I'll finish the papers and you couldn't be as sick of me as I am you. You'll take all the proceeds from the CD's, Howard. just wait for the house to sell, but I do need a few thousand dollars to live on for now. Three thousand."

"What about all this furniture? It's both of ours, but you could sell some. Ought to get three thousand easy." Howard sneezed again. "Damn."

"Everything in this house is mine now, you can forget it. Would you just sit down? There's nothing here for you to drink. I'll make some instant coffee for you and hot tea for me, then you go to bed. I want you packed and out of here early in the morning. Go wherever you've got Samantha stashed."

Carol Ann went to the stove and flipped a control knob, checked that the gas flame had caught, then placed a teapot on the burner. She drew water from a tap at the sink and half-filled a small kettle, then put it onto another burner and flipped its control knob, again, checking that the blue flame had caught.

"These the papers?" slurred Howard, reaching for the divorce papers Carol Ann had worked on, shoving her purse aside as he flopped into a chair at the kitchen table. "All filled out, huh?" he sneered, trying to read the small writing, squinting his blurry red eyes.

"Yes, and you can forget the three thousand dollars. I'll live on my credit cards. You're really an ass, Howard. Don't worry, though, I'll delete the part on there about me getting part of the proceeds from the CD's the minute you're out of here. Martin Bishop will be here tomorrow night and I'd like to offer him a place to stay for a few days. You know he won't stay in this house for ten minutes if you're here. So be out by noon tomorrow and that's final."

"Cozy little plan you got," sneered Howard. "Old Martin bouncing up and down between your legs, huh?" he chuckled, then sneezed and dropped the divorce papers to the floor. "I just can't imagine that, can't get the picture."

"Creep," snapped Carol Ann, flipping off the burner under her teapot, then kneeling to pick up the scattered sheets of paper at her feet. "You can fix your own coffee. There's a jar in the one of these cabinets. I'm going to bed."

Howard, after a fit of several sneezes, wiped his eyes and watched Carol Ann until she disappeared at the top of the stairs, remaining at the table until he heard her bedroom door slam closed. "Hmmm. So, it's your house, huh?" he whispered. "Maybe, but maybe not. The insurance settlement just might be all mine. Well, and Samantha's, too," he mumbled, then jumped up and flipped on the burner beneath her teapot, leaned over and blew out the flames under both the water for the tea and his coffee. But like tiny explosions, the burners burst into flames, again ignited by the pilot lights. "Bad boys," he scolded, sneezing, a finger shaking at the stove as if it were a disagreeable child. "You can't fool old Howard," he said, then lifted the teapot and doused both burners, the flames dying with snakelike hisses.

Howard, hurrying as he did, searched through Carol Ann's purse for the keys to her Tempest. No luck. "Shit," he mumbled, folding over with another sneezing fit. "Damnation, where, where, where to look?"

Howard ran to the garage and swung the driver's door of the Tempest open, finding the keys in the ignition. Hurrying again, he ran upstairs and pulled his old army duffel bag from under his bed, then stuffed everything he could into it and a small suitcase he'd always used for his toiletries. As he worked, he imagined he could hear the gas spewing from the burners, even smell it rising from the stove, boiling over like a witch's brew, noxious vapors rolling up the stairs to get him. He hurried; snapping the little suitcase closed, then grabbing shirts and pants from the closet, socks and shorts from dresser drawers and throwing everything into the duffel bag.

Once downstairs, his bags sitting in the kitchen by the garage door, Howard ran back upstairs to search for the bottle of Soma pills that Samantha had brought him. Unsuccessful, but knowing she had surely brought more he ran back downstairs, grabbing Carol Ann's purse just as the gas blew.

First, the downstairs area of the house, filled with the highly flammable natural gas, exploded like a dozen sticks of dynamite, then a fireball, searching for an escape, blew out windows and flew through the roof, lighting the night sky like the morning sun. The sudden explosion blasted Howard into the closed door that led to the garage then immediately enveloped him in hot hungry flames. Carol Ann, shocked and confused, was knocked from her bed. By the time she got to her feet, the whole bedroom a giant furnace. "Howard," she screamed, stumbling to the door, opening it just long enough to see a wall of flames boiling up the staircase. Carol Ann slammed the door closed, screaming as she ran to her bedroom window.

t was quite unusual for Karla to want to sit in her mother's lap, but the morning itself was unusual. The little girl awoke in a strange place. Nothing was familiar to her. Her mother had slept fully dressed and champagne bottles were in the kitchen. That bad man who picked them up at the airport was here last night. Something was wrong.

Samantha awoke at eight, her nerves yet shattered. She was feeling Karla's fixed stare, the fear telegraphing from her eyes. The little girl was sitting on the floor next to the bed, legs crossed, also fully dressed. It was obvious she'd been crying. "Honey," moaned Samantha, yawning, shaking with fear herself. She had done it, but…"I know you're confused," she said, wondering if she herself might fold from the guilt, the uncertainty, the crippling feeling of being everything, alone in this heinous act of treachery. "We're going home today," managed Samantha, willing herself to her feet.

"Is our home still the cabin?" asked the little girl, her voice quivering.

Samantha, weak and feeling a rush of dizziness, sat back down on the bed and lifted her daughter into her lap. "Sure, it is, Honey. Mommy explained that we just had to come here for a day or two. You remember that don't you?"

"Uh-huh," agreed Karla, nodding in confirmation. "On business. Is it all over with now? I don't want to see that Howard man anymore. He's bad."

The little girl had wanted to sit in her mother's lap all morning and it was no different the minute Samantha took the chair beside Mr. Russell's desk at the Republic National Bank this afternoon. Karla helped some while loading the bags into the Buick, but had she only done so because her mother seemed incapable, too nervous, or afraid of something? At the restaurant, she wanted right back into her mother's lap.

Samantha knew the instability of the situations she had involved her daughter in was scary. She had thought about it all morning. She had to admit that running from the confusion in New Jersey to the unknown in Lost Mountain Park, then this horrible scheme in Dallas, could have an enormous impact on her own life, as well as Karla's. Everything had to change again, a better resolution must be found and it could be found, decided Samantha, while endorsing the big check. Yes, and she would get started as soon as Mr. Russell got back to his desk with the receipt. It would take but a day and a half to drive back to Lost Mountain Park where Karla felt comfortable, then the move to the West Coast could began with a long trip by car, possibly a new one, up through Northern California, Oregon and on to Seattle, Washington. The trip might just be what Samantha needed, too. How wonderful it would be and how welcome the hassle of relocating if the cabin could be sold while they were gone.

"Okay. Simple enough, Mrs. Valentine," said the banker, smiling, taking his chair gracefully. He was a handsome man of at least fifty. A younger Uncle Hiram, advice as immediate and natural as a greeting. Samantha had seen Howard Lane's evil eyes in almost every face she'd encountered today, his shadow at every turn, but Mr. Russell seemed to be only sending her sincere messages. "Today's deposit brings the balance to two hundred twenty-two thousand, eight hundred sixty-one dollars and seventy-nine cents," he reported now. "Surely, Mrs. Valentine, you'd like me to find some safe fund where you can park some of that money until you need it, wouldn't you?"

Unlike Uncle Hiram, Mr. Russell spoke through a professional smile, but with almost the same degree of assurance, it seemed to Samantha. "Well," she began, but paused for thought, then was interrupted.

"Mommy," whined Karla. "When can we go? I wanna get..."

"I know, Darling," interjected Samantha, interrupting also, looking about the bank for what? For who? Howard Lane? "It's a long way to Disney Land, but it won't be long until we're shaking hands with

Mickey Mouse," she contrived, smiling apologetically to Mr. Russell. "Sir," she addressed him. "I've been thinking about asking someone for information on something safe that would provide a monthly income. Are you aware of anything like that?"

"Why certainly, Ma'am," responded the banker. "You could say it's a fiduciary responsibility of mine to inform all of our major depositors of safe investment funds. One that immediately comes to mind is a particular fund managed by the bank's trust department. The fund offers an almost zero risk investment that could be arranged to disperse over a thousand dollars to you monthly if you let me transfer two hundred thousand dollars into it for you. Would that interest you?" Mr. Russell paused then addressed Karla. "You haven't even said hello to me, Hon."

"Sir," broke in Samantha. "I need to take out travel money and enough to buy a car here in Dallas, but what do I have to do to set up two hundred thousand dollars in that income fund? Is it possible that the monthly income amount could be transferred to my bank in New Mexico?"

"That's all part of the service our bank offers, Ma'am, and if you'd care to finance that new car, we'd love the chance to do that for you, too. I can refer you to several automobile dealerships the bank does business with, every make and model. However, there's a Chevrolet dealership on Lemon Avenue where I've purchased two new cars over the years. I highly recommend you consider buying there. I'm sure you'll be satisfied."

Chapter 14

Martin Bishop wasted no time. It was intuition, he said. Adam, his nephew, wanted to wait until at least seven that evening they arrived at Love Field, but the minute Martin tried to phone Carol Ann and only got a disconnect message, he was convinced that something had gone awry and insisted on renting a car. "Gees, Unk, you're a hung-up dude," said Adam.

Martin appeared nervous and had the grim look of utter exhaustion about him. "Evidenced by my being here, I'd say, Son. I'll phone you tomorrow."

"No way," exclaimed the young soldier, beginning to feel that his uncle might not be capable of driving around a big unfamiliar city. "What have I got to do? I sure as hell am not in a hurry to reenlist, if I ever do. Besides, planes leave for Philly twice a day. Let's go find your friend. Mom said she's a looker."

Adam took Martin's credit card, rented a car and got a street map at the Hertz counter. Insisting on doing the driving, he and his uncle set out to find the Lane home in Oak Cliff. It was after eight when they found Kiest Park, immediately seeing the commotion at the site of the burned out home. Martin moaned, a guttural sound. "I knew it," he said, as Adam idled toward the burn site. "That fuckin Howard did something."

There was substantial damage to the roof, but the garage seemed to be the only part of the home that was completely destroyed. Carol Ann's Tempest was a blackened heap sitting on a cement slab partially covered with broken bricks and structural material from the house. "Damn it!" Exclaimed Adam, his eyes taking in the horror of scene. "I hope Carol Ann wasn't in there. Something exploded."

Martin wasn't looking. He'd buried his face in his hands. "Me, too, but she would have been and I'm gonna kill Howard if he…"

"The house doesn't look like a total loss," interrupted Adam, not wanting to hear the words he knew his uncle didn't mean. He parked the rental behind a municipal car, one of three, and jumped out. Martin stepped out, but knelt by the car, too weak to go further, assumed Adam.

There were two men kneeling by a pile of something in the front yard and several inside the burned-out home, two with rakes. One of the men kneeling, a burly man of middle age wearing a blue suit, stood and held up a hand as Adam approached. "That's as far as you can go for now, Sir. This should all be cleaned up tomorrow, but I can't let anyone disturb anything until the lab people and investigators get through here. Sorry."

"It's okay. What happened?"

"Natural gas. Probably from the kitchen stove. A tech told me he'd bet on that," explained the burly man.

"What happened to the people inside? Carol Ann Lane, or should I ask?"

"You won't like the answer, Son. I'm John Dickinson, who are you?"

"I'm Adam…"

"We're friends, Mr. Dickinson," interrupted Martin, stepping beside his nephew, hate oozing from his eyes like blood from a wound. "I served in Korea with Carol Ann's husband, Howard Lane."

"Sorry, Sir. He was dead when we got here early this morning, one thirty-six am to be exact," said Dickinson. "The woman lived about ten minutes after she arrived at Mercy Hospital." The investigator knelt by the man who was yet inspecting the pile of rubble. "Tragic," mumbled Dickinson, pulling a Cross pen from his inside coat pocket. "Look at this," he said, poking at a piece of melted metal. "It's the clamp to a purse. Sort of welded in one of the man's hands though. Makes you wonder doesn't it. The place is ablaze and it suddenly becomes real important to grab a purse."

"We'd better go, Adam," mumbled Martin, his voice like a growl.

"Huh?"

"Just a minute, Sir. I didn't get your names," said Dickinson, moaning as he got to his feet. "There's a question you might be able to answer for me, too."

Again, Martin knelt and covered his face with a folded arm. Adam turned to face the investigator. "He's Martin Bishop of Seattle. Retired colonel, U.S. Army. I'm Adam Richardson, Sergeant, U. S. Army, Fort Dix, New Jersey," he said, failing to mention that he was no longer in the army. "Need for me to repeat any of that?"

"No, just give me a minute, Sarge."

"What was the question?" gasped Martin, yet kneeling.

"Well, I've thought of a few more, uh, since you men are both from out of town, but the one I had in mind was, who's Samantha?"

No answer. Adam didn't know, but Martin's mind was asking questions instead of offering answers. How would a Dallas police detective know anything about Samantha Valentine? What could have been found in the house to involve her? Then, the answer came. Samantha was here and she might have the Buick. "Why do You ask, Officer?" mumbled Martin Bishop, his words groaned into his folded arms.

"Well," said Dickinson. "Mrs. Lane kept saying Samantha, Samantha, Samantha all the way to the burn unit at Mercy Hospital. I was just..."

"Samantha was Carol Ann's mother," sighed Martin, remembering the odd coincidence Carol Ann had mentioned. "Adam and I just stopped by to see Howard Lane. He and I are old war buddies. Were, I guess I should say."

"I see," responded Dickinson, sadly. "Yes, I understand."

"No, you don't," snapped Martin, his strength coming. "Where's the other car? They used to have an old Buick. Who identified the bodies? Who's making funeral arrangements? What happens next?"

"You sound like an investigator, Mister. Anyway, the neighbors who live right there are named Johnson," said Dickinson, pointing across Holiday Trail with his Cross pen. "He and his wife knew the couple, knew the man was retired army also knew the wife's mother's name was Samantha. They contacted relatives in Washington this morning. Fact is, I was hoping you and this young man were them. Maybe I just wanted to know if you knew some of the things a friend would. The other car, a Buick? Well, the neighbor, Grady Johnson, says it has probably been sold. I guess the Lanes had been trying to sell it for awhile. Howard offered it to Johnson for a thousand."

"We're on our way back to New Jersey," added Adam, laying a hand on Martin's back. "I'm stationed at Fort Dix, and he has to make arrangements to ship his furniture to Seattle. Most of it's in my mom and dad's garage. Uncle Martin just retired a few months ago himself. Commander, Fort Dix."

"Howard Lane was my XO," mumbled Martin, groaning again.

Dickinson made note of Martin and his nephew's addresses, then wished them luck and returned to his work. Adam drove to a Quality Inn he'd seen when leaving the airport. He kept an eye on Martin, but neither man spoke a word after driving away from the Lane home. While Adam was making arrangements for a room, Martin found a dark table in a lounge that was just off the inn's lobby.

"You okay?" asked Adam, joining him, dropping the bags in a chair.

"Never will be again." It was another mumble.

"Thanks for lying for me, and yourself." Martin hadn't had a drink, but already looked drunk. "You know that I know what happened," he whispered, looking into his big hands, opening and closing them slowly.

"No," said Adam, also whispering. "I'd say somebody got drunk and…"

"Howard could have been drunk," interrupted Martin, "but he and Carol Ann were actually murdered. Burned to death by a witch."

Adam leaned back in his chair, crossed his arms and looked at his uncle, sympathetically, but with equal confusion. "Well, I'm sorry as hell, Uncle Martin, but shouldn't you have told that Dickinson guy what you think?"

"Maybe, and maybe I will, but not yet." Martin closed his fists and lightly pounded on the table once, twice, the third time, then whimpered and rested his head on his folded arms. "Not yet," he repeated, a tearful moan. "I was so stupid. I believed that woman, and poor Howard must have, too."

Adam ordered a pitcher of draft beer, then sat and waited for a his uncle to rejoin the conversation, but Martin didn't move or make a sound. When the beer was brought to the table, Adam shook Martin's arm. "You need to get drunk, then go get some sleep," he said.

"Shut up." Adam ignored the meaningless affront. "What else you got to do?"

"Think," mumbled Martin, into his folded arms. "Maybe I'll fly commercial to Albuquerque and rent a plane, a Cessna one eighty-two, or something like that. There's some cabins somewhere up in the mountains north of there where an acquaintance of mine might live. You wanna go?"

"Rent a plane? Why not a car?" asked Adam.

"A plane," mumbled Martin, offering no explanation. "I'm licensed and fully qualified, but you don't have to go if you don't want to."

"Heck, I'll go. I'm standby to Philly, remember?" All kinds of visions of his uncle passed through Adam's mind. A beaten man deliberately crashing a small plane into a mountain. A crazy hermit living in a cave, hiding from his worst memory. "I'm free as a bird," he said, to extend the conversation, trying to get Martin to talk out his grief. "You want to tell me why the heck you'd want to go see some old friend at a time like this."

Again, Martin offered no explanation. "We'll spend a day in Albuquerque getting equipped, then..."

"Equipped for what?"

"The weather for one, but I wanna buy an oozy and a few rounds."

"An automatic assault weapon?" gasped Adam.

"Semiautomatic," corrected Martin, whispering again.

Chapter 15

The little Mexican bar was dark, smoky and uncomfortably cold, but remained busy with its lunch trade until a few minutes past two o'clock that afternoon. A steady stream of cowboys in denim jeans and jackets came in and took stools or tables close to the bar. They lit each other's cigarettes, joked and kidded among themselves in Spanish, but two spoke to Paul in English. "Damn cold isn't it," one said, then nodded to Ken while rubbing his hands and blowing into them. The other customer who spoke merely offered a greeting. He was an older man who smiled, but Ken detected that he exchanged a silent message with Paul, possibly questioning his reason for the stranger accompanying him.

Ken had noticed it when he and Paul walked in, but now the squeak of the front door was causing a certain tenseness to creep through him. The squeak announced everyone who came or went and Ken kept expecting some irate wild man to come running in, wielding a knife, or a blazing gun. He didn't know why he felt that way, but he could sense an uneasiness throughout the bar's patronage. Maybe this was a spot some local crazy considered his own private haunt and it wouldn't set well with him to see a stranger enjoying the services.

Ken's eyes kept automatically darting to the door every time he heard the squeak, but he wouldn't make eye contact with anyone unless it was absolutely unavoidable. Even a quick look in the direction of a female was out, he decided.

Several merchants with white shirts and dark colored parkas hurried in for a quick lunch, or to pick up carry-outs, the squeaking door grating on Ken like a toothache. His imagination was growing with each tense moment and now, he knew he was being appraised by a man who came in alone. He was at least sixty, very thin, wearing western boots with walking heels, a flat brimmed hat with a dozen or so shiny Mexican coins attached to the band. He wore a smart looking black corduroy suit and sported a well-trimmed goatee. A bullfighter. A slice of Madrid in the mountains of New Mexico.

Ken found himself flashing a smile of apology when making a split-second eye contact just as the distinguished Mexican man slid a chair out to join two men at a table by the door. The man did not return the smile, but remained standing, his eyes trained on Paul, eventually addressing him. "Pablo, nosotros conversar secreto," he said, then turned and walked through two swinging half-doors that appeared to lead to the kitchen.

Paul slid his chair back. "I'll just be a minute," he said, then hopped after the distinguished Mexican man. Ken wanted to head for the squeaking door, but didn't, feeling a confusing sense of immobility.

He had stayed with beer, but Paul had switched to coffee when he'd finished the chips and salsa. Feeling strangely alone and the need to do something, Ken raised a hand, deciding to speak to a young man who had just stepped through the same swinging doors Paul had passed through. The man's eyes cut straight to Ken, held a moment, then focused on the lady bartender when Ken smiled.

After moving down the bar, the man began helping the bartender with the cash register, apparently trying to get the drawer to stay closed. "Sir," summoned Ken, not knowing how he should refer to the young man. "Could someone bring me another bottle of Bud and give Paul a refill on his coffee?"

"Just leave it open for now," said the young man to the lady bartender, then turned and busied himself behind the bar, his hands not visible to Ken. Momentarily, he slid two shot glasses onto the bar, filled them from a near full bottle of brown something, then walked around the bar with a fresh cup of coffee and Ken's bottle of beer. He appeared to be eighteen or nineteen and looked as fitting as Ken felt he looked out of place. Although the bar and the weather outside was uncomfortably cold, the young man wore a black muscle shirt, shiny black trousers, black Italian shoes with sharp toes and had a tiny cross on a gold chain around his neck. The cross had different colored gems inlaid horizontally and vertically, making it appear like a four-spoke wheel. Through the languid light and hovering cigarette smoke, Ken could see that the young man's upper lip was dark with the beginnings of a new-growth mustache, his chin showing an attempt at a goatee. His hair was black and shiny, but too long.

Ken stood, stepped around a chair and reached for the drinks. "Thanks," he said. "Figure up what we owe, and I'll get you paid."

The young man neither spoke nor smiled, but handed Ken the drinks and returned to the bar, his hand going up to smooth back his hair. Ken turned his back and put the drinks down, then sat back down himself, facing the bar again. The young man, approaching from only a few feet away, stopped abruptly, leaned forward and slid one of the shots he'd poured a minute earlier onto the table in front of Ken. "Try this," he said, ready to drink the other. The kid's eyes were intense, large black pools of deep thought. "I always honor new customers," he explained, a hand smoothing back his hair again.

"What is it?"

"Bourbon. It's a man's drink."

"On the house?"

"No, it's on me," said the young man, his chin slightly raising in gesture, indicating that Ken should drink up.

"And, who are you?"

"Cash. What's your name?" said the young man, then threw back his head and downed the brown liquid.

Ken downed his shot, then introduced himself. Cash, as unemotional as a bailiff reading a verdict, slid out a chair and took a seat. "What's your business here?" he asked. "We don't often have distinguished visitors."

Ken sipped his beer, thinking, wondering why the sudden attention. He had gone all but unnoticed until the old man who led Paul to the back had come in and looked around. Now, this kid Cash was boring holes through him with the most intense eyes he'd ever felt. "I'm on my way to Oakland, California. Next stop, sunny Southeast Asia. Nha Trang to be exact."

"Oh, yeah? Vietnam via Travis Air Force Base in Oakland. The ugly city by the beautiful city by the bay," responded Cash. "Dirty hole," he added, again smoothing back his hair, a constant habit that was making Ken nervous. "You want one more shot, Man? I'll drink to you. A genuine war hero risking it all."

Ken had been careful with the beer and wasn't feeling it, nor was he about to get woozy on bourbon. One more would be the limit. "Thanks," he said. "I'll buy. Put it on my tab."

Cash snapped his fingers, his intense eyes remaining on Ken. The lady bartender, a heavyset woman with big red lips and thick black hair to her shoulders, hustled the drinks to the table, made no comment or eye contact before swishing her full dress back to the bar. "To Captain Killer," said Cash, offering a toast, followed by a sudden snap of his head to flip back his long hair.

Captain Killer, condescending thought Ken, as he clicked his shot glass to Cash's and swallowed the shot of bourbon. The kid waited for him to put the shot glass down, then took a sip from his and slid it onto the table, his eyes following the little glass for a brief moment, then returning to Ken. "So, you're a career man are you, Captain Valentine?"

"Not at all."

"Married?"

"That either."

"What brought you to Santa Cruz? Don't seem like it's on the way to Oakland from Fort Dix to me. A little off the track, wouldn't you say?"

"Fort Dix? It is, but I have a place in the mountains near here."

"A Place?"

"A cabin in Lost Mountain Park."

"Which one?" Ken found himself getting even more nervous under the intense scrutiny of the black eyes. "I didn't know they were numbered."

"No? I didn't know they weren't, but which one's yours? Where is it from, say the store, or the pier?"

"Three down from the store. It's one of the ones with a shed in back."

Cash nodded, his eyes moving around Ken's face, seeming to take a moment to evaluate what he'd heard. "If it's the third one down from the store, who's the pretty lady living there now? I hear she has a little girl."

"My daughter. The lady is my ex. How do you know all this, Cash?"

The kid smoothed his hair back and shrugged. "I can read, Man. Paul has your orders in the back." Cash smiled, almost apologetically.

"So, you own the cabin, but your ex plans to stay there until you get back from Nam, right?"

"Sorta," responded Ken, checking to see if Paul had in fact taken his orders to the back. "She wants the cabin, though."

"Think that's a good idea?"

"Why not?"

"Because, it's a bad idea. You plan to join Paul's mountain militia?"

The kid was cocky. "Are you involved?" asked Ken.

"Hell no, Man," exclaimed Cash. "I wouldn't give those creeps ten-day old tacos if they were starving. My kid brother got mixed up with'em, but that's gonna change real soon. Why the hell are you interested?"

Ken paused, letting a little accusing smile twist his lips as he scratched the stubble of his chin in thought. Cash himself might just have a stake in the Freedom Fighters. "Is your brother AWOL? What's his name?"

Cash didn't answer immediately, taking a long moment to reflect, his eyes yet intense, but his demeanor visibly softening. "My brother's dodging the draft. He's gone by the name of Gunner since he was twelve. I took him hunting and he shot a deer from over three hundred yards. A single shot between the eyes. He's a good kid, but the militia is no damn good for him, or anyone."

"You're pretty opinionated, Cash."

"That's a fair statement," said the young man, evenly. "Tell me something, Ken, what could those militants offer you? Are you planning to hide out to stay out of Vietnam?"

"You tell me something," said Ken. "How do you know the things about me that you do and, while you're at it, how old are you?"

Cash smiled as he reached for his wallet. "I get asked that a lot," he said, fishing a New Mexico driver's license from the wallet. "Twenty-six. I've seen the jungles of Vietnam. Packed a rifle up near the DMZ. It wasn't bad."

Ken absently perused Cash's license. "So, how do you know so much about me, Mr. Cash?"

"I'll tell you sometime. Sure you don't want another shot?"

Ken felt uneasy with the young man and the strange bar, but was finding the sense of challenge fun. "No more for me," he said, looking about, beginning to wonder if the little runt was going to come back to the table. "What was your unit in Nam?" he asked, wanting to maintain the conversation until he could find out about Paul.

"First Infantry. If ya gotta be one, be a big red one," said Cash, smiling a little. "You're really concerned about going aren't you."

"Sure," responded Ken, smoothing his own hair back, wondering why he felt it necessary. "I don't know one sane man who wants a tour in Vietnam?"

"The Freedom Fighters isn't the answer, Captain Valentine. In fact, there's only one answer. Do your duty, keep your head down and get back in one piece. I'd rather risk that again than join a bunch of radicals." Cash took another sip from the shot, then continued. "You're active military, Mister. If I thought you were really going to join some group and commit treason, I'd do one of two things. Shoot you in the head, or turn you in and hope like hell the AWOL Apprehension Board would throw you in the stockade for life."

Ken gave Cash a challenging look. "Heavy, Brother," he sighed. "Does everybody around here feel like you do about the Freedom Fighters?"

"Plenty do," responded the young man, nodding as he smoothed back his hair again. "They're dangerous. The men at the top are criminals."

"You don't turn 'em in on account of your kid brother, right?"

Cash stared directly into Ken's eyes. "Maybe, but we should talk about that, Captain Valentine," he said. "Tonight. Take Paul back to Pueblo Heights, then meet me here about nine. Okay with you?"

"I guess," agreed Ken, gesturing with his chin. "What's Paul doing back there with that man?"

"Papa? Papa? Oh, he and I own the Pueblo Heights. In truth, Papa and I just caught on to Paul. You can talk about it, but think it over first. You won't learn much if you mention our meeting tonight."

"Won't he find out about it anyway?"

"Probably, but by then we'll either have something to talk about, or we won't," said Cash, evenly again. "Pop and I don't have much room in our world for criminals. By the way, bring a coat, don't eat and maybe I'll introduce you to someone special. That's if you show," challenged the young man, smiling again, smoothing back his hair with both hands this time.

Ken waited at the table by himself until almost three. The bar was down to four drinkers and him when Paul hopped out from the back.

"You ready?" he asked, smiling like a happy child, one hand waving a one-hundred dollar bill, the other sliding Ken's orders onto the table.

"I'm plenty ready."

Ken started questioning Paul the minute they were seated in the convertible. The little man had gotten a twenty-five dollar a week raise, effective the first of last month. Confusing? Maybe. "Hey, Paul, why did you take my orders with you back there?"

"I knew my boss would want to know something about you, Man."

"Why?"

"Why not? You're a strange face."

"I was, but now I feel like I've been properly introduced, interrogated and all but fingerprinted. I don't give a shit though. Explain what a guy does after he joins the militia. Do most members live in one of those caves up on the peaks, or do they have jobs like you?"

"Maybe twenty-five have jobs, but most of are just fucked up losers who couldn't find work. They're on the run, hiding out, so they want to live up there. I had to stay for the training. A month. The headquarters cave isn't bad, but I'm not gonna put a foot in that one where the recruits live. Damn thing's just a crude hundred foot hole full of C-Rations, K-Rations, bunks and guns and explosives and about a thousand drums of gas. Gas like your car uses."

Ken, knowing he wasn't going to sleep in a mountain cave, nodded and continued, keeping his tone conversational. "What kind of training did you do?"

"The full-blown shit, Man. Rifle training, machine-gun training, mortar training, bivouacin and even survival stuff. Like eating bugs, hunting game and catching fish in the streams. That BB even made us learn to repel down the side of a cliff with a rope. Training was a big hassle, but I did it." "You aren't on the run or hiding out so what's in the militia for you, Paul?" asked Ken, then answered himself. "Oh, yeah, money for your dependents."

"Dependent," corrected Paul.

Ken nodded. "What did you pay to get into the Freedom Fighters?" Paul didn't answer Ken's question but explained more about the militia organization, BB's training program and Chief's lack of interest in it. "That smart ass Indian thinks he's got all the brains in the world when it comes to survival in these mountains, but he's full a shit. He's just a power-hungry little fart that's rat holing his part of the tuition money and donations that come in."

"Donations?"

"The strong arm kind, Man. You interested or not?"

Ken, playing Paul's same coy game, didn't answer his question, but asked his own. "Since the militia is funded mostly by charging new members with what BB and Chief refer to as tuition and protection money, plus these donations I guess, where do they keep all the cash?"

"Well," began Paul, then paused.

Ken used the pause to repeat his former question, one with less inference to his new interest. "What did you have to pay to get in? You never said."

"It went like this, Man," sighed Paul, his expression one of relief. "I brought in three new members and Chip kinda let me slide. I guess he's serving as the treasurer and he knew I was a producer."

"What's the chance of me getting in with something other than money?"

"Like what?" asked Paul, his beady eyes full of doubt.

"I've got a bronze statue by Remington at the cabin. It's worth way the hell and gone over ten thousand big ones."

"No shit?" mumbled the little man. "Whatcha doing tonight?"

Ken rubbed the stubble of his chin again, but didn't answer until he'd pulled in and parked by the manager's office at Pueblo Heights. "I'm gonna get me a nap first, but then I may drive up to Lost Mountain Park and look around."

"Yeah? Well, try to get that bronze. Thanks for the beer, Man."

Chapter 16

Samantha hurried out of the Republic National Bank in downtown Dallas, as if she'd just robbed it. Mr. Russell had made her feel so much better, but was she? She sped up Stemmons Freeway, 1-35 North, to Inwood Road, then east to Lemon Avenue and pulled in at Cotton Bowling Palace, remembering the big round neon sign from her days at SMU, particularly that long night when she met Ken at Victor's Restaurant and Lounge. Her nerves were finally beginning to settle, but she could still feel an evil presence. Howard was out there.

After parking the Buick in back, close to a fence between the building and the alley, Samantha and Karla walked, almost ran to Friendly Chevrolet, the dealership Mr. Russell had recommended, also remembering its close proximity to Victor's. There, after absently test driving but two cars, she bought a used 1966 Impala station wagon. Back at the bowling alley, Samantha transferred the bags from the Buick, wiped it down for fingerprints inside and out with a sweater, left the keys in the ignition and tore away.

Karla was talkative, but Samantha wasn't hearing. Beautiful green fields and big homes in peaceful settings were passing unnoticed, mere pickets in the fence that lined the long path home. Home? Where was home? Where the heart was? Where was that? It didn't exist. There were no open arms awaiting Samantha. Dr. Benjamin was the last person who opened his heart to her. A wonderful man who she would never allow herself to see again.

Tears were welling now. Karla was quiet, falling asleep, bored but peaceful in her innocence. Samantha reached up and pushed the rearview mirror against the headliner. She tried to imagine walking through a garden on a warm sunny day. A large garden, tidy with rose covered arches opening to meandering paths leading through huge beds of pink, gold and purple flowers. Beyond, swaying in the soft summer breeze and basking in the sunlight that pierced the limbs and leaves of tall trees that lined the big garden, was a sea of blood-red poppies, blurry, but stirring as if crossed over by an unseen whirlwind. No, it was only taillights and dancing neon signs along the streets of Wichita Falls.

After eating a late lunch, Karla crawled into the back seat and fell asleep. Samantha drove on, speeding along between seventy and eighty miles per hour. The sky was clear and the setting sun had a line of low wind clouds on the western horizon ablaze. While racing across the endless pasture lands of North Texas, there was no peaceful garden and Samantha's mind began to torment her. The old memories came out of the night and trapped her. She knew she had done something shameful, disgraceful and knew how humiliating it would be if she ever had to answer for her actions. It was satisfying to think she'd made a despicable rapist pay in some way, but it would always haunt her. Regardless, Samantha had to address all that remained to be done. If Howard's big check cleared without a hitch, knew away from Lost Mountain Park would be affordable and she knew that had to be done. A good life for her and Karla would never happen in Lost Mountain Park. If something very wrong wasn't going on there, it would always appear that way to Samantha.

The big wagon rolled along smoothly, eating up the narrow highways to Amarillo so quickly that Samantha hardly realized how much of the trip was behind her. It was only ten-fifty pm and she was hardly any worse for wear than when sitting at Mr. Russell's desk at the bank.

After refueling at a truck stop and checking on Karla, Samantha started out across the flat windswept Texas panhandle on Route 66. She turned on the radio, KOMA out of Oklahoma City, keeping the rock'n roll music soft and low, singing along with tunes she knew, keeping her mind busy. It didn't work long though and soon she was consumed in her thoughts again. Samantha felt she'd done the right thing in buying a newer car, maybe even the right thing in flying to Dallas. However, if Howard Lane was somehow able to find and challenge the income fund, prove the money was his, then what? Would he get the money back and Samantha herself be taken to jail? Who could be depended upon to take care of Karla?

The endless dark miles droned by, the yellow lines appearing unbroken as Samantha pushed on, trying to run away from the lonely solitude. The big rigs, in their own world, running lights like Christmas tree decorations, zoomed by unnoticed, part of the terrain. There was a westbound train in the distance to the right, its speed exacting that of the wagon. The passenger cars were yet brightly lit. Businessmen, soldiers, maybe honeymooners, thought Samantha, feeling a pang of despair, wondering if there would ever be a honeymoon for her. Would she again know love? Had she? "Yes," she whispered aloud. "I loved Ben and he loved me and one day I will know another love. One day."

Santa Rosa came and went like a blink, then a sign that read Moriarty 35 Miles, Albuquerque 73. Samantha stretched and yawned. Thoughts of the contingent outcome and consequence of unlawfully taking another person's money, regardless of the reason, was taking its toll. Her eyes were burning, beginning to fill with blinding tears. It seemed hypocritical to even pray about it, but she always prayed when she felt lost. "Lord, please find it in your heart to forgive me for knowingly and willingly breaking Your commandment," she murmured, ridiculing herself as she wiped tears from her eyes with the back of her hand. "I didn't know what else to do." Samantha ruffled through her purse until she found a Kleenex, then blew her nose and stuffed the tissue into a dashboard ashtray. "Help me, Lord," she whispered. "Help me. I need love. Everyone needs love. Help me, please."

"Huh? Are we almost home, Mommy?"

Karla climbed up front. "Hi, Honey. Did I wake you?" Samantha spoke while looking out her side window into the clear cold night. She wanted Karla's company, but didn't want her tears to upset the little girl.

"Yeah. I heard you singin a song."

Samantha had forgotten about the radio. "Well, let's get rid of the static and just talk for a little bit. Want to?"

"Yeah. How much longer til we're home?"

Samantha sniffed and wiped her eyes again, then pulled her daughter's head into her lap. "It's about three or four more hours, Honey. Do you want to stop and eat? Maybe go to the restroom?"

"Uh-huh, but can we drive on tonight? I can't wait to get home."

Samantha stopped at a service station just beyond Albuquerque on Highway 25 North. She refueled, bought soft drinks and snacks and was back on the road in twenty minutes. The first glow of dawn was just spreading across the slumbering mountain country. It seemed like awakening from a bad dream to Samantha. Having had little Karla to absorb her thoughts for the last few hours had made her feel better, also in a hurry to get home. The Chevrolet wagon drove like a dream, giving her confidence she didn't have with the old Ford. Except for the familiar smell of the mountain country, the increasing elevation was hardly noticed. The big wagon seemed to have power to spare.

Santa Fe, yet drowsing in the early morning, was in the rearview mirror before Samantha realized she'd gotten that far from Albuquerque. Again, tiny Santa Cruz came and went like a blink of the eye. The tall pines along the narrow road through the Santa Fe National Forest, standing like silent sentinels in the cold morning air, zipped by like the guardrails of a freeway bridge. By the time they wound through to Lost Mountain Park, appearing just like Samantha and Karla had left it, a busy morning was in full swing. The old Ford wagon was waiting in the yard, the Indian lady was fishing from the pier, appearing to be showing something on her hook to Sonny. Chip Parker's flatbed Chevy truck, again loaded with big gasoline drums, was parked by the store. He, Jay Redwine and little Jack Cox were looking under the hood while discussing something, but appearing to do nothing about it. Regardless of Samantha's dislike for the park, she had a sudden sense of relief and homecoming. It seemed immediate, a burden lifted as quickly as unexpectedly.

There was no wind and the placid water on the lake was a motionless yellow sheet in the morning sunlight. It was twenty past eight and Samantha felt better than she had in months, as if she had vindicated some terrible thing she had done and accomplished a great feat in the process. The little cabin looked like an awaiting embrace, familiar, something she owned.

While dragging in the bags, after getting her coffee on and starting a fire, the peace of the morning was suddenly broken when Chad walked around the corner of the cabin. "That was a quick trip."

His words and sudden appearance sent a shock of fear through Samantha like a bullet. "Oh, man," she sighed, dropping her suitcase. "I forgot all about you. Karla, come out here."

"Sorry," said the big blonde. "I've been staying in your shed and just didn't know how to let you know I was here without just stupidly moseying around front. How are you gals, anyway? Need any help?"

"We're fine, and now I could use some help," sighed Samantha, forcing a tired smile. "You almost scared the pants off me. Carry these into the den. I need to fix a little breakfast for Karla."

"Wow. I guess I'd better be a little more careful. A guy could get pretty embarrassed around you."

"I doubt it," sighed Samantha, realizing she would be getting dog-tired and weary as soon as the hyper feeling brought on by the long drive wore off. "Why am I glad to see you? I need to sleep for a day."

"Do it then. I'll be the guard," said big blonde Chad, smiling sincerely.

"What, Mommy?" asked Karla, standing in the open doorway.

Samantha explained that she just didn't want Karla to get the shock she did. "Do you remember Mr. Begay?"

"Uh-huh. Hi, Chad. Can I go to bed, Mommy?"

"You should eat a little breakfast first."

"But, I already brushed my teeth."

Chapter 17

Adam was as worried about the plan as he was his uncle. Although Martin had every right and reason to be saddened with the death of his fiancée, he sure wasn't making sense. It was seven Saturday morning. Last night, after a dozen glasses of beer, Martin mostly talked to himself, repeating over and over that he was definitely going to take an early flight to Albuquerque. He would buy an oozy, then rent a small plane and search the high New Mexico mountain country north of Santa Fe for some remote park. Adam sat and listened, getting less and less interested in going along with every passing moment. Why should he go? For the adventure? Hell no. He'd had enough of that while on search and destroy missions in the jungles of South Vietnam. Always ready to...to what? Shit, thought Adam, I don't want to go. I don't want Uncle Martin to go, but I can't stop him, so I have to go. What a mess. Uncle Martin's mind is a mess.

"Hey, Unk," he said, shaking him awake. "Get up. Get up and jump in the shower. I'll go after coffee and toast."

The morning sun was spilling through the motel room's curtained window as if Dallas was a war zone under siege. Martin opened his eyes, wondering where he was for a moment, then getting hit with the sudden realization. "Huh? Uh, who...Oh, okay," he sighed, sitting upright for a second, then lying back down, rubbing his face with his hands. "I don't know if I can make it."

"That's fine with me. How about we just fly to Philly and you stay with Mom for a week or so?"

Martin shook his head. "I'm going to Albuquerque."

"Well, get the hell out of bed then," ordered his nephew, tugging at Matin's foot, but wanting to slap him until he made sense. "I'll do everything until we get to the airport, then you're the boss. I say Philly, you say Albuquerque, but I'll do what you want. Come on," he coaxed. "Get yourself going. I'll be back in fifteen minutes."

Adam left the room. Martin rolled out of bed, stood and stretched. He moaned, feeling the swirl of a hangover and again, the crushing thought of Carol Ann actually being gone. Murdered. "Oh," he sighed, then knelt to a knee as if to pray, but only banged the floor with his fist once before stumbling into the bathroom. He didn't know what he would really do if he found Samantha Valentine, but he wasn't going to let her live. The woman, apparently a heartless evil bitch, killed Carol Ann and Howard Lane, who was probably completely innocent of half the involvement Martin himself had believed he had with Mrs. Valentine. Hell, he was thinking, while standing under the steaming shower, poor Ken Valentine was more than likely falsely accused, railroaded by me. I forced him into the duty in Vietnam. He might get killed and I helped his worthless wife get everything he had. She probably got half of what belonged to Howard Lane, too. "Bitch," he screamed, slugging the shower curtain, then ripping it from the rod. What a twist, he was thinking. A jury might give Samantha twenty years, but they wouldn't fry such a young mother, who the right attorney could make appear the victim herself. "Evil witch," he screamed again.

Adam had checked out and was waiting with Martin's breakfast when he stepped out of the bathroom. Scrambled eggs, bacon, toast and jelly, a pot of coffee.

"Feel better?"

"Huh? Oh. Yeah, I guess I do," responded Martin, drying his hair as he looked for his clothes.

"I packed your dirty stuff," said Adam. "Put on fresh. It's gonna be a long day and I don't want Mom seeing you looking like a street bum."

"Clean clothes? Yeah, I'd better," agreed Martin. "You can go see your mom. I'm going to Albuquerque. How far to the airport?"

"Five minutes," sighed Adam, giving up. "We're checked out and a guy at the desk gave me a list of phone numbers for the airlines. I'll make the calls?"

"Well, let's eat first."

"I already have, and if you're too damn stubborn to even consider going to Philly with me, I'll make our reservations for Albuquerque."

Chapter 18

Ken left the Pueblo Heights Motel under the cover of darkness, thick low clouds from horizon to horizon were hiding the moon and the stars. The temperature had dropped radically, well below freezing. After taking a nap, he had crept around the room like a spider, constantly checking to see if Paul was watching from the manager's office. He was wondering why the little guy had him so concerned, or was it the meeting at Cantina Clavado with Cash that had him worried. Why am I here? Ken parked his convertible in the shadows behind the little bar, stepped out, locked the door and opened the trunk lid. He took his nine-millimeter pistol from the brown satchel and slipped it into an inside coat pocket.

The familiar squeak of the front door spun heads like pages of a book blowing in the wind. Ken smiled at the faces, psychedelic in the reflection of flashing neon beer signs and the bright colors of the moaning jukebox. Where was Cash? "You lost, Gringo?" came from a dark corner.

Ken ignored the question, blowing into his hands as he moved around the crowded tables, looking about for an empty one. The place was cold, although packed to near capacity. Silent faces peering through the thick gray smoke that loomed overhead. A cold winter fog filled with big black derisive eyes, darts pricking at his skin. The music screeched and moaned like a dying man, Hank Williams could get along and be doing fine until he heard an old freight moving down the line. "Full on a Sunday? Shit," sighed Ken, unable to find a table.

Suddenly, while weaving his way back to the front door, a big hand grabbed Ken's left arm. "Have a seat, Man."

Ken looked down at the voice, that of a wide shouldered, dark-skinned man, grinning grotesquely, his teeth like the keys of a piano. "You mind?" asked Ken. "There aren't many places to park."

"Sheet no, Man. I asked you didn't I. Want a drink?"

Ken, nodding as he pulled a wad of bills from his front pocket, again feeling the eyes, told the man what he wanted. "Bud in a bottle."

"Hey, Tiny," yelled the seated man, holding up his hand. 'Two Buds and two shots of tequila." The man wore a black jersey, khaki pants with the legs rolled up and an ankle length trench coat, the size of a tent.

Ken took one of two unoccupied ladder-back chairs; the other was missing two of the three back braces. "I'm Ken," he said, extending a hand.

"Franco Ramos," said the grinning man, then shook hands with Ken. "What's your business?" he asked, the grip of his big hand like that of a small child.

Ken quickly withdrew his hand, then fumbled through his money to avoid eye contact with anyone. "I was looking for Cash."

"I see," responded Franco, knowing the reason for Ken being in Cantina Clavado. "Why do you want to talk to Cash? You looking for work?"

"No. Just army stuff. Old times you know."

"I see. You were in Nam then. Where?" Tiny, a giant Mexican, just over six feet, but well over three hundred pounds, brought the drinks on a small round tray, slid them onto the table. He was clad in denim overalls and a tee shirt. "It's seex dollars, Man," he said, his voice raspy, his tiny black eyes all but closed.

Franco tossed a ten-dollar bill onto the table. "Gieve de change to Laura."

With a big hand, Tiny swooped up the bill, his eyes squinting against the looming smoke cloud. "You're wastin your money, Franco. Laura's got a man now. Who's your friend?"

"Ken." Franco slapped Ken on the back. "Meet Ken de Gringo."

Ken stood, his eyes level with the big wide bartender's. Tiny, his lips tight, his big feet seemingly planted into the floor, just nodded. "Is Cash here tonight?" asked Ken.

Tiny's eyes squinted tighter. "Why do you want to know, Gringo?"

Ken looked at Franco, seeking support. "Well, he invited me to come by."

Tiny nodded. "Then, relax, Man," he said. "I'll see if he's comin out."

"Yeah, relax," repeated Franco, then to Tiny, "Send Laura, too. I ain't seen her in two years. Maybe I just wanna ask about her man."

Tiny responded with a frown, then harrumphed and returned to the bar.

It was a long wait. Franco Ramos only talked to other Hispanics at nearby tables, while downing the shot of tequila and sipping beer. Ken took a draw from his beer, then poured in the shot, cutting his eyes right and left as he did, noticing that the crowd was no longer staring at him. From a table by the jukebox though, he caught the eye of two young women, Mexicans in dresses, beauties, maybe working girls. One, appearing the taller of the two, had her long dark dress pulled to mid-thigh. She winked, shrugged with a wanton smile, raising a glass of draft beer, pointing into it. Ken nodded and held up a twenty-dollar bill, sensing that Tiny was observing.

"You just bought Rita a shot of tequila," said Franco Ramos.

"Rita who?"

"They used to call her Rita Franklin," said the big Mexican, raising his beer to acknowledge her. "She always wanted a hundred-dollar bill for all night."

Tiny was holding up the shot glass. "Franco, should I take the tequila to Rita?" asked Ken.

"Naw, Man. Stay put. She'll get it."

Rita slid from her chair like an awaking feline on the prowl, the nightly hunt, then proceeded to the bar, downing the shot when they handed it to her. While weaving her way toward Ken and Franco, she mouthed, "Thank you."

Ken got to his feet and held his chair, the good chair, for the approaching beauty. "Good evening, Rita," he said, holding her left hand as she graciously seated herself. "Would you like to invite your friend to join us?"

Franco answered. "No. She doesn't want her friend to join us."

Rita shrugged, batted her eyes and offered her hand. Ken, slightly caught off guard by Franco's curt response and Rita's disregard, was just about to take the broken chair, but remained standing until he had shook with Rita and kissed her hand. She laughed. "Are you French?" she asked.

"Texan," said Ken. "Houston to be exact."

Ken and Rita visited, exchanged phone numbers where each could be reached, then Rita returned to the table with her friend. Franco wanted to know if Ken was going to contact her. "Sure, why not?"

"No reason, except I was just wondering what kind of guy you are."

"So? Good or bad?" asked Ken, wanting the big Mexican's approval.

"How about stupid? You're a long way away from your friends, yet you're willing to get involved with a dangerous little devil."

"Well, Hell Fire," exclaimed Ken. "Is everything around here fuckin dangerous? That's all Cash talks about."

"What about the old soldier stuff?"

"Huh?" Ken, irritated at being questioned, shrugged and took another sip of his beer. "We'll talk about that tonight. Where the hell is Cash anyway?"

"Relax, Man," said Franco, his hands up as if his words were in plea. "He comes out when he wants to come out. I was just giving you a little advice."

"Okay, so what's so dangerous about Rita?"

Franco sipped from his beer while glancing toward Rita's table. "She has friends, Man. They'll rob you blind. Maybe beat the hell out of you in the deal."

Ken sat silently thinking for a moment, getting more irritated and more impatient to meet with Cash, considering whether to wait or leave. Rita kept acknowledging him with smiles and finger waves. Tiny was keeping a close watch on the goings-on throughout the bar, but especially between Ken and Rita. Franco, expressionless, kept his eyes glued to Ken's.

Finally, emerging from the back, through the swinging doors that led to the kitchen, Cash walked behind the bar to the cash register, opened the drawer with a ching, then took out a wad of bills. Ken tried to get his attention with a wave, but Cash hurried back through swinging doors. "He knows you're here, Man." said Franco, sourly.

"Yeah, well why doesn't the little fuckhead come out here then?"

Franco leaned forward in his chair, his big hand clamping Ken's forearm, pulling him against the table. "Show some respect, Man. This is Cash's place. You don't like something, you leave."

Ken tried to yank his arm free, but Franco gripped tighter, flashing his keyboard like teeth with a big grin. "Okay, okay," snapped Ken, his quick words attracting stares and muffled laughter from nearby tables. It seemed to him, that those who had overheard were awaiting a more violent reaction from the big Mexican. "I'll get us another round," offered Ken.

Franco released his grip. Ken picked up his money, then walked up to the bar, weaving around the crowded tables. Before he could order, Tiny held up two fingers, his eyebrows raised in question. Ken nodded, then looked back toward Rita, who was weaving her way toward him. Suddenly, pop, pop, two loud hand claps came from the end of the bar. Ken, startled, swung his head around to see what had happened. "Go home, Rita," said Cash, then to Tiny, "Ken and Franco's drinks are on me. I'll take coffee." Then to Ken, after a slight pause to smooth back his hair, "Let's go to your table, Man."

Ken's eyes followed Rita. "Hi, Cash. I'm back there," he said, a thumb over his shoulder. "It's getting late. Maybe I'd better..."

Playfully, Cash shoved Ken toward his and Franco's table. "You're just blessed with bad ideas aren't you. Let's talk first."

Ken led the way, taking the broken chair. Cash spun the good one around and straddled the seat. "Thanks, Man," he said to Franco. "I told you he'd stand out like a cow in a pig sty."

"No sweat."

Unbeknownst to Ken, Franco was in Cantina Clavado at Cash's request. Franco, now with the Department of Justice, was contractor for hire, overseeing the disposition of confiscated drugs and related paraphernalia by Border Patrol units in Texas, New Mexico and Arizona. He'd worked for Cash and his father once before. "Franco recovered a stolen delivery truck from a Jicarilla Apache policer officer for us. The police didn't steal the vehicle, but he wouldn't release it either. Well, he wouldn't until Franco explained why it would be wise to," explained Cash, winking at Franco.

The big Mexican didn't appear to be listening, but opened his long trench coat to show a federal badge and a pistol holstered under his left armpit. "My friend did the talking," he said, tapping the butt of the pistol. Ken reached into his coat pocket and massaged the butt of the nine-millimeter.

The DOJ contractor and Cash talked in Spanish for a moment, then Franco left for the kitchen and Cash turned to Ken. "Okay," he began. "Did you talk to Paul after you left here?"

"Yeah. Just about the militia though." "Doesn't matter. I need you to help Franco."

"You're kidding? The guy's a federal agent. What could I do?"

"Be a hero, Man," said Cash, smoothing back his hair, his voice dropping ten decibels, a mere murmur against the loud rumblings of the crowded bar. "You remember me mentioning my kid brother, Gunner?'

"Yeah. The deer hunter."

"I want him off that mountain. Paul will lead you and Franco up there and you guys are coming back with my kid brother and..." Cash, seeing no interest in Ken's eyes, explored another angle. "You men will be right where the Freedom Fighters keep their guns and ammo and drugs and money." Cash allowed a moment for that to soak in. "Get it?" he finally asked, checking the bait. "Real money? Cash money? All

I want is my brother outta there and off that mountain in one piece, but you guys might want something else."

Ken nodded, not really knowing, but wondering if Cash meant that there might be a lot of money to split between... Who? "Money is a little hard to spend when you're dead," he said, trying to appear at ease with the innuendo, as he had interpreted it. "Are we talking about a lot of money?"

"A lot by some standards," said Cash, having no idea. While assembling his thoughts and awaiting further comment, Ken sipped his beer and cut his eyes toward the jukebox, noticing Rita's empty chair. "What happened to the pretty lady?" he asked, an attempt to seem uninterested in getting involved with ripping off a bunch of radicals.

"Forget her, Captain Valentine," said Cash. "I didn't partake, but you can get all the strange pussy you want in Vietnam. Now, why don't you have something to eat, then go get some sleep. Franco will be knocking on your door at eight in the morning. If I were you, I'd be there. Otherwise, Papa and I will have to assume you're going to be the next Freedom Fighter recruit."

Ken cut a warning eye toward Cash. "Just don't go jumping to conclusions, Hot Shot. I didn't say I was joining the militia. What about Paul?"

"Depends."

Chapter 19

t was midmorning Monday, dull, cold and partially overcast, when Samantha finally decided to get out of the cabin. It had rained on Sunday, the sun peeking through the cloud cover only once in the afternoon. Twice last night, then again this morning, Samantha found herself sitting on the den sofa staring into the dead fireplace, her mind a whirlpool of disarray. Hours and hours of wasting time on useless thinking and planning. It was too late, after the fact. Nothing could be done now. She had gone to Dallas like some organized crime figure and extorted over two hundred thousand dollars from a man after drugging him. Regardless of whether or not she could justify it in her own mind, no one else would see it as anything but a criminal act.

It was time for Samantha to forget though. Forget Howard Lane and hope to never see him again. Was it possible, even though his chapter in her life was closed? It had happened with Dr. Ott when her Uncle Hiram forced him out of Dallas. And all dealings with Ken Valentine would conclude as soon as he picked up his Remington bronze. Samantha had to go on and live, do whatever was necessary to make a good life for her daughter.

Sunday afternoon, Samantha had wanted to sleep and lounge, weary from the long trip, but her torturous thoughts wouldn't let her. As much as she wanted to forget, she knew she needed to talk to someone about all that had happened, someone that would be objective, maybe assure her that she wasn't going to get in trouble, regardless of the outcome. Had the deposit had time to clear channels? Was Howard Lane hot in pursuit?

Samantha had been tempted to tell Chad Begay everything yesterday morning while making coffee for him, but caught the reflection of herself in the kitchen window. She was a wreck, the remains of one being driven by fear of having to one day answer for a deplorable act. Although Samantha needed to reach out to someone, she couldn't bring herself to talk to anyone in that condition. Plus, Mr. Begay had done nothing to indicate that he was or was not one she could trust. What would Uncle Hiram advise? *Remember, Samantha, everyone needs help from time to time and when you find that you do, the final responsibility is on your shoulders to get it.*

Samantha was all alone, feeling more alone with each passing moment, each troubling thought. In review of what had happened with Howard, the most troubling part was that the only proof that he had wronged her was her account and that of a child. A sudden chill rippled over her body, thoughts of prosecutors torturing Karla were sickening and being cooped up in the little cabin commiserating with herself was only making things worse.

Samantha took a long hot shower, washed her hair and put on a bright red sweater and white denim jeans. She stepped from the cabin and took in a big breath of the cool mountain air, shivering against the bite, but loving the vivacity it carried into her spirit, an odd moment of release, realizing a sudden sense of unfettered freedom. She drifted gratefully from the grips of cabin fever, a weight that had dulled her sense of well-being. However fleeting, Samantha wanted to cling to the moment as long as she could.

The park, though appearing dank and dreary under the broken cloud cover, had life and movement. Although no comparison to the high street bustle of Dallas and Houston, Samantha welcomed the sight just the same. Chad was sitting astride his big motorcycle in front of the store talking with Chip Parker and BB Douglas. Little frail Jack Cox and Jay Redwine were nearby, down on their haunches discussing something Jay was drawing on the ground with the blade of a knife. Suddenly, as if Samantha had called his name, Jack looked up, pointed at her and waved, then all but BB Douglas acknowledged her with a wave or a head gesture.

"Hello," mouthed Samantha, then looked away, across the road where the little round man and his big black dog were running down the middle of the grassy area, a happy pair playing with a stick. Out in the middle of the lake, calm and still, reflecting the blue and gray of the broken cloud cover, were two small boats side by side, two couples talking and laughing. Karla had been out on the pier with the old Indian woman since eight this morning. Where were Sonny and Ada? asked Samantha of herself, needing only the two of them to make the scene complete with about everyone she had seen or talked to in the park.

Samantha, her heavy thoughts washed away, leaving her tingling with energy, swung up onto the boardwalk and trotted across the big planks to the pier. Was she feeling so lively just because she had seen Chad? Surely not.

"Hey, Mommy," greeted Karla. "Chad found this fishin pole for me and that lady gave me a hook and some bait. It's bread. Fish eat bread, Mommy."

"Well, I didn't know that," said Samantha, kneeling by Karla. "Who's the lady who gave you the bait?"

"I'm Dolly," mumbled a toothless woman who was fishing from the opposite side of the pier from Karla. "You'f gotta fine little girl, Ma'am."

Samantha turned to face Dolly, but spoke while looking back toward the store, her attention drawn to the sound of Chad racing the engine of his big motorcycle. "Well, thank you, Dolly, and thank you for helping Karla with the bait. Excuse me, I'll be right back."

Chad had turned the bike around and was idling back toward the boardwalk. Samantha, automatically and wondering why, ran to meet him. "I thought you were going to Santa Fe," she said.

"I am, but I thought I'd ask how you're feeling. Not so glum, I hope."

"Not so much, I guess. How about you?" The big blonde, sitting straddle of the bike, arms extended, big gloved hands gripping the handlebars, had been appealing to Samantha from the moment she first saw him. Today, he looked like a real rebel in his thigh length denim coat, blue jeans and blue toboggan, his shades in a breast pocket. "You didn't mention it this morning, but isn't it freezing out in the shed at night?"

"Almost. Remember, we have a date tonight."

"I remember, but guess what?"

Chad released a hand control and shook a finger at Samantha. "You don't have anything to fix for dinner," he accused. "I'm sorry."

"Me too. Gees, and I was looking so forward to a home cooked meal."

"Maybe I can get something at the store, but..."

"Maybe I can bring something back with me. Sound better?"

"No," sighed Samantha, attempting a little smile of pity. "I'm doing dinner."

"Okay," said Chad, shaking his head as he began to turn the bike back toward the main road, but stopped. "Samantha," he said, his tone soft and serious. "Those men you talked to at the plaza in Santa Fe last week are going to be here in the park today. The art dealers?" he added, winking.

"Yes. Tall blondes. Father and son? Aaron and Lloyd something?"

Chad nodded. "Lloyd Bradley and Aaron Wright. No relation. Lloyd just lies to pretty women for the fun of it. He and Aaron are government agents."

Samantha gave that a moment of thought. "Are they coming to Lost Mountain Park because of the militia?"

Chad nodded again. "Yes, Ma'am."

Again, Samantha took a second for the fog to clear from what Chad was saying. "I see," she said. "You're a government agent, too. Am I right?"

Again, Chad nodded, but smiled and ran a finger across his lips as if zipping them closed. "Let's not talk about that, although everyone around here already knows."

"Okay, but do you know what I feel like doing right now, Mr. Begay'?" asked Samantha, keeping her voice low, stepping close to the big blonde government agent. She had no intention of doing what she felt like, but she was going to put her trust in him, cast her fears to the wind and tell him everything.

"Throwing up on my new denim coat?"

"Maybe, but hugging you and kissing you until you choke first."

"Okay. Do all of that, but not yet," whispered Chad. "For now, I want you to do me a favor. Don't do anything to indicate that you know Lloyd and Aaron and don't talk to those guys up at the store. That's if you can avoid it."

"I really don't care to, Chad, but I want to talk to you about something."

"I guess you want to do that right now?"

"If you have the time."

Chad shut off the big bike, leaned it on its kickstand, sat down beside it, folded his legs Indian style, crossed his arms and said "Shoot. I've got an hour."

An hour seemed like all the time in the world when Samantha began, but she quickly found that she had no time for interruptions. Twice when Chad asked her to repeat a name and once when he wanted to know the extent of her relationship with Dr. Benjamin at the clinic in Houston, she had to ask him to save his questions until tonight during dinner. When she finally finished, although he looked lost or vacant, the big government agent merely looked at his watch and asked that he be given an hour tonight at dinner for his questions.

"Okay, but I have a question. Have you ever been married?"

A head shake, a little bad-boy shrug and a wink was the big blonde's response, then, "I've always avoided pretty women and..." Chad hesitated, looking up at Samantha with a big smile. "Until now," he added, winking again.

"I like that, but aren't you going to arrest me?" asked Samantha, mock seriousness in her tone.

Chad got to his feet, then extended a hand to Samantha. "How about I do this?" he whispered, quickly kissing her lips. "You know," he said, straddling the big Harley. "I wish some of what you said wasn't true, but then I believe it is. I'm glad I didn't know that Dr. Ott and that wacko, Howard Lane. I'd be in jail right now. See ya tonight."

"Aren't you going to be too busy to have dinner? I mean with Lloyd and the other agent being here."

"You wish. I've got my question session coming and I'll be here. There's a friend of mine who's going to go into the militia camp and try to come out with a Mexican kid, then Lloyd and Aaron are going in with badges and try to make three arrests. If that goes okay, which I doubt, they'll lead a team of military police and DOJ agents in and offer a peaceful plan to dissolve the Freedom Fighters. With luck and a lot of cooperation, they can get those with any military obligation back to their various service branches."

"You keep saying they. Does that mean that you won't be involved?"

"No more than is absolutely unavoidable. I'm a short-timer."

"Well, I don't want you to go at all."

"I like that, and I definitely don't want to have to."

"Don't then, or can I not talk you out of it?" asked Samantha putting a hand over one of Chad's.

"I'd say no, but then…Well, you are one hell of a long ways from normal, Ma'am. See you between five and six tonight."

While walking back out to the pier, looking over her shoulder, watching Chad bounce and bump the big Harley up to the main road, Samantha felt as if she were floating. Drifting among small puffy white clouds, like sheep in a meadow on a sunny day. She was as high as a kite when she slid up onto the gasoline drum to watch Karla fish.

"Ain't caught nuthin," griped the girl, but Samantha didn't respond. Her mind was full of questions. Was she a complete idiot for telling a federal agent about Howard and what she'd done to him? Even if Chad was trustworthy, would he want to help her, or report her? Did she need help? When would she know? What is DOJ? Chad Begay must be like a cop but more, decided Samantha. *I trusted him not to ransack my place while I was away and not to ruin my life now that I've spelled it out for him. I did good. He even likes me.*

By noon, having had enough of the dank air, Samantha slid off the gasoline drum and knelt by Karla, arms wrapped tightly around herself. "Honey, I'm going inside. I'm cold. Aren't you about ready?"

"In a minute. Dolly said I gotta bite whalla go."

Samantha watched for Karla's line to move for a few seconds, then left the pier, skipping down the boardwalk, almost giggly until she encountered Jack Cox, waiting just beyond the landing. He was clad in khakis, including a matching snap-brim hat atop his small head. "Hi, Mr. Cox," greeted Samantha, happily. "I was on my way to the store just to talk to you," she contrived.

"Howdy, Ma'am. Can't make it tonight, huh?"

"No. I can't tonight, but maybe next week."

"Whatcha doin that's so important tonight?

Caught up in her giggly mood, Samantha spoke without thinking. "I'm having dinner with," she began, but stopped in mid-sentence, stepped back and put her hands on her hips, wondering where Jack's apologetic disposition had suddenly gone. "Why would you ask me that, Mr. Cox?"

Chapter 20

Saturday morning, the first available flight was at 9:20. Adam had to coax and push his uncle along, barely making it to the gate on time. One unexpected delay came when checking the car in at the Hertz counter, typical for a weekend, explained the clerk. Martin looked at her and smiled. "Huh?" Adam grabbed his arm and ran to the gate. His uncle hadn't been able to hear anything all morning. Maybe the guy was still drunk.

At thirty-three thousand feet, the big jet whistled across the vast Texas plains, hidden below the boiling gray froth of a thick cloud cover. Martin, lifelessly sitting beside his nephew, said nothing, did not even acknowledge the stewardess who offered coffee or juice. "He's fine. We've eaten," explained Adam, then shook his uncle to alertness, hoping his response would be something besides the usual blank stare. "Hey, Man," he said. "You've got me wondering if we should be trying to fly a plane ourselves. Look at this shit."

Martin looked at Adam instead. "I don't want anything to drink," he said, shaking his head.

Adam, getting tired of the baby-sitting, reached up with a thumb and turned his uncle's chin toward the window. "Look out there," he said. "Me and you can't fly a little plane through those clouds."

"Yeah. It looks pretty bad," admitted Martin, softly. "Maybe it'll be clear by tomorrow though."

"And, maybe it won't be," argued Adam, speaking to himself. He knew he'd only draw another huh and blank stare if he spoke to Martin.

Albuquerque was cold and windy all day Saturday. The cloud cover was yet thick and dark, too much for any pilot with no more airtime than Martin had, he even admitted, reluctantly, after Adam refused to talk about it. However, Martin seemed to perk up and feel better the moment he stepped from the plane. "Let's get our shopping done, then I'll buy you a big steak," he said, appearing lively and anxious.

Taking a taxi instead of bothering with a rent car, Martin dragged Adam around town all afternoon, gathering warmer clothing, buying an oozy and a set of high-powered binoculars, then unsuccessfully trying to arrange for a plane at Crawford Charter Service. The rental agent wouldn't let anything out until the weather service reported VFR, visual flight rating, conditions to the extremes of a pilot's flight plan, explaining, "It's company policy, but it's good sense, too."

The taxi driver suggested the motel, an isolated dump just north of the airport. The building tried to shake apart every time a big jet passed over. "You'd better sleep under the bed, Uncle Martin. One of these big jets might just hit us," Adam had warned.

If the motel would have had a restaurant that provided room service, Adam would have died of boredom Sunday. Since the cloud cover persisted and Crawford Charter Service grounded their rentals, Martin wouldn't shower, didn't want to shave, or get dressed, or even consider leaving the room. All he wanted to do was sit on the floor with nothing on but his briefs and plan his surveillance route to crisscross the Northern New Mexico mountain ranges. Between going out to get them, Adam made each meal last two hours.

That night, yet on the floor in his briefs only, his new binoculars hanging around his neck, Martin switched from mumbling to a map to studying the workings of the oozy. Adam, sitting across the room all day, decided to ask him what his intentions actually were. All day, his uncle had seemed to draw deeper and deeper within himself, not wanting to eat and never having anything to say. "Okay," said Adam, breaking a long silence. "I've figured out that we're not going to try to find some long lost friend of yours, or go hunting for bear, so how about you telling me what's really up, Uncle Martin. Who is it we're after?"

Martin lifted the binoculars and focused on his nephew, then pointed the oozy at him. "Bam, bam, bam, you're dead," he mumbled, distractedly. A child with a toy gun, pointing it at a fence post. "I'm going after Samantha Valentine, a stone-cold killer who murdered Carol Ann and Howard Lane. Two of my friends."

Adam didn't equivocate. "I don't like guns pointing at me," he snapped, crossing the room in three quick strides, then shoving the oozy barrel aside. "Point that somewhere else. You're going to explain yourself, or we're not going anywhere. Don't shit me. You were in love with Caro Ann Lane and didn't give a tinker's damn about her husband."

Vexed by his nephew's disrespectful outburst, accusing assumption and outrageous demand, Martin jumped to his feet, his arm back as if ready to strike Adam with the binoculars. "Boy," he snarled. "Don't you ever..."

Adam, the heels of his hands automatically striking like vipers, jabbed his uncle in the chest, then grabbed the oozy. Martin reeled back and fell to the floor. "I know what's wrong with you," said Adam, breathing hard. "You've gone plumb crazy."

Martin looked up at the blurry figure above him, pointed at his chest and shook his head. "Not me. It's you that's all bent out of shape, Boy," he said, smiling to ease tensions. "Sit down here. What do you wanna know?"

Adam tossed the oozy onto a bed, but remained standing, his attitude hostile. First, he asked who Samantha Valentine was, the details of how she became involved with Carol Ann and Howard Lane and how any of it could lead to murder. His uncle's explanations seemed unrealistic, but Adam let them pass as if he had no doubts of their veracity, his challenges to come later. "Okay, Uncle Martin. The woman, Samantha Valentine, is a conniving thief and stone cold killer. First thing Monday morning, let's call the sheriff of Dallas, or that detective, Mr. Dickson, and tell him everything you know. They'll pick her up in a heartbeat. I'll make the call myself."

"No," shouted Martin, then grinned and spoke in a calm manner. "You see, Adam, I know what happened, but everything I say will be considered an opinion. Investigators aren't interested in opinions. They want facts and it'll take hard facts to convince anyone that Samantha Valentine isn't just a sweet little angel. You'll understand when you see her. She's gorgeous and all together," explained Martin. "She has the kind of personality that takes everybody in, but she's a bloody witch. Adam. You and I can..."

"You and I can't do a damn thing, Uncle Martin," interrupted Adam. "You used to be the most sensible man in the world, but you're talking nuts now. Just think for a second. Think with your head and not your heart. Two people who you have no real ties to were murdered, if they were in fact murdered, and you think you know who did it and why. That's the only way you should involve yourself." Adam paused. Martin wasn't paying attention. He was trying to focus his new binoculars on a table lamp. "Listen," continued Adam, speaking slower, but in a louder tone. "In the morning, we can call that detective, then take the first flight back to Dallas and talk to him. There'll be somebody put to work on the case who's trained and being paid to solve it. I'm not going to fly all over New Mexico in a little single engine airplane and I'm not going to let you. You'll be a lot better off if we just..."

"You know," said Martin, interrupting, thinking out loud. "I had a set of field glasses like these when I was in Korea. You can go all the way to ten power. Not bad for twenty-two dollars."

"What a deal," sighed Adam, disgustedly, reaching for his coat. "I'm gonna walk over to that restaurant and get a beer. Do you want me to bring you one? Maybe a coke? How about cocoa? It's fifty cents."

"I'm fine." Martin had heard every word his nephew said. He just didn't want him to know. Nothing or no one was going to stop him from finding Samantha Valentine. Whatever the search took and wherever it took him. He even had a back-up plan to start on tomorrow.

Adam hurried back with the drinks, two beers for himself unless Martin changed his mind, but he did not. Not only did he not want a beer, he didn't want to talk, get up off the floor, or go to bed.

"Come on Uncle Martin," pleaded Adam. It was midnight and he had been watching his uncle from a chair he'd leaned back against the door. "You have to get some sleep no matter what you do tomorrow."

"I don't have to do anything," mumbled Martin, staring at the same spot on the map he had been for two hours.

Martin wasn't aware of the map he appeared to be looking at. His eyes were closed, but he couldn't see it even if they weren't. He was blinded by the process of his own metastasis. It began as an inner presence that slowly replaced his immediate vision with a moving montage of vivid pictures condensing his entire past to insignificance. There were moments of nothingness before he began to feel a slow deterioration of his mind, concluding with total numbness. Death.

Rebirth began with a tiny light and an almost inaudible hum, then louder and louder, brighter and brighter until all incapability and unawareness had been sensitized to pinpoint alertness and now he was capable of anything. Adam had not detected any of this. The transition was very subtle, no more sound or movement than a blink of the eye. Martin Bishop was no more. He would retain his name for now, but it would be only a metaphor for those who needed to gauge someone else. "There's a Martin Bishop," he said in thought, picturing that hallowed ceremony long ago when a young Martin Bishop pinned on his gold bars.

Adam couldn't take it anymore. There hadn't been sound or movement in the room for over an hour. He propped the chair back under the doorknob and sat down to finish the second beer. He wanted to shower, but felt too uneasy, choosing to silently watch his uncle until half past two. "Uncle Martin," he said, the one to break the silence again. "I don't care if you stay up three days. I'm not gonna let you go anywhere until you've contacted the detective in Dallas, so do whatever you want to."

No response, so Adam sat and watched until twenty-five past three, over an hour since the last big jet had rattled the little room. "Go to hell," he whispered, then reached up and turned off the night light by his bed, finally deciding to allow himself to sleep. He was dead within the hour. Martin slammed a pillow over his face at the same instant he rammed the hunting knife into his throat, holding the pillow tight until Adam's life had been snuffed out.

"You just didn't understand, Son," whispered Martin, looking over his shoulder as he slipped out of the room. "Nobody will tell me what to do again and nobody will stop me from doing anything. They can't."

Martin walked to the airport and rented a white four-door sedan. He had everything he'd brought stuffed into his duffel bag, his course planned and was on Highway 25 North to Santa Fe just as the morning sun was clearing the eastern horizon. He could still see the light and hear the hum. He was more alert than he had ever been.

Chapter 21

When Samantha asked little frail Jack Cox why he wanted to know her plans tonight, his answer was in the same apologetic tone she had come to expect of him. "Uh," he sighed. "Chip and BB was just a wonderin. They didn't say, but I figger they's wonderin if you was gonna be with the big Indin."

"If you're referring to Chad Begay, I'm fixing dinner for him," explained Samantha, evenly, but lightly resentful.

"They meant Chad Begay all right. Don't s'pose you'd be reconsider'n?" queried Jack, focusing on a small stone near the toe of his left shoe, his face shielded with the brim of his hat. "I wish you... Well, BB wishes you would cause he figgers maybe you don't know the man's not the kind you and your girl oughta associate with, Ma'am." Jack kicked the stone toward the road, then looked up at Samantha and removed his hat. "Begay's got a bad record. BB said he normally wouldn't make it any of his biness, but then he knows that Begay stayed at yore cabin while you was gone to Texas. Sonny tole me that the man just stayed in yore shed and I tole that to Mr. Douglas, but he figgered you might not even a knowed it happened. Mighta not tole Mr. Begay he could."

Texas? Samantha suddenly wondered how BB Douglas knew she had gone to Texas, but didn't pursue it. "Mr. Begay has a bad record?"

"Yes, Ma'am. BB and Chip knows about it. They tole me and I reckon they'll tell you whatever ya wanna know. I better run on and get a nap before the meetin. Hope to see ya there. I kinda hinted to Chief you'd come." Jack put his hat back on. "You kin ride with me'n Chip, if'n you come," he said, turning toward the store. "We'll be leavin bout four," he added, walking away.

"Just a minute," said Samantha, then paused and placed a finger at the side of her chin, thinking. She wanted to ask Jack to explain his insinuation in detail, but suddenly decided she knew all she needed to about Chad Begay and should only try to convince Jack she thought otherwise. "Wasn't Chad supposed to attend the meeting tonight? Isn't that why he's here at the park?"

Jack turned and took a step back toward Samantha, his features those of grave concern, actual fear in his eyes. "Ma'am," he said, his tone lower than before. "BB will have my head if I say too much, but…"

Samantha interrupted. She felt that Jack Cox was somehow compelled to always say too much and wanted him to continue, no buts. "Well, now I could be wrong, Jack, but I was under the impression that Mr. Begay was quite interested in joining…" Jack was shaking his head, his lower lip jutting out to emphasize his opposing opinion. "I see you don't agree, so why is he here?" she asked.

Jack looked over his shoulder, toward the store. "The man's DOJ," he whispered. "I don't know nuthin about it, but BB says he's here to investigate all us Freedom Fighters. BB, Chip and Chiefs gonna…Well, they can tell ya."

"BB and Chip are going to what?" exclaimed Samantha, feeling she should try to find out if Chad Begay was in some danger he may not be aware of.

Jack seemed to suddenly wilt, his demeanor like that of a child having to admit to a wrongdoing. "Ma'am," he began, shakily, then paused and wiped tears from each eye.

Samantha stepped close and spoke in a soft tone. "Mr. Cox, tell me what's wrong," she pleaded. "Are you afraid of something? Tell me what Mr. Douglas and Chip Parker are threatening to do to Mr. Begay. I know you want to tell me, because I'm going to have dinner with him. Right?"

Jack nodded, then looked over his shoulder toward the store again. "I can't say nuthin," he said, his voice trembling.

"Jack, are you afraid of Mr. Douglas and Chip Parker?"

The little man appeared to want to talk on, but did not. "I really gotta go now, Mrs. Valentine," he said, then turned and hurried toward the store, being met at the door by Chip Parker, who swung the door open and roughly dragged him inside.

Samantha trotted back down to the pier and got Karla, suddenly feeling that she should leave for Santa Fe immediately. Had she learned anything from Jack Cox that might help alert Chad? What had she learned? Only that something bad could happen in the park today, and she didn't want to witness it.

Samantha, nervous now, put Karla in the new station wagon, got her purse, locked the cabin, then drove away, noticing a tan Ford sedan pulling to a stop beside the store. Aaron Wright was in the driver's seat and another man was reading a newspaper, his face shielded. Lloyd Bradley? Samantha looked away. "You want to take a nap?" she asked of Karla.

"No, no," sang Karla, excited to be driving through the woods. Under the overcast skies, the little winding road was dark along the stretches between the tall trees. "Can we stop at that bridge, Mommy?" asked Karla. "Sonny said there's trout under the waterfall. In the stream, too."

"Honey, we're in a little bit of a hurry. We have to pick up our groceries and get back before dark. Mr. Begay is going to eat with us tonight."

"You mean Chad?"

"Uh-huh." Samantha wasn't in the mood to chat, but she knew Karla was going to. "Do you like Chad?" she asked, cutting her eyes toward Karla, trying to see if she might have some telltale expression.

"I don't know," said the little girl, her focus out the window. "Is a wolf somebody's dog that ran away? A mean dog?"

"I guess that's a good way for you to think of a wolf. Do you think Chad is a nice man? He seems like it to me."

"I don't know. Sonny said there's bears in the forest."

Unable to keep Karla's attention long enough to get a straight answer, Samantha reached across the seat and pulled the little girl against her. "You and Sonny talk quite a bit, huh?"

"Uh-huh. He's a good expert."

"An expert at what, Honey?"

"Army guns," said Karla, absently, her thoughts far away today. "One of those men up at the store taught him to shoot a big, long army gun. He can shoot a little bitty bird from way far off, too. Sonny told me that even experts can't do it, but he can. He's the best expert and he's gonna be my husband when I'm in the eighth grade."

"Oh, I see." Although Samantha felt this conversation wouldn't concern any other mother of a ten-year-old girl, she was undecided. "Whose idea was it to get married? Yours or Sonny's?"

"Mine and I'm gonna have four babies. Lucille and Madam Natalie and Miss Marilyn and Jacqueline Louise. They'll play together and go..."

"Just a second, Honey," interrupted Samantha, pulling to a stop just before the bridge. A muddy black Ford pickup was blocking her passage. Chad was talking to the two men inside, his motorcycle just off the road to the right, nosed into thick brambles between the tall pines. Several feet behind the truck was a canary yellow Ford convertible. "Ken?" exclaimed Samantha, grabbing her mouth as if she wished his name hadn't slipped out.

"Daddy?" questioned Karla, jumping up to stand in the seat. "Hey. It is my daddy. Look, Mommy. Who's that little man with my daddy?"

Ken waved as he stepped out of the convertible. "Stay here," he said to Paul Baldwin, then started toward Samantha's Chevrolet wagon. This is good, he said in thought. A solid Main Street American father, that's me.

Franco had already brought Chad up to speed on both Ken Valentine and Paul Baldwin. He and Chad were now checking the two-way field phones they were going to communicate with while Franco was in the militia camp. "Just a minute," said Chad, grabbing Ken's arm as he passed, then looking back at Samantha to see if she objected to him approaching her and Karla.

"It's okay," she sighed, stepping from her wagon, holding her daughter's hand as the little girl slid out of the seat and fought to get to her father. "Are you here to pick up the bronze?" asked Samantha of Ken.

"And see my baby," he said, kneeling and extending his arms. Samantha released Karla's hand and walked over to Chad Begay, threw an arm around his waist, then turned to face Ken and Karla. "Daddy, Daddy," yelled the little girl, diving into his arms.

Chad leaned down and whispered into the two-way field phone as if he was calling Samantha. "What are you doing?"

Samantha shrugged and took the phone from the big blonde. "I don't really know," she said, also whispering into the phone. "I guess I'm about half afraid of Ken, but I shouldn't be with all you men around."

Franco remained in the pickup, but Cash stepped out. "We'd better be on our way, Chad," he said.

"In a minute. Let's see what happens here." Chad walked over to his bike and slipped the phone into a saddlebag, then returned to Samantha's side. "Don't you think we have plenty of time, Mr. Mendoza?"

"I think it takes an hour just to get up to the peaks, Mr. Begay."

"You and I aren't going, Sir," said Chad. "Your man Paul will take Franco and Ken up. New recruits. Franco will hook up with a Mr. Bradley and a Mr. Wright. They'll deal with BB Douglas and Chip Parker. Chief, too."

"How about my kid brother?" whispered Cash, beginning to worry about all that might foil what he wanted to do today. He and his father, Don de Mendoza, had agreed to give Paul Baldwin a chance to redeem himself. As the night manager of Pueblo Heights, Paul had been as reliable as those before him.

Don de Mendoza had requested that Cash contact Franco Ramos a month ago. "A man who can get anything off the Jicarilla Apache Reservation can get Gunner off that mountain."

Cash contacted Franco Ramos the day his father suggested that he do so. Franco agreed to come take a look-see, but wanted to try and bring a team of DOJ agents with him and suggested that Cash learn all he could about the Freedom Fighters in the meantime.

Cash began inviting Paul Baldwin to join him for lunch at Cantina Clavado two or three days a week. While eating, he would ask about his brother, Gunner, and the militia meetings. It was general knowledge around Santa Cruz that Paul was involved with the Freedom Fighters, a group Cash and his father knew to be extremists preying upon many of the young men living in the mountain villages of Northern New Mexico, extorting money from them and their relatives.

Both Cash and his father had never served as army infantrymen. They were proud patriots and held deep resentment for any person or group who opposed military duty, or marshaled others for the purpose of an anti-government activity. They felt it a duty to report the Freedom Fighters as a subversive organization, but wanted to try and save Gunner first. That's all Cash had thought about for months. "Come on, Man," he requested of Chad, who seemed too interested in the pretty blue-eyed brunette. "Franco and Paul need to get started."

"Okay, let's go," agreed the big blonde. "Call me if there's trouble, Franco, and we'll plan something. If I don't hear from you in three hours, I'll…"

"I'll call," assured Franco.

Chad turned to Samantha. "What are you going to do, Mrs. Valentine?"

"What are we going to do?" asked Cash of Chad. He had set the plan this morning at breakfast, allowing Paul and Ken to choose, his way, or the way of the prevailing laws. Paul had made his mind up yesterday when Don de Mendoza talked to him in the kitchen at Cantina Clavado. He agreed to take anybody who wanted to go up to the Freedom Fighter's camp and try to bring Gunner back. Ken had agreed to help, but was only interested in the possibility of ripping off the militia's money.

Chad ignored Cash's question and repeated his to Samantha. "What are your plans right now?"

"I'd better stay here if Ken does."

Cash turned to Franco. "You haven't changed my plan, have you?"

The big Mexican wasn't anxious to walk into a militia camp, but he wasn't going to be alone. Lloyd Bradley and Aaron Wright would be there and they had experience with subversive groups. "No changes," said Franco to Cash. "I'm going after your kid brother just like I said."

"Okay. Let's go over your cover again," said Cash.

"I'm hot. Running from federal drug enforcement officers. Got busted in El Paso and came north to see my Nam buddy." Franco pointed toward Ken's convertible where Paul was waiting.

Cash summoned Paul. "Come up here," he said, waving an arm.

Paul hopped up to the front of the truck. Although Ken had been visiting with his daughter, he was listening. "How did I get here. he asked.

Cash deferred to Paul. "That's a good question. How did you meet Ken?"

The little man scratched his head. "Well," he began. "I used three different army lawyers when I was trying to get full disability. In fact, one drove me home for Thanksgiving when I was in the Veterans Hospital in Phoenix. Remember him? He stayed at Pueblo Heights."

"No, but I like the story," said Cash. "How about you, Ken?"

"I'm just plain AWOL. You guys go ahead. I'll follow along later. I need to spend some quality time with my daughter."

"What?" Cash threw up his hands in disgust.

"It's okay," interjected Chad Begay. "Paul can ride with Franco and I'll go up with Ken."

Franco waited for Paul to crawl into his pickup, then proceeded on to the peaks. Ken and Cash walked back to the convertible, then followed Chad, who followed Samantha and Karla back to the cabin. No one noticed the man in the white sedan who idled along a quarter of a mile behind Ken's Ford convertible.

Chapter 22

I t wasn't the trip up to the mountain. It never was. Chip actually loved the serenity, the mystery of the river canyons, the beauty of the big trees, the lay of the land, the chirping of the birds and especially the time alone to think. Jack Cox was in the passenger seat, but that was as good as being alone. The little man seldom made a sound unless he was spoken to. Chip Parker was thinking. He wasn't feeling so good right now, but he had more than that on his mind. The window was down, and the cool high mountain air was blowing into his face, but he couldn't wake up. He, Jack Cox and BB Douglas had just gotten together after long naps. A nap in the middle of the day never seemed to bother BB and Jack, but Chip himself always awoke feeling spent, depressed sometimes. It was meeting day routine though, and after all, he might not get back down the mountain before the wee hours of the morning. "It ain't that bad," he mumbled, thinking out loud, then spoke after unwittingly breaking the silence. "This road ain't that bad," he said, to Jack Cox.

Jack was clinging to his freshly cleaned M-14, his upper body swaying like a ship in the midst of angry swells; but he knew to take the middle road on any dispute that came up between Chip and BB, however insignificant it might seem. He had heard BB complain repeatedly about the condition of the road. "Can't say as I noticed," he said.

There wasn't enough traffic to keep the ruts worn down and BB wanted Chip to take a day and drag some crossties up to the camp and back until the road was fit to drive over. "Just get it done so I won't have to think about it, Chip," he'd said, just last night. "This damn road's beatin my truck to death."

Chip would take care of the road tomorrow if he could, but he was getting tired of taking orders all the time. BB wanted him to run sonny back and forth each day and Chief always wanted something done. "I'm gonna drag the road, but I couldn't today," explained Chip to Jack, sourly, then suddenly pointed forward and said, "I told that fuckin BB this was bound to happen. The members ain't been fed right and I knew they were just waitin for a chance to split."

"I figgered it, too," endorsed Jack Cox, turning around to look back at BB's truck, fifty yards behind Chip's. "I bet the sarge has an old fashion conniption fit, too."

Sonny had BB's attention, preventing him from noticing the loose line of armed Freedom Fighters hurrying out of camp, two and three abreast, Colonel Dan leading the way. Chief was up front, too, but he was gagged, and his hands were tied behind him. "Why's that?" Sonny had just asked. "Is there somebody suppose to be comin up here to the camp?"

BB, bouncing along the little one lane road, one hand on the wheel and the other out the window, was staring a hole through Sonny. "Just do what I say, Boy. I'm tired of you always askin me why about everthang." Sonny looked away, focusing on the small patches of ghostlike fog hovering over the ravines on the shady side of Maiden Peak. "What's wrong with you, Sonny?" snapped BB, noticing that the teenager was shaking his head slightly. "There ain't a better shot than you around, but you got me thinkin maybe you ain't man enough to look through the sights of no M-14 and pull the trigger if a man's the target?"

"I could do it," whispered Sonny, defensively. "I was just askin. Me'n Mr. Cox guard the gate all the time, but nobody ever said shoot nobody."

BB glanced forward and saw that Chip had stopped. "What's the deal here?" It was a quizzical murmur, followed by a shout. "Damn it."

Sonny whipped around to look ahead. "Where's everbody goin?"

The members had been fed up with BB and Chief for months. Gunner Mendoza proposed the plan the members liked best. Take up arms, then take Chief as a hostage for trade, then walk off the mountain. Colonel Dan had just added the spice. It was his idea to set fire to all the bedding in the caves. "Think about it, men," he'd said. "We gotta get at least a mile down the road and do it quick. It'll be a monumental blast when the gasoline catches in the little cave."

However, the end of the column wasn't completely clear of the gate when Colonel Dan ordered a halt. "Hold it," he bellowed, holding a 45 automatic to Chief's head. Jack Cox was wrestling to get a clip shoved into his M-14 and Chip Parker had stepped from his truck. "Lock and load," added Colonel Dan, and every Freedom Fighter who was armed leveled a weapon at either Chip's truck, or BB's.

"Put the rifle down, Jack," instructed Chip, then raised his hands and spoke to Colonel Dan. "This ain't gonna work. Better think about it."

Dan Newel smiled, then mimicked Chip. "This ain't gonna work. Better think about it," he echoed, then to Gunner Mendoza, who was about to step around him. "Blow a hole through anybody who tries to stop us."

BB Douglas was stepping out of his truck, bolting a round into the chamber of his M-14, which invited Gunner Mendoza to quickly fire his. *Crack*, reverberated off the big peaks and echoed through the canyons for what seemed like a full minute. The round was only meant to warn BB, but hit the outer most rear tire on the left side of his big dual wheeled truck. *Thud. Whoosh*, gasped the deflating tire. "Get back in that truck and go on, Mr. Douglas," ordered Gunner, his voice sternly serious, his eyes steely. "We're ready to kill or be killed," he added, looking over his shoulder, checking for smoke rising from the caves. There was none. "Make room," he said, absently to the men behind him.

BB turned and gently laid the rifle on the bed of his truck, then slid into the seat, speaking out of the open window. "Dan," he addressed. "I'll hunt you down if it takes me the rest of my life."

The members moved off the road to let Chip and BB pass, but kept their weapons at the ready. BB had a few scathing words for some of them, but mostly concentrated on getting the wounded truck up to the campsite. "Sonny," he snarled, pulling up behind Chip Parker at the big gate. "I don't want no back talk and no questions. Just get my M-14, then you and Jack man this post and shoot anybody comes up the road. Don't matter who it is either, Sonny. Just shoot and you tell Jack to do the same. Got that?" BB was mad.

Further down the mountain, the vehicles were proceeding with all-new caution. The shot Gunner Mendoza fired had sounded like a volley of ten or more. "Think we should call this off?" asked Paul Baldwin, of Franco Ramerez.

The big Mexican shook his head. "Nope. You might reach under your seat and pull out that double barrel twelve gauge and my 45 automatic though."

Paul pulled out the guns. "Is this shotgun a pump action?" he asked, as importantly as he could, considering his nervousness.

"Yep, brand new. Holds a shell in the chamber and four more in the magazine. Guess you better load up, shells are in the glove box."

Chapter 23

Samantha pulled around by the shed and parked next to her old Ford station wagon. Chad followed, leaning the big motorcycle on its kickstand close to the boardwalk. Ken stopped the convertible on the side of the road, then led Cash back to Samantha's new wagon. "What do you think?" he asked, running a hand along the hood. "I sure hope it didn't cost her sixty-thousand dollars."

"I think it's none of your business what your ex pays for a car," said Cash, upset with the way Chad Begay had changed everything.

Samantha ignored Ken's cutting insinuation. "Just come in and get your bronze," she said. "I'll make some coffee."

Karla grabbed Ken's hand. "Come on, Daddy. We got a fireplace. Come on. I'll show you your cowboy, then you gotta see my room."

Cash and Chad sat on the sofa. Neither said a word until Samantha asked if anybody really wanted coffee. Cash declined. "I don't want anything."

"Just a glass of water for me," said Chad, then to Cash, "I'm sorry, Man. I just didn't want you to go into a camp of crazies with some emotional war to win."

Cash got to his feet and knelt by the dead fireplace. "That was noble of you, Mr. Begay, but I make my own decisions."

Chad tried again. "Gee, thanks," he said. "Makes me feel proud. What do you wanna do? Go up the mountain carrying a white flag??

"That's better than being stuck here until Ken's ready and you decide I can go," said Cash, to the fireplace. "I should have brought my own car."

"Okay, okay. Take my bike," conceded the big blonde. Samantha brought Chad's glass of water and sat down beside him. "He can take my old Ford wagon, Mr. Begay," she suggested.

Cash spun around. "I'll buy it," he said, fishing a wad of bills from a front pocket. "How much?"

Samantha looked to Chad, who only shrugged. "Don't you plan to bring it back?" she asked of Cash.

"How much?" he repeated, dropping four one hundred dollar bills in her lap. "That enough?"

Samantha knew the old wagon wasn't worth half of Cash's offer. "Just borrow it," she said.

Cash took her right hand and put one of the hundred-dollar bills in it, then closed her fingers around it. "I'm renting it for a day. Where's the keys?"

Samantha thought for a minute, then went to her bedroom and brought back a big ring of keys, removed those for the Ford, then stuffed the key ring into her jeans pocket as she hurried outside, Cash and Chad following. While she got the strong box from the back of the old wagon, Chad made sure it would start. "Be careful, Cash," he said, turning the wagon over to him, then quickly turning toward the peaks. "Damn," he said, surprised. "Sounded like a rifle."

"It was," mumbled Cash, then climbed in the wagon and sped away.

Chad walked over to his motorcycle and opened a bulky saddlebag, took out a revolver, stuffed it into his belt, then pulled his vest over it. Samantha went inside to check on Ken and Karla. The little girl had given her father a tour of the cabin and they were standing by the fireplace. Ken had the bronze tucked under his arm. "I know Mom had more leather chairs. What happened to them, Samantha? How about all the glass and brass?" he asked.

"We gave 'em to the men?" said Karla, still excited.

"What men?" asked Ken, pointedly, cutting an eye toward Samantha.

She frowned with disgust, ignoring Ken's question as she continued through to her bedroom, putting the items she'd gotten out of the wagon into a dresser drawer. When she returned to the den, Chad was back inside, sitting on the sofa, his right arm resting across the back. His focus was on Ken, who was yet talking with Karla, promising to join her out at the pier. "You can show me in a minute. I'll be right out. I promise. Now run along."

"I know a little about you, Captain Valentine," said Chad, as Karla ran out the door. "I've been in touch with Mr. Ramerez since you two met. We're..."

"Government dicks, I know," interrupted Ken, sourly. "I'm impressed."

"That's good," said Chad, evenly. "Maybe you'll listen to some good advice. You've got your bronze, so finish visiting with your daughter, then climb in that yellow machine out there and head to Oakland."

"I plan to do just that, Mister," said Ken, then to Samantha, "I'll see you again, Dearest. How much did you get for Mom's stuff?"

"My stuff," said Samantha, avoiding eye contact as she sat down close to Chad, leaning back against his big arm.

"Oh?" responded Ken, his expression glowing with revelation. "You and the big dick here got big plans, huh? Take the money and run?"

Chad slid forward, elbows resting on his knees. "Ken, I really don't think you should start something here. You're right. I'm pretty big."

"I'll say. Samantha just loves big dicks. You two should get along fine."

Chad got to his feet, started to say something, but sat back down when little Karla burst through the door. "Come on, Daddy," she said. "Come watch me catch a fish. Can you stay for supper? Please, please," she begged.

"Just for a minute," agreed Ken, then to Chad, "Okay with you?"

There was a silent second, then Samantha spoke to her daughter. "Don't stay out very long, Honey. You still have to take your nap." Karla turned and ran out. "Don't keep her out there very long, Ken," repeated Samantha. "You could write from your next duty station though. Karla would love that."

"Oh, I could, could I?" Ken proceeded outside, speaking over his shoulder. "Samantha, you and the big dick better watch your steps."

Samantha looked toward Chad and shrugged. "You okay?" he asked.

"Hopefully my day's about over. How about you?"

Martin Bishop parked the white sedan by the road well beyond the store and picked up the big binoculars. He'd almost missed seeing the smoky old Ford wagon pull away, but it had to be Samantha. "What? That's Ken and the kid walking out to his yellow convertible," he whispered, tossing the binoculars onto the seat, then inching the car forward. "The bastard was probably in on killing Carol Ann and Howard."

Martin hadn't really slept since Friday night and that was only because he was drunk on beer. He needed a shave, a shower, had a headache he could hear and a stomachache that would double him over on any other day. But, this wasn't just any day. Sleep was no priority at all. It could wait until the mission was complete. "A good soldier doesn't make excuses and doesn't quit until the mission is in the books," he reminded himself, reaching down to the floorboard, patting the oozy as if it was a sleeping pup. "Wake up."

Chapter 24

It was little Jack Cox who saw it first. "Sonny?" he whispered, ruefully, pointing down the mountain. "Somebody's comin. Two men."

Sonny was up in the guard tower loading a second clip for the M-14, but when he looked up, there it was, big as life. Dropping the clip, he shouldered the M-14 and looked through the sights at the vehicle bouncing up the winding road to the camp. Mr. Douglas was right when he warned about the possibility of this on the way up. "Jack," said Sonny, softly, gloomily. "I don't wanna shoot nobody. No tellin what they want. Nothin probly."

"We gotta do it, Sonny. Mr. Douglas says we gotta shoot anybody who comes up here. Take aim at the driver. I'll get the other'n."

Jack grabbed his rifle and hurried up the tower, then shouldered the weapon and steadied it against a corner brace. "You ready?"

"Uh-huh, but I'm just gonna shoot between'em. Scare'em away."

"Better not. Cock yer rifle and take aim at the driver."

"No. I'm aimin at the mirror."

"Better not," repeated Jack "On three. One, two, three."

Crack. Crack. Sonny's round pierced the windshield, shattered the rearview mirror and exploded, sending fragments of shrapnel into both men's chests and faces. Jack's tore through the passenger's throat. The vehicle stopped as if hitting an immovable barrier. Suddenly, and only for a few seconds, quiet descended on the mountains. Time stopped for a moment, then the reverberating echoes bounced back from the rocky canyon walls, crack, crack, crack, ten times. "I was right on. The guy's dead, but yours is runnin across the road," whined Jack, sadly as he looked over at Sonny, who appeared about to cry. "I won't tell. You'd be in trouble if I told that you missed on purpose, but I won't tell, Sonny. Don't worry bout it. I promise." Suddenly, the guard tower shuddered, then there was a rumble, followed by a loud belch that came from the little cave. "What was that?" exclaimed Jack.

As if another echo, "What was that?" yelled Chip Parker. He was running out of headquarters cave looking over his shoulder, BB right behind him.

"There's a bunch of mattresses on fire down…" *Barooom. Barooom.* A huge cloud of black smoke erupted from the little cave, then barrels of burning gas shot up five hundred feet, flames that much more, black smoke churning angrily, reaching even higher. The whole mountain shook like Jell-O. The sky was on fire, a furnace filled with spinning cots, flaming mattresses and pillows and discarded clothing, pieces of furniture whistling as they sailed high into the boiling black air.

Jack and Sonny, knocked to their knees, were awestruck, entranced. Sonny was looking skyward, but Jack was looking for answers, whimpering and staring through streaming tears at Chip and BB. They were frozen, intently focused on the flaming mouth of the cave, disbelieving the horror, the roaring monster belching fiery death into the mountain air. "Oh no, why me?" wailed Chip, falling to his knees when headquarters cave blew.

Barooom. The explosion seemed no more than a firecracker compared to the little cave, where most of the gasoline drums were stored. "Look, Jack," said Sonny, pointing to the sky. "Them burnin barrels is gonna come fallin down on us. There's some dun landed by the road."

"Oh my God," sobbed Jack, then jumped from the tower. There was enough burning debris raining down to cover a square mile. "Come on."

"There'll be a forest fire like never been seen in these parts," said Sonny, then jumped from the tower himself. Jack was just helping him to his feet when Chip's truck slid to a stop by the tower. "Gimme that rifle and get yer asses in back," yelled BB, coughing as he held out a hand to retrieve his M-14. "We just gotta make it below Rainbow Canyon. Hurry up."

Sonny tossed BB the rifle, jumped onto the flatbed, then grabbed a handful of Jack's jacket and dragged him up. "Come on. Hurry up, Mr. Cox," he coaxed. "Don't cry. You ain't hurt, are you?"

Chip roared out the gate and down the mountain, trying to dodge the hail of fiery debris that was falling into the trees and peppering the road. "Watch out!" yelled BB.

Chip hit the brakes, then eased off the road to the right in order to get around a stalled vehicle. "Who were they?"

"I don't know," said BB. "The driver was missed though. Bet it was Jack missed him. Sonny woulda got'im."

Jack heard BB and started sobbing heavily. "Tell me...Tell me what we're gonna do now, Sonny?" he asked, in painful bewilderment. "Where we gonna live? The far'll burn everthang up. Even the cabins in the park."

"No, Sir, it won't. It can't jump Rainbow Canyon. Member? Mr. Redwine tole us that and Mr. Douglas just said it, too." Sonny stole a glance at the man Jack had shot, grotesque, head lying against the seat-back, throat opened up as if sliced with a jagged stick, blood yet oozing out the esophagus and trickling down the upper body. "We're leavin this mountain forever I hope," mumbled Sonny, then laid his head on his folded arms. "I wish you hadn't a shot that feller," he said, weakly and wistfully. "We didn't know what he wanted up here."

BB Douglas leaned out of the pickup window and pointed to the bloody corpse. "Hey, Jack, you can't hit a tree with a machine gun, but I bet Sonny can hit a sparrow in the eye from two hundred yards ever time," he said, then screamed when a bloody blur charged out of the tree line on the right side of the truck, "Son-of-a..."

Pop, pop, pop, pop, six times, point blank, three rounds hitting BB in the forehead. Chip Parker yanked the steering wheel to the left, but never made a sound. One of the rounds had hit him just below the right ear. The truck veered off the road, cutting between the tall timbers. Sonny dove out of the bed just as it moaned to a jerky halt in a big thicket of smoldering blackberry vines, sending a spiny porcupine scrambling into the woods.

"Ehhhhh," screamed Jack, then hit the ground running after Sonny, but was so blinded by his tears that he smacked right into a tree trunk. "Help me," he begged, his hands extended, his face contorted into a mask of agony.

Sonny yanked Jack to his feet. "You gotta stop that crying, Mr. Cox," he said, then held Jack's hand and pulled him along until they were deep into the woods and well hidden in undergrowth. "If the far don't get us, that guy'll track us down, Mr. Cox. We gotta get to that bridge over Rainbow Canyon somehow."

Chapter 25

Ken Valentine stepped from the cabin, then hurried out to his car and roughly deposited Karla in the passenger's seat. "Where we goin, Daddy?" asked the little girl. "Remember, I have to take a nap."

Ken shook his head and raced around to the driver's side. "Will we be back for supper?" Ken still didn't respond to the little chatterbox. He was embroiled in deep concentration. Not to be disturbed by one who couldn't help. Besides, the little brat was only being a nuisance because she knew she could.

"Daddy?"

"Be quiet, Karla," snapped Ken. "Can't I have just one minute to think?" Ken did need to think. He'd heard the explosions in the distance toward the peaks. What to do? There couldn't be much left of the Freedom Fighters. Was it time to pick up the spoils? Maybe Karla could be of help. Yeah. Who would dare put a child in danger? Ken dropped the convertible into gear and floored it. "You just sit down and be still," he snapped. "We're going for a ride."

"I was worried about that." Chad jumped off the sofa and was out the front door in two steps. Samantha hesitated a second, but was right on his heels. "Ken," she screamed, uselessly, then ran after Chad. "Let's take my car," she cried.

Chad was astride the big bike, yanking it around to face the road. "Go find a phone, Samantha. I'll be a lot better off on this," he said, engaging the starter.

Samantha threw a leg over the buddy-seat. "I wouldn't know who to call."

Chad paused for a split second, then shrugged. "I guess you've got a point. Hold on," he said, then slammed the gearshift into low and roared out to the road, but had to immediately stomp the brake, cut right and lay the big bike down to avoid a white sedan that was racing by. "That crazy son-of-a-bitch."

Samantha shrieked with pain. "Oh. Chad, my leg. My hip. Lift your bike up. It's smashing my leg. Hurry. Please."

The big man rolled off the bike and jerked it upright, then dropped it on its left side. "Tell me nothing's broken," he pleaded, kneeling by Samantha.

"I think I'm okay. It's just that I slammed against the ground and bruised my hip, then your old machine kind of smashed my keys into my right leg. Look."

Chad reached for Samantha's right leg. "No," she shouted. "Look at that white car. It's coming back," she said, then screamed. "He's got a gun."

Chad didn't look back. He scooped Samantha's little body into his arms like a toy, then ran to the back of the cabin. "Whether you're hurt or not Samantha, don't move, don't make a sound and don't get close to a window," he ordered, laying her on her back. "Keep as close to the wall as you can."

Samantha wasn't thinking of whether or not she was hurt badly. Her mind was busy trying to remember where she'd seen the man who tried to run her and Chad down. "I've got it," she suddenly said "The man in that white car is Colonel...Colonel, uh, he was..."

"Colonel who?" asked Chad, urgency in his voice, as he crept along the back wall, his revolver held in his right hand, pointed toward the Chevrolet wagon. "Think, Samantha. What son-of-a-bitchin colonel would try to kill us?"

"Colonel Bishop," shouted Samantha, recalling. "He's the post commander at Fort Dix. Howard Lane's boss."

"Howard? Yeah, Howard. The screwball in Dallas. How many of these crazies do you know anyway?"

As outrageous as the timing was, Samantha laughed through a whimper. "I wonder about that myself."

Martin had slid to a stop at the front of the cabin., then jumped out of the car and ran inside. Now he was tearing through the rooms like a man gone mad, screaming threats at the ghosts hiding in the shadows and the freaks looking at him through the windows. "Yeah. You're right. It's an oozy and I'm gonna kill the bitch. Just try to stop me." *Brrrp*. Martin sprayed the kitchen with a two second burst, shattering the windowpane, exploding drinking glasses, sending the coffeepot on a tumbling flight into the air, piercing the refrigerator and cabinet doors, covering every surface with shards of broken glass.

Chad, running in a crouch, rounded the house making his way to the front door. Samantha was sitting upright, her back pressed against the back wall of the cabin. She couldn't hold the same thought in her mind long enough to find a single answer. There was just too much. In truth, she'd failed. "Oh, God, what do I do?" she prayed, tears beginning to ease down her cheek. There was smoke coming from all around the big peaks. Samantha could smell it. She could see it right now. The wind was carrying it over the lake, over an old couple standing in an aluminum fishing boat, frozen in fear. Something had blown up in the militia camp and Ken was...Poor Karla, my little baby girl.

Brrrrp. Samantha's bedroom window exploded. A dozen bits of shattered glass shot all the way to the lake. *Splash, splash, splash*. The old couple dove over the side of their boat. This was mayhem. Samantha buried her face in her hands, pressed harder against the wall. "No, no, no," she whimpered, through muffled sobbing. "Please, God help me. Protect my daughter. I'll never again let anything..." *When you find that you need help, the final responsibility is on your...*Samantha fished the keys from her pocket, then sprinted to her car. *Brrrrp*. Martin put four rounds into the shower curtain, then ran into Karla's bedroom. *Brrrrp*. He was blind with rage, bent on revenge, but knew Samantha Valentine's death would be the resolution that could satisfy him.

Chad was at the front of the house kneeling by the cement slab when Samantha tore out to the road and sped toward the peaks. "Glory Be," he whispered, then looked up at the peaks. "My God. Those flames could spread all the way to this park." *Brrrrp*. Chad jumped to his feet and rolled through the front door.

Chapter 26

"We stopped when we saw that line of troops. Dan Newel surrendered, so Lloyd cuffed him and that Indian called Chief, then we left them on the road and came on up. That old couple at the store said BB Douglas and Chip Parker would be at the militia site until after midnight. The old lady said she didn't care if we killed BB Douglas and Chip Parker, but sure hoped we didn't have to hurt Jack somebody and a kid named Sonny."

"Well, Cash Mendoza has Mr. Newel and Chief now. He caught up with me in an old station wagon, so I sent him and his brother back down to Lost Mountain Park with your prisoners. They'll be there when we get back."

Aaron Wright's suit looked like he'd used two cups of all-purpose blood to wash it, his face a dermatology project. He was sitting on the road, staring back down the mountain, whispering to the wind. "We didn't see a thing. Lloyd was sitting there looking at the Freedom Fighter troops as we drove by. We had just passed the last few when he turned around and said something about the men at the end not having weapons, then *crack, crack*, the windshield shattered into a million pieces. He took a round right through the throat. Killed him instantly. I was in shock for a few seconds. Got splattered pretty good, but when I figured out I wasn't hurt so bad as it looked, I rolled out of the car and hid back up there along the road behind two big boulders. That's when the mountain exploded. I don't know what volcanic eruption sounds like, but that had to be pretty close."

"So when did you shoot those two guys?"

"Hmmm? Oh, they came down the mountain right after the blast. I waited until the truck was right by me and I could be dead sure it was BB Douglas on the passenger side, then I pulled off all six rounds," explained the grieving agent.

"I'm really sorry about your partner. Lloyd was an all right guy." Franco looked up toward the campsite, hidden in the boiling black smoke and raging flames. "Me'n Paul here'll go get his body. Ain't much else we can do. Look at the fire roaring out of those caves. We better get down the mountain before this whole range burns."

Ken Valentine was doing everything he could to get up the mountain. He couldn't believe Samantha's old Ford would have even made it, but, sure as hell, there it was. Cash was hogging the road, too. Ken pressed the accelerator down a little and held his course to the middle of the little logging road, letting Cash, and whoever the other hotshots with him were, figure it out for themselves. The winner of this game of chicken was going to be a canary yellow convertible.

Cash swerved right, only missing Ken's Ford by inches. "Go back, Man," he yelled as the cars passed. "The fire will be down to the bridge in no time."

Karla started crying, but Ken pushed on, soon meeting a solid wall of ragtag men. A jailbreak? A stampede? No. It's a foot race. Bar none, every bastard in the line was trying to outrun the fire and be the first one down the mountain. "The fuckin idiots are running over each other," mumbled Ken.

"Huh?" sobbed Karla. When Cash saw the bright glare reflecting off the windshield of the station wagon a quarter of a mile down, he slowed to a crawl and started looking for a spot to pull off the road. "Good idea," endorsed Gunner. "You coulda got us killed back there."

There was the bridge over Rainbow Canyon, then ravine after ravine after ravine and Samantha was almost on top of him before Cash finally found a spot wide enough for two cars to pass safely. He had stopped and was just stepping out to wave her down. "Wait. Stop," he yelled, as she roared by.

Samantha pressed the foot feed to the floor, zooming past the ravines. She was determined to get to her small daughter and had thrown caution to the wind. "Sorry" she whispered, looking back and seeing that Cash was okay and was proceeding on down the mountain.

Unknowingly, she had veered left and was still looking back when she felt a sudden sensation of flying. The wagon shot off the big plank bridge, sailing over the edge into Rainbow Canyon, down, down, down through the smoky haze it soared. Samantha let out a scream and held it until the big splash. *Ka-whoosh.*

Further up the mountain, undergrowth on both sides of the federal car had begun to burn before Franco Ramerez reached it. He eased to a stop twenty yards below and started to step out. "Turn this thing around," said Paul Baldwin. "We need to tear back down the mountain soon as we load him up."

"We'll put him in the back," said Franco, whipping the wheel as he backed off the road. "Damnation!" He explained, seeing black smoke rolling into the clearing he had just backed into. He slammed the big truck into low and lunged it forward. Paul was already hopping toward the smoking carnage.

Franco reversed back to the federal car, then he and Paul hastily threw the cadaver in the bed of the truck and raced back down the mountain. The car burst into flames before they reached Aaron Wright, who was walking down the road kicking rocks, talking to himself. "I didn't see a thing. I had no reason to think the camp would be protected by snipers. Lloyd said we'd already seen the whole Freedom Fighter army. He even told me…"

"Get in," shouted Franco, pulling to a stop beside Aaron. Paul jumped out of the cab and scrambled up into the bed with the cadaver trying to spare the young agent from a long ride down the mountain staring at his deceased partner. "You better get in, Sir", he said, looking back at the advancing fires. Aaron stopped, stared hypnotized, stunned with his disbelief. Ten yards back on the right, big roaring flames were climbing up out of a ravine, seeming to be chasing a little hog-nosed skunk and a pack of Kangaroo rats that bounced across the road. Above, there was a lone turkey vulture making wide circles as it soared higher, riding up on heat thermals to join a huge Golden Eagle that was hovering above the drifting smoke. A cloud of owls and hawks and smaller birds were heading due south, there shrieks and cries and flapping wings as loud as school yard mayhem.

Franco reached across and slapped the back of the passenger seat, a loud pop. "Get in, Man," he ordered of Aaron, his tone showing irritation.

Karla wouldn't stop her crying, but it had reduced to the hiccuping kind, tears and sniffs and jerks and whimpers that she was trying to hold back with a hand over her mouth. It wasn't bothering Ken though. He was mesmerized, driving along in the confusing obscurity of ecstasy. This was just too thrilling to fuck up with objectivity. It was awesome, better than what he'd read about Mauna Loa. Fire and smoke and no lava, a dash to the finish though, over the bridge and right through the flames to the top.

Ken sped across the bridge, past two rocky ravines, then another totally enveloped in flames. On and on through the gathering smoke, rounding a curve, then the straight shot to the top. It was looking worse up here, he was thinking, but not up at the crest of the big peak. No problem up there. That Cash Mendoza better not be pulling my leg about the Freedom Fighters having all that money hidden up there.

"Daddy?" whimpered Karla, pointing forward, her voice a squeaky mouse.

"Yeah, yeah, I can see it," snapped Ken, confused for a split second, then getting the picture. "Don't get rattled. A guy named Franco and another guy named...Come to think of it, what the hell are they doing?"

Ken had to pull over and ask what the deal was here. Franco's truck was blaring down the road like a derailed train. "Are we hic, hic, going home, Daddy?" asked Karla, speaking after Ken had idled to a stop.

"Sh. Be quiet. Let me talk to these men." Aaron Wright leaned forward and put a hand over his eyes like an Indian scout. "Why would a guy be up here with a kid?" he mumbled, then answered himself. "I don't know, but he shouldn't be up here with a kid."

Franco slid to a stop and jumped out, leaving the bumper of his truck a foot from the headlights of Ken's convertible. Paul stood up in the bed and looked over the cab. Aaron stepped out, planted his feet shoulder width apart and leveled his service revolver at Ken's head. "Hey, wait," yelled Paul.

Franco knocked the revolver to the ground and grabbed Aaron by the collar, then slammed him against the hood of Ken's convertible. "Aaron, you're just gonna have to get your head on straight," he said, then to Ken, "I don't know what you think you're gonna do, Ken, but I know what you are gonna do. You're gonna turn around and get down this mountain. You understand me, Partner?"

"Yeah, sure, Franco. I was just looking for a place to turn around."

"You found it. Turn around."

"Franco," summoned Paul. "Your walkie-talkie is squawking."

Franco hurried back to the cab and picked up the field phone. "Yeah, Chad, I'm here. We're..."

Franco was interrupted by Chad's screaming. "Franco, just listen. Ken Valentine kidnapped his little girl and is on the way up there. Samantha is after him in her Chevrolet station wagon right now. Be careful. Ken keeps a nine-millimeter in his car. If you can apprehend him, bring him down here. I'm in the mood to beat the hell out of him, but I'll settle for Samantha and Karla getting back down safely. I'll be on my way up there as soon as I can get my..."

Franco dropped the phone and raised his hands. Ken had an arm around the little girl's neck and was holding the nine-millimeter to her head. "You men will just have to throw your guns down. Over here," he instructed, adding a head gesture to indicate he wanted the weapons tossed at Karla's feet.

Ken's brain was taking a beating. Karla was crying hysterically. Chad Begay's voice was getting louder on the squawking field phone and Ken didn't know what to do, where to take this, or how to survive it. He didn't want to hurt the little brat, but it wouldn't be smart to let her go either. He had to get money somewhere. If not up here, maybe Samantha. Hell, he was down to six dollars, a tank of gas and a bronze that couldn't be turned to money overnight. Samantha had all of his money, over sixty grand of it.

"Now what?" said Franco, tossing the twelve gauge and Aaron Wright's service revolver by the squawking phone. Ken released the choke hold on Karla and clamped a hand over her shrieking mouth, then looked up at Paul. "You wanna go with me?" Paul shook his head.

"You got a gun on you?" asked Ken, then smiled menacingly when Paul tossed Franco's forty-five automatic down. "Thank you, Gentlemen," he said, as tauntingly as he could over the fear and uncertainty that was pulverizing his judgment. "Now, you may proceed. Get in the pickup and head down the hill."

Franco saw the fear in Ken's eyes. "Let us take the girl," he said. Aaron Wright, coming around, said, "Mister, whatever your intentions are, don't add to the problem by involving that little girl."

Paul wanted to make his plea, too. "Ken, I'll go with you if you'll let your daughter go with Franco."

Even the big blonde Indian was adding to the confusion. "Just hang in there, Franco. I had to tear the front fender off my bike, but I'm on my way."

It might not be wise to take Paul along. He didn't want to go and wouldn't be of help. More important, Samantha wouldn't be concerned for his safety, but Ken knew she'd pay big time for Karla's. He could always come back to look for the money. Come back when he didn't have a kid along to distract him. "Okay," he said, shakily, but having decided. "It goes like this. You guys are going to lead me down to the park, then keep going. I'll take my little girl back to her mother, and then I'll leave. Don't try anything or whatever I have to do will be your fault. Get going."

Franco and Aaron Wright crawled back into the truck. "Don't be stupid," said Paul, yet leaning over the cab, looking down at Ken and Karla. "There ain't nothin left of the militia camp."

"Ya'll just go. Like I said, I'm comin down." Ken held the gun to Karla's head until the pickup had moved around his car and was heading further down the mountain, then picked up the silent field phone and pressed the transmitter key. "Mr. Begay. Mr. Begay, this is Ken Valentine. Come in," he repeated over and over while gathering the arsenal that had been tossed onto the road by his car. Chad, knowing he'd accomplish nothing by engaging in negotiations with Ken, ignored his phone and sped up the logging road.

Chapter 27

Although she screamed all the way to the water, Samantha had the good sense to close her eyes, turn her head and push hard against the steering wheel, locking her elbows, taking a big breath and holding it just before the big splash. The wagon hit almost flat on its undercarriage, doing a right curl as it waffled to the bottom of the shallow river pond, hissing and groaning until it came to rest on its right side in a bed of gravel. Icy, crystal-clear water immediately filled the wagon through the open driver's window. Samantha was stretched out in the front seat, her hands yet gripping the steering wheel, her feet touching the passenger's door. She opened her eyes, let out a little air, then hoisted herself through the open window. She was just beginning to kick her feet to propel to the surface when her head popped into the air. Her feet hadn't cleared the window. "Oh," she grunted, looking up at the bridge, feeling a bump on her forehead. The bridge, only a few feet up a ridge beyond the wagon, seemed blurry and distant. "What else can I mess up?" whimpered Samantha, disgusted with herself, realizing she could have been killed and of no help to her daughter.

Samantha placed her feet securely on the wagon's slippery door, then stood upright. How was she going to get to shore and up to the bridge? Stupid, stupid, stupid. Never had she been so stupid. She had shown such irresponsible abandonment, but never had Karla been in such peril.

Three grown deer and a bobcat scampered out of an opening in the tree line and ran down the riverbank, shocking Samantha momentarily, but pointing out the way. The opening was a footpath, going over a rocky ridge and continuing up to the road just beyond the bridge.

She gingerly walked forward to the edge of the wagon's fender, watching the path for other animals, waiting and listening. A baneful birdsong, a lone whippoorwill, the sleepy river pond quietly trickling over her feet, the sky filled with fluttering fowl, rolling gray smoke, all sailing southward. "Oh," she whimpered, dizzily looking down at the blurry water, then jumping from the fender. She hit with a splash, dog paddled a few feet, then waded across the slick river rocks to shore, staring up at the menacing smoke, shivering and hugging herself. Now there were big billowing clouds of black boiling up from both sides of the footpath, rolling down Rainbow Canyon, following the river's course. What to do? Samantha couldn't use the path. She would have to climb the ridge right above her, she decided, willing herself to get moving, just as she heard the roar of a vehicle. Up on the road? Coming back down from the peaks? "Hey, hey. Please," she screamed, weakly, waving her arms, running back upriver, only to watch a black pickup zoom across the bridge. It was the one she'd seen the big Mexican man sitting in at the bridge earlier today. Why would it be going down the mountain? The fire. The mountain was on fire.

Ken and Karla roared across the bridge, following the pickup, just before Samantha had reached the base of the ridge. "Wait," she whispered, feebly crawling to the road.

Exhausted, her head and heart pounding like twin sledgehammers, Samantha fell to the ground. She was right in the path of the advancing flames and knew it, but exhaustion, despair, pain and a loss of will had overcome her. She rolled into a fetal ball and didn't move, imagining the snaking tendrils of the hungry flames eating through undergrowth, hissing like a thousand adders, ravaging everything with hell's hot death.

Too emotionally and physically spent to move, Samantha closed her eyes and lay motionless, drifting away, her mind a dartboard for the daggers of horror that stabbed at her will to go on. Poor Karla. How could Ken put her in harm's way? What happened to Chad and what madness could have brought Martin Bishop to the park? Were he and Ken really close friends? Had they conspired against her? For what reason?

Samantha had lulled herself into believing that Howard Lane had been the last page of a past she wanted to forget, but was it going to be one she could never expunge from her life? Would it be Ken? Would

Martin Bishop kill or badly injure Chad Begay? Where was Chad? Was all this her fault?

Chad was stopped along the logging road well below the bridge, sitting straddle of his motorcycle talking to Cash and Gunner, the field phone to his ear. All three men were listening to Ken Valentine's demands over Karla's loud sobbing. "Look, ya big dick," squawked Ken. "Nobody's going to get hurt. I just need to talk to Samantha for five minutes. Karla's fine. The fire just scared her."

"I want my mommy? Ha-hic, I want my, hic,...Is that a bear?"

"Shut-up, Karla. You still there, Dick?"

"I'm here. Where's Samantha and how did you get Franco's phone?"

"Haven't seen her. The big Mex will be down in a minute. He's..."

"I want my mommy."

"I said shut-up, Karla. You better listen to me, or you won't ever get to see your mommy again," snapped Ken, then into the transmitter, "Look, Dick, you let me come down without any trouble and wait at the cabin, then I'll talk to Samantha a few minutes and go. She owes me a little money. That's all. You can arrange that, can't you? You being such a big shot federal agent and all."

"I know you've got a gun, Ken. What about that?" asked Chad.

"I don't own one bullet. Honest. You can have the damn gun."

Chad thought for a second. He had rolled through the doorway of Samantha's cabin snapping off round after round, then jumped to his feet and ran back out to his bike. One of the rounds hit the crazy colonel in the right eye and another in the chest. The oozy was probably still in his hands. "Ken, I'm going to stay right here by the side of the road until you get here. You throw the gun out when you pass, then stop a ways down and let Karla out. You can go on then, but stay out of the cabin. I'll bring Samantha back and you two can talk out on the pier, then you go wherever you choose to."

Easy enough, thought Ken. He had the shotgun and the two pistols he'd gotten from the big Mex and Paul and that other guy. "I got your word on that?"

"You won't hurt Karla, or Samantha?"

There was a deal here, thought Ken, feeling better. "I wouldn't in a million years, Stupid," he said, into the transmitter. "They're my...Hell, you wouldn't understand. Just make way. I'm coming down."

Chad sent Cash and Gunner on down with instructions to wait at the store, then roared up the mountain. He had to catch Samantha before she encountered Ken and Karla. But, Franco, Aaron and Lloyd? What had happened? Where were they? asked Chad of himself, up shifting, then twisting the throttle for more speed, the big bike lunging beneath him.

He was leaning into a curve, dragging a foot for balance when Franco's truck appeared. It was just coming up out of a wash a hundred yards up the mountain. Chad slid to a stop. Franco pulled to the right, then stopped abreast of the bike. Paul spoke first. "Sir, Ken's gone crazy. He's right behind..."

"He's just scared," interrupted Franco. "He would have..."

"Where's Samantha?" interrupted Chad, revving the big bike. "I know she's not with Ken and the little girl."

"No one's with Ken but the girl," said Paul. "He took all the..."

"Chad," said Franco. "The guy isn't gonna use a gun for anything, but getting down without getting arrested. I could tell."

"I don't know," said Paul. "He's..."

Chad asked what guns Ken had, then told Franco to drop Aaron and Paul at the store, leave them and his truck there, and then go wait in Samantha's cabin until Ken showed up. "I'll try to get the little girl, then find Samantha," he added, over his shoulder as he sped up the road.

When Ken saw Chad's bike racing toward him, he pulled to the side of the road and stopped. "Get out and stand on the hood right now, Karla."

The little girl sniffed, whimpering as she climbed over the windshield. "L-like this?" she asked, her back in an exaggerated concave arch, legs straight, hands held stiffly at her side.

"My God, will you just relax a little," sighed Ken, shaking his head, exhaling in disgust, then, "Never mind. Just stay there and shut-up until I say get down." Ken knelt behind the right fender, pumped a shell into the chamber of the shotgun and held it across his knees. "That's the big blond bastard coming on that bike and you're going to ride with him."

"O-o-okay, hic, ha-hic. That's Chad, Daddy, but where's my mommy?"

"Just be perfectly still and don't ask questions. The big dick will take you to see your mother."

Chad idled to a stop. "You okay, Karla?"

The little girl jumped down and ran to the bike. "Hic, ha-hic, Daddy won't take me home and he's being mean. I want my mommy, Chad."

Ken stood, the shotgun leveled at the big blonde federal agent. We've got a brand-new deal, Dick. You take Karla and lead the way down. I'm going to the cabin to talk to Samantha, then I'll leave. No problems with that, right?

"Samantha is up here," said Chad, lifting Karla onto the buddy-seat. "I wanna know what you did with her. Where is she?"

"She isn't up here. I would have seen her."

Chad studied Ken's face, seeing the fear and confusion. Their eyes met, then he looked up the mountain, seeing the advancing fire, its flames reaching above the tall trees beyond the river canyon and the angry black smoke filling the sky. "Mister," he sighed. "You go do whatever you want, but I'm going to take your little girl and go look for Samantha. If you've done anything to her, hurt her in anyway, you won't be able to..."

"Cut the bullshit and go look for yourself, Dick," "Samantha is not up here and that's a fact. I don't know where she is, but I'll wait at the cabin." Ken gestured with his head. "Go ahead," he said, patiently.

Chad was idling forward, hoping to find another road, one that Samantha might have taken up to the peaks. "Chad, Mommy really isn't up here," said Karla. "Me and Daddy didn't see her nowhere."

Chapter 28

There was a bottle of wine on the mantle, cooling in a sleeve. A fire raging in the fireplace, popping and hissing, but he added another log, then turned to face her. "You know I love you," he whispered, his giant features psychedelic behind the brightness thrown from the crackling fire, his shadow dwarfing all else. "I will until I'm dead and buried."

It was so hot, so loud, her lips were very dry, but it didn't matter. The time with him was so precious. It wouldn't last. It couldn't. She kicked off her heels and began to unbutton her blouse as he approached. "I know you love me."

He scooped her into his arms, kissed her lips, each cheek, then buried his face in the small of her neck. "This is a moment I would have died for if I had too, Samantha. I pray you won't regret it. I know I won't."

He lay her on the carpet, finished undressing her, then himself. They lay nude in the dancing light of the fire for several quiet minutes, both enjoying the special moment. Neither felt a burning need for the coming sexual encounter. It would only be an answer to love's purest calling. An exchange to gratify the other, to temporarily invest in them, to express the most feeling one could for another when there was no chance for a future.

Her hip was hurting and there was a deep bruise on her right thigh, but she opened her arms to him, wanting all that the moment held. He came to her, bracing his big body on the carpet with his elbows resting at either side of her waist, then moved his lips across her nipples. They responded, hardening and tingling with his every touch. His right hand slid under her back, then down between her buttocks and the carpet to her left thigh, caressing it, then working his strong fingers gently against the muscle. "Think we should do this?"

"I want to, but go slow, Ben. I'm so out of practice."

"Mrs. Valentine. Mrs. Valentine." It was a distant cry. "Come on. Hurry up, Mr. Cox. It's Mrs. Valentine."

"No. We gotta go on down the mountain, Sonny."

"Mrs. Valentine. Are you hurt?" Louder, closer, fast steps splashing through water. "Oh, Mrs. Valentine. Your poor head," moaned Sonny, kneeling beside her, startling her awake. He and Jack Cox had struggled through the woods to the river canyon and were making their way to the road from the other side of the bridge when Samantha sailed over the side.

"Sonny? I thought you were..."

"You ran off the road, Mrs. Valentine," said the boy, bug-eyed with concern. "You hurt your head. Did you know it?"

With Sonny's help, Samantha, yet woozy, sat upright and felt the knot on her head. "Yes, and I bruised my hip. My leg, too. Have you seen Karla?"

"Is she in a yeller car?"

"Yes. Where did you see her, Sonny?" Samantha tried to get to her feet, but faltered, ending up on her hands and knees.

Sonny grabbed her shoulders. "Be careful, Mrs. Valentine. You okay?"

"I think so."

"Anyways, I saw Karla and a man go down toward the park in a yeller car."

Jack, distraught and weak with fear, fell feebly to his knees a few yards up river. "Sonny, I can hear that Mr. Begay's motorbike. Can't you?"

Chad was idling across the bridge. "Mr. Begay," screamed Sonny.

Karla heard Sonny's loud scream and looked over the bridge, first seeing the wagon submerged in the river, then Jack Cox and Sonny, then her mother, on hands and knees in the rocks between the riverbank and the tree line. The three of them were only a matter of feet from a wall of churning black smoke that was boiling from a footpath and down the river canyon. "Mommy, Mommy. It's Mommy. Stop, Chad," shrieked the little girl, tugging at his arm.

Chad stopped the bike on the bridge, then carried Karla in his arms as he ran, jumped, stumbled and slid on the seat of his jeans until they were down the ridge to the riverbank. "Hold on," he said, then lifted her to his shoulders.

"Mommy."

When Chad reached Jack Cox, he took Karla from his shoulders and let her run ahead of him, then he, Sonny and Jack silently watched the tearful reunion. The little girl slid to her knees a foot from Samantha. "Mommy, Daddy's bein bad. He tried to scare me. Said I was never gonna ever see you anymore. Hey, you gotta big bad bump on your head."

Samantha reached out for her daughter, laughing through tears. "Oh, Sweetheart, your father is just scared, too. I'm so happy to see you."

"Our new car ain't no good now, Mommy."

Chad suspected Samantha ached from head to toe and felt the little girl should be cautioned, but her and her mother's embrace looked too pure to disturb and he needed to deal with Ken and the dead colonel. Franco and Aaron Wright would have to handle the prisoners and the militia. "Samantha, we need to get you and Karla up to the road, a safe distance from the fire. Jack, will you help me and Sonny?"

"You mean just...I can do that," responded Jack. Sonny helped Samantha to her feet, then he and Jack alternated pulling Karla along by a hand.

Chad lifted Samantha and carried her, struggling part way up the ridge, then sat her on her feet. "Karla is having a hard time getting up the hill, Samantha. If you can make it on your own from here, I'll carry her on my shoulders?"

"Of course, I can make it on my own."

Once up to the road, Sonny led the way down the mountain while Chad pushed his bike along behind until everyone was beyond the bridge. "We'll send a car back," he said, straddling the motorcycle. "Come with me, Sonny. I may need some help."

Sonny was dogged with deep regret about that poor guy Mr. Cox shot, but he turned and walked back to the bike with a proud swagger in his step. He had a friend who was an important agent. Bet he had killed plenty a times. Bad guys though. "Sir?" he called. "Can Mr. Cox ride along? We need to tell…"

"No," cried Jack. "I better stay here with Mrs. Valentine and Karla."

Down the mountain, Franco Ramerez turned around in front of the store, stopped, jumped out of his truck and gazed out over the park. A line of dwellers on both sides of the lake were out of their cabins, their eyes fixed to the west, watching the setting sun sink into the boiling black and orange sky above the blazing peaks. "Paul, go inside and get Cash," said Franco. "Gunner, too. They can unload Mr. Bradley back there. Have'em bring us some guns. I don't care what they are as long as they will shoot. Hurry it up," he snapped, then pointed to Aaron Wright. "Take my pickup and go see if Chad needs any help, but don't mess with that guy in the convertible."

Cash, Paul Baldwin, Gunner and Ada Redwine brought out four rifles, then the men carried the body back inside. "You're a mess," said Ada, of Aaron Wright, then offered to clean him up and paste on a few bandages.

"Thanks, but not now, Ma'am" said Franco, shaking his head, then speaking to Aaron. "Get going." Aaron checked the load of a rifle he had been handed, then climbed in the truck and sped toward the logging road.

Franco threw a rifle over his shoulder and sprinted down to Samantha's cabin. Old Jay Redwine was trooping through the kitchen, assessing damage, hands in his pockets, a deer rifle hooked under an arm. Martin Bishop's body lay face down in a pool of drying blood in the bathroom doorway, the oozy a few feet to his right. "I don't know who you are, Mister, but I'm tellin you to get the hell outta here," ordered Franco of Jay.

The old man hurried out the door without a word. The big agent kicked the oozy next to the cadaver and covered them with a throw rug. He returned to the den, pushed an armchair next to the fireplace and sat down, the rifle he'd gotten from Gunner across his knees.

Aaron Wright met the yellow convertible after encountering the long loose line of ragtag militiamen again. Ken, idling along behind them, pulled to the right, smiled and waved with the nine-millimeter automatic. He was shaking with fear and doubt, very aware that he was in over his head. Vietnam didn't sound so bad after this, but he had to have money. Just a few thousand would do for now.

Chad and Sonny had left Samantha and Karla with Jack Cox and were tearing down the mountain. As soon as Sonny hopped onto the bike, he began telling the big federal agent about Jack shooting Lloyd Bradley. "Mr. Douglas told us we had to shoot anybody who came up the mountain, but I didn't want to," yelled Sonny, hanging on tight, leaning into the curves.

"What?" exclaimed Chad, snapping his gaze around to Sonny's face for a split second, then quickly facing the winding road again. "Jack would do that?"

"Well, Mr. Cox was just afraid not to," defended the boy.

Chad was concerned about Jack Cox being back at the river with Samantha and Karla. "Sonny, has Mr. Cox seemed...Is he acting weird?"

Sonny answered immediately. "No, Sir. I don't think so," he said, his tone appearing an attempt at being helpful. "He's a good guy. Just real scared."

When the lead militia troops cleared the tree line, they spread out on the grass across from the store. Ken pulled around the ones who trailed and sped to Samantha's cabin, parked right in front, shut the car off, stuffed the nine millimeter in his belt, carried the shotgun and ran inside. "Hey wait," he said, dropping the shotgun, smiling as he raised one hand like a child in class.

Franco was holding a rifle leveled at him. "Where's the pistol?" Ken fished the pistol from his belt and tossed it at Franco's feet, his expression one of surprise. I just can't believe there was a gun in my belt, it was saying. "You guys got it done, huh, Franco? Cash's brother, okay?"

"You stupid shit," sneered the big Mexican. "Why don't you just shut-up and find a seat. I don't want to hear a peep outta you until Mr. Begay gets here."

Chad stopped along the road when he met Aaron Wright. He instructed him to pick up Samantha, Karla and Jack Cox, then return to the store. Aaron told him that Franco was armed and waiting in Samantha's cabin, then left for the bridge. Chad and Sonny continued down the mountain. Up at the bridge, Samantha and Jack Cox were trailing along behind Karla. Jack had wanted to talk the minute Chad's bike was out of sight. Samantha hurried along listening while he told about shooting Lloyd Bradley in detail. She took a deep breath. "Jack," she said, exhaustively. "If you're wanting my advice, then here it is. You have to tell Mr. Begay. You shot and killed a federal agent. Don't try to get away with it. You won't."

Samantha and Jack walked along in silence for several minutes, then the little man spoke, soft and sorrowfully, "Mrs. Valentine, I hate what I did, but I can't change it. What do ya think will happen to me?"

Before Samantha could answer, Karla yelled from a few yards further down the road. "Mommy, there's a pickup coming."

Aaron Wright saw the little girl standing in the middle of the road and stopped, turned the truck around and waited. Samantha and Jack ran to Karla and led her to the truck. The agent smiled, but with impatience. "Get in."

Samantha and Karla climbed into the bed. Jack Cox hesitated for a moment then opened the passenger side door and slid into the seat. The federal agent, yet a bloody mess, took a long look at him, then sped back down the mountain. Neither man spoke until they were halfway to the park, the agent eventually mumbling dully, "What's your name? 1 know you were in the back of that pickup with the boy when I shot BB Douglas and Chip Parker."

The little man nodded. "I'm Jack Cox, and yes, I was in that truck," he mumbled, then plowed on with his story again, ending it with the same question he had for Samantha. "What's gonna happen to me?"

"I'd kill you right now if it was up to me, but you'll have to face trial with Dan Newel and your little Indian leader."

When Aaron reached the cabin, Chad and Ken Valentine were out front, sitting on the hood of the rented sedan Martin Bishop had driven. The colonel's body, wrapped in a sheet, was laying across the trunk. Franco, Cash and Gunner were moving Dan Newel, Chief and the ragtag militia troops down the road to the hangar. Sonny, Jay and Ada Redwine were passing out slices of bread, milk, cookies, chips, canned food, fresh lunch meat and other food items easily carried and eatable. "Just stay put," said Chad to Ken, getting to his feet. "You've embarrassed yourself enough for one day."

Samantha was standing in the bed of the truck, dusting off the seat of Karla's pants. Chad helped the girl climb down, then offered a hand to Samantha. When Jack Cox stepped from the cab, Aaron Wright frisked him and told him to stay in the truck, then turned to Begay. "Is that it?"

The big agent shrugged and echoed. "Is that it? Dead or alive, you and Franco have what you came for. You've got your men. You can take this white car and the body with you. Maybe I'll give you a report on what happened here someday. The corpse, Colonel Martin Bishop, U.S. Army, retired, has all the identification on him you'll need for now."

"How about that one?" asked Aaron, gesturing toward Ken.

"The captain there? Oh, he's just a goofball on his way to Oakland, then sunny Southeast Asia. I'll handle him."

Chapter 29

A Saturday in late November
Hilton Hawaiian Hotel
Honolulu

It was the fourth day at the resort. Samantha and Karla were walking briskly through the lobby to board an elevator for a trip up to their room. They were hiding their hair with a single page of a newspaper. Two army captains on R & R from Vietnam waved and nodded. "Bet they just got their hair done," said one, then the two of them hurriedly began helping Sonny and Chad with a small flat white box, a strand of black ribbon and a sheet of shiny silver gift wrap.

Excluding using Samantha's old Ford wagon to make two trips to an FBI field office in Albuquerque, Chad remained at Lost Mountain Park for three weeks after the episode with the militia. Franco Ramerez and Aaron Wright had collected what government property they could identify, then disposed of the Freedom Fighters, releasing most without charges. Dan Newel, Chief, Jack Cox and seventeen of the line members were transported to the FBI field office for processing. The bodies of Lloyd Bradley, Chip Parker, BB Douglas, and Colonel Bishop were taken to the airport, then flown to Washington DC. Cash, Gunner and their father helped the remaining militia members with transportation needs lodging and phone access until they could get back to their homes. Chad, Sonny, Jay Redwine, Dolly, the little round man with the black dog and Samantha put her cabin together. Ken's bronze statue went back onto the mantle. He had sold it to Samantha for three thousand dollars and was overjoyed when Chad sent him to his duty assignment in Oakland. Jay and Ada offered forty thousand dollars for Samantha's cabin, but the park seemed much different to her without BB Douglas, Chip Parker and Jack Cox lording over it.

When she couldn't make up her mind, Chad offered the trip to Hawaii. Jay and Ada paid Sonny's way, gave him two hundred dollars to spend and promised him a job when he returned. He would be assisting with the mail run, taking care of the trash in the park, collecting for utilities, mowing and doing general maintenance work around the cabins they owned. The round man with the black dog offered Sonny his shed to live in and Chad was strongly considering giving the kid his Harley.

This was the big day. A first. Chad and Samantha had shared evening meals, shared the stories of their lives and if Sonny wouldn't have interrupted, they might have shared a night of intimacy that began under a full moon out on the pier. The big blonde had grown dangerously fond of the pretty blue-eyed woman and he was a pushover for little Karla.

"It's a beautiful gift now, Sir, but it still needs something," said one of the captains, then tied a little bow with the ends of the black ribbon. "How's that?"

"Thanks." Chad held the little package up for review. "Think she'll like it?"

"Hell yes."

"I know she will, Mr. Begay," said Sonny, his tone bordering on over confidence. "I ain't never seen nothing like that." "

Okay then. It'll have to do. Who wants me to buy'em a drink?"

Chad was stalling and the soldiers knew it. They exchanged dubious looks, then, "Maybe just one," said the soldier who had tied the ribbon.

Samantha and Karla hurried to their room and began getting ready for dinner. Chad and Sonny had escorted them to a different resort, beach party or ocean side luau three of the last four nights. One whole day was spent in a Volkswagen convertible, touring Pearl Harbor, a dozen piers and docks, the lush countryside, rain forests, cane fields and rugged coastlines on the trade winds side of the island. While eating breakfast this morning, the big blonde man suggested a day of rest, free time to shop, lay in the sun, stay in the room and sleep, but he promised a surprise for tonight. Samantha and Karla spent the morning at the beach, then the early afternoon shopping and had just come from a beauty salon in the Islander Hotel lobby. To prepare for the surprise, the little girl wanted to have her nails done, wear lipstick and dress to the nines, which Samantha agreed to allow and do a little of the same. Their nails and lips would gleam fire engine red tonight, their brunette hair, parted in the center, had been done with big coiling curls bouncing to their shoulders. The dresses they chose were sleeveless red muumuus decorated with a hibiscus flower pattern. Karla wanted to wear island thongs, so Samantha bought them and picked out a similar pair for herself. "I want to eat a fish again," said the little girl, running naked to beat her mother to the shower.

"Whoa," said Samantha. The child had been overly excited since takeoff from Los Angeles, appearing almost awestruck from the moment the flight attendant announced, *All carry-on items must be stored under your seat or in the overhead bins.* "You take a bath, Karla. I don't want you to ruin those curls. Today will be the last time we see the inside of a beauty salon for awhile."

Samantha had definitely overspent, rationalizing that she was only rewarding herself and Karla for finally having closed the book on a past that could be interpreted as a bit tawdry by some.

As it turned out, Ken's leaving for Vietnam didn't ease the guilt Samantha felt about her role in all that had happened to her. It came with what Chad learned when he tried to get in touch with Howard or Carol Ann Lane. Unable to reach either, he asked a young FBI associate in Dallas to look into the matter and contact him through the field office in Albuquerque. "Sir, would you tell me why you want to know?" asked the agent.

Chad asked the young man to hold and allow him to change phones, which he did not, nor need to. He needed to think. The young agent's question was generic in a way, but there was something in his tone. Martin Bishop again? The FBI field office director had already told Chad that the crazy retired colonel was somehow involved in the murder of his own nephew, a young man found stabbed to death in a motel near the airport in Albuquerque. And, Samantha had told him of her acquaintance with Howard Lane, of Howard's with Martin Bishop, or Martin Bishop's and Ken Valentine's purported brotherhood-like bond.

It was clear. Martin Bishop had done something bad enough to Howard and Carol Ann Lane to involve the FBI.

"Find out everything you can and I'll tell you what happened. I'm retiring in a month, Kid, so it can be your bust. I couldn't care less."

There was one minute of phone silence, then the young agent's voice whimpered across Texas like an exhausted sigh against a hard wind. "Well, Sir, they're, uh, both dead and buried. Murdered, uh, victims of arson, I think."

Willing to contrive, planning to truncate and make himself believe, for the sake of closure with Howard Lane for Samantha, Chad chose the story he would live with forever. Who would be the worse? No one. "Young Man," he said softly. "I'm the man who shot Martin Bishop, a retired army colonel whose dying words were a bunch of garble about getting even with Howard Lane. I didn't find out who Howard Lane was until yesterday."

The young agent wanted a statement from Chad, which he immediately completed and mailed. That night at the dinner table, he told Samantha what had happened to Howard and his wife. She was visibly moved and retired to her bedroom early. The next night, while Chad was sitting out on the pier with his feet dangling over the side and watching the moon crawl over the distant mountains to the east, Samantha walked up from behind and sat down beside him. "It's so peaceful," she said, an observance, her tone not needing a response.

Chad leaned back, palms flat on the big planks, arms extended, elbows locked. Samantha was leaning forward, arms at her side, hands resting on the big planks, feet dangling over the pier with Chad's, slowly moving back and forth, back and forth. Her long auburn hair, damp from a recent shower, was glistening against the soft radiance of twilight. She was in her typical evening attire, sandals, jeans and a loose pullover jersey. "Mr. Begay," she said, softly, looking out over the calm water. "You've done a lot for me and my daughter and I've thanked you personally, as well as in my heart. Be that as it may, nothing impressed me as much as you trying to contact Howard Lane. I would never have had the nerve to. I'm very sorry he and his wife died so tragically, and I can't say that I won't think of them off and on for awhile, but at least I know the day will come when I won't. Thank you for that, too, Sir."

"Okay, I didn't want to be so formal, Ms. Valentine, but I'll say you're welcome. That's from the heart, too, Ma'am. Now, what are you going to do with your cabin?"

"I'm sorry. I know that I don't need to call you Mr. Begay. It's just that you seem bigger than life sometimes. You'll be Chad from now on. Anyway, I'll sell the cabin to Mr. Redwine in time, I'm sure. I just don't know where I'd go. It won't be Texas, or New Jersey, but those are the only places I've eliminated."

Chad was enjoying looking down at Samantha's heart shaped bottom and the back belt line of her jeans, gaping open with her forward lean, the top two inches of her white panties showing. "You know," he said, leaning forward, putting an arm around her waist and pulling her closer, "we have a similar problem. I sold my house in DC and my last day of employment with the U. S. Government is December thirty-first of this year. I haven't decided where I'm going to live either, but I do have an idea. A place I plan to look."

"Where?" Samantha wriggled closer, her hip and right leg touching his left, her head laying on his big shoulder.

"Someplace beautiful and pure. Like you, Samantha." Chad put a hand to her cheek, lifting her chin, peering into her blue eyes for a long moment, then kissing her awaiting lips even longer. "That was nice," he whispered. "I think I'd like to live in Hawaii. Want to go take a look? You said Ken never took you there, and since I've been twice, I'd love to be your guide."

Down in the bar of the Hilton Hawaiian Hotel Chad was drinking and thinking, hearing less and less of Sonny's conversation with the two soldiers. He had spent the entire morning with a real estate agent, looking at house after house, three different apartments and two different grade schools for Karla. Tomorrow morning at eleven, the agent wanted to pick him up and take him to see a huge bungalow on Waimanalo Bay, the east side of the island, currently vacant, just perfect, he claimed. Things were moving fast, but Chad was ready for that. "Let me have the address. I'll take a look myself, then call you."

In the gift box, resting beside him on the seat cushion of the booth, was his surprise for tonight. He loved it. "Sonny," he said. "Now, you do know where to go and what to do tonight, right?"

"Yes, Sir. I'm taking Karla to see a fella named Don Ho, then to the luau right out there on the beach. Think I better go get ready?"

Chad's plans for the night weren't so simple as a short walk up the street to see a show, then back to eat Bar-B-Q pork. He had chartered a sunset helicopter ride, one that would take him to the bungalow in Waimanalo. He had ridden in helicopters before, but hopefully it would be a first for Samantha.

While he and Sonny were dressing for dinner, he explained his plans for the night and warned that he and Ms. Valentine might be late. "Midnight at the latest," he said. "Can you keep Karla busy that long? She can go for a swim if you stay with her."

Just before the big fiery sun sank into the Pacific for the night, Chad and Samantha taxied to a pad at the south end of Waikiki Beach. The chopper was waiting, sliding doors open, engine at high idle, and its big rotor blades buzzing in the damp evening air. When Samantha stepped out of the cab, she immediately screamed, then grabbed her muumuu. "Oh, no." The rotor wash had sent it over her head and her curls into a feverish spin. With her feet dancing like in hot coals, bikini panties shining in the dimness of dusk, bringing smiles, claps and nods from the late sun worshipers, whistles and comments from a group on a passing catamaran, Samantha grabbed the flapping muumuu. "Hey, Mister. Love your lady's muumuu," came from atop a lifeguard tower.

Chad, ignoring the comments and catcalls, helped Samantha with her hair until she had her dress under control, then tucked the gift box in his belt and swooped her into his arms, ducked his head and ran under the whirling rotor blades. "Sorry, Samantha," he said, into her ear. "I should have warned you about that."

She slapped his backside, playfully, but hard. "Darn you," she gasped, fluffing her hair. "How embarrassing. I think you planned that little show."

As soon as Chad had sat Samantha in the back and climbed in himself, the pilot turned around and checked the tightness and security of the buckles on her shoulder harness. "Yours okay?" he asked of Chad, yelling over the sounds of the noisy craft. When Chad nodded, the pilot handed him two headsets. "Help her with these," he yelled, winking this time.

The pilot had already gotten an eyeful and Chad wasn't about to share what he had to say to Samantha with him. "We won't need them," he yelled, returning the headsets.

The pilot shrugged, then turned to his controls. After pulling on tight gloves, he rolled the throttle, increasing engine and rotor speed, then lifted the collective, bringing the vibrating craft to a hover. Samantha leaned into Chad, then took his hand. "This is scary," she yelled, then suddenly grabbed her hair again. "Can we close these doors?"

Chad yanked at a door, watching for a reaction from the pilot. He was pivoting the aircraft in place. After a half turn, the nose dipped forward and the beach suddenly sank, disappearing as the craft lurched up and out across the water. "The doors are pinned," yelled Chad.

"Ooooooh," screamed Samantha. "Here goes my stomach."

"You'll be all right, Samantha," yelled Chad, then held his hand over her mouth until the craft smoothed out high over the bay in straight and level flight.

Samantha pulled Chad's hand from her mouth. "Wow," she sighed. "That was thrilling, but…Ooooooh." The pilot banked left, then leveled the craft again, appearing to be on a direct collision course with the top of Diamond Head.

"Close your eyes," yelled Chad, then pulled Samantha against his chest, burying her face in the small of his neck. "Better?" She nodded.

The pilot cleared Diamond Head and set an eastbound course, just Kuliouou on the left, then on to Koko Head Park. Over the park, as the pilot banked left, Chad leaned away from Samantha and asked her if she was going to make it.

She was fine, she claimed, smiling, looking about, across the island to the blood-red horizon, then east, an endless black vista as the Pacific stretched to the states. "Nothing seems real up here, Chad. Thank you for this. It's wonderful. Look at the lights. They seem to… Ooooooh…"

The pilot was banking left again, more radically this time, looking back at Chad and pointing down. "I'll have to approach to a hover over the water," he yelled. "Otherwise, the rotor wash will kick up the sand and blind us."

Chad cupped his hands to his mouth. "How will I know which bungalow?"

"There's only six. You'll find it."

The pilot rolled the craft out of the hard left bank and lined it up east to west over the water, heading right to the beach, descending steadily, his landing light showing the way. "Don't worry," he yelled, over his shoulder. "The water is only about two feet deep where I'll let you out. I'll be back at exactly eight."

Samantha shook her head and leaned into Chad. "I'd rather walk."

When the pilot had approached to a hover, Chad tapped his shoulder and told him that he and Samantha would take a taxi back. "Good luck," he yelled, hands steady on the controls, eyes fixed to a point on the beach.

Chad jumped into the shallow water, secured the gift box in his belt, then extended his arms to Samantha, rotating his hands, encouraging her to jump down beside him. "Come on. I gotcha."

"Okay," she yelled, rigid, hesitating, watching the wash from the whirling blades eddy the water around Chad's legs, lifting it, creating a dense mist.

Splash. Samantha hit the water to Chad's left, lifted her muumuu to her thighs and high-stepped it to the beach. The pilot blinked the landing light, turned the craft around and roared out over the water.

The beach was almost totally dark, deserted, the only visible lights further up the beach. Beyond, hard rock music drifted from a small building lined with cars and trucks. "That was fun, but why are we here?" asked Samantha, looking back at Chad as he waded to shore. "This seems like a beach for the locals."

Once at her side, Chad took Samantha's hand, sat down in the sand and pulled her into his lap. "Samantha," he began. "I spent the morning looking at places to live. Houses big enough for the three of us. A real estate agent told me there was one here that would be perfect. That's why we're here."

Samantha thought for a moment, then got to her feet. "What's in that box you've been carrying since we left the hotel?"

Chad pulled her back into his lap and handed her the box. "I love it," he said. "I hope you will."

Samantha ripped the ribbon off and tore away the paper. Do you know that no one has given me a wrapped gift since Karla was born?"

"That's hard to believe."

Chad had selected gold earrings and a gold chain necklace with dangling sapphire droplets, perfect matches for Samantha's eyes. "They're really beautiful, Chad," she whispered, wiping her eyes with the back of her hand. "I don't know what to say."

Chad got to his feet, then lifted Samantha to hers, slipped the necklace over her head, kissed her quickly, then started up the beach. Samantha tagged along behind until she had her new earrings in place, then ran after him, jumping on his back when she caught him.

"Hey." Chad sunk to his knees.

"Mister," said Samantha, rolling off Chad's back. "I'll be happy to go look at the house, but can we talk for just a minute first?"

Chad sat cross-legged, ready to listen. "Go ahead."

Samantha lay on her back and stretched her legs out, her upper body propped on elbows, head back, her gaze fixed on the starry heavens. In no way was she lost in thought, but chose to appear so. Her mind was free, free to roam, to plan, to create and to love. "You're being too nice to me, Chad." It was a soft murmur. "My aunt and uncle were always wonderful to me because they loved me. Dr. Benjamin, too. What's on your mind?"

"Just you."

Samantha shook her head, one slow move to the right, then back to the left, eyes yet focused above. "That's no answer."

"Well, I did mean the whole package, Samantha. You and Karla, life on the island and..."

"Come on, Chad. You can do better than that."

"Okay, so I'm a thinker and not a talker. If this agrees with you, I'd like to find a house we can rent for a while. Then, I'd like for you and Karla to stay here on the island and enjoy yourselves, while I go back to the mainland to sign some final papers. I'll take Sonny along with me, and if you'd like me to, I'll sell your cabin to the old couple at the store while I'm there. I'll sell your furniture, too, the old Ford wagon and that bronze. You hate my bike, so I'll give it to Sonny for helping me, then…"

"Chad," interrupted Samantha. "You're leaving something out."

The big blonde thought for a minute, knowing full well what he hadn't said, but he never had, when he meant it, when it meant something. "Samantha," he finally said, his tone a soft plea. "I love you. You've probably heard that from a dozen men, and they probably knew how to say it better, but I don't. You probably think…"

Samantha giggled, amused, but pleased to hear the big man express his affection for her. "I'm sorry," she said. "Go on."

"Go on she says," whispered Chad, a conversation with himself. "Go on and make a fool of myself. Okay, I can handle that. Samantha Valentine, I, Chad Begay, want to spend my next life with you. I want to marry you whenever you're ready and wherever you are at the time. I love you, I love you and I'll do everything to prove that…"

"Okay, Mr. Begay," said Samantha, then got to her feet. "Those were very sweet words and I hope you meant everything you said." Samantha bent down and kissed Chad's lips, a light peck. "Thank you," she whispered, then fell to her knees beside him, pushed him back onto the sand and lay her upper body flat against his. "You should go on back to the states and do whatever you have to." Samantha's eyes were locked with the big man's. "I love your Hawaii," she whispered. "So does Karla and we need to spend a little time together, just the two of us. We'll stay at the Hilton while you go do what you have to do, but please hurry back. You see, Sir, I just might be in love, too."

www.ingramcontent.com/pod-product-compliance
Lightning Source LLC
Chambersburg PA
CBHW071238300726
48975CB00002B/463